CRY OF METAL & BONE

EARTHSINGER CHRONICLES BOOK THREE

enelope

Song of Blood & Stone
Breath of Dust & Dawn
Whispers of Shadow & Flame
Hush of Storm & Sorrow

Cry of Metal & Bone

EARTHSINGER CHRONICLES
BOOK THREE

L. PENELOPE

ST. MARTIN'S GRIFFIN NEW YORK

This is a work of fiction. All of the characters, organizations, and events portrayed in this novel are either products of the author's imagination or are used fictitiously.

First published in the United States by St. Martin's Griffin, an imprint of St. Martin's Publishing Group

For information, address St. Martin's Publishing Group, 120 Broadway, New York, NY 10271.

www.stmartins.com

Designed by Steven Seighman

The Library of Congress Cataloging-in-Publication Data is available upon request.

ISBN 978-1-250-14811-7 (trade paperback)
ISBN 978-1-250-14812-4 (ebook)

First Edition: 2020

10 9 8 7 6 5 4 3 2 1

For Paul, who took the leap of faith first

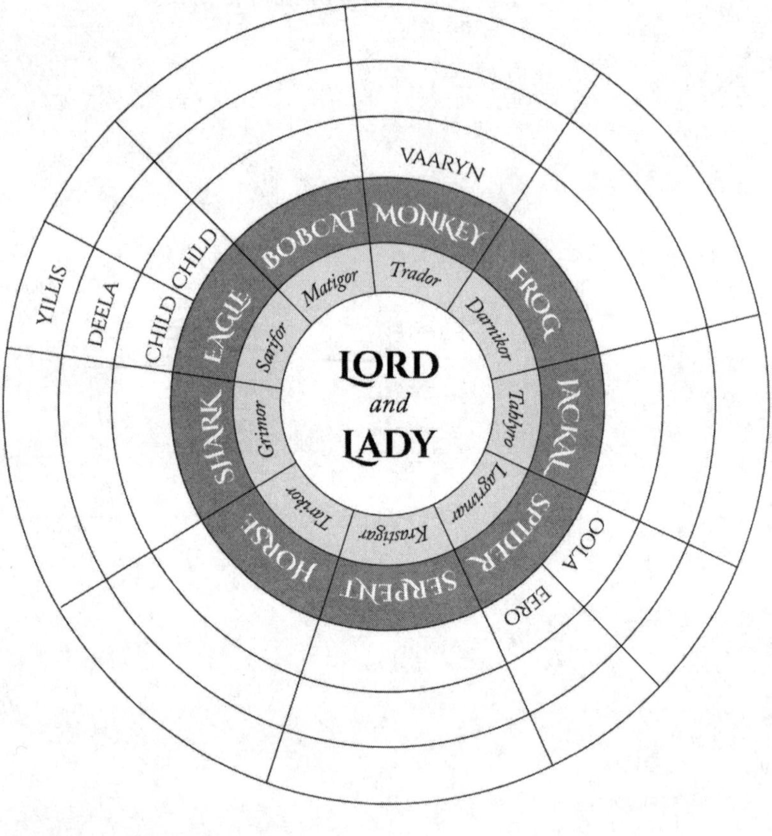
LORD and LADY
Sarifor
Matigor
Trador
Darnikor
Tablyro
Lagrimar
Krastigar
Tarikor
Grimor
EAGLE
BOBCAT
MONKEY
FROG
JACKAL
SPIDER
SERPENT
HORSE
SHARK
VAARYN
CHILD
CHILD
DEELA
YILLIS
OOLA
EERO

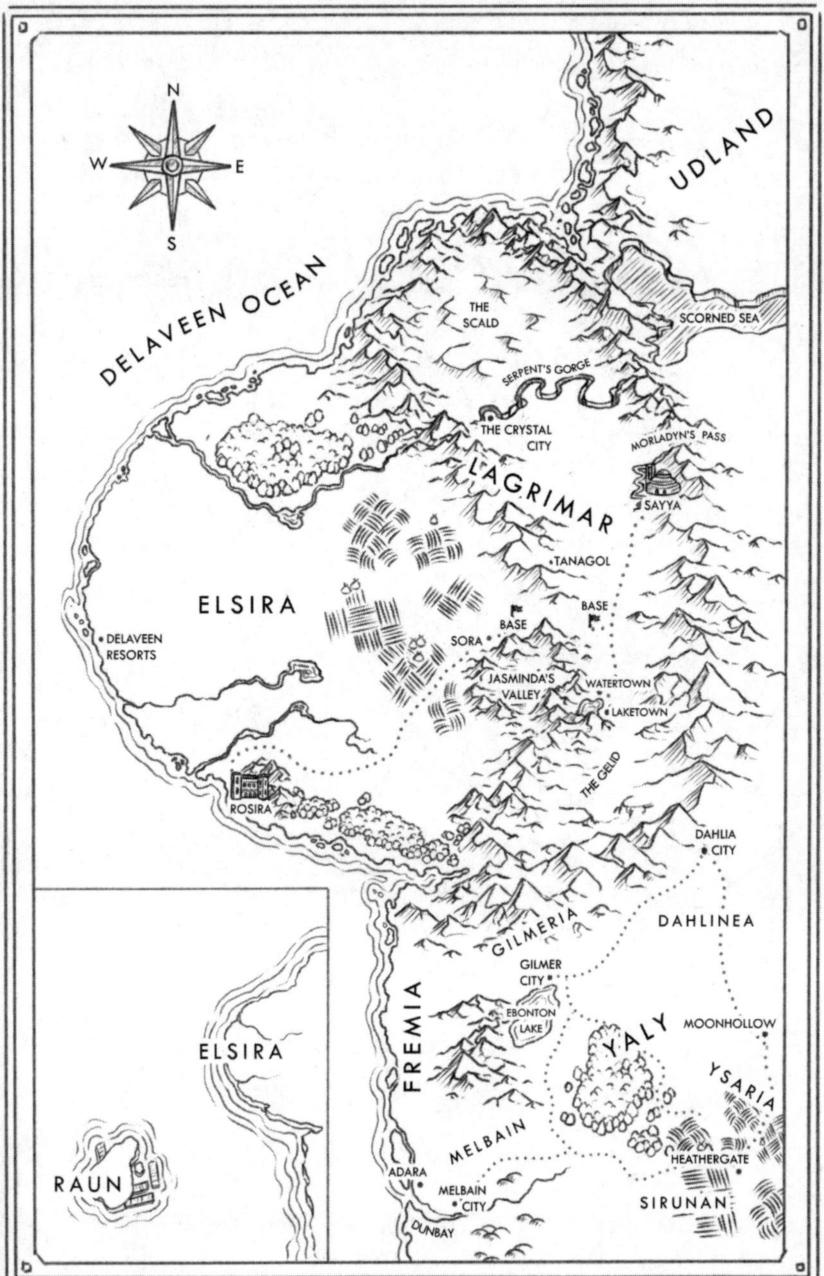
N
W
E
S
UDLAND
DELAVEEN OCEAN
THE SCALD
SCORNED SEA
SERPENT'S GORGE
THE CRYSTAL CITY
MORLADYN'S PASS
LAGRIMAR
SAYYA
TANAGOL
ELSIRA
BASE
BASE
DELAVEEN RESORTS
SORA
JASMINDA'S VALLEY
WATERTOWN
LAKETOWN
THE GELID
ROSIRA
DAHLIA CITY
GILMERIA
DAHLINEA
GILMER CITY
FREMIA
EBONTON LAKE
YALY
MOONHOLLOW
ELSIRA
YSARIA
MELBAIN
HEATHERGATE
ADARA
RAUN
MELBAIN CITY
SIRUNAN
DUNBAY

CRY

OF

METAL

&

BONE

PROLOGUE

"Blessing from the Goddess?" The little girl's voice wobbles with apprehension. She is eight or nine years of age with coppery hair pulled into a topknot, mimicking the style of the women of the Sisterhood. Perhaps she is an aspirant. She bends her body at an awkward angle, in a sort of half curtsey, her little limbs stuttering either from holding the position or from nervousness.

I touch my thumb to her hairline and trace it across her forehead. Blessing bestowed.

There are others, so many others, waiting for their chances. The temple seethes with them—a swarm of busy insects climbing over themselves, reaching for me, yearning, hoping. Precisely what they believe a brush of my skin against their skin will accomplish, I do not know.

No, that is not true. I understand who they believe me to be. And though it pains me, I answer to the name they have given me, the Goddess Awoken, just as I did the previous moniker of the

Queen Who Sleeps. I sleep no more; instead I walk among them offering their faith a rare embodiment.

Beside me stands the new queen of my people. Jasminda's calm and placid exterior masks the swirling doubt that has yet to abate. I do not know the cause, but her constant uncertainty is a pinprick needling my side. She asked to accompany me today, to better understand the people whom she is to rule.

I abdicated the throne I never wanted in the first place nearly as soon as I was free. She and Jaqros will share it now. It is better this way.

Have you seen enough, Jasminda? I call to her using my Song.

She looks up sharply, tearing her attention away from the retreating figure of the little worshipper.

You do this every day? Her inner voice is incredulous, though the only external indication is a slight widening of her eyes.

The people come every day. So I do, as well.

It must be exhausting. She scans the vast temple interior. White marble stretches out around us. Every inch is filled with people—my followers. There is no seating; the crowd stands facing the raised dais where we loom above them, surrounded by blue-robed members of the Sisterhood.

Before I awoke and left my prison in the World Between to return to my body here in the Living World, the worshippers would drag their blankets and mattresses to one of many temples erected around the country and sleep, hoping to have their dreams graced by me. The Sisterhood would preach words attributed to me, words I never said, and tell tales of deeds I never did. But their belief gave them hope and peace and joy. I watched over them, spoke to those I could in dreams, guided them when possible, and withstood the aching loneliness and solitude.

And the followers did not question what they were told. Centuries passed, and my life, my own existence, faded into myth and, even worse, ideology.

It does not tire me, I tell Jasminda. *We all do what we must.*

These people, the descendants of those I knew and loved, are all that are left for me. If I did not become the goddess they expected, what else would I do in this new world? Who else would I be?

I am no longer a girl called Oola who ran across this land when it was little more than wilderness. I am no longer the woman whose people made her queen so she could stop a war she was responsible for starting when I gave my twin brother, Eero, a taste of my power and it drove him mad. Turned him into a despot—the True Father. Caused him to rend our land in two, separate our people, and reign with terror for five centuries. But there is no one left who remembers who I was.

It is almost as if I have been erased.

The woman I was before is no more. These people only see the goddess they have made me. Perhaps some hint of the truth remains in Eero's mind, somewhere inside the madness. He corrodes in the palace dungeon, not speaking, not eating, while the people he tormented burn him in effigy and curse his name.

Meanwhile, I repent and mold myself into an idol, a version of myself that bears little resemblance to reality.

The crowd teems and pulses, and my senses skate over them. I recognize a few individuals whose dreams I visited, back when I had no control over where I went and with whom I spoke. The hope and expectation in their hearts slice through me.

With my Song, I extend my awareness beyond these walls. The city bristles with people. The press of so many consciousnesses in such proximity is unnerving. In my youth, there were not so many alive in the entire land as there are in these ten square kilometers.

The gathered throng ripples and spits out another devotee. An elderly man seeking a blessing steps up to the dais. He greets Queen Jasminda with a stiff bow before turning to me. The worshippers hum with a hopeful anxiety. Their emotions press against me, thick as the crowd itself.

My Earthsong-fueled awareness narrows to a fine point. I block out the swarm of bodies, even the seeker before me and the girl-queen next to me. There is someone here quite unlike the others. Malice pulses through his pores. Bitter hatred twists his energy. I cannot locate him in the crowd; I merely feel the strong sense of malevolence. Drawing deeply from my connection to Earthsong, I focus my inner Song until the man's intentions come into clearer resolution, so clear it's almost like hearing his thoughts.

I snap back into my physical senses and look at Jasminda beside me. Her brow is already furrowed. Her weaker Song may have picked up on the danger, but she is slow to process it and appears confused.

"Queen Jasminda is leaving now," I announce to the Sisters nearby, punctuating the statement by pushing a sense of alarm into them. The Royal Guardsmen assigned to Jasminda rush out of the shadows and surround her, whisking her off down the aisle of the temple before she can even protest. I give an extra mental nudge of anxiety to the guards, and they take off at a near run. It is impolitic to make them pick up the queen and haul her away bodily at such a pace, but there is no time to waste.

The old man still stands before me, his perplexed expression mirroring Jasminda's from a moment ago. Hundreds of people fill the building, but it would be impossible to get them all out in time. Their last moments should not be spent in a panic. So I do not tell them what is coming. Instead, I lean forward and press my thumb against the man's forehead, bestowing my blessing, for what it is worth.

It turns out to be worth very little. Only a heartbeat later, the bomb planted in the temple explodes.

CHAPTER ONE

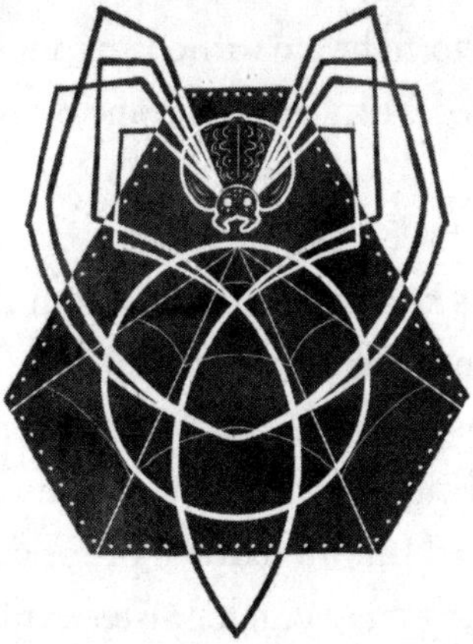

Look to the beginning to find the end. The venerated matriarchs who held us in their wombs and nurtured us in their bodies could not bear to let us falter. To them we dedicate our praise, for they were First. What shall be Last is still unknown, but the journey of the seeker is not yet ended. May she uncover the truth before the end of things.

—THE AYALYA

Tai Summerhawk stalked through the streets of Portside, adjusting to the feel of solid ground under his feet after so many weeks at sea. The stench of horse dung mixed with diesel exhaust and a hint of sewage assaulted his nostrils. He longed for the equally foul, but far more familiar, odor of the selakki oil that filled his ship.

His first mate, Mik, matched his stride, his eyes constantly roving, searching for threats, as was the man's habit. The last time Tai had been in Portside, he'd nearly been killed.

The silence between them was not the comfortable kind, but Tai relished the break in his friend's constant haranguing. He'd almost rather have to fight a cutthroat or angry dockworker than listen to any more of Mik's admonitions on how foolish this trip was.

"The king will have your head," the man had stated almost daily, scratching his bushy green beard with thick fingers. "She'll put you back in irons when she finds out."

Tai had merely shrugged. The last time he'd seen his mother, the current king of the island nation of Raun, was two years ago when she'd sentenced him to hard labor for defying her as well as his part in thwarting his younger sister Ani's apprenticeship to a rival captain. He'd served his time, not focusing on the back-breaking work, the heat of the sun, the stink of the vicious selakki that the chain gang fished from the ocean for slaughter and harvesting, or even his anger at his punishment. His only thought had been of fulfilling the promise he'd made to a dead man.

Mik knew exactly why this trip was so important. He'd been there and heard the dead man's final words, knew of Tai's vow. That was why Mik had been waiting with Tai's ship, the *Hekili*, the day Tai was released, with a course already charted for Elsira. Ever cautious, the exhaustive warnings were just a part of his makeup. As *cautious* was not a word ever used to describe Tai, they made a great team.

The Portside neighborhood in the capital city of Rosira was different from what he remembered. There were still people from every nation on the continent mingling in the streets and pubs, but far fewer than normal. Entire sections of the dock were empty, whereas just a few years prior it would have been difficult to find a place for even his small ship.

"Rather deserted around here, isn't it?" he asked Mik.

His friend nodded. "Elsira's harvest has been small so far this year. Not as many vessels going from here to Yaly. Add that to your mother's embargo and things have been slow to say the least. We'll likely see very few Raunians here."

His people were deeply involved in the commercial shipping business—both legal and illegal—across the Delaveen Ocean. Tai wondered how the Elsirans were getting on since King Pia's edict barring trade in Rosira. That wouldn't stop the most stalwart of smugglers—it certainly hadn't stopped him.

"And on top of all that, they've got internal problems," Mik said, motioning toward a group of men on the corner holding picket signs. As Tai drew closer, their chants rose over the din of horse-drawn carts and autos clogging the street.

"Elsira for Elsirans! *Grols* go home! Cull the herd! *Grols* go home!"

Tai caught several passersby looking askance at the protesters. One man, an Elsiran judging by his reddish hair and anemic coloring, scowled and muttered under his breath.

"What's that all about, eh?" Tai asked him in the Elsiran tongue.

The man shook his head. "Damn fools don't appreciate peace. Civilians, the lot of them. If they'd fought in any of the breaches, they'd be singing a different tune, I'll tell you that. They're afraid the refugees from Lagrimar are here to take something from them. Those poor souls just want to live free like the rest of us." He spat on the ground. "The war is over!" he shouted at the protestors before walking away.

This land had changed much in a few short weeks. The Elsirans had been at war with their eastern neighbors, the Lagrimari, for centuries. But the war had ended six weeks ago when their deity, the Queen Who Sleeps, awoke from Her magical slumber. Even in a prison an ocean away, Tai had heard tale of the wondrous event. According to Mik, the Queen, now known as the Goddess Awoken, had ordered the two lands to be united into a single country. Lagrimari refugees were pouring in from their desert land into resource-rich Elsira in search of a better life. But the drought and the economic downturn, along with many lifetimes of hate between the two peoples, made unification a difficult proposition.

Tai regarded the protestors, a sour taste filling his mouth. "I need a drink."

"That's the first sensible thing you've said in weeks, mate," Mik replied.

They entered the nearest pub and sat at the bar. The crowd was light, and the mood inside somewhat somber. Maybe it was because of those idiots shouting in the street. Elsirans had always been small-minded and bigoted. Tai had been here countless times but never stepped foot outside of Portside. Until recently, the city's strict immigration laws had always prevented foreigners from violating the hallowed ground and entering the rest of Rosira.

A surprisingly pretty barmaid set a cold beer in front of him, smiling suggestively as she did. He winked and brushed her fingers with his as he grabbed the tankard. Then again, not all Elsirans were bad. The promise in the young woman's eyes and the refreshing liquid soon eased his ire. He would find out when her shift ended, but for now he needed to focus on why he had returned to Rosira.

His fingers moved to the pouch around his neck, the kind all Raunians wore. It carried his birthstone, given to him on the day he'd come into this world and to be sent back to the sea after his death, but it also carried another stone. One that was bloodred in color and had powerful magic locked inside. Its origin and purpose were unknown to him, but the journey he'd taken to retrieve it had been harrowing. His sister had risked her life fishing it out of the ocean, and Tai had watched a Lagrimari man and his two sons give their lives to protect it. All on the orders of this Goddess Awoken.

Tai had no allegiance to the Elsiran deity, but he had sworn an oath to complete the mission and deliver the strange stone to the Sisterhood. Now he might be able to give it to the Goddess directly. His vow would likely land him back in prison for defying his mother's wishes and daring to travel to Elsira—in violation of the embargo and new travel restrictions—but it was a small price to pay. At least he'd be alive. Dansig ol-Sarifor and his twin sons had not been so lucky. Their bravery still humbled him.

Somehow he had to find a way to contact the Goddess. Once he gave her the stone—a caldera was what Dansig had called it—the deaths of the family he'd known only for a short time but would always respect would not have been in vain. His sister Ani's pain—she'd lost not only her hand in the blast that had killed the three on the *Hekili,* but also the boy she'd hoped would one day be her husband—would not have been in vain.

Mik was quiet beside him. The low drone of the pub settled Tai's nerves. He caught the barmaid's attention and ordered a second beer.

"Sure thing, sailor," she replied, her voice husky. He grinned, admiring the cleavage she had on prominent display. Mik snorted next to him, and Tai chuckled.

"When's quitting time?" he asked as she set his drink before him.

She propped her elbows on the bar top and leaned forward, lazily looking him over from his freshly dyed blue hair to the tattoos covering his cheeks and forehead. By the way her eyes danced across his sun-toasted skin, he suspected she was after the novelty of sleeping with a Raunian. That was fine by him. He would give her plenty of stories to tell about her night with a "barbaric" foreigner.

He raised the mug to his smiling lips, but it fell from his grip when the pub shook and rocked. The roar of an explosion caused immediate panic as glasses toppled from the shelves, and he and the other patrons dove to the ground as the smell of smoke invaded the air.

CHAPTER TWO

From the roots of the tree sprang three branches, each vying for water and light. A fruit blossomed—a girl child—though withered and failing. She was plucked too soon and left to die. But Siruna the Mother found the babe, healed her body, and claimed her as her own. She named the girl Ayal, and on her back would rise a nation.

—THE AYALYA

Darvyn ol-Tahlyro rounded the corner of the busy street that divided Portside from Lower Rosira. He ran through the gate separating the two parts of the city, easily bypassing the guards who normally stopped him on days like today when passage by non-Elsirans was still forbidden. They were too busy staring at the billowing blaze not three blocks away.

The Queen's Temple—the Goddess's Temple now—was on fire.

Thick black smoke shot from the ruined entryway. The normally pristine, white marble facade with its square columns and carved landscapes was completely destroyed.

He sprinted up the street, barely aware of the line of black vehicles he passed until a familiar figure stopped him in his tracks.

"Your Majesty," Darvyn said, breathing heavily. "What's happened?"

Queen Jasminda's face was pinched, worry and shock vying for dominance across her features. Her beaded silk dress was rumpled and a smudge of ash marred her cheek. "I need to get in there, but *She* must have brainwashed my guards. I didn't even know She could do that. Can you help?"

Darvyn noticed the phalanx of Royal Guardsmen lining the sidewalk and blocking off the new queen's access to the blast. Each man had a determined set to his jaw that brooked no opposition. Darvyn reached for his Song, tapping into the infinite flow of Earthsong and drawing it inside himself. The guards' emotions were clouded and difficult to parse, something he had seen from those who'd had recent contact with Oola, the Goddess. She had not taken over their free wills but had pushed an emotion into them so strongly that the men were slavishly committed to a course of action beyond reason or rationale. Intense fear or pain could create such a reaction in people.

Darvyn dropped a sudden cover of darkness around himself and Queen Jasminda, blocking them from view. The Guardsmen froze, blinking rapidly as if trying to understand why a black void had opened up before them.

Jasminda sighed with relief and took Darvyn's hand, pulling him toward the destruction. "I wish I could do that," she said wistfully.

"Once you have a better hold on your Song you'll be able to."

Jasminda had been a weak Earthsinger all her life until gifted additional power by Oola when the Mantle fell and the war ended. The new queen was still learning how to use so much power, and Darvyn, the only adult Earthsinger they knew of a similar strength, had been helping her.

He had spent the past weeks in Elsira advising his friend Jack, the new king, along with his soon-to-be bride, Jasminda. The task was made more complicated because he also sought to avoid the elders of the Keepers of the Promise, the Lagrimari rebels who had worked so long for freedom for their people.

His overall faith in the group he'd been part of for practically his whole life had been shaken deeply. Not only had the elders lied to him about his mother—hiding the fact that she'd tried to contact him for years before her death—but one of their own had betrayed him, resulting in his imprisonment and torture by the True Father's agents.

Now the True Father was locked in the dungeon, and the Lagrimari people had been liberated only to become refugees in this land of their former enemies. The Keepers were on the front lines of advocating for their people, a goal Darvyn shared, but he would no longer blindly trust anyone.

And nothing he did, no plans he made or aid he rendered, could distract him for long from the thoughts of the Lagrimari woman who had stolen his heart. The falling of the Mantle had been bittersweet for him. Kyara—fierce, lovely, strong Kyara—had disappeared into thin air that day and hadn't been seen or heard from since. Darvyn's feet moved forward, but his heart and soul were trapped in the past—with her. She haunted his every breath.

As he and Jasminda rushed toward the destruction, she explained to him how Oola had forced her out of the temple without a word just moments before the blast and how She had stayed behind.

"I've been healing those I could reach with my Song. There is so much pain and hurt," Jasminda said as they came up on the edge of the smoke.

Since the Great Awakening, as the end of the war was being called, the city's temples were always packed to capacity. Most Elsirans had spent their lifetimes worshipping Oola, and the opportunity to do so in the flesh caused a kind of spiritual exhilaration in many that he found somewhat distressing.

Darvyn had fought in the Seventh Breach, had seen the kind of animus the magic-fearing Elsirans harbored against the Earthsinging Lagrimari. But the fact that their Goddess was the most powerful Earthsinger alive did little to sway their devotion to Her. It also did little to curb their lingering hatred of the Lagrimari. The irony was potent and daunting.

Regardless of Her devotees' human failings, Oola visited the three Rosiran temples built to honor Her every day. Hundreds would have been inside when the explosion hit.

As Jasminda and Darvyn reached the edge of the destruction, he stretched his Song farther, feeling for the wounded. "There are so many injured; we'll have to go in."

Jasminda nodded. Without another word, she hiked up her expensive, delicate skirt to reveal sturdy black boots and plunged into the darkness. Darvyn followed, climbing over the rubble to reach what remained of the temple.

Immediately, they were struck by a pungent odor. *Palmsalt,* Jasminda said to him using her Song. *The explosion must have released it.*

Darvyn sang a silent spell to create a bubble of fresh air around his head. When burned in large quantities, the substance released a fast-acting deadly gas, and if anyone survived the blast, the palmsalt would finish them off.

It's just beginning to spread outside the temple. Can you trap the gas so it doesn't escape with the smoke? Darvyn asked. *I'll see if there are any survivors and send anyone I can out to you for healing.*

Jasminda nodded and stared up at the smoke billowing into the sky with tense concentration. Darvyn turned away and hastened farther into the temple. He scrambled over a sickening jumble of bloodied bodies that had been crushed by the collapsing walls. He drew Earthsong to him until his Song was ready to burst—the fast-moving torrent of life energy battered him as he stood amid its turbulence. The power crashed against him, and his Song absorbed the energy and held it, ready to use.

Gloom surrounding him, he scanned the nearby bodies for any signs of life. A hush blanketed the space, interrupted by soft moans that drew him forward toward several survivors in the atrium. Their injuries were serious, but it would only take him a few moments to set their bones, staunch their blood loss, and boost their internal healing ability, allowing their bodies to fight off the poison.

Earthsong rippled and flowed like white-capped waves refusing to be stopped. Life energy was drawn to life and it wanted to rush out full force and face down any challenges to itself, but Darvyn had to be careful. There was much to do here, and he needed to be judicious. Even his strength had a limit. When his Song was tapped out, it would be many hours before he'd be able to sing again.

Once he cleared what was left of the doors to the inner part of the temple, the crush of the palmsalt lifted from his senses. He released the bubble around his head to find the air clean and fresh. A soft glow illuminated the space, and he did a double take.

Oola—he refused to call Her the Goddess Awoken—floated in the air, Her skin radiating a gentle light. His connection to

Earthsong crackled and pulsed; somehow he could feel the great quantities of energy She was pulling into Her Song.

One temple wall had fallen away, disintegrating into rubble, but the others and all the columns had been frozen midfall. Chunks of marble hovered in midair. A spray of dust hung midarc overhead. It was as if time had stopped. Everywhere people were unharmed and awed, staring above them with jaws open, many prostrate and kneeling.

Darvyn, these people must go. I cannot force them all to leave and hold the building up at the same time.

He stepped farther into the room, gingerly avoiding the prone bodies of those amazed by the display around them. *What of the palmsalt?*

Trapped for now.

How long can you hold off the collapse?

Long enough for them to evacuate. But they will not go.

"You must get out of here," Darvyn shouted in Elsiran and then in Lagrimari, noting a mix of races among the followers. "The Goddess demands that you get to safety."

A few heads swung in his direction, but most kept their eyes firmly on their deity.

I have tried that. They will not even listen to me. Oola's inner voice was wry. *You must* force *them.*

I don't believe in that, Darvyn said. He'd witnessed Her take over a man's will and had no desire to ever do something so invasive with his Song.

It is not puppetry. It is merely an emotional kick. You cannot force a man to do what he would not. You may, however, impel him to prioritize certain actions.

It isn't right, Darvyn said.

It is necessary. Or they will all die in awe of my great and limitless power. Oola's eyes flashed. Darvyn had long ago grown used to Her peculiar sense of humor. She had been communicating with him from the World Between since he was a child.

He looked around and bent to the nearest devotee. Tears shone in the woman's eyes as she stared at Oola. Darvyn picked the woman up and carried her toward the atrium.

You will carry four hundred people out of here? Oola asked.

Your power dwarfs mine. I know I couldn't hold up this building for more than a few moments. Can you not hold out for as long as it takes?

The others would die for their reverence of me, and you think I do too little. Her inner voice snorted. *This building is heavy, Darvyn. The palmsalt is not dissipating inside its containment, but rather its poison is battling my spell. Jasminda's spell was not strong enough to control the smoke along with the gas escaping into the air, so I am reinforcing hers, as well. Would you have it all be for nothing because you want to prove to me how moral you are? That you are ethically superior to me?*

Darvyn set down the woman in his arms. He clenched his fists, fighting within himself about the right thing to do.

Let us agree that you are the more honorable of us, She said.

Flaring his nostrils, he came to a decision. He would not do what She asked. It was too much. Instead, he focused on his Song, bringing the mighty stream of Earthsong to heel to control the air around them. Oola had told him that was the way She lifted herself and appeared to be flying. He had never been particularly interested in flying about himself, but now found the will to try.

The woman he'd just set down rose into the air, feet hovering above the ground and eyes widening with fear. He didn't waste any energy soothing her emotions, he merely pushed her across the open space and toward the exit.

Next, he worked on two people at a time, finding his rhythm with the new technique. Soon he was able to lift half a dozen at a time. As the crowd watched people floating by them, more and more awestruck worshippers scrambled to their feet.

Some began to file out under their own power while Darvyn carried the others away with his Song. Sweat broke out on his forehead. Thank the seeds most in here had only minor injuries; he wasn't sure he'd have much Song left for healing once he was done. Soon enough, the interior of the temple was nearly empty.

How is Jasminda doing? he asked.

She is helping lead them out and healing the injured.

Darvyn oversaw the final worshippers' exit and then climbed out without looking back. Oola could take care of Herself.

Outside, the Elsiran army had arrived and was maintaining a perimeter of safety around the temple.

"Have the nearby buildings been evacuated?" Darvyn asked one of the soldiers.

The Elsiran looked at him askance. "Who wants to know?"

Darvyn took a deep breath to hold in the retort he wanted to spit out. Jasminda appeared at his side, and the soldier bowed.

"He is assisting in the rescue, Captain. Please treat him as an extension of me." Her voice was hard.

The captain visibly paled. "Yes, Your Majesty. The entire block has been evacuated."

"Good. The temple will collapse at any moment." Darvyn stared at the captain until the other man looked away. Darvyn knew what the soldier saw: a Lagrimari, someone who until a few weeks ago would have only been met in battle on the other side of a war that had been going on for far longer than either of them had been alive. Even now, in peacetime, the Elsirans were able to accept a Goddess and a new queen with the same skin color as the Lagrimari, but that seemed to be the end of their tolerance.

The shock of discovering Oola's appearance had been overcome quickly by the faithful. The Elsirans had worshipped Her for centuries, believing Her to look like them. Those whose dreams She visited never got a clear picture of Her. They only heard Her voice and listened to Her counsel and advice. Darvyn couldn't help but wonder if Oola could have done more to foster acceptance from Her prison in the World Between.

After all, She'd visited him, as well. For reasons She claimed not to understand, She could visit his dreams at will—and he could seek Her out—unlike most, for whom visits were a random happenstance. And he alone had been able to see Her clearly. In his more cynical moments, he suspected She didn't show Herself to the Elsirans on purpose, knowing that they would reject Her, the way so many were now rejecting the Lagrimari who were flooding Elsira. This soldier's reaction wasn't anything unique.

Beside him, Queen Jasminda gave orders to another soldier. Though she looked just as Lagrimari as Darvyn, her mother had been Elsiran. She was a child of both people, both nations, and now, thanks to Oola's abdication, she was also the queen. In a few days, she would marry Jack, the former Prince Regent and now king of what was slowly becoming a united land. But it would take more than a declaration from a goddess to consolidate two former enemies.

Darvyn turned toward the rubble as it groaned and shook. Oola was releasing Her spells and allowing the destruction to take its course. He'd just begun to think about who the explosion had really meant to harm—the new queen, the old one, or both—when Oola emerged from the building, floating on an agitation of air currents.

She drew nearer, carrying something in Her arms. She settled down before them, and his stomach turned as recognition dawned. The body of a small girl lay cradled in Oola's hold. She was Elsiran, her copper hair tied in a topknot.

Darvyn approached Oola as She knelt, not letting go of the child. He reached out with his dwindling Earthsong to the girl, even knowing it was futile. Death had already taken her.

"There's nothing that can be done?" Jasminda whispered, kneeling next to them.

"Even Earthsong cannot bring one back from the World After," Oola answered. She laid the child on the ground and rose, turning to survey the gathered crowd of worshippers and onlookers to the tragedy.

The ones who did this watch us, even now. Her thoughts touched his mind via Earthsong.

Darvyn stood and took in the hundreds of faces staring back at them—some in horror at the destruction, some in rapture at their Goddess. But there must be someone here looking on in satisfaction.

Who did this? he asked.

Oola remained silent, observing the crowd intently.

Jasminda shook her head and crossed her arms. Her dress was ripped and dirty, but an air of regality persisted. She may have only been queen for a few short weeks, but she was well suited to it.

This is a message. Someone will take responsibility for it, and then we'll know exactly what they thought they were saying, Jasminda's inner voice said.

A bomb laced with palmsalt placed in a temple full of people, both Elsiran and Lagrimari, was not just a message. It was a declaration of war. And Darvyn knew about war. He'd been fighting his whole life, and it had cost him everything—his family, his childhood, the woman he loved.

Peace was a fragile creature; its tiny heart had barely even begun to beat in the weeks since the Mantle fell. But his people finally had a real chance, not just to survive but to thrive. This was the future he'd been fighting and sacrificing for all his life. Yet there seemed to be no end in sight.

He sighed and scrubbed a hand over his face. He would make another vow to add to the others slowly filling his heart.

Find those responsible for this destruction and bring them to justice.

Find the man who murdered his mother and avenge her death.

Find Kyara, the woman who owned his heart, and never let her go.

I will find them all, he swore. *Whatever it takes.*

CHAPTER THREE

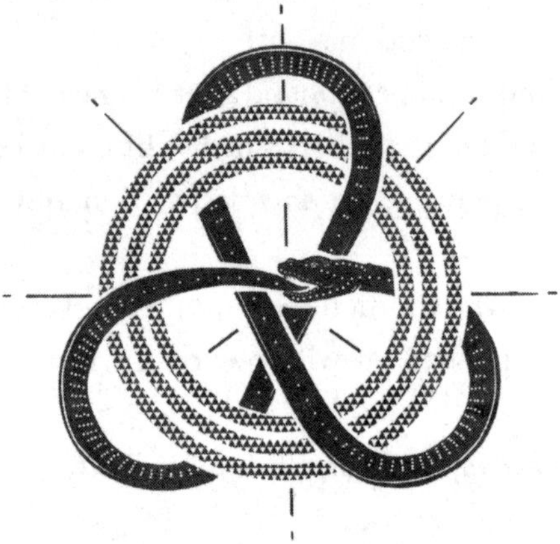

There were no thrones, no dynasties, for the matriarchs had warned against it. Those lessons echoed in our ears for a time, but years pass and memories blur until voices, once clear, turn to whispers and then fade entirely.

The branches of the tree spread further apart and the roots began to wither and die.

—THE AYALYA

Kyara regained consciousness in stages. A droning, tinny sound reverberated in her ears. It slowly faded, replaced by a voice speaking in a language she didn't understand. Her eyes twitched before clamping tightly shut, impaled by the brightness surrounding her. Leather bands cut into her forehead, wrists, and ankles, locking them in place. She could wiggle her toes, but her fingers responded sluggishly. A warm liquid coated her palms, and her chest ached, the coppery scent of blood tinging the air.

She stilled her movements and reached for her other sight, but her Song was silent. Panicking, she tried again and again to access her power, fearing for a moment that it was gone, truly gone, forever. But wasn't that what she'd always wanted? To be rid of the dreadful power to command Nethersong, the energy of death. Her Song had done nothing but cause her sorrow. It would be a mercy to have it stripped away. However, something was wrong—different than she'd expected.

And then she felt her Song, finally, resting inside her, though shrunken and emaciated to almost nothing. Instead of a snarling beast trying to rip through its leash, it resembled an abandoned pup, left to fend for itself without the skills to hunt or survive. Kyara's entire body was weak, her mind a fog. As the foreign voice rumbled on and on, her memory of how she got here started to return in patches.

She recalled standing on the streets of Sayya and losing control of her power. Watching in horror as her unchecked Nethersong caused every living thing around her to collapse. People had fallen where they stood or had slumped in carriages and rickshaws. Horses had keeled over. Birds had dropped from the sky. The only sound had been the cracking and splintering of wood and metal when out-of-control vehicles collided. Grief and pain . . . that's what she remembered.

She had killed before. Many times. Her years of forced servitude as the True Father's assassin had left her all too familiar with the taking of human life. She had always struggled to control the unruly power inside of her enough to make sure only those she was commanded to kill were slain. But she'd failed.

And worst of all, she'd failed *him*.

A vision of Darvyn lying in a heap with his two friends assaulted her.

She'd killed him.

A sob escaped Kyara's throat. Nearby, the foreign voice paused, then continued.

She pulled at her bonds uselessly and risked opening her eyes again, forced them to withstand the blinding light until they adjusted. A ceiling of dark, paneled wood hung high above her. With her head locked in place, she only had the use of her peripheral vision. People sat on tiered benches, wearing cloaks of varying colors, many of them staring at her. She was at the front of an auditorium or classroom of some kind.

The sight of the blood on her hands, seeping from wounds in her palms, cleared the fog of her memory in one burst.

Raal, one of the mages who called themselves Physicks, had magically transported her from Lagrimar to . . . wherever she was now. Somewhere in Yaly, she remembered being told, nestled deep in the vast country where the Physicks had originated. She'd been locked in a cell, believing that Raal would do what he'd promised: remove her Song and free her from its lethal power.

But somewhere along the way, the plan had changed. Ydaris was here, too, revealing herself to be Yalyish and not the Lagrimari Earthsinger she had pretended to be for so long. And the former right hand of the True Father was still controlling Kyara through the blood spell carved into her chest. Kyara was bound to obey Ydaris's commands just as she had been since the age of eleven when the nonhealing wound had been inflicted on her.

Whatever sort of lecture or gathering this was, whatever they were doing to her, lasted for hours, though there were no windows by which to mark the passing of time. The brilliantly lit room was filled with hundreds of people, mostly in their late teens or early twenties, Kyara noticed. The stone table she was dragged and strapped to was eerily similar to the one in Ydaris's library back in Sayya on which so many horrors had been wrought.

The mages had called this place the Academie. It must have been both a school and a prison. As the blood trickled from her hands, her Song grew weaker, as did her body, and she would inevitably pass out. That was what happened every time.

Every few days she was shackled and brought here, to this room, to this table, to be observed by apathetic students her own age, none of whom even looked askance at the woman chained before them.

The blood draining from her was courtesy of an elderly man who would pierce her flesh with a knife made of bone. Instead of stealing her Song outright, the way the True Father had with his people, the Physicks would drain it from her slowly, just to the point where her Song was barely there, and then they'd give her some time to allow it to regenerate. Though Ydaris's command restrained Kyara from singing, over time her Song would grow strong again. And when she reached full strength, she'd be carted away again for a repeat performance. Like today.

Her eyes fluttered open as students began to file out of the classroom, climbing down the stairs and leaving through a door she couldn't see. She must have lost consciousness again. Once the crowd was gone, footsteps neared the table, and then two guards loomed over her. They released the binds, but her limbs were too weak to even attempt escape. Instead, she submitted to being shackled, hand and foot, and led from the room to a comparatively dark hallway.

Every wall they passed was paneled in rich wood. In the stark desert of Lagrimar, such a thing was decadent, but in resource-rich

Yaly it must have been the norm. The floors and ceilings of the halls were covered in the same material, polished to a high gloss. She passed doors every few paces, most with glass windows embedded in them but shaded by fabric so she couldn't see inside.

Each passageway looked just like the others, and she struggled against the weariness, trying to find some difference, some way to identify her surroundings and perhaps find an exit. Eventually, she gave up and let her heavy head hang down. So much energy was required to keep it upright.

A clank of metal roused her. Somehow she'd fallen asleep while walking, and she awoke back in the prison. The door to her cell slid open on its own—perhaps using some kind of magic—and Kyara was deposited on the floor in a heap. Another clang and then the pounding footsteps of the retreating guards sounded. Always different men, all with shaved heads marked with the same blocky symbol tattooed on their scalps. She'd gathered that the insignia marked those who were not Physicks but merely servants.

She crawled onto her bed and let out a sigh. The only bright spot in this whole ordeal was the soft, pliable mattress. It was the most comfortable thing she'd ever slept on. The irony was not lost on her.

"Anything new?" a hoarse voice asked from the cell next to hers.

"Let her rest. Can't you see she's exhausted?" The second voice was identical to the first, but the difference in attitude identified the speaker.

"Nothing new, Roshon," she said, not bothering to open her eyes and regard those with whom she shared the otherwise empty prison. Roshon grumbled under his breath. He was the more ill-tempered of the two teens. His twin, Varten, was the personable one. Both bore the ginger hair of their Elsiran mother and looked nothing like their Lagrimari father, Dansig, who shared their larger cell. His dark, tightly coiled hair had gone silver at the temples, and kindness shone from ebony eyes.

Kyara rolled to her side and looked over to find their concerned gazes on her. Even prickly Roshon looked anxious. She forced a grim smile to put them at ease. Varten returned her smile, then lay back on his bed. He'd grown increasingly weak these past few days. A healthy seventeen-year-old, even one who had been locked up for two years, should not spend so much time sleeping. But every day he grew paler and seemed to have a bit less energy.

She shifted into a sitting position and forced herself to recall what she could of the trip from the classroom. "We go the same way each day from what I can tell," she whispered to them. "The guards take eight hundred seventy-four steps from the dungeon staircase to the auditorium. The number of turns are the same, too, and we never encounter anyone else in any of the passageways."

She leaned against the wall and closed her eyes, massaging her temples to take away the fatigue when she realized she was merely spreading blood across her face.

"Come, let's clean you up," Dansig said. Kyara crawled off her bed and made her way to the vertical bars separating the cells. She sat resting her head on them and pushed her arms through, allowing him to rinse her hands off with a cloth and water from the sink bolted to the wall. Then he bandaged her palms using supplies that one of the servants always brought with their meals.

"I'll try harder next time to find information we can use. Someday one of them will make a mistake that we can use to our advantage," she said. "We *will* find a way out of here."

Dansig hummed as he tied off the bandage. She stared at his lowered head.

"Varten's getting worse?" she whispered for his ears only. Dansig's pain-rimmed eyes met hers, and he nodded grimly. Both their gazes fell to the ruby-red bracelets adorning each of his wrists. The calderas were much like the collars that the Cantor used in Lagrimar to subdue Earthsingers. Bespelled by blood magic, they blocked Dansig's Song so that he could not heal his son or escape using his power.

After weeks spent in such proximity, Kyara had learned much about the family. For most of their incarceration, Dansig and the twins had been studied and used in experiments. Interrogated endlessly, pumped with drugs, coerced with the Physicks' amalgam magic, and brutalized. Each of them still bore scars from the encounters. Much of it had been done in an attempt to learn the location of the death stone, a caldera of great power.

Kyara shivered at the thought of the Physicks getting their hands on such a thing. The family protected the location of the death stone without even knowing its purpose. She'd revealed to them that the caldera contained the trapped Song of a Nethersinger. Possessing it would give the Physicks the same power over death energy that Kyara wielded.

Dansig, Varten, and Roshon had never broken, not telling their captors anything about the death stone, but they had all paid dearly for their silence. And now the only bright light in all of this was that Kyara's arrival had shifted the mages' focus to her. Except having her around was almost as bad as having the deadly caldera.

She took a deep breath, willing strength into her worn-out muscles. She would gladly succumb to her eventual death, as she did not think she could live through the process of having her Song drained repeatedly for much longer. But Dansig and his sons did not deserve to die in prison. They were a good and loving family, and they needed to get out. Right now, Kyara was their best chance of that happening. She was the one who left the cell regularly and could gather intelligence to form an escape plan.

“I won’t give up, Dansig,” she said as she struggled to her feet and back to her mattress. “I’ll find a way out of here for you. I promise.”

CHAPTER FOUR

The Mother kept her daughter cloistered, protected from a world which had already proved false. But cocoons were meant to be escaped. A shelter, too long occupied, becomes a tomb.

—THE AYALYA

Lizvette Nirall turned the dial of the radiophonic next to her mother's bedside, changing among the four channels and turning away from the unyielding voice of the newsreader recounting the events of the day. That would only aggravate Mother, who was breathing peacefully now after tossing and turning for the past quarter of an hour.

The classical music station would soothe Marineve Nirall's nerves and hopefully put her in a better state of mind to heal from her sudden illness. The palace physician had said nothing was wrong with Mother's body, and Lizvette agreed. It was the woman's heart that had broken, and Lizvette bore part of the blame.

A knock sounded at the door. Before she could even utter the words to invite entry, her cousin Zavros Calladeen strode in, eating up the floor with his commanding walk. Lizvette took a deep breath before he drew too close. He tended to suck up all the air in the room. She suppressed an inappropriate chuckle as the thought of her entering a room in such a manner popped into her head. Being ladylike and proper required a soft shuffle, not a commanding gait, no matter how many times she wished otherwise.

Her cousin acknowledged her with a mere nod of his head before kneeling at his aunt's side and grasping her hand in his much larger one.

"How is she?" His voice was a low, deep rumble.

"Much the same," Lizvette replied. "She sleeps most of the day away and is fitfully awake much of the night."

He searched the face of his beloved aunt. "And the physician?"

"Had nothing new to say. He prescribed a few tinctures to add to her tea and said I should try to get her to eat more, but it's not a physical ailment . . . I think we both realize that."

Zavros turned to look at her for the first time. "Have you heard from him?"

She reared back from his question as if she'd been struck. "Father? No, of course not. If he had contacted me I would have alerted someone. Do you honestly think I wouldn't?" She pursed her lips to keep them from quivering as he paused to consider.

"I'm not sure what to think of you, Lizvette." Her cousin's cold tone was no surprise. He and Father had often bumped heads, and while Zavros was no supporter of the unification, it was Father who was wanted for treason after spreading rumors about and threatening the life of their new queen. And for her part in Father's ploy,

Lizvette was on house arrest, confined to her family's apartment in the palace, where she'd lived nearly her whole life.

She swallowed the burning in her throat that arose whenever she dwelled on her situation. Though she wore no physical chains, regret bound her heart. She deserved the punishment, she couldn't deny that, but weeks of pacing the floors, feeling claustrophobic in a place that once had given her joy—on top of watching her mother deteriorate slowly from shame and heartbreak—had taken their toll.

Zavros squeezed his aunt's hand again, then rose, motioning brusquely for Lizvette to do the same. She narrowed her eyes at his haughty manner but still followed him out of the bedroom into the sitting room, closing the door behind her.

"You won't stay longer?" she asked, though she was honestly glad to be rid of him. "Mother so enjoys when you read to her. I think she likes hearing a man's voice."

"I wish I could, dear cousin, but the principality—I suppose we should be a kingdom now, shouldn't we? At any rate, things are in flux just now. There's been a bombing at the Southern temple."

Lizvette gasped. "A bombing? What in Sovereign's name?"

He nodded. "Yes, not an hour ago. We're keeping the press at bay for now until we know more. Of course, the wolves are salivating at the door. Both the Goddess Awoken and our *dear* queen were inside when it happened."

Lizvette cringed internally at the cold tone he used when referencing Queen Jasminda. "Were they hurt?"

"Certainly not. Their magic sees to that, doesn't it, Lizvette?" He raised an eyebrow. "Were you hoping, perhaps, for some harm to befall the queen and place you back into the affections of King Jaqros?"

Her mouth hung open. She was quite literally rendered speechless by the horror of his implication. She snapped her jaw shut and breathed in deeply, flaring her nostrils. It was her own fault. Most people who knew of her downfall likely would have asked the same question. She *had* tried to force Jasminda to leave and position herself as the most likely contender for Jack's heart. But Lizvette would never have tried to intentionally hurt or kill another person. The thought made the burning in her throat flourish to an inferno.

When Father had told her that sending Jasminda back with the Lagrimari refugees after their despicable king, the True Father, had demanded his people be returned was the best way forward, Lizvette had believed him. The men she'd hired to kidnap Jasminda were not supposed to injure her in any way; she'd made that clear. But none of that mattered anymore. Regardless of what happened, Jack would never choose her now.

Her heart clenched painfully. Her own loveless engagement to Jack's older brother had ended with his death. And Jack had never loved her either and never would. Perhaps the problem was her.

Zavros was still talking dispassionately about the horror at the temple. "The Sisterhood will likely be appealing for funds to rebuild," he said with derision. "And we will have to hold a national funeral service for the dead. More distractions from the real work the Council needs to focus on."

"And the injured?" she asked. If her cousin had any humanity left, it was buried deep inside, far beneath his ambition and political cunning.

"There are very few, almost none seriously so." He shrugged as if it was of little importance.

"I suspect the queen and the Goddess healed a great many."

Zavros waved this off. Anything good about the magic of Earthsong fell on deaf ears when it came to him. Most Elsirans feared Earthsong, and not without good reason. While the magic could not be used to harm directly, the Lagrimari army had used it to create all types of mayhem—from mudslides to earthquakes to fireballs—during the many breach wars. But Earthsong could also be used benevolently.

"The Council will form a committee to oversee the investigation into the bombing," Zavros said. "These are changing times we live in, cousin. Changing times. I must go. Send word if Aunt Mari's condition worsens."

"Of course."

He bowed stiffly before disappearing through the main doors. The guards assigned to her quarters were visible in the hall until the door shut.

Lizvette turned to the balcony and walked out to stand in the crisp fall air. *All those people . . .* Her heart ached at the senselessness of the deaths—what sort of evil could be responsible for such horror? Was there no good left in the world? She stood lost in thought for so long that her fingers grew numb where they met the cold, stone railing.

Winter was on its way. Where would she be come spring? Her future was uncertain. Charged with treason, she would not face a regular trial. The king and queen themselves would decide her fate. Considering her history with Jasminda, even her longtime friendship with Jack was unlikely to aid her. Though he had promised her exile instead of the possibility of death. She had to be grateful for that.

She drew away from the railing and rubbed her hands together as an intense melancholy consumed her. If she could go back in time and change her behavior she would. But her father's malevolent whispering in her ear had swayed her. Thank the Sovereign that the Mantle had fallen, ending the long war the very day the refugees were to return to Lagrimar. When Lizvette looked back at her actions, she could not speak against her punishment. She deserved every moment of suffering.

She had actually liked Jasminda at their first meeting, though the jealousy had quickly arisen when Jack's feelings had become clear. And though Lizvette still loved Jack as much as she had since childhood, she was a pragmatist. She bet his heart had belonged to Jasminda from the day they'd met. The memory of the way he often gazed lovingly at his soon-to-be bride was etched in her mind.

There would never have been a time when he looked at her that way. Her own fiancé had not looked at her that way when he'd been alive, and it was unlikely a man ever would. Even before her crime, she was a tool in the hands of powerful men. Her father had wanted her to become a princess; he had pushed and wheedled until she was betrothed to Prince Alariq, no matter who her heart longed for. Alariq had wanted her to be a symbol for the people. No one had cared what she wanted.

Without anyone around, she let her guard down, let the tears fall that she would never allow another soul—including her mother—to see. Niralls didn't cry. Her parents had reinforced that childhood lesson with a switch across her legs. In fact, it was her very first memory. *Never cry. Never show any emotion at all.* It was so deeply ingrained in her that even alone, only three tears made it down her cheeks. Yet, it was more than enough to shame her.

She wiped them away and turned to go back into the apartment, when an odd chirping caught her attention. The sound was unnatural and metallic, like no birdcall she'd ever heard, and indeed, the creature that landed on the terrace ledge certainly looked like no bird she'd ever seen before.

At first she thought the thing was some kind of windup toy,

but it had gotten all the way to the second story of the palace on its own. Crafted from heavy paper and thin plates of metal, it hopped from foot to foot in jittery motions. She peered closer to view the tiny screws that kept the whole thing together. The bird resembled a sparrow but with little gears visible inside its chest that were slowly winding down. When its mouth suddenly opened, she stared in shock.

"Lizvette, my dear." She stumbled backward upon hearing her father's voice coming from the contraption. "I hope this message finds you and your mother well. I apologize for not having been able to communicate with you before now. I am saddened to hear of your house arrest. A cleverer girl would have been able to avoid such a thing and exploit your connections to help get you out of that rat's nest, but that ship has sailed, as they say. At any rate, if your mother has any intentions of the religious variety, bid her to make her prayers from home today. The temples are not safe. As long as there are unsavory elements in control of our great land, safety is simply not guaranteed. Probably best that you are confined to your rooms. Make sure Mother doesn't stray far, either. My thoughts are with the both of you. Rise above your dull tendencies and exceed my expectations, dear girl. Ta-ta for now."

The bird shut its tiny beak, and the gears inside crawled to a stop. Lizvette had just moved toward the thing to pick it up and inspect it when a strange clicking sound rang out and smoke began pouring from it. The entire contraption vibrated before exploding in a burst of sparks.

She raced back inside and slammed the terrace door, peering through the rattling glass as the haze cleared. It had left nothing behind, not even so much as a gear. Lizvette looked around wildly, half expecting that someone had snuck in to witness the strange sight, but she was still alone.

The radio purred from the other room where Mother slept. Lizvette sank onto the couch. Eventually, her shaking subsided and she pondered her father's message.

Mother had always been a devoted follower of the Queen Who Sleeps. Since the Goddess's awakening and Lizvette's arrest, Mother had visited the temple daily until she grew too sick to leave the palace.

Zavros's news echoed in her mind. The Southern temple would not have been Mother's first choice, being so near the dangerous neighborhood of Portside, but all the temples were so packed these days, and that one was the largest. Mother could have very well been present for the bombing—and Father knew it. His warning had likely arrived later than intended, and Lizvette's heart sank at the realization that her father's treachery had not ended now that he was in hiding. He had known about the bombing beforehand. Could he have had something to do with it? She could not deny her suspicions, as horrible as the idea was to contemplate. As for the rest of his message, *Safety is simply not guaranteed* . . . Did that mean more attacks were coming?

Her hands shook as she gathered her pen and paper to send a note to the king requesting an audience. She had to warn Jack about this and needed to see him in person to do it.

CHAPTER FIVE

Those who met the child saw our future in her. Hamish the Warrior pronounced her brave. Rhys the Spy praised her inquisitive nature. And Atar the Organizer admired her circumspection. But Neftet the Merciful questioned her courage saying, "The line between prudence and cowardice is drawn in smoke." Her words were wind battering the flames of our hope.

—THE AYALYA

Ella Farmafield grasped the bar under the window as the bus took a turn at high speed. Her stomach lurched and she was quite certain that at least one of the vehicle's wheels had left the ground. When it thumped back on the pavement, she bounced on the seat, gasping. She couldn't find her breath to send a whispered prayer to Saint Maasael, the patron of travelers. This was nearly worse than the journey she'd made to Elsira on that dreadful steamer ship.

The woman at the bus's helm, an elderly Sister with a snow-white topknot, had to be one of the worst drivers Ella had ever seen. They had been in no less than three near collisions and hopped the curb at least four times. But the shuttle the Sisterhood offered from Rosira to the refugee camp on the outskirts of the city was the best way for her to get there. The distance was too far to walk, and a taxi would have been impossibly expensive.

The other volunteers on the bus clutched their seats or chests in alarm. Fortunately, the turnoff to the little dirt road leading to the camp was just ahead, and this terrifying trip was nearly over. However, a deeper fear tightened a fist around Ella's chest. If today's visit was unsuccessful . . . She shook her head, unwilling to imagine the consequences.

Under normal circumstances, Ella would have leaped at the chance to answer the Sisterhood's call for volunteers to aid the Lagrimari refugees—she herself had emigrated over six years ago from the neighboring land of Yaly. Not to escape a brutal dictator, true, but to find a better life with her Elsiran husband, Benn. Ella knew exactly how mistrustful of foreigners people in this country could be and had great sympathy for the cause of the Lagrimari.

But while her desire to help the refugees was sincere, it was not her main reason for coming to the camp this day. Today was about justice.

As the city of white tents came into view, so did the sounds of shouting. A small group of protesters, perhaps three dozen, had amassed at the entrance to the camp.

Ella blew out a breath. The woman across the aisle from her sighed. "Don't they have anything better to do?" she muttered.

These anti-refugee protestors were everywhere these days. On street corners, crowded into meeting halls, filling the airwaves with their hateful opinions on the evening news broadcasts.

Ella squinted at the signs some carried with racist slogans like CULL THE HERD and GROLS GO HOME. Home? From the little she knew, Lagrimar was a vast wasteland, a desolate desert where the Lagrimari had been trapped for hundreds of years by the magic of the Mantle, and suffering under their immortal dictator the True Father.

Since the war and the fall of the Mantle, many Lagrimari had left their hardscrabble lives for the promise of something better in Elsira, and Ella for one was happy to have them. The presence of the other Elsiran volunteers on the bus was evidence that not all citizens felt such animosity toward the newcomers.

The bus careened past the knot of protesters and the handful of soldiers keeping them at a decent distance from the tents. They pulled to a jerky stop in a makeshift parking lot that held mostly Sisterhood trucks and a few army vehicles. When Ella disembarked and placed her feet on solid ground, she barely resisted the urge to kneel down and kiss it.

She scanned the surrounding area, which was free of any Lagrimari. They seemed to keep to the tents mostly, she'd only seen a few on the two other trips she'd made to the camp.

A group of Sisters approached, royal-blue robes swishing as they walked. Their neat topknots appeared to be achieved without the aid of pomade—Ella was impressed. Two acolytes shadowed the group, the preteen girls wearing the lighter blue dresses of initiates adorned with white pinafores. The Sisters greeted the volunteers warmly and began assigning them duties around the camp.

Ella stayed to the back of the small crowd, her eye on one of the Sisters. The woman was shorter than average, with frail, birdlike limbs and narrow features. She looked like a strong sneeze could blow her over and vibrated with nervous energy. Her topknot held hair of a dark auburn verging on burgundy and her eyes burned a pale gold.

Sister Rienne was the real reason Ella was here. For the past six weeks, Ella had been trying, and failing, to find someone not browbeaten into silence. If just one soul would speak out about what had been going on behind the scenes in the Sisterhood, she was certain others would join in. But if she couldn't convince Rienne to help, then Ella had very little hope left.

Ella caught Rienne's eye and smiled enthusiastically, but the woman's gaze darted away. She was more skittish than a barnyard cat, but Ella was persistent. And stubborn.

She successfully ensured a place in the group of volunteers that Rienne oversaw and followed her through the orderly aisles separating the tents. Every now and then a curious head would peek out, but for the most part, the residents stayed away from visitors. The group entered a large supply tent near the edge of the camp.

"These crates hold the shipment of textbooks we've been waiting on," Rienne said in her papery voice as she pointed to a small mountain of wooden boxes. "There are Elsiran language books as well as history, math, and science. We'll need them unpacked and organized by subject with children's books here and adult books here. Each stack will be put in its own knapsack to be distributed to the schools in the camp and in the nearby overflow locations."

Ella rolled up her sleeves and got to work. To her dismay, Sister Rienne hovered just out of casual-conversation distance.

The first time they'd met, Ella had merely wanted to take the woman's temperature and try to develop a rapport. But it was their second and last meeting that caused the Sister's current avoidance of her. Ella had come on too strong, something she didn't usually do—it's just that she was growing desperate.

After nearly an hour of working, her first opportunity to speak with Rienne alone arrived when the Sister slipped out of the tent. Ella grabbed several empty crates and took them outside to the rubbish pile.

She looked around anxiously, finally spotting the Sister's small form bobbing down a nearby aisle. Ella ditched the crates and broke into a jog to try and match Rienne's pace. Though Ella had at least two heads of height on her, the woman was quick.

"Sister Rienne, a word please?" she called out, keeping her voice pleasant.

Rienne whipped around, exasperation creasing her forehead. Ella paused, her chest heaving from the exertion of the chase. They were deeper inside the camp now; large signs marked the rows with numbers for the north-south routes and letters for those going east-west. "I need to speak with you about the matter we discussed last time."

Rienne clasped her hands and tightened them. "Mistress Farmafield, I don't think it's appropriate—"

"I realize that the memories are difficult to rehash, but . . ." Ella's eyes entreated the Sister. She took a step forward and lowered her voice. "The High Priestess of the Sisterhood has hurt many people. Corruption corrodes the organization. She's torn apart families. Ruined lives. Your family is not the only one."

Rienne turned her face away, pain tightening her features.

"Someone has to stand against her. Tell their story. Together we can take her down. Don't you want justice for Lyza?" Ella whispered.

Shaking, Rienne cut her eyes at Ella. "How do you know the things you claim to?" She held up a hand when Ella went to respond. "It doesn't matter. I don't think I want to know. What you ask is impossible. The High Priestess is untouchable. What happened to my daughter was an abomination. But Lyza has found peace in the World After. The Sisterhood is all I have left. If I go against the High Priestess, I'll have nothing."

Rienne's eyes filled with tears, and Ella's heart cracked. She'd heard the same from the other women she'd approached over the past few weeks. Women who had grievances against Syllenne Nidos, the High Priestess of the Sisterhood. Taking her down had been Ella's driving goal since the Mantle's fall. She had her own reasons for doing so, and had been arrogant enough to think it would be relatively easy. Syllenne had made many enemies during her ascension over the past decades and Ella knew so many details . . . but could never reveal how exactly she knew.

There had been backstabbing, theft, blackmailing, threats, assaults, and heartbreaking abuse. Rienne's poor daughter Lyza, only nine years old and an acolyte to the order, had been beaten and brought to the brink of starvation, all as punishment for her so-called high spirits. Syllenne had overseen the discipline back when she'd merely been a temple priestess off in the far east of the country.

Young Lyza had died of an easily treatable infection when Syllenne had denied her medical treatment. Rienne's grief made her a shell of her former self.

"There are others," Ella pleaded. "More like you who've been affected. Alone your voices may not carry, but if you raise them together . . ." She clasped her hands together to emphasize the unity.

Rienne just shook her head. "Syllenne knows everything. I'm sure she knows you're here now speaking with me. Besides, don't you think the Goddess can sense the heart of Her own High Priestess? If something could be done, wouldn't She do it?" A deep frown descended across her drawn features. "As powerful as the High Priestess was before the Great Awakening, she is that much more untouchable now. And if the Goddess Herself has not seen fit to replace her . . ." Rienne spread her arms apart in a defeated gesture.

Ella took a deep breath, gearing up to press her case, when a figure appeared farther down the row, approaching with speedy footsteps. A dense foreboding caused Ella to hold her tongue as she recognized the feline grace of the Sister drawing near them. Golden-red hair and a face carved with otherworldy beauty came into view—Sister Gizelle.

Rienne noticed Ella's aggrieved expression and looked over her shoulder at the newcomer. When she turned back around, her face was ashen. Gizelle was one of Syllenne Nidos's lackeys and her presence here underscored Rienne's point—the High Priestess was always watching.

Gizelle had been the one to kidnap Ella's newborn nephew—on orders from Syllenne Nidos—moments after her sister died. The baby was held for days until Ella discovered his location and reclaimed him. Now he was safely out of the country, out of reach of the High Priestess and her machinations. For if Syllenne ever discovered the secret hidden in the baby's blood, he would never be safe.

And now, if Gizelle reported back that Ella had been targeting Rienne, things could very well get worse for the timid Sister. Ella cursed herself for not expecting something like this.

Sister Gizelle glided to a stop next to them, her perfect face arranged in the most vicious scowl. "Mistress Ravel, whatever are you doing here?" Even her voice sounded like melted gold, the steely unfriendliness in it notwithstanding.

Ella gave a broad grin. "It's Mistress Farmafield. In Yaly, married women keep their surnames. I seem to have gotten a bit lost in this tent maze you've constructed." She motioned to Rienne.

"This Sister was so kind as to stop to aid me; I'm really quite a dullard about directions."

Gizelle eyed them suspiciously. "Where precisely are you trying to go?" Though at least a decade her senior, Sister Rienne shrank away from Gizelle, whose gaze had narrowed to a flinty point.

Voices rose from around the corner. A small crowd seemed to be headed their way. "Please keep up," an exasperated woman called out. "No more stragglers if you please."

The group emerged in the intersection Ella and the Sisters were standing in. Close to a dozen Elsiran men and women led by one harried, middle-aged Sister. The woman's face was plain and round; her no-nonsense manner put Ella in mind of her mother-in-law. Ella didn't recognize any of the people from the volunteer shuttle, and she hadn't met a male volunteer, yet several men were present. Most appeared middle class, well dressed, and not like they expected to pick up trash or unpack crates. Quite unlike the plain frock she'd worn to do odd jobs around the camp.

The new Sister eyed Ella, Rienne, and Gizelle curiously.

"Here they are," Ella said brightly. "One row looks just like another here."

Gizelle's eyes widened a fraction. "You are here with Sister Moreen's candidates?"

"Oh yes," Ella said. "I just got a bit turned around."

Sister Moreen sighed dramatically. "We don't have time to chase after those who fall behind. Stay close to the group. This way, please." She began walking backward, leading the men and women deeper into the camp.

"Thank you so much for your help," Ella called out, moving off to follow. She planned to track them for a while and then make her way back to the tent she'd been volunteering in. However, while Sister Rienne disappeared so quickly Ella thought she must dabble in magic as a hobby, Sister Gizelle fell right in line, apparently determined to ensure Ella made it to where she'd claimed she was going.

Ella was only mildly curious as to where that was, but her interest was piqued when they approached a tent much larger than the rest at the intersection of rows AA and 49.

She ducked into the entrance and blinked as her eyes adjusted to the lower light. Gas lamps illuminated a space that was even bigger inside than it had first appeared. This looked to be some sort of meeting area, done in the Lagrimari style with cushions on the ground around low tables instead of regular tables and chairs.

Seated in orderly rows in the middle of the space were at least thirty children ranging in age from about three years to young teenagers. All had the same mist of melancholy clinging to them. These children, down to the youngest, had seen far too much in their few years of life.

Folding chairs had been brought in for the Elsirans, and Sister Moreen herded them to the seating area as the children looked on. Gizelle stayed, standing near the entry most likely to prevent Ella's escape from whatever it was that she'd gotten herself into. Ella sat at the edge of her chair, taking in the details of her surroundings and trying to listen in to the people around her. She couldn't afford to ask them what they were doing here when it was something she should obviously know.

Moreen stood in front of the chairs and the chatter quieted immediately. "Thank you for heeding the call." Something close to a smile graced her stern face. "The need for families to adopt the Lagrimari orphans is great. It far exceeds those willing and as such, you all are truly to be commended. I believe I speak for everyone in the Sisterhood when I tell you how grateful I am.

These children represent just a small fraction of those who need stable homes with upstanding families."

Ella looked at the people around her in a new light. Men with collars starched and pressed, women in what may well have been their best dresses, hoping to make a good impression. And the children, sitting still as stones in their neat little rows. Faces scrubbed clean and eyes—well, if not hopeful, then nearly so. Ella's heart tore. She focused back on Sister Moreen.

"Now there is a language barrier, but the children are learning Elsiran quickly. Their minds are so pliable and while it's not possible for us to learn their language, which apparently was created via witchcraft, we have no doubt that most of them will be fluent in a few short months. Many have already made astonishing progress. With care and attention, these children could be a part of your family."

Everything else faded away as Ella considered what she'd stumbled into. Six years of marriage had not blessed her with a child. Adoption was always a possibility, and one she'd considered, but it had never seemed to be the right time. Her and Benn's finances were a mess, they lived in a one-bedroom flat over a corner bodega, and Ella hadn't been at her job for very long; however, something deep within her bloomed and blossomed at the thought of bringing one of these children home.

Oh dear, what will Benn say?

The Sister spoke for a few more minutes, and then it was time for the children and adults to meet. Awkward tension filled the air at first, with both groups unsure of how to proceed. A gray-haired Lagrimari man appeared, a box of toys in the crook of his arm, and Sister Moreen helped to distribute them on the low tables scattered around the space.

Ella moved to kneel at one such table and picked up a cloth doll.

It bore flaming-red hair and skin the color of aged parchment—nothing like any of the Lagrimari children. She made a mental note to send away for dolls from Yaly, where the people's appearances, and as such the toys, were not so homogenous.

A handful of tin soldiers had been placed on another table. A small boy of around eight sat on a cushion nearby, his huge eyes almost comically round. Ella scooped up one of the soldiers and held it out to him, but he reared back as if it would strike him.

Vexed with herself, Ella cursed silently. Of course the boy wouldn't want to play with a soldier. St. Siruna only knew how Lagrimari soldiers treated their people, and the Elsiran ones had been little better.

She put down the toy and picked up a truck instead. This time the boy smiled.

"Oh, isn't he precious?" a voice behind her cooed. A young couple hovered nearby, both beaming at the child, who had the presence of mind to grin back.

Ella gave him a wink before rising and allowing the couple to sit and play with him.

Near the entryway, Gizelle stood giving the whole gathering the evil eye. But Ella barely noticed her; instead her gaze was captured by two girls clinging to each other in the corner. Both appeared frightened, though the elder of the two was obviously trying to look tough.

As Ella approached, a shrill voice behind her caught her ear. "The little one is pretty as a picnic, but the older one does nothing but glare, and look, she's covered in scars." Disgust colored the woman's tone, and Ella noted the marks on the elder girl's arms.

"I wonder if they're sisters?" the woman murmured. The Lagrimari man with the toy box happened to be passing by.

"Yes, sisters. And they won't be split up," he said gruffly. "A few couples have been interested in the younger girl, but she won't leave her sister."

"As well she shouldn't," Ella said, unable to keep the thought to herself. Why would anyone want to split up sisters? The children had already been through so much.

Feeling the scrutiny of the adults, the older sister straightened and arranged her face so it didn't resemble a glower so much as a sulk.

The woman who had asked about them turned away, pulling her husband with her. "Perhaps we should keep looking."

The older girl's posture slipped, her expression turning crestfallen. A hollow opened up in Ella's chest causing her eyes to burn. She approached the girls and crouched, coming to eye level.

"Hello, I'm Ella."

The younger one smiled and brought her hand to Ella's forehead. Ella looked up, surprised.

"It's how we greet one another in Lagrimar," the man said from behind her.

Ella grinned and touched the girl's forehead.

"This is Ulani, she's six," he continued. "And the older one is Tana. She's eleven."

"Pleasant to meet you, Tana," Ella replied, and touched the girl's forehead. The settler translated her words into Lagrimari.

Tana's expression was carefully blank but Ella sensed curiosity from her. Up close, the network of scars covered not only her arms but her legs as well. The girl tugged the three-quarter sleeves of her dress, trying in vain to cover her arms.

"I had an older sister, too," she said. "She's gone now, and I only really started getting to know her after she traveled to the World After, but I understand how important sisters can be. You two should never be separated."

Tana blinked rapidly, her clouded expression lightening. Ella sat back on her haunches, regarding the girls as a feeling of rightness drenched her like a warm summer rain. How was she going to break the news to Benn? Because these two had already stolen her heart.

CHAPTER SIX

Even the matriarchs could not claim perfection, so for us to do so would sully their memory. A seeker was needed, and Ayal was chosen. As hero, as offering, as gift, as sacrifice. She would journey to remind the people of the land that the past should not be repeated, and to join the branches of the tree into one, sturdy trunk. A firm foundation that would not fail.

Not again.

—THE AYALYA

Jasminda ul-Sarifor could still smell the smoke in her hair. She'd scrubbed herself raw after finally returning to the palace from the madness of the aftermath of the temple explosion, but the acrid tang of smoke and bitter palmsalt clung to her nostrils. Perhaps the scent no longer permeated her skin or clothes and was only in her mind.

She wound down the hallways, barely noticing the passersby who stopped and bowed or curtsied at her with murmurs of "Your Majesty." Ever so slowly, she was getting used to the idea of being the queen of Elsira. Though if she stopped too long to think about it, raw terror still seized her as the consequences of her failure played out in her mind.

No. Failure is not a possibility. She squeezed her hands into fists, crushing the piece of paper clutched in one of them. Holding on to her anger kept her mind clear. Rage burned at whoever had set the bomb that had destroyed so many lives and forever scarred their land. And a bitter resentment bubbled over the sender of the note slowly turning to pulp in her grip.

Her mama would have been disappointed in her. She was the most even-tempered person Jasminda had ever known. Even Papa had not been prone to rages, so it was a mystery as to where she and her brother Roshon had gotten such fiery tempers. Her other brother, Varten, had taken after their parents—sweet and even-keeled.

Eyes still sore from exposure to the fire stung as the loss of her entire family slammed into her like a wall. There were days when the grief was barely a whisper on her skin, and others, like today, when it threatened to immobilize her. Fury closely chased its heels. She had to overcome the desire to punch something, and she absolutely could not cry. Especially not here in the palace hallways. It was unladylike, and certainly unbefitting a queen.

She paused to gather herself, closing her eyes and breathing deeply. *One task at a time.* She counted to ten and back down to one, willing calm to infuse her bones.

When she opened her eyes again, a butler was headed her way, concern painted on his face.

"I'm all right, Renard," she said, waving him off. "Thank you."

He bowed and stepped aside, still watching her warily. Jasminda forced a smile—a brittle, crackling thing—to hopefully relieve his alarm as she continued on her way to Jack's office. When she arrived, she nodded at the secretary seated in the outer chamber before heading in.

King Jaqros Alliaseen stood when she entered. He looked as dashing as ever, if quite rumpled with his shirttails having escaped his trousers and his hair sticking up in all directions. The tight knot inside her loosened at the sight of him and her lungs were able to fill completely.

That morning, he'd raced to the temple once he'd discovered she was there and attached himself to her side. The worshippers had long been cleared out and the building sundered to rubble; investigators from the Intelligence Service were poring over the ruins, collecting evidence. Jack had refused to let her go, giving orders and answering questions with Jasminda nestled firmly in the circle of his arms.

He'd needed to reassure himself that she was all right. And she'd needed the comfort. But his face as he regarded her now seemed leaner somehow. Deep shadows hollowed his eyes. The stress of the day was taking its toll. Jack had not bothered to rest or change his clothing since returning. He'd poured himself into his duties—probably to stave off panic.

Only after she'd crossed the threshold and was halfway into the office did she notice the second man standing in the room. He was an imposing man of middle years with a great walrus mustache overtaking his face.

"Director Dillot," she said, inclining her head toward him in the way she'd been advised was queenly.

Luqos Dillot, Director of the Intelligence Service, bowed deeply. "Your Majesty," he said in a rumbling baritone. "I was just advising His Majesty of the latest development in the investigation."

"What development?" Jasminda asked, sitting next to Jack on the settee. Dillot settled back into the armchair across from them.

"A group called the Hand of the Reaper has taken responsibility for the temple bombing. They've sent these letters to the major newspapers, demanding they be printed." He handed over a single typed page. Just three paragraphs of text that sickened Jasminda's stomach.

"Who is this group?" she asked.

"A secret society that has operated in the shadows, meddling with our culture and government for decades," Dillot said flatly.

Jack rubbed his forehead. "The group is said to have been started one hundred and fifty years ago by Prince Niqolas."

"The same Prince Regent who was beheaded in a coup?" Jasminda asked.

"The very same." Jack's voice was grim. "Niqolas had a strong distrust of foreigners."

"As would anyone kidnapped as a child and forced to live among the savages of Raun, Your Majesty."

"The Raunians weren't responsible for kidnapping him, Director," Jack replied. "The True Father hired mercenaries to do that. In fact, it was Raunians who saved his life and returned him to his home, did they not?"

Dillot nodded his assent, but still wore a sour expression.

"At any rate," Jack said, "the experience left Prince Niqolas with quite the jingoistic streak. At some point before his brother led the coup to depose him, he created the secret society with others sympathetic to his cause."

"For what purpose?" Jasminda asked.

"They're nationalists first and foremost," Jack replied. "It's said they're responsible for coining the phrase 'Elsira for Elsirans.' In the beginning, they worked to control public opinion and promote the idea that a war with Yaly was necessary."

"Just because Niqolas hated foreigners?"

"He hated the Lagrimari specifically for orchestrating his kidnapping. He thought that he could go through Yaly to attack Lagrimar from its eastern border. No one was ever certain that the Mantle stretched that far since those mountains are impassable. But apparently, Prince Niqolas believed it was nothing a few tons of dynamite couldn't solve."

Jasminda's brows rose.

"Luckily for Elsira," Jack continued, "the army's High Commander was not as malleable as the populace. After the coup and Niqolas's death, the Reapers were quiet for a time, but reemerged to oppose the plans for a national railway."

"*They're* the reason we have no railroad?"

Dillot spoke up. "There was always opposition to the idea of blighting our country with great steam-pumping iron beasts. Farmers would lose valuable land, and the whole thing would be an eyesore."

Jasminda shook her head in disbelief. "A railroad track takes no more space than a road. And think of the convenience."

"Most Elsirans do not agree with you, Your Majesty." Dillot appeared to be one of them.

"Likely because there was a sustained campaign to poison the people against it," Jack replied. "Every form of popular media seemed to coalesce to oppose a railway: newspaper articles and editorials, plays were written parodying the idea, music halls were filled with songs deriding it. I once came across an old math textbook with an equation about how many acres of land would be ruined by the construction of a train station. There was a concerted, directed assault and those who care to study such things point to the Hand of the Reaper as its source."

"So because the trains and engines would have to be manufactured outside of Elsira, the group contested it?" Jasminda asked.

Elsira was an insular country that was being dragged into the technological age kicking and screaming. They'd adopted some modern conveniences such as electricity, automobiles, and telephones, but every time a railroad was proposed, or an airship field, or any number of other updates, the plans were vehemently opposed. Compared to some of their neighbors, Elsirans lived in the dark ages.

Jack shrugged. "Foreign tycoons have never been well thought of here. Had the steam engine been an Elsiran invention, we likely would have railway tracks crisscrossing the country. We're quite lucky that an Elsiran devised his own automobile design."

"No one knows who they are, and how they accomplish such things?" Jasminda asked.

"They are cloaked in secrecy," Dillot responded. "We believe the group is headed by five members and the bulk of their work is carried out by independent cells."

"Perhaps without knowledge of the other cells or even who they're working for," Jack added. He looked like he was going to say more, but then thought better of it.

"And are they known to be violent?" Jasminda said, her voice lowering.

Dillot fidgeted with the folder in his hands. "Not that we know. But again, their activities are by and large hidden. There have been theories about their accountability for various unexplained deaths over the years, but they have never before taken responsibility for an event such as this."

Jasminda regarded the letter she held, reading over the hateful words again. “They say there will be another attack,” she whispered.

Jack nodded. “If we don’t do what they ask.”

A knock at the door forestalled further conversation and Jack’s secretary entered. “Your package has arrived, Your Majesty.”

“Thank you, Netta.” He rose quickly, his expression inscrutable. “Keep me apprised, Dillot. When the evening papers hit the stands with this letter printed, we need to be prepared for the fallout.”

Dillot rose. “Yes, Your Majesty. Quite right.” He seemed flustered at being dismissed so quickly. However, with another bow, he was gone.

Jasminda turned to her fiancé. “Should we stop the papers from printing it?”

“The people will find out anyway. These things tend to spread.”

She dropped the page onto the coffee table and the other crumpled paper in her hand fell as well. She’d forgotten she was holding it.

“What’s that?” Jack said, moving to grasp it.

“Lizvette has sent you another message.”

Jack froze midreach. “I promise you I don’t know why. We’ve both made it very clear—”

“I’ll handle it. I just wanted you to know.” Her previous irritation at Lizvette’s persistent attempts to communicate with Jack had vanished for the moment, replaced by a sad emptiness in her belly. Another attack was in the works—when would it end?

Jack ran his hand through his already disheveled hair, which was longer than usual. He’d been scheduled for a haircut that morning.

“Do you think we should postpone the wedding?” she asked.

Shocked eyes regarded her as the bookcase in the corner of the room slid open. Jasminda tensed, but Jack placed his arm around her, pulling her closer.

"It's just Benn," he said. "And no, of course not. The wedding goes on as planned." He gave her a squeeze and then rose as Lt. Benn Ravel stepped into the room from the hidden entrance to the office.

Jack's friend and former assistant brushed off the dust that clung to his black uniform as the secret door slid closed. "Your Majesties," he said with a bow.

"Benn." Jack motioned him forward. "Thank you for coming. Sorry about the subterfuge, those passages weren't too narrow for you?"

Benn was quite a bit stockier than Jack's lean form. The tiny secret hallways that ran through the palace would have been a challenge. His expression was sardonic. "I may develop claustrophobia after that experience, sir."

Jack chuckled and the men sat.

Benn had recently transferred from the army to the Royal Guardsmen, but as far as Jasminda knew, he hadn't been assigned any sort of traditional guard duty. He was, however, one of the few people Jack trusted implicitly, and though she didn't know him well, that was enough for her.

They briefed Benn on the Hand of the Reaper and showed him the letter.

"This reads like a manifesto. They want Elsira for Elsirans and"—he peered more closely—"they're calling for a separate state to be established for the Lagrimari?" His perplexed expression was almost comical. "I'd thought that was Lagrimar?"

Jasminda laughed bitterly. "Keep reading."

Benn scanned the page. "'We acknowledge that the country of Lagrimar is untenable and humbly suggest the less populated land in the north of Elsira as the location for a new Lagrimari state. Our only mandate is that it be separate and independent so as not to sully the purity of Elsira.' Hmm." He grabbed his chin, rubbing at the stubble there.

Beside her, Jack was stiff. "There have been other calls for a separate state. If I had to guess, I'd say the Reapers have been sewing the seeds of this idea ever since the Mantle fell."

Benn shook his head. "That's ludicrous. Split the country in two just so they don't have to deal with the refugees and make them citizens? But what about the Goddess? She's the one who called for a united land for Elsirans and Lagrimari. What does She have to say about this?"

Jasminda thought of Oola standing on the platform at the temple moments before the bombing, always so mysterious and close-lipped. "The Goddess has always been clear. We were one people once and She wants it to be that way again. A two-country solution is not on the table."

"But She has not weighed in on this demand," Jack said. "And She has steadfastly avoided providing counsel to us on any matter at all. Each request for advice on decisions from small to large have been denied." His voice was acerbic. The Goddess's abdication of rule had been maddeningly complete. Her past weeks had been spent either at the temples or entirely absent, unable to be located by anyone.

Jack tapped a rhythm out on the arm of the settee. "The Council will no doubt want to consider all possibilities."

Jasminda blinked rapidly, not believing her ears.

"I'm not saying that it's a good idea, but as rulers we need to weigh every option." His voice was conciliatory, but Jasminda couldn't shake the dread overtaking her.

"You would consider bending to the will of terrorists?"

Jack clenched his jaw. "It's not just the terrorists calling for two countries."

"Yes, it's the worst of the Elsirans. The nationalistic, small-minded people who think there's such a thing as Elsiran purity. The ones being manipulated by an insidious cancer that's already claimed dozens of lives this morning alone." Her voice rose with each declaration.

Jack stared at her, eyes wide. So her anger hadn't left after all. She turned to face Benn, who looked uncomfortable witnessing the disagreement between the two leaders.

She and Jack would discuss this later. "So why did you force poor Benn here to brave the dusty secret passages?"

Jack took a deep breath. She could feel his gaze lingering on her but couldn't look at him right now. His voice was low and measured. "Do you think the Hand of the Reaper could be responsible for my brother's death?"

Jasminda startled. Weeks ago, Benn had come to Jack to confide that his wife Ella believed Prince Alariq had been murdered. Her only proof lay in the memories of her dead sister, memories she'd been able to access via a magical spell. Benn hadn't thought Jack would believe him. Little did the man know that the new king and queen were very well acquainted with magical memory spells.

Alariq had died in an airship accident—or so the nation believed. The idea that it had been murder had shaken Jack to the core. Ella believed that Syllenne Nidos, High Priestess of the Sisterhood, along with a mysterious man from Yaly were responsible for the killing.

Jasminda chanced a glance at Jack; his face was troubled. "The letter mentions further attacks, but also hints at past ones," he said.

Understanding dawned. "If Alariq was murdered," she said,

"then it stands to reason it couldn't have happened without at least the knowledge of the Reapers, if not their approval."

"We have to assume they have their hands in everything," Jack said, voice tight.

Benn stared at the ground, considering. "Ella is sure a Yalyishman was the one who approached Syllenne with the plot. If this Reaper group hates foreigners, then wouldn't it be unlikely for them to have worked together or even approved of an assassination?" He shook his head. "It doesn't track."

"The truth is we have no idea of the identities of the Hand of the Reaper or anyone they may be working with or what they're truly capable of," Jack said. "I asked you to come in secret because, with the exception of Usher and Darvyn, the people I trust completely are those in this room. And I'd prefer to keep you as anonymous as possible to prohibit any reprisals. We have to assume that every institution from the Council to the constabulary is compromised."

Benn nodded grimly. "I understand, sir. What do you want me to do?"

"I'd like you to lead your own investigation into this. You can move around to places we can't and you have connections we don't. And your wife has proved very resourceful."

"That's one way of putting it," he chuckled.

"There will be another attack. We believe that the Reapers use independent cells. If we can find the people actually responsible for the bombing, that will get us closer to being able to stop another tragedy."

Benn looked somewhat pale.

Jasminda was still upset at Jack's willingness to even consider two countries. But her admiration and appreciation for the speed of his mind was greater than ever. She leaned forward. "It's a big task, Benn, but I agree with Jack. There's no one else we'd entrust it with."

"It's one I'm happy to do, Your Majesty. I just hope that I'm up to it. I promise I'll do my best."

She smiled. "I don't believe any of us feel up to the roles we've been assigned. I certainly don't. Your best is all we'd ever ask."

Benn took a deep breath, which seemed to re-inflate his resolve.

"Thank you, Benn," Jack said. "These times will sorely test us all."

Jasminda felt that truth deep in her bones. As she sat back against the cushion, the smell of smoke wafted up from her hair. She wondered if it would ever leave.

CHAPTER SEVEN

The seeker was uncertain, unconvinced of her talents, and wavering in her resolve. She begged the Mother to task someone else and lift this burden from her neck. But Melba the Judge raised a sapling in one hand and her axe in the other. "There is change and rebirth or there is death."

—THE AYALYA

At the northwestern-most edge of Portside, Pier Road dead-ended in a vacant lot. No warehouses stood here, and the shoreline was too rocky for ships to safely dock. Massive boulders rose from the ocean to meet the edge of the mountain ridge that surrounded Rosira.

Darvyn took in the fresh scent of the ocean only a few dozen paces away. The black waves, sparkling in the moonlight, mesmerized him. The day he'd arrived in Rosira and seen the vast, unfathomable ocean spread out before him for the first time, he'd nearly cried. It still overwhelmed him.

"Strong as sand and weak as water," he called out in Lagrimari. His voice carried to the two women and one man he felt waiting in the shadows of a small wooden shack. Upon hearing the code phrase, the figures peeled away and walked toward him. Darvyn raised his hand in greeting to Rozyl ul-Grimor, who stood at the head of the small group.

"Darvyn?" she asked, squinting at him.

"You look surprised to see me."

"Didn't expect the mighty Shadowfox to grace us with his presence is all," she teased. "If the people knew who you were, there would be a riot."

Since the fall of the Mantle, his alter ego, the legendary folk hero known as the Shadowfox, hadn't been needed, at least by the public. There were no fields to plant here with his Song, no skirmishes with corrupt soldiers, no one to save from having their Song stolen, no pull on his incredible power. Until the temple explosion that morning, that is.

Rozyl turned to give a hand signal to the woman next to her, Sevora, who disappeared into the darkness, likely to do another scout of the area. The remaining man was Darvyn's old friend Zango, who crossed his meaty arms in front of him, nodded in greeting, but remained silent. All had served in the Keepers of the Promise with Darvyn, fighting for freedom from the True Father's rule.

"Considering what happened this morning, I wanted to be here—in solidarity. But do you really think all this secrecy is necessary? You know the king and queen won't retaliate against a group of Lagrimari having a meeting."

"You and I may know that," Rozyl said, "but the people don't.

Not yet. Concealing the meeting is just a way to make them more comfortable to come out and speak their minds. And there's the rest of the Elsirans to consider."

She tilted her head and the moonlight illuminated the jagged scars on the left side of her face that had been made during a bobcat attack in her childhood, an incident she didn't speak of. They gave her a fierce appearance, one backed up by the actual ferocity of her personality.

"Did you hear something?" she asked, her body preternaturally still.

Darvyn opened his Song. The dark, empty lot stretched out before them, hiding the gathering of close to one hundred people just beyond. "Sevora frightened a water rat. Are you the one cloaking the meeting place?"

Rozyl gave a brief nod.

Sevora reappeared, giving the all-clear signal, and they gathered together. The energy from the nearby people beat a tempo in his head. The meeting was hidden from their eyes and ears by a clever spell the Keepers had been using for years. It required an Earthsinger to gain entry, and those attending tonight's meeting had been instructed to approach in groups so that one of the few who'd retained their Songs could lead them in.

They walked a few dozen paces, and then Rozyl extended her arm straight out. Her fingertips brushed against gravel, causing a ripple. What had appeared to be an empty lot with nothing but crushed rock underfoot was revealed to hold a tent, gravel clinging to its exterior to make it look like the ground in the distance. The optical illusion was simple but effective.

The mirage pulled away like a curtain to unveil the tent's interior. Darvyn and the others slipped into a crowded space filled with Lagrimari men, women, and older children packed in a tight spiral of bodies. A petite woman standing on a wooden crate at the center of the space held their attention.

"We will not trade one prison for another! We will not barter away our futures!" Talida was an elder of the Keepers. A middle-aged woman with steely, bright eyes, her silver locks were interwoven into thick coils streaming down to her waist. Her throaty voice thickened the air.

"We have just as much right to be in this land as anyone else. *Our* ancestors transformed the earth beneath our feet from desert to plentiful. It is only through the treachery of one of *them*—the True Father—that we were separated from this land. Why should we be cast off to some far-off corner with scraps and told to begin anew?"

Shouts of agreement rose from the crowd.

"Why not open the doors of employment instead of slamming them in our faces? Why not allow us to fill in the gaps here? We are a hardworking people; we are not looking for handouts because we are lazy. The doors of acceptance rattle in their hinges from the force used to shut them!" A chorus of cheers rang out.

"And what of justice?" Talida continued, when the crowd died down. "It cannot be put off forever. Why has no one seen the True Father?"

She paused to spit after saying his name. Many others in the crowd followed her lead. "They say he rots away in the deepest part of the dungeon, but it has been weeks since any have beheld him. Where are the Cantor and her agents? Those who have terrorized us for generations? What of the trials we have asked for? When will we see the villains punished?"

Shouts and applause sounded as Darvyn began working his way through the throng. Talida's words were rousing, but something about them sent a sliver of unease down his spine. Still, it warmed his heart to see so many of his people here, looking well fed and full of hope, regardless of their meager circumstances.

He made it a quarter of the way around the outside of the crowd when a familiar gravelly voice stopped him. "Didn't think you'd make it here tonight, *oli*."

Darvyn turned to find Turwig ol-Matigor leaning casually against one of the tent's support posts with his arms folded. An observer would simply see a grizzled old man dozing off in the back. But Darvyn knew better. Turwig was the closest thing Darvyn had to a father. He had been the one to take him from his mother's home when the True Father's threats against him forced her to seek safety for her son among the Keepers. Turwig had taught Darvyn everything, and Darvyn had always considered him family.

But the elders had kept him from his mother, purposefully, seeking to sever his connection to her and hone him into a tool for their use. That revelation had left him unmoored, floating adrift from everything he'd once thought to be true. He looked upon the old man differently now.

"Why is everyone so surprised I'm here?" Darvyn muttered.

"You have to admit, you've been scarce."

"Do you blame me?" Darvyn arched a brow. Turwig had the decency to look somewhat abashed. Darvyn wasn't certain he'd been one of the elders who'd kept his mother away, but the old man must have known about it.

Another round of cheers rose from the audience as Talida finished her speech. Darvyn turned to watch her climb down from the crate. She was aided by a scowling man with a bushy beard; Darvyn held back a groan. "I was hoping Aggar would be otherwise occupied tonight."

"Where else did you think he'd be, *oli*?" Turwig gave a wry grin.

"Literally anywhere else."

The old man snorted.

Aggar climbed onto the crate, which barely looked able to hold his weight. "What do we fight for?" he cried.

"Justice! Justice! Justice!" the crowd responded. Darvyn moved off to get closer to the makeshift stage.

"The streets must run red with the blood of the monsters who starved us, who stole our children, who enslaved us!"

The responding voices grew frenzied.

"Every pay-roller who benefitted from our suffering! Every Enforcer and Collector! Every Golden Flame!"

Aggar's gaze locked with Darvyn's, and a dangerous light appeared in the man's eyes. "I believe that we have with us tonight someone who many of you will want to hear from."

Darvyn froze. He reached out with his Song for the other man's emotions. Excitement. Eagerness. A thread of animosity directed at him that was even stronger than normal.

"Throughout the bleak years, there was one figure shining in the darkness, defying the madness of the ruling regime and sparking hope in all of our hearts." Aggar's voice was rich and engaging, so different from his corrosive personality. The listeners hung on every syllable.

"The need for secrecy is over, the time for hiding done forever. I cannot allow us to go to our beds without giving you the gift of meeting the Shadowfox."

A gasp rose from the audience. People looked around, trying to figure out who among them was the legendary rebel.

The identity of the Shadowfox had always been protected for Darvyn's safety since the True Father had been after him his entire life, eager to steal such a powerful Song. But no one had reached out to Darvyn about announcing his identity at this meeting.

He looked back at Turwig. The old man's facial expression did not change, but Darvyn felt the denial of his knowledge of this in his dark gaze.

Aggar's eyes glinted in challenge as the assembly became more and more excited at the prospect of finally meeting the famed Keeper. Though only a few years older than Darvyn, Aggar had been raised to the level of elder, a distinction the man had earned, but one that still rankled. Now he was provoking Darvyn, creating a spectacle. He could simply leave, refuse to play this game of Aggar's. Making himself known now, without a plan or considering all the consequences, wasn't wise.

But the crowd vibrated with hope and energy, and by the smirk Aggar wore, it was clear he expected Darvyn to duck out and disappoint everyone. Perhaps he thought such a thing would bring the Shadowfox down a few notches in the eyes of the people. Jealousy pulsed through the man's other emotions.

Wise or not, Darvyn made the decision. Aggar's years of baseless mistrust could not triumph here.

Darvyn had worked in darkness and stealth his entire life; now he would step forward into the light. With a deep breath, the weight of expectation once again on his shoulders, he made his way to the center of the gathering.

Nostrils flaring and eyes narrowed, Aggar stepped down from the crate to stand next to Talida. His shock and anger beat a cadence against Darvyn's senses. Darvyn brushed by him and took his place.

The wood creaked beneath him, but if it had held Aggar's heavier weight, it would hold him. He looked up to find every eye trained on him.

Fear ballooned in his middle. The quiet stretched on and on.

Then the audience began to cheer.

Shouts and applause lasted for several minutes. Every time Darvyn raised his arms to quiet the people, the jubilation only increased. He caught sight of Rozyl, Sevora, and Zango in the back. The connections to his trusted friends set him at ease as he waited for the audience to quiet down.

"My name is Darvyn ol-Tahlyro, and I am the Shadowfox." The cheers began again in earnest and took even longer to die down this time.

"Though you never saw my face, I have met and aided many of you. It was my honor to do so. I am . . . humbled by your regard and grateful for your attention. It has been a long journey up to this point." He scrutinized the careworn faces looking up at him. "Much has been lost, but there is also much to be gained here. I look forward to our future in this new-old land of our origin."

Zango began to clap and others followed suit. Darvyn didn't know what else to say. He'd never had cause for public speaking before.

"What does the Shadowfox have to say about our benefactors?" Aggar shouted from just behind him.

Darvyn clenched his jaw. What was he playing at? "I . . . I urge patience. It has only been a few weeks. Housing is being built. And schools. The call to separate us into another land is only being broached by a few. The king and queen support unification. As does the Goddess Awoken. The Sisterhood and many others are coming to our aid. Jobs will come. Our battle against the True Father was not won in a night and neither shall be our integration into this new land."

The audience nodded and murmured their assent. Many Lagrimari had fallen into the reverence of the Goddess Awoken in the past weeks, now that they were free to worship as they chose, while many others were still circumspect of organized religion.

"I encourage everyone to learn the Elsiran tongue. To not engage those who would speak poorly of us and hold fast to the knowledge that the Goddess would not have led us here if things were not going to improve. Already the weather is better, is it not?"

Laughter rang out.

"Our place here is being created. We will not have to wait forever, but we must give them time. The king and queen are aware of our needs. Neither they nor the Goddess will abandon us. Thank you!"

He jumped off the crate and was immediately surrounded by people patting him on the back or greeting him with fingers pressed to his forehead.

"Thank you," people repeated over and over again.

An elderly woman stopped him with a palm to his chest. "You came to our village and restored my husband's garden after the soldiers had salted it. We were able to feed the entire neighborhood after the ration decrease. Bless you, *oli*." Son, she called him. He smiled at the woman and ducked his head in acknowledgment as tears pricked the edges of his eyes.

His movement through the crowd was stymied by many such testimonies. One woman's children had been saved from starvation by the secret potato fields he'd planted. He'd led a team of Keepers to rescue a caravan full of children who'd been stolen by nabbers to be sold to the highest bidder. His intervention had saved a group of teenagers' Songs from tribute when they were children. The list went on and on. He held back the tears as the people expressed their gratitude.

"And what of justice, Shadowfox?" Talida's voice rang out, causing the group that had gathered around him to turn. Standing on the crate again, her face was strangely blank. Sadness poured from her, and his heart clenched at her pain. "You urge us to wait for the Elsirans and say that change is coming, but the Elsirans blame us for taking food off their tables when the king and queen feed us. They call us criminals and savages when the real criminals sit in the dungeons of the palace being housed and fed when their lives should be forfeited." Her voice carried over the now-quiet group.

"The Enforcers. The Collectors. The Golden Flames. Should they not be held accountable?" Pain laced her gaze as their eyes locked. He did not know her story, but every Lagrimari had either experienced some form of cruelty from the government, or watched someone they loved do so.

"There will be trials for those who have harmed us." He spoke more to her than to their audience.

"Will we trust the Elsirans to provide our justice? We have no say in their courts."

"All of that will be worked out. The Mantle fell a mere six weeks ago." He spread his arms, pleading.

"And yet we still suffer." Her voice was hard.

"You have the ear of the king," Aggar said, slicing him with a razor-edged glare. "Are you truly our advocate?"

Talida's hands fisted. "Justice must be swift. And it must be ours to mete out."

"The king is a fair man and eager to do what is needed for the unification," Darvyn said. "And the queen has been on our side since before the Mantle fell." He was confident that the rulers would do whatever was necessary to provide closure to the people.

"Lagrimari should be involved in deciding the fates of those who tormented us and sit in prison," Talida said. "And for those who are in hiding, still hoping to escape justice . . . we want to hold their trials in absentia." Her voice grew stronger with each demand. "We should not have to wait for months and years to heal these wounds."

Darvyn sighed as the silence around him indicated that every man, woman, and child present was hanging on his answer. "I will bring this to the king and queen."

"We should start with a symbol of the True Father's thirst for blood—his most beloved assassin."

Darvyn stopped breathing at her mention of Kyara. As Talida spoke, Aggar's cold eyes bored into him like a drill, menacing and mean.

"The first to be tried for crimes against the people of Lagrimar should be the Poison Flame!" she shouted.

A deafening cheer went up among the crowd as Darvyn's vision swam. His heart tore in two. Muscles rigid, his gaze never left Aggar's.

So this had been the game. Reveal the Shadowfox to the people, force Darvyn to show his face to them, accept their praise, and then back him into a corner he'd have difficulty escaping.

Talida's emotions were shielded. The woman still had her Song, though she was not a strong Singer. Her shield was flimsy, and though Darvyn could have broken through it if he'd wanted, he left it intact. Her refusal to look at him any longer let him know that she, too, knew exactly what her demand would do to him. Both she and Aggar had witnessed Darvyn's meltdown when the Keepers had threatened to execute Kyara in Lagrimar. Aggar had even ordered Darvyn to be collared—fixed with a device that prevented access to his Song—briefly.

Cries of "Justice! Justice!" rang out. Darvyn spun around, beset on all sides by people when all he wanted to do was escape into the fresh air.

Hands reached out to him, words of gratitude barely reaching his ears. Someone gripped his arm and dragged him away while they murmured thanks to the people still surrounding him. Then he was outside, gasping in the crisp, sea-salty air, fighting the terror that clutched him.

Zango stood before him, concern etched in his gaze. Rozyl spoke in a harsh whisper behind him, but Darvyn was still drowning in a sea of sorrow.

For the first time since Kyara had disappeared from the streets of Sayya, Darvyn was glad. He hoped she was far away and safe. He could not imagine a choice more difficult than one between the people he'd spent his life protecting and the woman he loved.

CHAPTER EIGHT

"A riddle will I offer, to help you find your way," said Crispis the Entertainer. "What is freely given but expects a reward?"

Ayal would ponder the answer for a very long time.

—THE AYALYA

A pounding at the door roused Tai from fitful dreams. He shook his head to clear it of the hazy images of broken bodies, rubble, and chaos. The scene from the morning's bombing had invaded his troubled sleep. He and Mik had only gotten a glimpse of the destruction, but it had been enough to see that there was nothing they could do to help. Besides, when Elsiran soldiers had caught sight of them, they'd been pushed back beyond the gate into Portside.

The sobbing and wailing of the onlookers and survivors still clamored in his ears, mixing with the sound of someone beating on the door, and forced him off the lumpy inn mattress. Mik snored loudly from his bed in the corner. The man could sleep through a tsunami . . . and had.

Tai peeked out the window to see that night had fallen, but he had no idea of the time. They'd rented the room and fallen asleep in the early afternoon, weary from the voyage. He'd intended to go find that barmaid again but had opted for a nap first. Now he wrenched open the door, expecting to find a squad of grown men—perhaps those he owed money to—by the intensity of the knocking. His last retreat from Rosira had been made in haste, without a chance to settle his debts.

Instead, a teenage girl stood at the threshold, perhaps his sister's age. She was Lagrimari, and her dark eyes held shock, as if she wasn't certain he was actually going to answer her belligerent thumping. She lowered her fist and took a hasty step back. That's when Tai noticed the girl wore the light-blue robes of an initiate to the Sisterhood with an odd little white apron attached. She'd wrangled her springy black hair into an approximation of the topknots the Sisters all wore, but instead of the calm, serene expressions they assumed, astonishment froze her features. Perhaps she'd never seen a Raunian before.

Her gaze was locked on his shock of blue hair and the tattoos swirling on his face. He reached up and traced the newest ones, which spread from under his left ear to the middle of his cheekbone. The two barely healed lines indicated his years in prison. His forehead bore the insignia of his rank as captain of his own vessel, along with his family's pattern, and his chin bore marks displaying his right to use the communal waterways surrounding the island of Raun.

He gave the girl time to look her fill and watched the embarrassment settle over her. He racked his brain to remember the few words of Lagrimari he'd painstakingly learned from the passengers of his ill-fated voyage two years prior.

"All is well?" he said, struggling with the guttural pronunciation of the language. It had taken nearly as long for him to learn to speak the sentence as it had for him to master Common Fremian.

The girl's eyes widened, and she rattled off a string of words. He held his arms out and shook his head.

"Sorry, but I don't understand." He tossed out the phrase in the four languages he spoke fluently, but she showed no recognition.

She pulled out a piece of paper and handed it to him. Written in Elsiran were the words:

The Goddess Awoken requests an audience with Master Tai Summerhawk. Novice Zeli will guide you.

Tai's breathing hitched. One hand went to his birthstone pouch. He read the note three times before handing it back to the girl, Zeli. Well, this was a stroke of luck. Then again, maybe he shouldn't be surprised that someone as powerful as the Elsiran Goddess could find him. Holding up a finger, he bid the girl to wait while he ducked back into the room for his shoes and coat. He considered waking Mik, but instead scribbled a note and placed it on his friend's nightstand. Then he left the room to follow Zeli and meet the Goddess.

A black, gleaming town car idled on the street outside the inn. Somewhere a clock chimed nine—not as late as he'd thought. Zeli motioned for Tai to enter first, then climbed in behind him. The auto took off and passed through the Portside gate, waved on without inspection by the soldiers manning it.

Tai had seen Rosira dozens of times on approach from sea, but this was his first up close glimpse of the city. From the water, it appeared as though the buildings climbed straight up the mountain. Nearly all the structures bore distinctive stucco facades in soft pastels with clay-tiled roofs.

Winding switchbacks in the road made him slightly dizzy as the auto zoomed around the corners, rising higher and higher. Zeli grasped hold of her seat, as well, her eyes closed as if this trip was no easier for her than it was for him. Tai wondered where the Goddess Awoken intended to meet, at the peak of the mountain? But it turned out to be the next best thing, as the town car passed through the gates of the Rosiran palace and pulled to a stop.

White as bleached bone and lit with hundreds of electric lights, the palace stretched out on either side of him. It was only three stories high but at least a cable-length wide. Zeli was out of the car before he had a chance to really take in the exterior. They passed under pointed arches and an abundance of carved marble as he followed her quick pace inside. None of the black-clad guards stopped them, which was just as surprising as finding himself inside the home of the king and queen in the first place.

Zeli strode through the snarl of opulent hallways, never pausing or appearing confused. The only time she stalled was at an intersection of the corridors to allow a group of soldiers to pass them by. Tai observed the precision of the soldiers' movements and was surprised to find a willowy young Elsiran woman in their midst. Her head was held high, her hands clasped before her with no chains or shackles affixed, but Tai could see the metaphorical prison bars around her clear as day.

She did not so much as glance in his direction, but he could not keep his eyes off her. She was regal in bearing, and her fancy Elsiran gown and perfectly coiffed reddish-blond hair were at odds with the armed men guarding her. He couldn't say how he knew that the guards were not so much for her protection as for her confinement. Perhaps it was just one prisoner recognizing another. He wished he could have handled captivity with the quiet resignation apparent in the woman's demeanor. But though his mother had won the kingship of Raun when he was a teen, there was nothing royal or dignified about him.

He shook himself and peeled his gaze away from the group, hurrying to catch up to the Lagrimari girl who was already a dozen paces ahead. Thoughts of the delicate Elsiran woman and her strange circumstances consumed him until Zeli wrenched open a door, revealing a stone staircase leading down.

Tai's curiosity grew, along with his trepidation, as he was led into the bowels of the palace. His uneasiness multiplied when they paused at the brass gate leading to the dungeon. Two years of hard labor had left him with little desire to step one foot farther. Zeli turned for the first time, her squint of confusion transforming to an expression of understanding. She shook her head, pointed to the bars, and swept her arms apart, indicating no. She fished the note from her pocket, pointed at it, and gestured down the dim hallway.

The Goddess was in the dungeon?

She motioned him forward. Tai took one wary step and then another as tension stiffened his muscles. Zeli slowed her pace to match his. Consciously avoiding the eyes of the prisoners, he made his way down the passage. He felt the men behind the bars staring at him and felt shame at his cowardice, but freedom was still too new for him to have the courage to look at any of them straight on.

The dungeon was divided into corridors, and Zeli led him deep into its belly. The damp, close air was musty and cool. A Guardsman unlocked a creaking gate revealing an even darker chamber.

Illuminated by flickering candlelight was a woman who could only be the Goddess Awoken.

She stood before an imposing wooden door leading to what he thought might have been a storage room as it was clearly not a proper cell. Nearly as tall as he was, the Goddess had thick dark hair that sprouted out in a riot of unrestrained curls falling past Her shoulders. She wore a flowing white dress but no other adornments.

Her simplicity momentarily shocked him. The Raunian deity, Myr, was always portrayed bedecked in precious jewels—rings on every finger, throat held up by his many necklaces, wrists laden with bracelets. And though Myr had not walked the earth for eons, Tai had expected the Elsiran Goddess to be similarly arrayed. Her presence, however, was potent. Power seemed to crackle off Her skin, and Her gaze raked over him, leaving a prickling sensation in its wake.

Her voice burst with musicality when She spoke to Zeli in Lagrimari. Then the girl curtsied deeply and left. Tai bowed stiffly, unsure of how to address the deity before him. He knew only a little of Her lore, and most of it had come from the time when She had slept and spoke only to Her followers via dreams.

Glittering, dark eyes peered into his soul. When She turned back to the door, Tai nearly slumped with relief.

"Come forward, Tai Summerhawk," She said in Elsiran, inclining Her head slightly. He took a few steps forward, then a few more until they stood side by side. The Goddess smelled like power—that was the only way he could describe it. Being near Her reminded him of the stormy sea in the moments before a crack of lightning would rend the sky. The hairs on his arm stood up from their proximity.

He looked through the small, barred window leading into the

room. Empty shelves lined the walls, lending credence to his guess that this had once been a storage room. But now it bore a cot on which a man was lying, his back to them. Limp, russet-colored hair pegged him as an Elsiran, most likely. To be kept apart from the general prison population must make him either especially well connected or especially dangerous. Based on the Goddess's presence, it was probably the former.

"I would like for you to tell him your story. He has always liked stories." She motioned toward the man in the cell.

The request was odd, but such were the ways of the powerful. The prisoner wore what was once a fine shirt and trousers, now ragged and encrusted with dirt. Tai could see nothing but his back and longed to ask who he was, but he swallowed the question. "Which story?" he asked instead.

"The story of how you acquired the death stone."

The pouch around his neck seemed to pulse, though Tai was certain it was his imagination. *The death stone.* That was what Dansig had called it, as well. Tai pulled on the cord, freeing the pouch from behind his shirt, but the Goddess raised a hand to stop him.

"The story first, if you please."

"How—how did you know about it?"

Her gaze seemed to puncture his skin, leaving him somewhat breathless. The corners of Her mouth shifted slightly, but he could not call Her expression a smile. "I had a long time to watch the world. I saw many things."

Tai exhaled when She turned to motion him to a stool in the corner of the small chamber. He felt awkward sitting in Her presence, but She apparently preferred to stand. Tai sat obediently and thought back to the events of two years prior.

He told of how he and his sister, Ani, had been here in Rosira, negotiating a deal to sell some merchandise he had come to possess.

A fellow Raunian named Bor was the buyer, but the deal had gone terribly wrong. So wrong that it ended in a chase through the streets of Portside followed by Bor and his men.

In the ensuing confrontation, a woman of the Sisterhood had been shot and killed as she stood on a street corner alongside a Lagrimari man and two Elsiran teens. It turned out they were father and sons, and the boys, twins, were half-Elsiran and half-Lagrimari. The dead Sister had drugged and kidnapped them from their home far away, based on a message she'd claimed she received during a Dream of the Queen.

He paused his tale, eyeing the Goddess for any reaction. She hadn't moved, so he continued.

Fleeing the violence, and with no time to discuss a plan, all five of them had escaped to the *Hekili* and headed out to sea, only to be chased by Bor's ship. They finally managed to elude their pursuers, but returning to Rosira was impossible.

The father, Dansig ol-Sarifor, and his sons, Roshon and Varten, had reluctantly decided to complete the mission the deranged Sister had kidnapped them for—to find a magical stone lost in the ocean's most dangerous waters.

After much convincing, Tai had agreed to sail them to the Okkapu, a section of the sea feared by Raunians, and after a harrowing search, they had retrieved the death stone. But before they could sail away, a rival captain had found them. He'd been hired by a Yalyish mage who had been seeking the same magical object.

Ani had hidden the death stone, and Dansig had elicited a promise from Tai that if something happened to him, Tai would ensure the stone found its way to Rosira and to the Sisterhood. When the mage couldn't recover his quarry, he'd captured Dansig and his sons. Tai had fought to save them, but the mage had ignited some sort of explosion, killing both him and his captives, and maiming Ani.

Tai's mother's punishment had waylaid him for two long years, but he was now able to keep his promise and give the death stone to the Goddess Herself, now that She'd awoken.

He finished his story and looked over to see that the man in the cell had not stirred. The Goddess Awoken peered at the prisoner with some unfathomable emotion in her eyes. Tai wished he knew what it was.

"Show it to me," She said.

He jumped to his feet, freed the stone from the pouch around his neck, and held it out to Her.

"I cannot touch it." She kept her distance but peered at it fiercely.

Though Tai, Mik, and Ani had been able to touch the death stone with no ill effect, Dansig had been beset by horrible visions when he'd held it. Perhaps it had to do with Earthsong magic.

"What does it do?" Tai asked. "Why was it so important to retrieve this bit of rock?"

The Goddess clasped Her hands before Her and looked off down the corridor. Her bearing and manner had not changed, and Tai couldn't get a read on Her. "They live still. The mage did not kill Dansig and his sons."

Tai gasped and nearly dropped the stone. "You're certain?" Ani had been convinced that the three had somehow lived, but he'd thought it wishful thinking.

"Would you like to help save them?" She tilted Her head and slayed him with another penetrating gaze.

"Of course. Where are they? How did they survive? I-I saw them . . ." He could still feel the heat of the blast in his face. It was he who had bandaged what remained of Ani's arm after the explosion had taken her hand. And though the damage to his ship had been minimal and the detonation oddly contained, he didn't understand how anyone could have survived being in the midst of it.

"This task would put you at odds with your king, would it not?"

He sighed heavily. "I am already at odds with her. I will face whatever punishment awaits in order to free them." He owed them that much. They had been on his ship, under his protection when they had been attacked. In a short time, they had become friends, and Ani's connection to Roshon made them family, as well. If the young man had not disappeared, he and Ani would be nearly wed by now.

The Goddess smiled slightly, but the action only made Her appear sorrowful.

"Jasminda does not know her family lives, and I would like to keep it that way until they are retrieved successfully."

"Jasminda? Dansig's daughter? He spoke of her often—they all did." His mind caught up as the pieces fell together. "She is the same Jasminda that is the new queen?"

This was good news. Dansig had often worried as to the fate of his only daughter, left behind when the Sister kidnapped him and his sons. There had not been time to get word to her after their trouble on the docks, and the man's greatest wish was to complete the mission and return to her. She had only been seventeen then and alone in the world.

"Y-Your Majesty . . . why not tell her? I'm certain she would be greatly relieved to know—"

"She will learn when the time is right. For now, she has many other concerns to occupy her mind." Her tone brooked no opposition, and Tai clamped down his argument.

"But why me?" he asked. "Surely there are others you could send."

Her forehead creased slightly, and She tilted Her head to the side, almost looking through him as though She were seeing something else. "I believe having a Raunian along will be useful to them."

Then She blinked and Her eyes refocused on him. Her words made little sense. Raunians had no magic, unlike the Lagrimari or the Physick mages. True, Tai was resourceful and could think on his feet, but that didn't seem like such a rare talent. Though She wasn't *his* goddess, it was clear that She had a wealth of knowledge at Her fingertips. He would have to trust in that and not second-guess this chance to make things right.

"You will receive further instructions shortly," She said mysteriously.

Zeli reappeared bearing an ornately carved wooden box. She motioned to the stone still in Tai's outstretched hand. He recalled just then that the Goddess had never told him what the stone did, what the true purpose was of the object that had caused so much heartache, death, and destruction. He gently placed the mysterious bit of rock in the box, careful not to touch Zeli in the process. She slammed the box closed, the sound echoing against the ancient walls of the dungeon.

Zeli motioned for him to follow her. Grateful to leave the oppressive atmosphere, he trailed her, looking back only once to see the Goddess still standing before the cell of the mysterious prisoner, Her hand gripping the door handle.

CHAPTER NINE

"A compliment, charity, a helping hand—all freely given, but expecting reward," Ysari the Artist said, trying to come to Ayal's aid.

But the Entertainer was not satisfied, none were the answers he sought. "You must come to the solution on your own," he advised the seeker, "lest you be led astray by the kindness of others. For our greatest battles are always fought alone."

—THE AYALYA

Lizvette clenched her hands at her sides as she walked through the halls of the palace surrounded by four Royal Guardsmen. It was a bit much, she thought. She wasn't a hardened criminal.

Their footsteps disappeared in the plush carpeting, and her nerves grew with each step. She had not seen Jack since the day he'd stormed into her apartments waving a letter written in her own hand that had put the woman he loved—and their new queen—in danger.

Her father's words echoed in her head, telling her that she could still be the princess. As if *she* had been the one who wanted to be princess in the first place. That had always been Father's dream—and Mother's. Yes, she had gone along with it, but not because she'd had any desire for power or prestige. She did what her parents told her to, an obedient, proper daughter. And look where it had gotten her.

The guards led her to the royal receiving room. Alariq had preferred using this chamber for official business, as opposed to the ornate throne room. She had never seen Jack using it; he favored his office in the adjoining wing of the palace. But many things had likely changed in the weeks during which Lizvette had been on house arrest.

She took a deep breath as the Guardsman before her rapped on the door. Lizvette heard nothing, but apparently the guard had, for he opened the door and ushered her in.

She brightened her expression, affecting a demure smile for Jack—one that froze in place when she came face-to-face with Queen Jasminda.

A scowl marred the queen's beautiful visage. Her dark eyes sparked, and Lizvette fought the urge to take a step back, to run out into the hall and flee the woman's obvious rage.

Instead Lizvette fell into a curtsey, as deep as she could manage, and stayed there.

Jasminda's steps sounded on the marble floor. "Get up, for Sovereign's sake."

Lizvette rose, keeping her head down and staring at Jasminda's shoes—heavy-soled boots that were at odds with her ruched silk dress adorned with hand-sewn beading. An exquisite piece that the new queen seemed uncomfortable in.

Jasminda paced back and forth for a few moments, and the quiet in the room, except for her footsteps, set Lizvette's perfectly coiffed hair on end.

"This isn't the first message you've sent to him." Jasminda's voice was hard and cold.

Lizvette looked up, startled.

"And I believe I clearly stated that I didn't want you to have any communication with him, didn't I?"

Lizvette dropped her head again in deference. At the beginning of her arrest, she had sent letters to Jack, filled with her apologies. She'd received nothing back for the first week until a very short missive appeared, telling her to stop in block letters.

"Your Majesty," she began, then paused when Jasminda stopped pacing directly in front of her. Lizvette chanced a glance at the queen's face before dropping her eyes again. Still angry. She cleared her throat. "Your Majesty, I . . ."

"Spit it out, Lizvette. What do you *want*?"

"M-my father sent me a message. I thought that you both should know."

"Ah, but your letter wasn't addressed to both of us. It was addressed only to King Jaqros, was it not?"

"I did not think you would appreciate a message from me, Your Majesty."

"And why did you not forward on this message from your father?" the queen asked before stalking away.

"It destroyed itself." Jasminda stopped, and Lizvette looked up. "It was an amalgam." The queen's frown indicated she wasn't familiar with the mech. "A little mechanical bird that spoke with my father's voice. Such things are common in Yaly. They have many creations there made by mages known as Physicks."

"Why have I never seen one?"

"The Elsiran people hate magic, as I'm sure you've experienced. They're also highly suspicious of any foreign technology. Amalgams are a mix of both, and there are laws forbidding them in Elsira."

Lizvette's gaze followed Jasminda as the queen strode over to the window. "Alariq thought it was ridiculous," she piped up, feeling a little braver and excited to be useful, educating the queen on something. "He wanted Elsira to open its borders and be more accepting of innovations, but the Council did not approve."

Jasminda stood in profile, tapping her fingers on the window ledge. A wave of sadness swept over Lizvette. She had stood here many times with Alariq, talking over his ideas and plans for the nation. Though theirs hadn't been a love match, they had been great friends. With him, she'd had a purpose. A bright future of service to her people had stretched out before her. Now she spent her days idle, trying to keep her mother's spirits up, as well as her own.

"And what did your father say in this amalgam message?" The queen's tone was less angry now, more resigned.

"He warned my mother and me to stay away from the temples today."

Jasminda whipped her head around so fast, her neck cracked. Her eyes bored holes into Lizvette, who was so entranced she couldn't even drop her head.

"It arrived before the bombing?"

"No, afterward. But I believe it was delayed and intended to be delivered beforehand."

The queen looked off to the side. "Nirall knew about the attack before it happened?" she murmured, almost to herself.

Lizvette nodded sadly. Jasminda shook her head as her fingers worried themselves picking at her nails.

Courage spurred Lizvette forward. "Your Majesty, I-I think I can find him. The newspapers say that the Intelligence Service has had no luck sussing out his location. If he's in Yaly, I believe that I can draw him out and perhaps help bring him to justice."

Jasminda's expression did not change. A tick in her jaw was her only movement.

"And what would you want in exchange for bringing in your father?"

"I only want to prove my loyalty to Elsira. My patriotism. I'm not a traitor, Your Majesty."

Jasminda's brows shot up, and Lizvette ducked her head.

"I have never had the opportunity to apologize to you in person, but I am deeply sorry for my actions and the harm they caused you," Lizvette said. "My greatest wish would be to go back in time and never have taken you from the safety of the dungeons and sent you back to Lagrimar with the refugees. My only defense is that I was led to believe—" She blinked against the stinging in her eyes. "I believed I was doing what was best for my country. Which I love."

Jasminda stepped toward her and reached out to draw Lizvette's chin up so that their eyes met. Her touch was gentle but firm. "And Jack?"

Lizvette gulped. "E-excuse me?"

"Did you do it for Jack? Are your feelings for him what they once were?" A crack in Jasminda's rigid mask revealed the briefest glimpse of vulnerability.

Lizvette's heart fluttered. Admitting her feelings for Jack now would do nothing to help her cause. Besides, the queen certainly had nothing to worry about in that regard. Jack was relentlessly in love with her. "I-I did it for my people. I can prove that I am loyal, that I don't deserve a lifetime of exile."

Jasminda stepped back, releasing her. "And how do you plan to bring your father to justice?"

Exhaling heavily in relief, Lizvette considered. "He trusts me. At least I think he does. He knows I've been arrested, and he did send that warning message. He could only have obtained the amalgam messenger in Yaly or Fremia, but it stands to reason that he would be in Yaly as it's a far larger place to hide and he has developed many connections there over the years. I suspect his good friend Rodriq Verdeel may be helping him."

"The ambassador to Yaly?" Jasminda asked, her expression skeptical.

"Yes, Your Majesty."

"He's been questioned extensively and claims to know nothing of Nirall's location." She crossed her arms but appeared to be considering Lizvette's theory.

"He could be protecting Father. I've known Uncle Rodriq my entire life. I believe if I can convince him that I'm loyal to my father, he will help me find him."

The queen's eyes narrowed. "And how do I know that you're not really loyal to him? That this isn't just a plot to escape your punishment?"

That stopped Lizvette cold. Her mouth opened and closed. How could she get the queen to trust her now? She'd befriended Jasminda when she was new to Rosira and stuck out sorely among the aristocracy of the palace. But it had been a means to an end. Blast Father for sowing the seeds of treachery in her mind. If she were as strong as Jasminda, she would never have been so easily led astray.

She shook her head. "I do not know what I could say to make

you trust me, Your Majesty, when you have every reason not to. Only this: search my heart. You have that power, don't you? I've heard that Earthsingers can tell when someone is lying and can see the intentions in one's heart. If you feel that I am lying, so be it. But I swear to you on my life that I am telling the truth."

She steeled herself, grasping for the hardened shell she used to protect against the pain of her parents' constant disapproval. Unwilling to display the weakness her father always decried her for, she would be as strong as Jasminda had been when the new queen had saved their land and helped awaken the Goddess.

"I will consider your request," Jasminda said regally, then turned away, effectively dismissing Lizvette.

Lizvette curtsied anyway, though it was to the queen's back, and returned to her contingent of guards who led her to her rooms, praying the whole while that the queen believed her and could one day find it in her heart to forgive.

CHAPTER TEN

"Best sleep on it," Keyes the Dreamer counseled. "Untangling the snarls of our consciousness is best done in slumber, when the veil between worlds is thin. There we can flow with the stream and not battle the currents of our minds."

—THE AYALYA

Every silence had its own unique signature, and the one surrounding Kyara now made the hair on the back of her arms stand up. She stood in the dark, her hands and feet free of their shackles, yet she felt caged all the same. Turning around in a circle, she noted the strangeness of her surroundings. She could see herself clearly, but endless black stretched out beyond. No light source was visible, and the silence was a shroud.

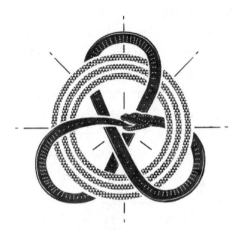

Then the whispers began. First one voice, then many, speaking in another language. Though she couldn't make out the exact words, she recognized the tongue of the Cavefolk. Those grotesque, ancient creatures that lived underground waiting, they'd claimed, for her.

The warning they'd given her lingered, coming to mind often during the long quiet stretches she spent trapped in her cell. It was they who had told her of the death stone and that it somehow had a part to play in the war to come between the three worlds—the Living World, the World Between, and the World After. According to them, Kyara and her ability to manipulate Nethersong would be needed. But if the Physicks kept up their ministrations, she might not have any Song left. There might not be anything left of *her* at all.

The whispering voices went on and on, muffled as they muttered something she couldn't comprehend. She thought of Murmur and the other Cavefolk, with their repulsive translucent skin and colorless eyes.

The whispers quieted when a woman's voice rang out. "They were not always so hideous."

"Who's there?" Kyara asked, turning, trying to locate the speaker in the persistent gloom.

"Once they looked as normal men do. Quite pale, to be certain, but perfectly ordinary." A figure separated itself from the darkness, cloaked in the very gloom itself. Kyara's eyes skimmed over the suggestion of a woman's form, but nothing was clearly visible. "You should not judge them so harshly," the stranger said. "They are friends."

The woman's voice was like music lingering in the air after the last note is played. A hushed but resonant sound laden with sadness as if misery were etched into every fiber of her being.

"I don't know about that," Kyara said. While the Cavefolk hadn't been hostile to her, they had nearly killed Darvyn. She wasn't inclined to trust them. "Who are you? Where are we?"

The sad woman's head tilted to the side as if she were listening for something. In the silence that stretched between them, the whispering began again. The woman convulsed, shudders racking her body. "They're coming."

A roar arose, like the wind scourging the countryside, and more figures began to emerge out of the darkness. The first was a little girl of eleven or twelve, a ragged dress clinging to her thin frame.

Kyara gasped. "Ahlini?" Her childhood friend had died ten years earlier. The incident had begun the long, strange journey of Kyara's life, leading her to a bleak existence in service to the True Father.

Ahlini stared vacantly at Kyara. The whites of her eyes were fully black, the way they'd turned when she died. "How could you, Kyara?" Ahlini cried. "I thought we were friends."

"We were!" Kyara said, her eyes stinging with burgeoning tears.

Next to the little girl, an emaciated man appeared, his hair matted with dirt and grime. It was the man who had broken into the harem and attacked Ahlini. Kyara had been trying to protect her friend when her power had first engaged. She'd killed both of them before she knew what she was doing.

"I was driven mad with hunger, living on the streets of Sayya," the man said. Kyara felt his black gaze boring into her. "I only wanted food, not to hurt the girl, and yet you killed me."

Kyara shook her head. "You were choking her. I-I wasn't *trying* to kill you."

Another man and woman stepped forward, holding hands. Kyara recognized the woman as the kindly merchant's wife who had taken her in when she'd been thrown out of the glass castle of Sayya with nothing, not even the clothes on her back.

"I tried to help you," the woman said, shaking her head. "And you repaid me by murdering me and my husband."

“He was beating you,” Kyara tried to explain through her tears. “I didn’t have control. I didn’t know what I was doing.” It had taken her years to manage her Song and not accidentally kill anyone in the vicinity when she used her power.

More people stepped into the light, encircling her. More of her victims. Men who would have hurt her or sold her to even worse men as she had made her way alone down the Great Highway. Innocent bystanders, too close to the epicenter of her power’s discharge. Those whose lives she’d been ordered to end by the Cantor and the True Father. More and more of them clambered forward to tell their stories and demand accountability for what she’d done.

Kyara fell to her knees, squeezing her eyes shut and covering her ears to block out their testimonies and questions. The words were a clanging chaos and felt like fingers all grasping for her, even though the dead themselves stayed a good ten paces away. She gasped in a breath and shook, cowering on the ground.

Then the voices stopped.

She looked up to see the shrouded, sad woman standing alone, her body even dimmer than it had been before, like a shadow visible in the darkness.

“You must embrace the Light if there is to be peace.” Her voice was barely audible and sounded pained.

Kyara shook her head and rose. “I don’t understand.”

“Embrace the Light,” the woman breathed out again before she disappeared.

Kyara sat up in bed and threw off her thin blanket. She scrubbed the tears from her cheeks, struggling to bring her breathing under control.

“Was it the same dream?” Dansig asked quietly.

She turned to find him sitting at Varten's bedside. Both boys were asleep.

"Always a version of the same thing, but I never get used to it." Every time she was brought back from having her Song drained, she had the dream with all her victims showing up to accuse her and the Sad Woman repeating the cryptic phrase that made no sense.

"I wish I knew what 'embrace the Light' meant," Kyara said, rising to pace her cell. Though she was bone tired, getting back to sleep after the dream was impossible. "And *he's* never there," she whispered, staring down at her hands.

"Who?" Dansig asked, breaking out of his fog.

She shook her head, unable to even speak Darvyn's name. "One of the last men I killed." She hadn't meant to kill any of them, but her power had been uncontrollable. She must have wiped out half the city when she'd lost herself. She supposed there was a chance that Darvyn's Earthsong could have protected him from her. Could he really still be alive? Or was his spirit too disgusted to even visit her dreams?

She crouched in the corner of her cell and rubbed her eyes. "My mother isn't there, either." Kyara had accidentally killed her mother while still an infant, or so Ydaris had told her.

Dansig's eyes crinkled sympathetically. "Maybe they aren't spirits, just embodiments of your guilt, and you can't see her because you don't recall what she looked like."

Kyara had thought the same thing before. But if this were all just a product of her imagination and a result of the remorse she bore, she would actually feel better. Something about the dream—its consistency and the fact that it was so much more real than any other dream she ever had—made her doubt that it was merely her conscience having its say.

"Or maybe the Sad Woman is your mother," Dansig suggested. "You say it feels like she's trying to help you, right?"

Kyara shrugged and stared out into the dark hall. There were no other prisoners in this section. She wondered if there were others here somewhere and she'd just never seen them.

Varten moaned in his sleep and turned fitfully. Dansig brushed his son's hair back and watched him until he settled.

"He isn't getting better," Kyara said, her voice soft.

"No. And he sleeps longer and longer each day, though he never seems rested."

She sighed heavily and leaned her head back against the wall. Dreams and guilt aside, she needed to focus on a way out of here before it was too late.

CHAPTER ELEVEN

Phelix the Mystery looked on in silence, bathing the seeker in a pure, hypnotic light. Receiving this benediction, Ayal found comfort in the unknown. To step away from home was to embrace the unfamiliar, to be held in the arms of the enigma. Honor those who ask the questions, *the Mystery revealed,* and beware those who offer answers.

—THE AYALYA

"That is not how we do things," Pearl cried, slapping his palm against the thick, polished table. The smooth mask obscuring his face quivered with anger that he was barely reining in. "How dare you use our name in such a manner? And without the permission of the collective?"

Jade's masked form was preternaturally still. It stood to reason that breath was entering and escaping his body, but his chest gave no sign of movement. "New times require new methods. Has no one here noticed that our country is being overrun? You are happy for me to utilize my resources to take the action, but not take credit for it? The people must know what we face. We will need to recruit soldiers for the battle ahead."

Before Pearl could bluster up a response, Diamond held up a hand. His silent authority rippled through the others. His mask was the most monstrous of them all, with bugging eyes and a grotesquely shaped mouth. He spoke with a graveled voice bearing a lethally sharp edge. "It has already been done, so we have no choice but to move on. However, in the future, this body must come to agreement on matters such as these. Announcing ourselves in the newspaper has a rippling effect of consequences that we could have prepared for. Consensus, not unilateral action, is how we operate. If you wish to continue to be a part of this collective, you must agree to abide by our ways."

A crackle from a device in the center of the round table issued Amber's reedy voice amid a soft hiss of static. "And now that you have 'outed' us, so to speak, what is the next step, Jade? Do you intend to publish our photographs in the newspaper? Perhaps have 'wanted' signs printed and posted in the local constabularies?"

Jade steepled his fingers, covered with blue gloves edged in gold piping—blue and gold, the colors of Elsira. "You recruited me to this organization because you needed fresh blood. New ideas."

Sapphire spoke up. "We recruited you because a hand must have five fingers. And our fifth member met an untimely end, leaving a seat open. I, for one, was not a fan of your membership. I don't trust you. But I was outvoted. Because we vote, that is how we come to decisions."

"I appreciate your beneficence," Jade said derisively. "To be effective, we must rally the people to our cause. Is that not the purpose of this body in the first place?"

Pearl snorted. "How likely are they to support us knowing that friends and family members perished because of an act we admit to perpetrating?"

"We seek those who are already mistrustful of the status quo," Jade began coolly. "Those disinclined to step foot in a temple and worship a power they can never obtain. The others are expendable."

"Those temple-goers you cast off so easily still make up the majority of the population," Sapphire said through clenched teeth. "The loss of the temple was strategic, even I can admit to that, but you cannot discard the opinions of the populace. The will of the people is where our power lies."

"Yes, and we create the will of the people," Diamond announced. "They are the canal waters and we the locks that move it into position."

"Aye," responded Jade, betraying his lower-class roots. "We must guide their thoughts and direct their actions. My way is just a jump start to that end. You will see."

"Clean up the loose ends," Diamond directed. Jade raised a hand in acknowledgment. "And consult us before using our name again."

Jade ignored the older man's imperious manner, but Sapphire seemed ready to argue the point some more. Diamond raised his voice a notch. "We must trust one another to complete our given tasks. That is the only way to move forward." His tone indicated the time for discussion of this matter was at an end.

Sapphire's narrow shoulders sank.

"And now," Diamond continued, "how goes the fundraising, Amber?"

The peculiar device on the table coughed up a crackle. "Slowly. Our contacts here are not suitably motivated to assist, but I am still working diligently on the matter."

Diamond nodded. "Pearl, any updates?"

"I'm closely monitoring my assignment. Nothing new to report as of yet."

"Very well then, things seem to be moving apace. The time and place for our next action must be decided upon once we've gathered the needed intelligence."

Discussion continued around the table, but Jade leaned back in his chair, listening quietly. He hadn't been sure about joining when he was recruited, but had been curious enough to plod through the tedious layers of initiations necessary. Now he was glad he'd done so, but not, he suspected, for the reasons anyone here would suspect. No, the old guard's time had passed; what no one here but him seemed to realize was that their tactics were already obsolete.

There was more than one way to attack the threat that faced the land. And in order to cull the herd, they would need sharp tools.

"I'm not so sure about this, seashell," Benn said as he and Ella stood on a street corner in West Portside facing a nondescript, three-story building. The bleached bricks were beginning to crumble and the windows had been sealed and painted over in a dreary mud brown. Behind them, the narrow street bore few signs of life, though it was just a little past the breakfast hour and the rest of the city was bustling. Rubbish littered the gutters and putrid smells wafted out from darkened alleys. The taverns they'd passed on the way had no names, just increasingly lewd graphics on the signs above the doors distinguishing one from another.

"Did you think someone dealing in illegal substances would have an inviting lair?" Ella asked.

"I'm not particularly enthused about visiting a lair at all." Benn's voice was dry. "Are you sure you trust that old man?"

"As much as anyone can trust a professional smuggler." She smiled up at him and was met with a worried look.

The Intelligence Service report stated that the temple bomb had included close to half a kilogram of palmsalt—far more than could be acquired aboveboard. With only one distributor in the country legally permitted to sell the deadly material, and only in tiny quantities, Ella had reasoned that those responsible for the temple bombing had procured it on the black market. She'd taken Benn to visit an acquaintance of hers, an elderly Raunian "import-export man," at his regular breakfast spot.

Old Nir had been seated at his usual table in a darkened corner of a dingy tavern, and had brightened when they'd arrived, happy to share his meal with someone. She thought he must be quite lonely and spent a while just chitchatting before getting down to business.

"Are you a fan of fireworks, Nir?" she'd asked.

"Hmm. Can't say that I am. Awful lot of noise they bring," the old man said. "Colored lights popping up all around to stun your eyes . . . No, I can't say I'm a fan. But you young people do love your bright and shinies."

Ella suppressed a smile."Yes, I think they're exciting. But they're quite hard to come by in this country. I'm planning a birthday party up the shore, before the weather turns, and thought a man with your connections would know how I could get my hands on a few fireworks for the party."

Nir wiped his mouth, his calculating eyes flashing in the dim light. "I don't trade in such things myself. Dangerous to transport on a craft such as mine, powered by a thermo-engine. You'd need a cold-powered vessel. Wouldn't want all those bright and shinies bursting on board and releasing all that bad air." His gaze turned suddenly shrewd. "My ship could come down around me like that temple up yonder."

Ella held his eyes, not flinching under his perusal. A lonely old man, but not a stupid one. Palmsalt's main use was in fireworks. When small amounts were mixed with various other chemicals, it created pretty, multicolored flames. But when burned in large quantities, the gas it gave off was deadly, which was why its sale was strictly regulated in most countries.

Nir peered at Benn who sat by Ella's side but had remained quiet, allowing her to take the lead. However, under the old man's sharp stare, Benn tensed. Ella put a hand on his thigh to calm him.

"I don't think I can help you," Nir said slowly, scraping the eggs on his plate onto his fork. "Minding my own business is more than enough work for me. Can't keep stock of everyone else's too."

Disappointment held Ella in its shadowy grip, but she wasn't going to give up. Benn had the look and bearing of a soldier or a lawman. Though they were dressed casually in street clothes, Benn's hair was regulation short and his posture arrow straight. And asking about palmsalt the day after an attack, Nir likely thought they were working with the police. And who would want to implicate their countrymen in something as horrific as the bombing?

"A salesman isn't responsible for what his customers do with the merchandise." She leaned forward, keeping her voice even. "The customer is the only one to blame. The only one who might be sought to answer for their actions. One might never recall the salesman at all. There would be no need."

She sat very still as Nir mulled this over. Tension radiated from Benn in waves.

"A man's livelihood is sacred," Ella continued. "There's no justice to be had in taking that away. But those people who died yesterday—so many women and children, merely worshipping their goddess in a place they thought safe—those people deserve justice. I'm just looking for information on a customer. Nothing more. I give you my word."

She didn't dare look at Benn, though she suspected his expression might be clouded with disapproval. But their goal wasn't to identify who sold the palmsalt, merely who bought it.

After a prolonged silence, Nir sat back in his chair. "I knew there was something about you, missy. Remind me of my auntie. More stubborn than a barracuda, she was." He sighed deeply.

"No one with any sense would sell much more than half a kilo at a time," he said. "The only two men I know with the stones for such are Bor Wintersail and Hak Floodhammer. I don't do business with Bor myself, and he ain't in the country anyways, but I can tell you how to find Hak."

Nir had directed them to the old, brick warehouse, only a few blocks away from the tavern where he ate every morning. Staring up at the building, a flurry of nerves overtook Ella.

"Well let's get this over with," Benn said, taking her hand and moving forward purposefully.

They'd only taken a few steps when the main door to the warehouse opened and two figures rushed out. Both appeared to be young men, dressed in brown coveralls with billed caps pulled down over their faces. Ella got a quick flash of chin as the men sped by, heads low. They moved so quickly they nearly mowed her down. Benn swooped her out of the way just in time.

Neither man apologized or even looked up as they hastened off down the street.

Ella looked after them, then back to the warehouse door, which hung open. A tight sense of unease squeezed her chest.

Benn was on alert, too. He pinched the bridge of his nose. "A deal gone bad, maybe?"

"Perhaps." Caution overtook nerves as they approached the door. Nir had given them a coded knock to use, but it wasn't necessary.

Benn pushed the door open the rest of the way and looked inside. The front room was a small antechamber, empty except for an unoccupied desk and chair. The only other exit was a single door, which must lead to the interior of the warehouse.

Benn turned the knob warily, keeping himself between Ella and whatever was on the other side. The door glided open easily. On its other side were no less than half a dozen deadbolts and chains. "I take it this door is usually locked," he said dryly. "Is there any way I can convince you to stay outside?"

"You should be glad I brought you along in the first place," she quipped.

They were a team—and a good one. Ella hadn't blinked when Benn returned from the palace entrusted with this mission. And when she'd brought up adoption, he'd seen how serious she was. He'd gazed around their tiny, one-bedroom flat, no doubt wondering where they would store two growing children, but immediately agreed to meet them on the next visiting day. Ella was sure he'd fall in love just as she had. So though her apprehension multiplied, there was no way she was leaving.

She reached into her bag and retrieved her shael, the short, weighted club she carried with her at all times. Benn eyed the weapon and shook his head, but retrieved a revolver from the harness at the small of his back.

He closed the door and engaged one of the locks. She raised an eyebrow. "Don't want any surprises at our backs."

Ella nodded and then took in the vast space before them. Rows of metal racks took up the shadowed interior. Crates and boxes of all sizes filled the shelves with labels in languages from every country on the continent.

Hak Floodhammer's operation was immense. She couldn't imagine the contents of all those shelves nor estimate the amount of money that must flow through this place.

Benn took in every detail and motioned to the corner a hundred paces away where a glassed-in office glowed orange from its overhead lighting.

The quiet and emptiness of the place sent a chill up her body. There should be activity here—loading and unloading of goods. The chatter of workers. Something. Instead, an unsettling silence permeated the air.

When they neared the office, the reason became apparent. Three men lay prone, just outside the door, blood pooling around their heads from their slit necks. Each bore the green or blue hair the Raunians preferred. The dark lines and curves of a tattoo graced the cheek of the man whose face she could see.

Ella gripped her shael tighter, though by now, she felt the danger had passed. It had, most likely, bumped into her out on the sidewalk a few moments ago.

A great sadness welled inside her at the sight of these dead men whom she did not know.

"Are you all right?" Benn asked, voice low.

Her jaw quivered but she nodded. She'd seen a dead man

before, knifed in the street after a pub fight several years ago. Benn squeezed her arm.

"Stay here."

She looked up sharply, attention torn from the tragedy before her. "Where are you going?"

"Just want a look around the office. Then we need to leave."

"Should we call the constables?"

"When we get home, we will," he said, then sidestepped the bodies to enter the office.

In her homeland of Yaly there was no saint of death. The closest was Saint Phelix, the champion of mysteries, who interceded when one gave oneself up to the unknowable nature of things. The World After was arguably the biggest mystery of them all. No one had ever come back to tell its tale. Ella sent up a prayer to Saint Phelix to guard the mystery of these men and to Saint Neftet to provide them mercy and peace.

When she opened her eyes, Benn was there holding a stack of large brown notebooks. He peered at her, concern etched in his gaze. She straightened and wiped at her eyes, which had begun to leak.

"What are those?"

"Ledgers," he responded. "Looks like Hak kept track of his transactions, but they're all in some kind of code. Better to keep these out of the hands of the constables or Intelligence Service if they may be compromised."

"I wonder why the murderers didn't take them," she asked as they made their way back to the main door.

"They were in a hidden compartment in the desk. Easy to find if you know what you're looking for. But I don't think these killers were professionals."

He listened for a moment at the door before opening it. The

entry chamber was as they'd left it. Ella peered through the peep-hole of the outer door. "Street's clear."

Once outside, Ella longed to rush away, but Benn advised they should avoid anything that would make them stand out. Best move at a lethargic crawl like everyone else in West Portside.

The ledgers were a tight fit in Ella's bag and weighed it down. Benn offered to carry it for her, but that would look even more odd, a man with a lady's purse, she reasoned as their painfully slow pace made her feet itch.

"They must have been tying up loose ends," she said, voice low.

"It would seem so."

He put his arm around her so he could grab onto the shoulder strap and relieve some of the weight. If only he could do something about the dense load of melancholy that had descended on her heart.

CHAPTER TWELVE

Accepting the course which lay ahead, Ayal was finally ready to embark. "But how can I bring the people together? What do I seek?" she asked. "And when will I know I have found it?"

The Mystery radiated an eternal glow, lighting the way and creating harsh shadows.

You are now on your way.

—THE AYALYA

Darvyn made his way through streets clogged with celebrants waving flags, tossing flowers, toasting one another with the cups of ale being given out liberally at every tavern. The joy in the air was infectious as both Elsiran and Lagrimari stood side by side raising cheers to the wedding of Jack and Jasminda. A glimpse of a true unification that was still a long way off.

The wedding was supposed to have taken place at the Southern temple. However, after the bombing, the event was moved to the Eastern temple, a much smaller space. Few places would have been large enough to hold all who had wanted to attend. Security had been an intense challenge, but every Earthsinger the Keepers had was on hand monitoring the crowd for any hint of wrongdoing.

The unfamiliar Elsiran marriage ceremony had been short, especially when compared to the three-day ritual the Lagrimari practiced. The spectators were a mix of aristocracy in their finely wrought clothing, working-class folk dressed in their best, and the Lagrimari refugees, cleaned and pressed as best they could manage.

Jasminda's green silk dress was embroidered in gold. It was done in the Lagrimari style and made her skin glow. Jack's medals shone on his military uniform and Darvyn's heart swelled with affection for both of them. The queen was a symbol of hope to his people—a Singer who looked like them, leading this land that they were meant to share. And a king, honorable and just, who only wanted the best for his people.

Oola officiated the ceremony, held in both languages so that all could understand. Jack and Jasminda had transferred the contents of tiny glass bowls filled with various materials to a larger bowl. The bowl of brown earth symbolized the foundation of their union, water was for the fluidity required to shift and change to face new challenges together, oil to fuel their bond, and finally, fire to light their way until they left this world.

Then they had blown out the flame and Oola had bound their hands in multicolored ribbon. The crowd thundered their approval as the bride and groom retreated to the waiting town car and the procession that was now taking them through the city.

Before Darvyn had left the temple, a familiar voice pierced his mind.

Meet me at the palace. I have need of you.

He'd groaned internally and searched for the speaker, finally spotting Oola amidst a swarm of worshippers. Her dark eyes flashed at him before returning to Her disciples.

He wanted to refuse Her command, though he knew it was useless. The Goddess Awoken was not easily ignored.

When the deluge of wedding guests in the temple had thinned to a trickle, Oola had flown off on an air current. Now, Darvyn fought against the throngs as he made his own way back to the palace, ever vigilant for signs of a threat. Drunken revelers and pockets of people singing and dancing in the middle of the roads as they followed the processional of the royal motorcade hampered him at every turn.

What did Oola want now? What task had She cooked up for him and what would be its cost? He was sorely tired of Her manipulations, they had been going on his whole life.

Two hours later, he finally arrived at the palace. Battling the carousing hordes had shrunken his patience to almost nothing. As soon as he entered through the opulent doors, he found a girl waiting for him. Tarazeli, a Lagrimari teen who'd joined the Sisterhood immediately after the fall of the Mantle. Many orphaned Lagrimari girls had apparently done so, likely in awe of Oola's magnificence.

"You seek the Goddess?" Zeli asked. Irritated, Darvyn nodded and followed her when she began to move.

"Are you Her personal servant?" he asked.

The girl brightened with pride, misinterpreting his question as praise. "I'm Her robe mistress. I'm still learning my duties, but it's a great honor to be chosen."

"To be sure," Darvyn said, trying to hide his exasperation with

Oola. He had no idea if the girl was an Earthsinger or merely perceptive, for she frowned at him.

"I have dreamed of Her my whole life," he said by way of explanation. "She has often required things of me. Far more often than I would have liked. Our relationship is . . . complicated."

She nodded, but it was clear she didn't understand. No one did. Following Oola's directions had gotten people killed. Her plans may have helped bring the Lagrimari freedom, but at a very dear price.

They stopped before a door guarded by two Royal Guardsmen. It opened by itself, and Zeli motioned him forward.

The room was a parlor of some kind, filled with polished furniture inlayed with gold. A collection of porcelain vases rested on the mantel, and Darvyn kept a wide berth of the delicate display. Oola stood at the window with Her back to him. The terrace faced the grand gardens of the palace, beautiful and green even though winter's chill was nearly upon them.

He stalked forward to question her. "What do you want?"

Oola did not turn around. "Always to the point, Darvyn. So refreshing. I shall be direct as well. The time has come. You are needed to guide the others to rescue Jasminda's family."

His anger and frustration abruptly fled. On the day the Mantle fell, Oola had come to him. He had been outside the city of Sayya, waiting for Kyara, who, of course, had never arrived. When he wanted to search for her, Oola had prevented it, saying that he was needed by Jack and Jasminda. That it was time for Jasminda's family to come home.

He had put it off as long as he could, stubbornly staying to search for Kyara. But there had been no trace of her. And so he'd finally gone to Elsira and met Queen Jasminda, then quickly decided to help her and Jack achieve unification. Oola's cryptic words had faded from his mind.

He'd known that Jasminda's mother died many years earlier and her father and twin brothers disappeared two years ago and were presumed dead. As a fellow orphan, he felt for her—before becoming the queen, she had lived alone as an outcast until meeting Jack and setting off a course of events that led to Oola's awakening.

Darvyn stared at his hands, the weight of this new task settling onto him.

"This journey," She said, finally turning to face him. "It is one I sense that will lead you to whom you seek."

His head shot up, and his breathing stuttered. "You know where Kyara is?" His emotions tangled into a knot of hope, joy, betrayal, and rage. "You knew and prevented me from searching for her all this time? Now you dangle her like a carrot before me to get me to repay a debt that *you* owe to Jasminda."

He was shouting and inhaled deeply to calm himself. "I will run your errand because if our new queen's family is alive and can be brought home, it would be a blessing. Why do you feel you have to bargain with me so cruelly?"

Oola blinked, slowly. Her impassive expression was impossible to read. "You so seldom ask anything of me, Darvyn. You are a rare one, indeed. Everyone else only *wants*. They wish to take and not give. You are right to be angry, as I have slighted you. For this, I apologize."

Darvyn's mouth hung open. He could not recall Her apologizing to him before. "Th-thank you."

"Kyara lives, of that I am certain, but since awakening, I can no longer see what I once could. And even I cannot sense the life force of a Nethersinger." Her voice almost held a trace of emotion. Was it regret?

Darvyn blinked, all his anger fading away at her admission.

"However, I know that Jasminda's family is being held in Yaly by the Physicks."

His nostrils flared at the mention. A Physick named Raal had been responsible for his mother's death, purposely infecting her with the plague as part of some sick experiment his people did on those they considered expendable. The same Physick was one he suspected of being involved in Kyara's disappearance. Raal had met with Kyara shortly before the Mantle fell, offering her some kind of deal to take away her power. If she was in Lagrimar or Elsira, Darvyn knew she would have found her way to him by now. But if she was in Yaly, perhaps against her will . . .

"You think they have Kyara, as well," he thought aloud.

She spread Her arms and gave an almost imperceptible shrug. "I do not want Jasminda to be given false hope, in case your task fails. She is to know nothing of her family until they are found. As a cover, you are to join another mission in Yaly. Only you and the Raunian know of this additional plot. Once you are there, I am sure you will find a way to save the day. It is what you do, is it not?" She raised Her eyebrows.

He wasn't sure if that was a jab or not. He'd always tried to use his strength for the good of others. "Do we not have a responsibility to serve and help those weaker than we are? Isn't that why we have this power?"

She turned away again, Her voice growing oddly hollow as She spoke. "My power was not unusual in my time. I was as everyone else was. It is only now that it sets me apart."

"But you were queen of your people. Of all the people," he said, not understanding Her sudden change of mood.

She straightened Her shoulders. "Go now. The king and queen are expecting you in the throne room. You will gain more information there."

The dismissal was complete, but for the first time, Darvyn saw the Goddess as She really was, all the honorifics stripped away. She was a woman out of time. The only one of Her kind left in the world. Her power so immense as to be unfathomable, even for him.

He left the room, leaving Her to Her solitude. Perhaps he had judged Her too harshly all this time.

Lizvette suppressed the anxiety rising within her as the Guardsmen led her into the royal throne room. She'd been summoned from her apartment with no warning and no explanation. The room was empty, and she was left alone when the guards retreated. She stood for several minutes, staring at the dual thrones carved out of mahogany and embroidered in blue and gold. The second throne was a new addition. It was identical to the first, but brighter, its wood glossier in its newness. Perhaps it had been in storage for use as a backup if something ever happened to the primary throne.

Until the Goddess awoke from her centuries of slumber, the country had been ruled by a series of Prince Regents. This was the first time since the Goddess Herself was crowned queen five hundred years ago that the land was ruled by a full monarch, much less two.

The door behind Lizvette opened, and two Elsiran women were ushered in. A Sister in a blue gown, red-gold hair in the customary topknot, entered alongside a shorter woman whose hair was cut into a brutal bob. Lizvette averted her eyes quickly so as not to stare at the burn scars crawling down the Sister's cheek to meet her jaw. Her companion was dressed in trousers and a leather jacket, and grinned broadly at Lizvette, who nodded back with less enthusiasm.

"I don't think I've ever been in the throne room before," the second woman gushed, rubbing her hands together like she thought she might settle in and stay awhile. "What do you think this is all about?"

The Sister shrugged, and Lizvette couldn't find her voice to respond that she had no earthly idea, either.

Moments later, a young Lagrimari man entered, his face locked in a frown. He was lean with striking cheekbones, and he bowed politely to them before going to stand off to the side of the room. Tension radiated from him as he scanned the room, taking in every detail. Every so often he would pull at the collar of his button-up shirt, appearing uncomfortable in it.

Aside from Jasminda, Lizvette had never been in the company of a Lagrimari before. His constant vigilance and the way he stood with his back ramrod straight put her in mind of a soldier. But the idea of a Lagrimari soldier in their midst was disturbing. For all that she supported the unification, the history between the two nations was bloody. Certainly this man was too young to have committed any atrocities in war. She looked away, feeling a bit guilty at her gut reaction to the newcomer.

Her discomfort only grew when an even stranger man was led into the room. His shockingly blue hair and bronzed skin marked him as a Raunian. Tattoos decorated his forehead and chin, and two parallel lines graced his cheekbones. She recognized him as the man she'd seen a few days prior, the last time she'd been summoned. His presence in the palace had astonished her then.

For a moment, when their paths had crossed in the palace corridor, Lizvette had hoped the man was an emissary from his people, sent to negotiate an end to the crippling embargo Raun had placed on Elsira. But it had been late at night and he had not been flanked by dignitaries or guards, only by a single novice to the Sisterhood. He'd sparked a jolt of fear in her. Raunians were notorious the world over for their barbaric traditions and uncivilized society. Known as a nation of pirates, they were led by a king selected by some sort of game of strategy, one who could be male or female . . . something about their language having no grammatical genders. They ruthlessly ruled the seas, as well as a good portion of the international shipping market, and were said to be hotheaded and belligerent. Even their women learned hand-to-hand combat, if the stories were to be believed.

Now, when the Raunian's gaze slid over her body for quite a bit longer than was decent, Lizvette shifted closer to the two Elsiran women. Her cheeks flamed and she turned away, determined to ignore such behavior. Whatever the king and queen had gathered them here for, she hoped it would be over quickly. As much as she appreciated a reprieve from the boredom of her rooms, this was all a little too bizarre.

The door behind the two thrones opened, and Lizvette dropped into a deep curtsey, a pang going through her heart as Jack and Jasminda strolled into the room, hand in hand, still dressed formally in their wedding attire.

Jack was arresting in his black coat fringed with gold epaulets, his military decorations and medals gleaming in the soft light. His face was sharp, just this side of severe, but today it was lit from within with joy as he beamed at his new wife. Jasminda's green gown was gorgeous—exotic and beautiful, just as she was. Together they were an odd sight, but somehow a perfect one.

Lizvette pushed down the jealousy that sparked. Earlier, she'd listened to the ceremony on the radio with her mother and been grateful her house arrest had prevented her from attending.

She rose from her curtsey with the others and held herself so tightly she feared her bones might break, but she refused to allow even a sliver of emotion to show. She'd hidden her feelings for Jack all her life, had planned to hide them forever when she married his brother. It would not be so hard to continue to do so.

For the briefest of moments, she considered if exile to Fremia would be such a bad thing. At least there she would be spared the sight of him—that striking jaw, those lips that constantly threatened a smile. She would not have to watch his happiness grow with another. But no, Elsira was her home, and if a lifetime of heartbreak was part of her punishment, she would bear it.

Between one blink and the next, the Goddess Awoken appeared. Lizvette wasn't sure if She'd come through the door behind the thrones or emerged from thin air, but Her presence thickened the atmosphere in the room. Lizvette had not seen Her in person before and found herself enthralled by the deity she'd worshipped her whole life. Power seemed to radiate from Her pores.

As the king and queen sat, the Goddess stood next to them, peering at those gathered. Lizvette held her breath when Her gaze grazed her, and her eyes darted to the ground, staying firmly locked on the tiles until she felt the Goddess's attention pass.

Jasminda did not look in Lizvette's direction, but Jack glanced at her quickly, no emotion in his eyes. She stiffened as another piece of her heart disintegrated into ash.

Queen Jasminda gestured them all forward before speaking. "We have taken a break from our celebration and asked you all to come here for a very important purpose. The need is immediate and could not wait another day. Lizvette Nirall"—Jasminda motioned in her direction but still did not look her way—"believes she has information that will assist us in finding the perpetrators of the temple bombing."

Lizvette's face heated, her blush riding high in her cheeks as the attentions of the others scoured her. So the queen had decided to accept Lizvette's offer. A tiny flicker of hope lit within her.

"We have reason to suspect that her father, Meeqal Nirall, is working with the Hand of the Reaper. Since more attacks have been threatened, time is of the essence. I ask that you all accompany her to Yaly to investigate and, hopefully, bring Nirall back here for interrogation and to stand trial for treason."

The Raunian man sucked in a breath. Lizvette darted a glance at him, surprised to find pity in his eyes. Unlike the rest of him, which appeared alien and fierce, his eyes held a warmth she did not expect.

Jack spoke up, his voice resonating in the marble room. "The Intelligence Service has had no luck locating Nirall. For those who do not know, he was a former member of the Council of Regents, a trusted advisor who actively worked against me in secret and threatened Jasminda's life. If he has any connection to the Hand of the Reaper, then it is likely that he's being apprised of the ongoing investigation."

"That is why this cannot be considered an official mission," Jasminda added. "Aunt Vanesse, you and Clove are traveling to the Yaly Classic Air Race, which takes place in a few days. I would ask you to transport the others. Their cover will be as race attendees."

The Sister nodded, her scarred face beatific when she smiled. This was Jasminda's aunt. Lizvette recalled that the queen's mother had been from a prominent Rosiran family. "Of course," the woman said.

The shorter woman, Clove, also grinned infectiously. "Sounds exciting."

Lizvette smothered a small smile. Their unquestioning enthusiasm was refreshing, and neither had looked upon her with scorn for her father's actions—or her own, which had been publicly detailed in the press.

The queen continued. "Darvyn ol-Tahlyro is a trusted friend of my husband's and of the crown." She motioned to the Lagrimari man who seemed uncomfortable with the praise. "And the Goddess has recommended Tai Summerhawk to accompany you, as well." Jasminda's voice held no uncertainty, though she didn't elaborate as to what the Raunian's skills were or how he was to assist. "We are in your debt, Master Summerhawk."

The Raunian tried to hide the look of surprise on his face and bowed deeply. He hadn't spoken yet, and Lizvette wondered what his voice sounded like. Deep and gravelly, she guessed, as that would best match his build. Taller than she was by at least two heads, he was larger and broader than most Elsiran men. The loose collar of his linen shirt revealed a well-muscled chest, and thick, woven breeches covered strong legs.

He caught her appraisal of him and raised his eyebrows as if to ask, *Do you like what you see?* Lizvette snapped her head forward, embarrassed by her lack of propriety and irritated with his impertinence.

"There is a contingent of Foreign Service agents stationed in Yaly," Jack said. "They have just been deployed in the past two weeks, chosen from men I trust in the army; however, they don't know the particulars of this mission. The fewer who know the better. If an arrest or additional security is necessary, call on them. They understand that this is classified."

A heavy solemnity hung in the room, and Lizvette felt the weight of what was being asked of her. She hoped she was up to the task.

The Goddess stepped forward, capturing everyone's attention. "All know the part they are to play," She said. Lizvette scanned the faces around her, which all held some level of confusion. It appeared the Goddess was overestimating the knowledge of those present. "You must leave immediately and work diligently to accomplish your tasks."

Lizvette bowed her head in deference. If their Sovereign believed they could do this, then they must be able to. After answering a few questions about logistics, the king, queen, and Goddess exited through the same door behind the thrones, leaving the rest alone.

"Clove Liddelot. Nice to meet you," the shorter woman announced, holding her palms out in greeting. Lizvette pressed her palms to Clove's.

"Vanesse Zinadeel," the Sister said, and Lizvette repeated the greeting. While not aristocrats, the Zinadeels were wealthy merchants. Both daughters had chosen to join the Sisterhood, but it was not widely known that the family had cut off the eldest after she had left the order to marry a former Lagrimari prisoner of war.

Lizvette wondered as to the story behind the burn scars on Vanesse's face but would never pry. Then she startled somewhat to notice that Clove and Vanesse held hands after they'd made their introductions. Their body language and constant eye contact seemed rather intimate, but before she could decide if she was reading too much into things, Darvyn approached.

"We are to travel by airship?" he asked in heavily accented Elsiran. She was glad he spoke the language. She hadn't even considered the communication barrier.

"Aye," Clove said. "The king has lent me the royal airship for the Yaly Classic."

"Clove is a pilot. She's come in the top ten for the past three years," Vanesse said proudly, squeezing her hand.

There was definitely more than friendship between the two women. Such pairings were seen with regularity in Fremia, where

Lizvette had attended university, but Elsira was a far more conservative country. Then again, much was changing. Only weeks ago an Elsiran and a Lagrimari would not have been in the same room together. She shook her head slightly in wonder at it all.

Only then did Clove's words hit her. "Alariq's airship?" Lizvette said with a gasp. Clove's enthusiasm paled a bit. "The one that killed him?"

Clove and Vanesse shot one another wary glances. Vanesse came forward, placing a hand on Lizvette's arm. Instinctively, Lizvette wanted to brush off the contact, unused to such familiarity, but she held herself still so as not to offend.

"It's been fixed and fully inspected. Clove has flown it several times since then and will go over the mechanics again before we take to the air. She's made sure it's safe."

"And we won't be flying into any thunderstorms, either, be sure of it," Clove added.

Alariq had died in such a storm . . .

Lizvette knew their words were meant to calm her fear, but her chest tightened anyway. She had lost her fiancé and her future in one of those contraptions. Alariq had never shared the common Elsiran view regarding foreign technology. He had been forward-thinking, excited about new advancements, and look where it had gotten him.

Lizvette nodded and smiled in an effort to put the others at ease. Vanesse and Clove mimicked her actions, appearing relieved, though Darvyn peered at her closely. She suspected he was an Earthsinger and, as such, would be able to see through her lies, but she couldn't worry about it. She would have to steel herself against her fears and rise above them. It was necessary to complete this mission, return some honor to herself, and avoid exile.

Darvyn and the women talked among themselves, discussing

what needed to be done before they could take flight. The Raunian, Tai, who had stood somewhat apart from them until now, sauntered over to Lizvette. A smattering of dark hair dusted the visible skin on his chest. She tore her gaze away only to be drawn in by his hands, which were palms out, ready to greet her in the Elsiran way. His fingers were thick and calloused, likely from years of labor. She hesitated before raising her own hands and touching his palms as lightly as possible. A strange sensation—something like static electricity—greeted her, and she jerked back.

Tai chuckled at her skittishness, but a shadow seemed to cross his eyes. His reaction was curious, but the expression dissolved into a smirk before she had decided what it meant.

"Well, duchess, it looks like we'll be spending some time together."

"We don't have duchies any longer in Elsira," she snapped, more forcefully than she had intended, annoyed by his smug tone. "'Duke' is a ceremonial title reserved for the king. And of what use will you be on this mission? How is this any of your concern? We are currently at odds with Raun."

"I'm not here in any official capacity," he said with a grin. "Think of my participation as more intimate in nature." He swaggered deeply into her personal space.

She leaned back, torn between stubbornly standing her ground and maintaining a respectable distance. Raunians didn't acknowledge the rules of polite society. She hadn't thought the Lagrimari did, either, but Darvyn had been nothing but respectful and polite so far. Quite unlike this coarse pirate.

"I'm good at finding things, duchess. Maybe I'll get the chance to show you sometime." He winked, and heat trailed down her body followed by a spike of anger. How dare he? She was far too well bred to slip down to his level, however. She spun away and stood closer to Clove, listening in on the conversation she and Darvyn were having about travel times.

Lizvette's skin prickled at the thought of the Raunian who remained behind her. It would be quite a long mission with him around.

CHAPTER THIRTEEN

Maasael the Traveler accompanied the seeker as she took her first steps into darkness. He provided a boat and wind enough to carry her away.

Alone she sailed until the placid sea was interrupted by the emergence of a fin. "Where are you going?" called a shark through his razor grin.

"To prevent the repetition of the past" was Ayal's reply.

—THE AYALYA

Tai gripped the edge of his seat as the airship took off from the roof of the Elsiran palace. He'd never been in one of the contraptions before and would have happily spent the rest of his life with his feet firmly planted on the ground or on the deck of the *Hekili*.

Mik had shivered when Tai had told him of the upcoming journey. "Wingless, featherless men were not meant to race through the skies, mate," he'd said. Tai agreed, but there was nothing to be done about it.

Clove and Vanesse sat in the tiny cockpit. The rest of them had piled into the airship's narrow cabin, which featured four plush seats, two on each side, and was lined by windows. Tai had no desire to watch the earth grow farther and farther away, so he stared straight ahead at the woman in front of him. Lizvette.

Her name fit her. She was every bit the picture of Elsiran aristocracy he'd supposed her to be—nose upturned slightly at the end, delicate, nearly golden eyes framed by full lashes. Her strawberry-blond hair was swept up into an elegant knot at the back of her head. She kept trying to avert her gaze from him, and a strange satisfaction filled him every time she failed.

Often her glances were filled with annoyance, which delighted him even more. Elsirans were obsessed with manners and "proper" behavior. Tai knew enough to realize that staring was considered rude, but he didn't care. Partly because he liked the color her cheeks took on when she caught him and partly because he just liked looking at her. Finally, she held his gaze a bit obstinately.

He grinned broadly, pleased at the hint of fire in her personality. "So, duchess, I take it you've been to Yaly before."

"Yes. When I was a child, we would travel there frequently to visit my Uncle Rodriq, the ambassador. He isn't my uncle by blood, just a close family friend. I haven't been back for several years." She stopped, seeming to realize she was rambling. Tai tried to hold back his amusement, but by her pinched scowl, he wasn't doing a good job. "Have *you* been to Yaly, Master Summerhawk?"

"To be sure. I sail there frequently. It's the vilest place on earth," he answered in Yalyish.

Her eyebrows raised, apparently surprised that he had enough intelligence to learn an additional tongue.

"Is that their language?" Darvyn asked in Elsiran.

Tai turned to him. "You don't speak Yalyish?"

Darvyn shook his head. The two had only spoken briefly before the trip. The Lagrimari man had approached Tai after they'd been dismissed by the rulers of Elsira and confided that they were the only two who knew about the mission to save Queen Jasminda's family and the Goddess wanted it to stay that way.

From the corner of his eye, Tai caught Lizvette's frown.

"Neither do I," Clove piped up from the pilot's chair. "You can always purchase a translation amalgam."

"What do you know of Yaly?" Lizvette asked, turning toward Darvyn.

"Not much. We had limited contact with them—trade only. Lagrimar exported the iron ore and precious jewels found in our eastern mountains and received shipments of goods we couldn't produce. I've only ever met one Yalyishman." The last was said with venom.

Tai's gaze was drawn to Lizvette's lips when she placed a finger to them in thought. "How did you trade?" she asked. "I thought Lagrimar was entirely cut off from the world except for during the breaches?"

"Morladyn's Pass. It's a river that was created from generations of slave labor—Earthsingers blasting their way through the eastern mountains. A cable runs through from end to end and pulls unmanned barges."

"But if there's been a path through the mountain all this time, how is it that the True Father never went through or tried to invade Yaly?" Lizvette asked.

Darvyn's lips twitched in the beginning of a smile. "He tried, once, after the pass was completed. No one alive but him knows what happened, only that he did not succeed. I've heard tales from the elders that all but three of the soldiers who went with him were lost, and the three who returned went mad. But history has a way of disappearing in Lagrimar, so the truth will likely remain a secret."

Tai had never given much thought to the isolated desert country. Tales of the True Father's cruelty and the pitiful state in which he kept his people were known the world over, however his exploits rarely impacted anyone but the Elsirans. It had been 250 years since the Fourth Breach, or Iron War as it was called, that saw Elsira fighting both Yaly and Lagrimar. Raun remained neutral in such conflicts, though Raunian mercenaries were often hired by foreign navies for special missions.

Tai couldn't imagine being stuck in one place his whole life, never having seen other lands, learned other languages, or met different kinds of people. He felt a deep compassion for the Lagrimari, just now being introduced to the rest of the world.

Darvyn rubbed his hands across his face. "So what is the plan to find your father?"

Lizvette's posture grew even more rigid, if that were possible. Tai could only imagine what was going on inside her mind to hold such tight control of herself.

"I want to start with my uncle. He's been itching to retire but has stayed on as ambassador since his wife is Yalyish and has no desire to go to the 'hinterlands,' as she calls Elsira."

"Imagine what she'd think of Raun," Tai muttered. Lizvette almost smiled. "Well, I think we should start with a Dominionist gathering," he went on, watching her brow lower.

"Why start there?" she asked, her voice shrill.

"Because your uncle seems like a weak lead. Certainly if they are such good friends he would not give your father up. However, the Elsiran temple bombing follows the pattern of similar attacks against Yalyish devotionaries perpetrated by the Dominionist sect. There have been close to a dozen bombings over the past five years, each escalating in damage and intensity. Palmsalt has never been used before, but other similar toxins have been."

"So you think the Hand of the Reaper may have been inspired by the Dominionists?" Darvyn asked.

Tai shrugged. "Inspired by, colluding with. The Dominionists are well-known haters of magic and would have motive for assassinating the Goddess and destroying a place of worship. Nirall could be working with them."

Lizvette tapped a finger against her chin before shaking her head. "The Dominionists are a foreign group that's begun to gain a foothold in Elsira. I don't think a nationalistic faction like the Reapers would associate with them—assuming Father is a member of the Reapers. Uncle Rodriq is the far more logical choice. If I convince him that I'm loyal to Father, he will help me."

"Zealotry is rarely logical, duchess," Tai said with a smirk. "Those with common enemies often work together. But how about this, let's test out your acting abilities, shall we? Convince me that you like *me* and I'll believe you can pull this off." He sat back, crossing his arms.

Her nostrils flared, and her jaw was clenched so tight he feared she might break a tooth. Tai's blood warmed at her reaction, but disappointment descended when she began breathing deeply and regaining her icy composure.

"And are you going to waltz into a Dominionist gathering and demand an explanation for who bombed our temple? Will they answer a blue-haired Raunian, or will they throw you out on your . . . your keister?"

"My keister?" he repeated incredulously. "I'll have you know that this blue-haired Raunian is an expert at negotiation, able to make deals and maneuver in every society, in a variety of languages at docks all around the world." He instantly regretted allowing her to see how her disdain affected him. He may be a smuggler by trade, but he was a bloody good one and well versed in the art of getting men to talk. Though even he wasn't sure if that was why the Goddess had included him.

"I still have not heard a plan yet, Master Summerhawk. And I'm not certain why you are even on this mission. I know my father and how he thinks. I am the best person to locate him and bring him back for justice."

"Your Goddess apparently believes that I have some value or else I would not be here. And why are you so quick to turn against your own kin anyway?"

Her lips tightened and her neck elongated as her chin shot up. Ah, that was a sore spot. He well understood. His father was a bone of contention with him, as well.

"My father," she said through clenched teeth, "is a traitor to Elsira. I, however, am a loyal patriot, and it is my duty to bring him in."

"A loyal patriot on house arrest for the past few weeks?"

He regretted the words the moment they were past his lips, but he couldn't take them back. Lizvette's facade remained a stony mask, but her eyes revealed that his jab had hit its mark.

She swallowed and dropped her gaze to the floor. "I believe that I was put in charge of this mission, and I say we are starting with Uncle Rodriq." Her words were quiet yet still charged with authority.

"I'm not sure why you think you're in charge, duchess. I know you're used to the world dropping at your feet and commanding the masses with a crook of your pinkie finger"—he waggled his in example—"but I have more experience in this kind of thing. You start with the uncle and your father may run. We should start with the Dominionists."

She leaned forward ever so slightly, her carefully managed exterior now shored up and showing no cracks. He leaned in, too, drawn by the force in her expression. But before she could say another word, a powerful blast of air pushed them back against their seats. Tai struggled against it but could not move.

Outside, the clear blue sky was marred by a curious crack of lightning. In the pilot's seat, Clove jumped. Vanesse turned around to glare at Darvyn.

"I apologize. I just needed their attention," Darvyn said.

"Please be careful," Vanesse said, then turned back and placed a soothing hand on Clove's arm to still her frantic movements.

Tai's brows lifted. He was cold from shock. Darvyn looked back and forth between the two of them. The tight band across Tai's chest pinned him in place, and Lizvette's wide eyes must've meant she felt the same thing.

"Is that . . . is that Earthsong?" she whispered.

Darvyn nodded solemnly, his eyes firm but not unkind. "This whole mission cannot be spent bickering. Do you two understand?"

Lizvette gulped and looked away. When Darvyn's gaze moved to Tai, he cracked a smile if only to hide the terror that the display of magic had ignited.

The pressure lifted and he could finally move, breathing deeply and hoping his relief wasn't too apparent. Lizvette swallowed and rubbed her breastbone.

"We will start with her uncle," Darvyn said, then leaned back in his seat and closed his eyes.

Lizvette shot Tai a smug expression, a small smile playing on her lips. He twirled his hand and bowed at her exaggeratedly from his seat, mimicking a fancy blue blood. When he straightened, her smile was gone and a pang of loss throbbed through him. She should smile more. Maybe then she'd be tolerable.

He settled back in his seat and closed his eyes. Getting some sleep seemed like a good idea.

Lizvette stepped from the cool interior of the airship onto the blazing-hot tarmac at the air station. The square of flat, paved land had been cut directly into the center of Melbain City in the western part of Yaly. Towering buildings of steel and glass rose overhead, and the air was clogged with smoke from innumerable factories.

She winced as the volume of the city pummeled her. Was it the voices of millions of people residing in a few dozen square kilometers? Or the autos that filled the streets, which hadn't seen a horse or cart in decades? She looked up into the perpetually gray sky but found no answers there.

Though the official capital of Yaly changed at the whim of each elected president, such fluctuations were inconvenient for the rest of the world, so the ambassadorships of all the nation's allies remained in the commonwealth of Melbain. The current president hailed from Gilmeria far to the north, and Lizvette was glad not to be going to that frigid place. Each commonwealth claimed to have a unique character and culture, but she found them all tediously similar. All had megacities in which the vast majority of the population lived and worked, and surrounding territories for farming, mining, and such. But a country as large and as productive as Yaly still had to import many of its resources. Elsira did a large trade of agriculture with the superpower, but the recent drought had affected both lands.

She took in the towering airships parked around them. Most were commercial vessels carrying dozens, if not hundreds, of people. There were only a few smaller crafts in the crowd. Her party stood around Clove, who mimed in frustrated communication with the Yalyish attendant who came to see to the ship. Tai stepped in to translate, smoothing out the tense moment.

Lizvette took a moment to regard him while he was otherwise occupied. The Raunian was keenly intelligent, to be sure, but she still wasn't certain what he was doing here. The Goddess couldn't have chosen him simply because he had a good head on his shoulders. But it was useless to speculate on Her reasoning. Lizvette would just have to trust in Her.

The conversation between the pilot and the attendant went on and on, and Lizvette shifted uncomfortably. Her traveling gown was far too heavy for the heat wave Melbain City seemed to be having. Sweat trickled down her back and between her breasts, leaving her flushed.

After an eternity, the attendant moved away, grumbling under his breath.

"What was that all about?" she asked Vanesse as the group returned.

"Clove is very particular about the maintenance of the ship." She rolled her eyes, then gave a yelp and jumped. Clove appeared from behind her and winked. Lizvette blushed, averting her eyes.

Tai sauntered over and stood next to her, rocking back on his heels.

"Yes?" she hissed.

"No luggage, duchess?" His dark eyes twinkled. The others were carrying their bags. She swallowed, not wanting to meet his gaze. Carrying her own luggage had never occurred to her, but there were no servants on this trip.

She marched away from him and picked up her traveling case. It was far heavier than she would have packed it if she'd thought she'd have to haul the thing herself. She struggled to lift it and walk back with some sense of decorum, cursing herself all the way for bringing so many dresses.

Tai merely smiled and turned around, following Clove and Vanesse off the tarmac and into the main building of the air station.

The load lightened suddenly and Darvyn was beside her, taking the case from her hand.

"Thank you," she said. He merely nodded and walked ahead, leaving her in the rear.

Lizvette felt ashamed and weak. They must think her coddled and spoiled. Yes, she had been born to privilege, but none of them had witnessed the darker sides of her upbringing. She squared her shoulders and marched into the station, determined to show Tai and the others that she was more than a pampered aristocrat.

They breezed through customs, having to stop only for Darvyn to receive an inoculation against the plague.

"They don't vaccinate in Lagrimar?" she asked.

He gave a humorless chuckle. "Even if they did, I wouldn't have taken a dose away from a non-Singer."

"So the plague wouldn't affect you?" Her curiosity was piqued.

"I would heal it before it could do any damage." His face tightened as if the subject pained him, so she let it drop.

Outside the station, they piled into a taxicab, fortunate to find one large enough to seat all five of them. Then they were off to the hotel where Clove and many of the other Yaly Classic racers were to stay.

The sun had just dipped below the horizon, and electric streetlights flickered on. Pedestrians crowded the sidewalks, and vehicles vied for space on the congested roads. Darvyn leaned his forehead against the glass, his eyes wide.

She wondered what it must be like to live in a desert under the rule of a madman. "Very different from Lagrimar, is it not?" she asked.

He looked over to her, a smile breaching his grim expression. "I don't understand how anyone could endure this. They literally live on top of one another," he motioned to one of the enormous towers as they idled at a stoplight.

"Personally, I don't understand how anyone could live this far from water. All this solid ground makes me landsick," Tai muttered.

"You all don't know what you're missing," Clove said. "There is never a boring moment in the megacities. Excitement on every corner. Shows and parties and festivals and dancing. You could live here your whole life and never dine in the same place twice."

Vanesse looked a bit skeptical, as did everyone else in the cab.

The streets were filled with a multihued variety of people, so unlike Elsira. Yaly did not have strict immigration laws, plus their population boasted three races: the Daro, lighter-skinned nomads native to the land; the Summ, a dark-skinned race that at some point had migrated from the east; and the Pressians, who vaguely resembled the deeply tanned Raunians and had sailed from the far west to settle in Yaly hundreds of years ago.

Early wars among the three groups had raged but had been sorted out long ago as a common religion spread and united the races. Lizvette had studied *The Ayalya* in university, the beloved book detailing the nation's creation myth. The vast majority of Yalyish worshipped eighteen saints, and each saint had a commonwealth established in their honor. Melbain was built in tribute to Saint

Melba, champion of justice. Statues of the woman abounded in parks, on street corners, and on building facades, and they were etched onto the currency.

Soon enough, they pulled up to the hotel and tumbled out. It was a midrange lodge, quaint and homey, nothing like the luxury establishments where Lizvette was used to staying. Still, it was clean and the staff pleasant. The trip and her upcoming task had drained her energy, and she wanted nothing more than a good night's rest. But due to the airship race, the place was too booked to give them all separate rooms. Luckily, Clove had been able to change her reservation to a suite. They entered a small sitting area with a bedroom on each side and a shared bathroom.

"Boys on that side, girls here," Clove announced as she strode inside.

The room Lizvette was to share with the other women had two double beds. Vanesse sat on the one closest to the window and began rifling through her bag. Clove sat next to her, and Lizvette stood awkwardly in the doorway.

"Perhaps you would prefer that I sleep in the sitting room. I don't want to intrude on your privacy."

Vanesse smiled generously, and it lit up her face. The more Lizvette looked at the woman, the less she saw the burn scar marring her skin. "It's all right. I'm sure you'd be far more comfortable on a real bed than on that couch."

Neither seemed to think the sleeping arrangements an issue, and Lizvette did not want to make a big deal of it. They were, after all, doing her a kindness in helping with her mission.

As she washed up in the bathroom, she thought of how Mother and Father would react if they knew she was sharing a room with two women who were obviously in a relationship. Father would be the most vocal, but Mother would let her displeasure be known in more subtle ways, as was her habit. Passive-aggressive comments were her style.

At least she was free from her mother's snobbery for a while. Lizvette had enlisted her maid to sit with Mother during the trip, and Zavros would check on her as well. A tendril of guilt worked its way through her, but she shook it off. Mother's illness was mostly in her mind—her body was not sick—and if Lizvette could restore some iota of honor to her family and avoid exile, a miraculous recovery may be in store. She chuckled to think about it.

She changed into a fresh gown for dinner before returning to the bedroom to free up the bathroom and spend several minutes repinning her hair. The door was slightly ajar, and she looked up to find Tai standing there staring at her.

She raised an eyebrow at him. "May I help you?"

"Just admiring the view," he said with a cheeky grin.

She flushed, then marched over to the door and slammed it in his face.

CHAPTER FOURTEEN

A storm pummeled the boat until it crashed upon a shore, and Ayal stepped foot onto sand dark as tar. There she met Woman-With-Eyes-Like-Fire digging for clams in the mud flats. "Come and share my meal," the woman said, and Ayal was grateful, for she had never had a friend.

—THE AYALYA

Kyara looked up when the door beyond the cells opened on quiet hinges. A guard entered, and the wound on her chest began to pulse.

Ydaris appeared and approached Kyara's cell. With a wave, the woman dismissed the guard, who left without another look. As chillingly beautiful as ever, Ydaris wore one of the elaborately embroidered dresses she'd favored in Lagrimar rather than the long, red coats the Physicks here seemed to prefer. Her golden gown was delicately beaded and her head was covered in a matching wrap, which was common among both Physick men and women.

"Kyara," Ydaris said with a glacial smile. Her emerald-green eyes shimmered in the low light. "I could not have imagined how helpful you would be. We are closer now than we've ever been. I should thank you."

"Closer to what?" Roshon asked from the cell next door. Kyara was curious, too, and Ydaris seemed to be in a chatty mood, but she knew better than to expect any direct answers from the woman.

Ydaris ignored Roshon and gripped the bars with one hand, idly fingering the medallion around her neck with the other. Kyara had never seen the woman without it—not once in ten years—though it was usually hidden beneath her dress. Anxiety for what was about to come twisted Kyara's stomach.

"I forbid you from accessing your Song in any way," Ydaris said.

The searing pain on Kyara's chest flared quickly before dying away, and she clenched her teeth until the agony was over. She wasn't sure why Ydaris felt the need to reinforce the binding spell every few days. Once the commands were spoken, they were in effect until Ydaris gave a new order. At least that's how it had always worked in Lagrimar. Had something about the spell changed?

Ydaris turned to leave and the questions bubbling up inside Kyara had nowhere to go but out. "Why don't you just drain my Song and be done with it? Why keep me here, day after day? Take it and be done!" she cried.

Green eyes peered at her coldly. "Removing your Song entirely can happen but once. This way, while less efficient, is far more advantageous. You are stronger than anyone thought you were. But take heart. We are almost done with you, my dear." Her lips curled into a terrifying smile before she continued to the door and the guard let her out.

Kyara slumped on her bed. She'd theorized that whatever they needed her Song for was best achieved with it attached to her. Otherwise they *would* have removed it as Raal had promised. But what was their goal? And would they really accomplish it before the process killed her?

The outer door opened again, this time admitting an old woman dressed in servant gray and stooped over a meal tray. Kyara looked at her dubiously; she normally received two meals a day and it was hours yet until the next one.

From the corner of her eye, she saw Roshon sit up sharply. A change in the routine was certainly something to take notice of.

The old woman placed the tray on the ground and slid it through the narrow opening in the bars.

"Why an extra meal?" Kyara murmured.

"Do you think they're trying to poison you?" Roshon asked.

She snorted. "I should be so lucky."

The servant clucked her tongue. "You're being given extra rations to bolster your strength."

Kyara froze as the reedy voice floated to her. "You speak Lagrimari?"

The woman kept her head down and remained slumped, though the tray no longer weighed her down. Wrinkled, paper-thin ebony skin stretched over gnarled fingers that retreated into the folds of the servant's robe. "You'll need to be strong to face what comes."

Kyara scrambled off the bed and over to the wall of bars. "Why? What's coming?" The only thing she knew of the Physicks' plans was what Raal had told her back in Sayya. The mages were searching for immortality. Though why anyone would want to live forever was beyond Kyara. This life was difficult enough.

"Does what's coming have to do with the war among the three worlds?" she asked.

Her question seemed to shock the servant. The old woman reared back and raised her head. Dark-blue eyes clouded with age gaped at her. "How do you know of this? Saint Dahlia save us, can you truly speak to the spirits?"

Now it was Kyara's turn to be shocked. How could this woman know of her dreams? She shook her head. "I-I don't know."

"Eat." With a wary eye, the woman began backing away. "Build your strength, girl."

"Wait!" Kyara said, pressing against the cold iron. She hadn't been able to communicate with anyone other than the family in the next cell since she'd arrived. Ydaris didn't count, and Kyara hadn't seen Raal since her first day here. There was so much she wanted to know, but before she could get out another question, Varten began coughing.

Dansig, who had not left his son's side, rubbed the boy's back as Varten coughed up blood. Alarmed, Kyara met Dansig's eyes.

"Can you at least tell someone in charge that Varten needs help?" Kyara pleaded. "Something's very wrong with him."

The old woman nodded and eyed the ill teen with sympathy. She rapped on the outer door. Just before the guard opened it, Kyara got out one final question.

"What's your name?"

"I am Asenath," she said. "I will ask a physician to see about the boy."

And then she was gone through the thick metal door.

Ella was swaying on her feet. The beauty shop was busy with the normal Sixthday rush. Everyone wanted to look their best for Seventhday, which for most workers was their day off. She'd been at it since the shop opened without so much as a lunch break and now the late-afternoon crowd was thickening.

Her sleep had not been easy since she and Benn had come across the dead smugglers two days ago. She'd checked the newspapers but there hadn't been so much as a line about the murders in the crime section. Which meant the constables were helping to sweep it under the rug.

Plus, she hadn't heard anything more about her request to visit the children with Benn. Sister Moreen said it would take a few days for approval, but now Ella worried that her vendetta against Syllenne Nidos was going to be an issue. Were Syllenne's spies scuttling her chances? Tana and Ulani should not be made to suffer for things they had no control over. Ella couldn't get the girls out of her mind.

The door over the shop jangled for the hundredth time, causing her to wince. She looked into the mirror at the newcomer and couldn't suppress a cringe.

"You didn't tell me Vera was coming," she whisper-shouted to Doreen, the hairdresser at the station next to hers.

Doreen glared. "You expect a rundown of my entire schedule on a daily basis?"

Ella tightened her jaw, then pulled the curling iron from her client's hair just as it began to smoke. "I would appreciate a heads-up when my mother-in-law is expected."

Doreen merely rolled her eyes and turned to meet her client. Vera Ravel was a steam engine of a woman whose force of will Ella would have admired had she not been the victim of it. Vera's opposition to her younger son's marriage to a foreigner had been vociferous and unyielding. There were very few people whom Ella couldn't manage to soften toward her, but Vera was one.

The woman marched past her, then paused, turning stiffly in her direction. "Ella," she said, acknowledging her with a nod of her head.

"Good afternoon," Ella replied, holding herself rigid. Thankfully, the woman continued on her way to settle into Doreen's chair as if it were the throne in the palace, sparing Ella any more of her civility.

"Mistress Ravel, how are you today?" Doreen said cheerily as she draped a cape around the woman's shoulders.

"Fair to middling, I'd say. Not looking forward to having to trek all the way to the Northern temple tonight, that's for certain." Her voice was all starch and vinegar, even when she was engaging in what for her was pleasant small talk. Ella forced herself to remember that Benn loved his mother, so there must be something about her that was lovable.

"Imagine the gall of bombing a temple," Doreen said, clucking her tongue. "I've never understood how there could be such evil in the world."

"Aye," Vera responded. "Too many folk have lost sight of their faith, that's part of the problem. Instead, they're taking up with that lot down at the docks. Those Dominionists," she sneered.

Doreen turned up her nose. "Wish I knew where people's good sense has gone. The Goddess is right here in front of everyone where they can see all Her wonders in the flesh."

Vera hummed in agreement. "Though She looks like a *grol,* there's a difference between Her miracles and witchcraft. People can't see that, then they're dumb as doornails. 'From the beginning, you heard, and saw, and touched that which was put before you by our Sovereign, and still you did not understand.' That's what it says in *The Book of Her Reign.*"

Ella was unable to keep herself from snorting. Both Doreen

and Vera shot hard glances her way. She ducked her head to hide a smirk.

"All this talk of a separate country for the *grols* though," Vera said. "It makes sense. Since they can't abide the country they already have, why not spare some of the land up north for them? That way they can go about their business and we can go about ours. No one's saying they didn't suffer under the True Father, but we shouldn't have to tear ourselves apart to accommodate them."

Doreen shrugged. "I don't know. The Goddess wants unification. Don't see why we can't all live together. It works here in Portside."

Ella froze for a moment, comb wavering in her hand. Doreen was often mean-spirited and snobbish. Who could have suspected she would support unification?

Vera waved a hand. "We've had our fair share of trouble with the rabble here in Portside over the years, but the Lagrimari are different. Knowing they could let loose a stream of witchcraft any time they want, I'm not sure I could sleep at night if one lived too close to me." She shuddered.

The bell over the shop's door rang out again, punctuating Ella's anger at her mother-in-law's intolerance. She looked up from force of habit and then did a double take. The woman in the entry was almost certainly not here for a color, cut, or relaxer. Sister Rienne had traded her blue robes for an embroidered, white muslin day dress and her hair was in two braids twined on either side of her head like earphones. She searched the faces of the women in the shop until she found Ella, then her whole body relaxed—a marked contrast to the tension she'd entered with.

They locked gazes in the mirror and Ella motioned down to the woman in her chair, hair half-full of curls. Rienne nodded and took a seat in the waiting area, absently flipping through a magazine while Ella finished up with her client.

Twenty minutes later, Ella hurried over to Rienne. "What's the matter? Has something happened?"

"I need to speak with you. Privately." Sister Rienne's voice trembled, and Ella grew even more worried. She led the woman beyond the washing stations to the storage room, looking behind her to make sure they weren't being monitored. Once closed in the small room that smelled strongly of pungent chemicals, Rienne took a deep breath.

"Some . . . information has come into my possession. I wasn't sure who to go to, but I thought that you—that is, your husband is a Royal Guardsman, is he not?"

"Yes." Ella nodded slowly.

"Then perhaps . . . You see I'm not certain I want to be involved."

"Slow down, Sister Rienne. What information has come into your possession?"

She pulled out a small notebook that had been lodged in her bosom. Ella's brows rose at her choice of hiding place. "Since the bombing, all of the Sisterhood operations have been moved to the Eastern temple. I was setting up the volunteer management office there when I found this mixed in with our paperwork."

"What is it?"

"An account registry. It contains records of supplies purchased for the temple: food, linens, cleaning supplies, things like that." She opened the small book and flipped until she'd found the page she wanted.

"Look there." A thin finger pointed to a line of cramped handwriting.

"Item: p. salt. Vendor: B.W. Quantity: twenty-five kilos?" Ella looked up, shocked. "This is dated three weeks ago."

Rienne nodded. Ella peered at the registry again. The entry

was in the same slanting script as all the others, buried amidst purchases of flour, potatoes, and heating oil.

"The quantity is far too large for cooking salt," Rienne said. "I looked through the whole book. We never buy more than a kilo at a time in bulk for the discount. I think it's palmsalt. And look at this." She fished a folded square of paper out of her bosom. "It's a letter from the High Priestess. Every Sister receives one on the anniversary of her vows." Rienne snorted. "She's thanking me for my diligence and service. But you see the signature."

A slanted, thin script neatly spelled out *Syllenne Nidos.* The handwriting matched that in the ledger.

"But how would the High Priestess's private account book make its way to the volunteer office?" Ella asked. "Especially when it contains such damning information, so poorly concealed?"

Rienne shook her head. "There has been a lot of confusion in the move. The Southern temple was home to nearly a hundred Sisters who've had to be rehoused along with a dozen offices for various outreach projects. We've been in chaos for the past three days."

Ella hummed in response, her mind racing. Was this the proof that she'd been searching for? A way to take down the High Priestess? But why would Syllenne have bombed her own temple? If she was a member of the Hand of the Reaper, why choose the seat of her own power as a target?

She couldn't put anything past the woman. Ella was certain that if Syllenne felt she could gain more power by destroying the Sisterhood whole cloth, she would do so. Still, something about this evidence of Rienne's felt very convenient.

According to Nir, no one would stock or sell such a large quantity of palmsalt. One stray spark and an entire city block could be filled with poison gas. And if the vendor initials B.W. stood for

Bor Wintersail, then he hadn't even been in Elsira three weeks ago to make such a sale. After the murder of the smugglers, Benn had investigated the other potential palmsalt lead. Wintersail's ship had departed from Elsira two months earlier, port reports stating he was headed for the Southern Seas. Something wasn't adding up here.

"You could go directly to the constables with this," Ella said.

Rienne dropped her eyes. "And what if nothing comes of it? What if she's too powerful to take down or the government officials cover for her? I can't take the chance of being the one to turn this in—look at what she's already done to me and mine."

Rienne had no idea of the tragedy Syllenne had brought down on Ella's own family, but she at least had the courage to stand up to her openly. Sucking in a breath, Ella squared her shoulders. "All right. I'll make sure this gets to the authorities. Your anonymity will be preserved."

Rienne murmured her thanks. "By the way, you should receive approval for the adoption visit later today. Sister Moreen is sending out couriers with the information. There are several steps before you can take the children home, but the process has been started."

"Thank you for telling me." Ella gripped the woman's thin hands. "And thank you for bringing me this." She held up the tiny journal.

"You are a good soul, Mistress Farmafield. I know you won't rest until justice is served."

As they made their way back into the beauty parlor's main area, her words echoed in Ella's head. She was starting to fear that justice would be far more complicated than she'd thought.

CHAPTER FIFTEEN

Woman-With-Eyes-Like-Fire took Ayal back to her family, a rowdy group of nomads who roamed the coast weaving nets and catching what sea creatures they could. "We make pilgrimage to Nikora the Weaver year after year," they explained, "and She blesses us."

Ayal felt their many years of homage cast a shadow over the bright day.

—THE AYALYA

Lizvette threaded her fingers together and clasped them tightly in her lap as the motor coach rumbled along the streets of Melbain City. Captain Jord Zivel of the Elsiran Foreign Service sat in the driver's seat, nimbly steering the enormous vehicle through the heavy morning traffic. Another of his men, a lieutenant whose name Lizvette couldn't recall as it had been rattled out so quickly, sat in one of the more functional than comfortable bench seats, along with Tai and Darvyn.

Zivel had arrived at breakfast to introduce himself and offer his men's assistance in any way required. The vague plan forming in Lizvette's mind had solidified. Though the men wore no uniforms, their closely shorn heads and exacting demeanors practically screamed military. Exactly the types to escort a recently exiled Elsiran citizen on a visit to the ambassador's home.

"I really don't know why you two felt the need to accompany us," she said to Darvyn, waving her hand to include Tai, as well. "It isn't as though you can come in." Bringing a Lagrimari and a Raunian along when she met with Uncle Rodriq was too strange to contemplate. Even the Foreign Service agents were merely to accompany her as part of her cover story. They would not be privy to her conversation with Rodriq.

Tai opened his mouth, no doubt ready to argue, but Darvyn cut him off with his calm, even tone. "We'll need to stay close in case something goes wrong." He winced and rubbed his head. She'd noticed him doing that a lot since they'd arrived in Yaly.

"Are you all right?" she asked, lowering her voice.

"Lagrimar is a small country. Even Sayya, our capital, does not have as many people as one of these city blocks. Rosira is busier, but still so much smaller than here. I feel the presence of millions." He squeezed his eyes shut. "They're like a sandstorm beating against me constantly, even with my shield."

Lizvette frowned, studying his pained expression. What must it be like to have magic? To feel the energy of every living thing around you? She caught Tai staring at Darvyn, looking like his thoughts were running along the same lines as hers. Their gazes glanced off each other, and for once, his held no mischief or accusation, only concern for Darvyn.

"I've known Rodriq since I was a baby," she said. "Don't worry. There won't be any danger. Stay outside and nearby if you must, but everything will be fine. I'm certain of it."

Her confidence faded as she was led through the dim townhome by a stony-faced maid. A solemn quiet enveloped the house, making their footsteps sound like the clattering of hooves. Zivel and his man stayed in the hallway. Lizvette stepped into Uncle Rodriq's office.

She swallowed her astonishment at the sight of him. His once full, rosy cheeks were now gaunt. What little hair he had left held far more gray than red. Worry for his health peppered her. He sat behind a great mahogany desk that overwhelmed the small room. The maid notwithstanding, the place smelled dusty, like it could use a deep cleaning. The shades were drawn, and only the small desk light illuminated the space.

"Uncle," she said, throwing her arms open, expecting her usual hug from him. Instead, he looked up at her, annoyance in his gaze.

"Lizvette, what a surprise." He did not sound like it was a pleasant one. He stood stiffly and rounded his desk to greet her, giving her a very weak hug and tapping her on the head absently. "I'd heard you were on house arrest in the palace. How is it that you are here now? Why did you not tell me you were visiting?"

She tamped down her disappointment at the tepid greeting and launched into her story. "The king and queen have passed down their sentence on me. I am exiled." Tears would be too much, even in such a situation, but she did allow her lower lip to quiver as if she were overtaken by emotion.

"I did not receive a dispatch on this," Rodriq said, affronted. He shuffled through the papers on his desk as if searching for a memo. "I should have been notified."

"It happened just yesterday, after the wedding," she said quickly.

"I suppose the new queen felt . . . jealous of me." The words burned coming out of her mouth.

She glanced toward the doorway and drew closer, lowering her voice. "The Foreign Service insisted on escorting me here as if I'm a common criminal." Her eyebrows drew up dramatically, and Rodriq sighed.

"That's the procedure. A sitting ambassador may only have limited contact with exiles." He glanced toward the door then shook his head and lowered himself into a high-backed chair next to his radiophonic. His office was decorated in a heavy, masculine style that felt oppressive. It was all leather and dark wood and thick brocaded drapery.

"I need your help," Lizvette said, approaching him and kneeling by his feet. She took his hand in hers. "I need you to help me find Father. At least get a message to him about my situation. He is all I have left now. If anyone has been in contact with him, it's you."

Uncle Rodriq had always been far kinder than her own father. His mild voice and gentle words were at odds with her parents' pernicious disappointment. It was no secret they had wanted a boy. Having failed at being born the proper sex, and committed the unforgivable sin of being an only child, Lizvette could do little else right in their eyes. But Rodriq could be counted on for a kind word. He used to ply her with the books she adored, toys that Father said were useless, and candy Mother feared would affect her weight.

"Don't you think if I knew where he was I would have turned him over to the authorities? As should you." Rodriq's voice was cautious.

"He's being charged with treason," she whispered. "The punishment is death." A true shiver racked her form. Though it was likely what he deserved, he was still her father. She took a deep breath, gathering the real emotion to help sell her performance. "How could I ever subject my own father to such a fate? After all he's done for Elsira?"

As a child, Lizvette would pray to the Queen Who Sleeps that some scandal would erupt and reveal that Rodriq was her father and not Meeqal Nirall. But now he pulled his hand away and scratched at his beard.

"You always were a loyal girl," he muttered. "Almost to a fault. Meeqal used to say that you were lacking in the brains department, but I never agreed. A sweet child always trying to please. Even now."

She was taken aback by his words. "Isn't it a child's duty to be loyal to her parents? Her family?"

"You are not a child any longer, Lizvette. And your father doesn't deserve the loyalty. Meeqal was right about one thing: if you had been a boy you would have gone far in this life. A son would not accept such treatment." He stroked his chin again.

Lizvette sat back on her heels, stunned. She'd done everything she could to win her father's respect. She had nearly been the princess of Elsira. She would have served the role well, no matter what her heart wanted, and it still would not have been enough. What more did he want from her?

Traitorous tears burned the borders of her eyes, but she would never let them fall. Instead, she stood abruptly. "Do you know where he is, Uncle?"

Rodriq shook his head and stared into the distance. On the bookcase behind his desk was a framed photograph of the two families. Father, Mother, and her, standing stiffly for the formal photograph along with Rodriq, his wife, and their two young sons, who were now off at boarding school in Fremia.

"I have not seen him in months," he said, voice flat. "You would be better served going to Fremia to serve your exile there. Searching for your father is a fool's journey. I have never before believed you to be a fool, Lizvette. Am I wrong?"

A tick in her cheek jumped involuntarily. "I am sorry to have disturbed you. Thank you for your time."

She left the room quickly, allowing the door to slam behind her. The maid who had led her in was nowhere in sight, and Zivel and his man stood still as statues. When she marched down the hallway, they followed close behind.

She wrenched open the front door. The dull glow of the sunlight filtering down through the smog surrounding the city reached her, along with the noise and the peculiar odor in the air. A wave of nausea struck her, but she pushed it down. Tai and Darvyn buzzed on either side of her asking questions, but the rushing in her ears drowned them out.

Uncle Rodriq had always been her salvation. His kindness had carried her through the times when Father had ignored her and Mother had been too busy with the demands of high society. When their cold disregard made her resolve crack, a considerate word from Rodriq had made it better. And now he seemed to share her parents' low opinion of her. Why? What had happened?

She was no closer to finding Father's location, so perhaps she was as useless as he'd always claimed. The warning he'd sent in the amalgam bird had not even been for her, it had been for Mother. True, Lizvette was on house arrest and unable to leave the palace, but the message had not been a greeting or an apology over her current situation. One that *he* had led her to. No, it was merely a warning for his wife that he was about to do another terrible thing for which he felt no guilt.

If her father was a monster who could have had a hand in the murder of innocent people worshipping in a temple, what did that make her?

Her eyes felt bruised from holding back the tears. She clenched her fists around her skirt. Real exile still faced her, and shame surrounded her. What had made her think that she would be able to do this? Find Father and bring him in? Prove her loyalty? Perhaps she was a fool after all.

When a single tear escaped her eye, she did not even wipe it away. It lay there, a badge of dishonor and failure to go with all the rest.

Lizvette's brittle exterior was beginning to scare Tai. He knew she was tightly wound, the way all the upper-class citizens tended to be on the mainland, but now she vibrated with tension. Yet alarm still filled him when a tear escaped her eye. What in Myr's name could have driven her to tears?

Darvyn frowned, also studying Lizvette. She didn't answer either of their queries. It was as if she couldn't hear them. The two ruddy Elsiran military men stood off to the side next to the vehicle.

"What did he say?" Tai asked for the second time.

Finally, she shook herself out of the fog enveloping her and stumbled. When Tai caught her arm, she jumped. He removed his hand quickly. Frightening her hadn't been his intention. She swallowed and smoothed her skirt, appearing to be obsessed with the pleating.

Darvyn moved them out of the way as the sidewalk filled with pedestrians. "What happened in there?" he asked.

She shook her head. "Nothing. He told me nothing."

"Do you think he knows anything?"

Her bottom lip quivered so slightly that Tai thought it might be his imagination. When he blinked, the shudder had stopped but something in Lizvette's eyes had dimmed. Their amber depths were pools of sadness. How had he not recognized that before? They truly were windows to her soul and told a tale of sorrow he wasn't ready to hear.

"You were right, Master Summerhawk," she said. "We should locate and investigate a Dominionist meeting. Perhaps we'll have better luck."

Tai shook his head. "No, I think you were right. If he shut you down so sharply, he must be hiding something. We just need to figure out what."

Darvyn looked up abruptly. Perhaps the man's magic clued him in to Tai's plans. It was obvious this *uncle* of Lizvette's had upset her, and for some reason, Tai couldn't let that stand.

"What is going through your mind? Your face is full of mischief." Lizvette's brow furrowed dramatically in the prim, demure way that he expected from her. That was better. Anything but that loss and hopelessness.

His face split in a huge grin. "Sometimes it takes a bit of mischief to get things done." He spun around and headed for the steps to Verdeel's town house. Protests rang out behind him, but he was deaf to them.

Instead of ringing the bell or picking up the heavy door knocker emblazoned with a fish wrapped around a tree—the Elsiran symbol—he pulled at the latch, which no one had bothered to lock after Lizvette's exit. With a glance over his shoulder at his dumbfounded companions, he entered the darkened interior of the home.

The hallway stretched out before him, quiet as a tomb. He'd thought these fancy folk would have their homes lit with every electric bulb they could afford. The coolness of the marble beneath his feet sunk in through the thin soles of his boots—better suited to the surface of his ship than the halls of the wealthy. He cocked his head to the side, listening as he walked silently down the hall. A clanking in the kitchen caught his attention, but the thumping from a room off to the side was likely what he sought.

He stopped in the doorway of a finely decorated office watching an Elsiran, who must be Verdeel, stuffing papers into a briefcase. The man looked up, startled, as Tai entered and closed the door behind him.

In the distance, footsteps approached. Darvyn and Lizvette must have decided to join him. He didn't necessarily want them to see this, so he locked the office door.

Verdeel's eyes rounded, his cheeks blew in and out like a fish's.

"Where is Nirall?" Tai asked, cracking his knuckles. The world believed Raunians to be nothing more than brutes and pirates, and Tai had used this to his advantage before. Oftentimes, soft, rich men like this needed only the threat of violence to part with their valuables. Information was all he sought *this* time, but he was certainly no saint.

"I-I have no idea. How did you get in here? Who are you?" he sputtered.

"Scream for help and this will end badly . . . for you."

The door rattled behind him. "Tai," Darvyn said quietly.

"I'll just be a moment," Tai answered in a proper-sounding voice. "I'm having a conversation with Master Verdeel here." He turned back to the man who was now red-faced. "Just a little easy conversation where you tell me what you said to Miss Nirall to make her so upset and why you wouldn't tell her where her father is when it's clear you know."

The ambassador sputtered again and backed away, keeping his

briefcase against his chest as a shield. Tai took another step forward until Verdeel was flush against the wall with nowhere else to go.

"Where. Is. He?"

The men were nose to nose, and Tai raised his arms to cage in the shorter man. When Verdeel didn't respond, Tai placed his forearm on the man's throat and pressed, closing off his windpipe.

"Tai." Darvyn's voice was in the room, directly behind him now. He could smell the light scent of Lizvette's perfume, as well. Fresh and clean with a hint of fruit.

She would be horrified, of course. Then again, this was who she already thought Tai was so what did it matter? They all must play their roles.

He pressed against Verdeel's neck even harder. The man's red face turned purple. He sputtered a few words, and Tai let up.

"Ready to tell me what I want to know?" Menace dripped from his voice.

The man nodded. "M-Meeqal was b-blackmailing me. He'd discovered some information I didn't want shared and swore me to secrecy regarding his location, forcing me to keep it from the Elsiran Intelligence Service. I thwarted their investigation."

"So he is here in Yaly? In Melbain?" Lizvette asked from behind him.

"Y-yes. He's here," Verdeel confirmed. "Though I don't know where. He contacts me when he needs something. I have no way to contact him."

"Did you know about the temple bombing?" Lizvette's voice trembled.

"What do you mean *know about it*? I heard of it on the news."

Tai stepped fully away from Verdeel, and the man sagged, coughing dramatically. Tai rolled his eyes.

"But not before it happened?" Her voice was stronger now.

"What are you saying? No, of course not." Verdeel straightened his suit coat as if insulted at the idea. "Who *are* these people, Lizvette? What further trouble have you gotten yourself into?" He glared at Darvyn, but his gaze wisely stayed away from Tai.

Lizvette shook her head. "You and Father are the oldest of friends. He confides in you. You must know something else."

Verdeel let out a humorless chuckle, raspy from the pressure on his throat. "That friendship died the moment he threatened to go to the authorities on me. Self-preservation, Lizvette. That is what is needed in this world, not your misplaced loyalty. If indeed that's what it is." The venom in the man's tone made Tai step toward him again, scowling, enjoying when he shrank back against the wall.

Tai turned to find Lizvette's eyes wide and pained. Verdeel's words had hurt her. He still could not fathom why this made him want to strangle the man for real this time. He moved to the cold fireplace to gather his thoughts, tightening and releasing his fists.

Lizvette looked around the room as if lost before turning toward the hallway. "Captain Zivel?"

Verdeel's eyes narrowed. "What are you doing?"

"Captain? We need your assistance in here."

"You're really going to turn me in, child? What of the loyalty you spoke of?"

She looked over her shoulder and snapped, "I've had a change of heart." Then she turned her back on the man she'd called uncle.

When he made as if to speak again, Tai took a step forward. "Don't talk to her. Don't talk at all."

Verdeel clamped his mouth shut. Tai turned back to the fireplace and leaned against the mantelpiece. He beat his fingers against the wood to calm the rage that had again risen. A shiny, polished chrome vase on the mantel allowed him to see a reflection of the room behind him. Lizvette went into the hallway to speak with the Elsirans in low tones. Darvyn stood in the center of the room, his arms crossed. Verdeel was trying to surreptitiously slide his briefcase behind the bookshelf to his right. Tai let the man think he'd succeeded. There was something in there he was obviously trying to hide.

Lizvette led the Foreign Service agents into the office. "Ambassador Verdeel must be placed into custody." She motioned to the man in question. "The three of us are witnesses to his confession of obstructing justice and aiding a suspected traitor to the crown."

Zivel produced a pair of handcuffs and approached Verdeel. "We should inform the Melbain police as a diplomatic courtesy," he said. "They will likely want to hold their own investigation."

Lizvette tapped her lips. Tai could practically see the gears turning in her mind. Would the involvement of the Melbain police scare off her father? "That's fine," she said after a moment. "Call them."

Zivel moved to the phone to place the call.

The police arrived shortly thereafter, and the house staff gathered in the hallway to watch the commotion. While the lead officer held Lizvette's attention, Tai slid across the wall to retrieve the briefcase from its hiding place. Darvyn's sharp eyes didn't miss a thing, but the Lagrimari man said nothing.

The police stayed to search Verdeel's home, though the Elsirans escorted the ambassador out in handcuffs. He would be taken to Elsira for trial.

"Do you think we can trust that Zivel fellow?" Tai asked on the cab ride back to their hotel.

Lizvette shrugged. "Jack—I mean, the king does. Besides, he's dealing with the Melbain police directly, to keep them away from us. That will be helpful."

"You handled that well, Lizvette," Darvyn said. A blush was her only response.

"Yes, very coolheaded, duchess."

Lizvette's bashful expression changed to a frown. "What did you take from the office?" she asked.

"You saw that, did you?"

She pressed her lips into a thin line and stared at him.

"He was stuffing things into it when I arrived for our . . . chat. I think it may hold something of interest." He grinned and readied himself for her reprisal.

But she surprised him by merely crossing her arms and peering out the window at the dusk falling around them. "That was quick thinking, Master Summerhawk. Your presence on this mission is becoming easier to understand."

While not exactly praise, it shocked Tai to the core. He could come up with nothing else to say for the rest of the ride.

CHAPTER SIXTEEN

Walking barefoot on the sand, Ayal stepped upon a shell that sliced her foot open. Her cries of pain brought the people to her, but as they were the prized of the Weaver, Dahlia the Healer would not come.

—THE AYALYA

Ella gasped and clutched Benn's hand as the shuttle bus careened around a curve in the dirt road. Her alarm was not at the driving skills, or lack thereof, of the elderly Sister at the wheel, but at the number of protesters teeming outside the refugee camp. The group had doubled in the past few days.

Scores of angry people, shouting slogans and carrying signs, crowded the perimeter of the parking lot. A pitiful few soldiers were all that stood between the demonstrators and the camp.

The bus was met by a contingent of grim-faced Sisters, with

Sister Moreen at their head. Prospective parents filed off the vehicle amidst the clamor of "Keep Elsira Elsiran!" from less than one hundred paces away.

Ella kept her hand in Benn's as they followed the Sisters deeper into the camp, until the shouting turned into a muffled murmur. Her chest remained tight as they entered the same large tent she'd visited before, where once again the orphaned children were seated in sober rows.

A slow smile spread across her face when she spotted Ulani and Tana, seated near the back. Ella tugged Benn forward, eager to greet the girls, when Sister Moreen's sharp voice brought her to a stop.

"Today you will have supervised visits with the children to ensure your suitability as parents. Please gather here to be matched with your chaperone."

Sucking in a breath, Ella checked her enthusiasm. She was glad the Sisterhood was taking care in placing the children, even if it collided with her eagerness. But when she met the Sister who would be overseeing her interaction with the girls, her spirits took a nosedive.

"Sister Gizelle, what a surprise," Ella said through clenched teeth.

Gizelle's eyes narrowed. But her expression smoothed when she turned her attention to Benn. She looked him up and down with a gaze just shy of lecherous. "You must be Master Ravel. I don't think I've had the pleasure." She held her hands out to Benn for a greeting. Ella gripped her husband's hand tighter.

Taking the cue, he ignored the young woman's outstretched hands and bowed to her instead. He was well aware of the history the two women shared.

Gizelle chuckled and dropped her arms. "We take our duty

to the orphans seriously. We must be certain that our adoptive families are of the highest moral character, as I'm sure you can understand." Her voice oozed honey.

"And I'm certain you're the perfect person to judge high moral character." Ella's words were tipped in frost. They had the desired effect of wiping the smugness from the Sister's face.

"It isn't at all clear Mistress Ravel—excuse me, Mistress Farmafield—whether a foreign citizen is even permitted to adopt in Elsira."

"Well, since the children aren't Elsiran, I don't see why an exception can't be made."

Gizelle tilted her head. "Laws are not made to have exceptions, I'm afraid. It's what separates us from the animals."

Ella geared up for a retort when Benn's deep voice broke in. "'Laws writ by men contain all the flaws of man. The sun needs no law but to shine.'" Ella stared at him.

"*Book of Her Reign,* chapter nineteen," Gizelle murmured. She straightened her shoulders and looked around the room. "Well, let's get this over with."

Ella grinned at Benn. Leave it to him to defuse a situation with something a Sister couldn't argue with—scripture. Still, it would be so easy for Syllenne, and Gizelle by extension, to deny her the ability to adopt the children as retribution. Had she gotten her heart set on something destined to be impossible?

Nerves fluttered on delicate wings in her midsection as she approached the table where the girls were sitting ramrod straight, barely moving a muscle. She'd never seen children be so still and take up so little space, but all the young Lagrimari present seemed to have mastered the technique.

Ella folded herself onto the cushion; it took Benn a bit longer because of his bad back. She smiled at the girls. "Do you remember me?"

Ulani nodded, but it was Tana who spoke. "Ella."

"Yes, and this is my husband, Benn." She brushed her hand across Tana's forehead, then Ulani's. Turning to Benn she said, "This is how you greet someone in Lagrimar."

"Yes, I know." He chuckled. Ella had forgotten Benn had worked near the Lagrimari settlement in the east for years and must know far more about their culture than she did.

They sat, doing their best to communicate with the girls, though it was slow going. Today, two translators rotated among the tables, aiding in the interactions. Both were settlers—former Lagrimari prisoners of war who had been in Elsira for years. Benn greeted each man warmly when he came by to help.

Together, they played with the provided toys, and worked on teaching the girls a handful of new Elsiran words, all under Gizelle's watchful eye. Thankfully, the Sister didn't appear to hold any animosity toward the children and kept her attitude in check. She even went as far as to play with Ulani, who marched a toy horse up the Sister's arm.

All too soon, the visit was over. Ella hugged each girl tight, tears clogging her eyes when she had to say good-bye. Tana clung to Benn; she'd opened up more with him, even gracing him with a rare smile—one Ella hoped to see a lot more of.

Ulani spoke to one of the settlers, her voice pitched upward like a question. "They want to walk you out," the man said.

Ella looked to Sister Gizelle and held her breath. The Sister's expression was glacial, but she gave a subtle nod. Grinning, Ella took Ulani's hand as Tana held on to Benn and they made their way back into the day's dying light.

The warm glow of the visit cooled rapidly as the sounds of the protestors grew louder. Once they reached the parking area, it was clear that even more had amassed over the past two hours and they'd moved much closer, spilling onto the gravel, unfettered by the ineffectual guards.

Ella stopped short at the unfolding chaos. Ulani's hand in hers turned to stone. The little girl may not have been able to understand all the words or read the signs, but she could see very well the vitriol on the demonstrators' faces and hear their barbed tones.

Adopting and caring for these girls didn't just mean sheltering, clothing, and loving them. It would also mean safeguarding them from the embedded hatred in their new land.

Some of the protestors began pointing to where Ella and the others had emerged from the rows of tents. The demonstrators began marching forward at an alarming pace.

"Take the children back," she called out to Gizelle, who had been steps behind them. She pushed Ulani back, placing her body between the child and the approaching mob. Then she turned and picked the girl up, intent on carrying her back to safety. Benn was already hustling Tana away.

A *bang* sounded behind her along with the spray of gravel. Anguished cries rang out. Ella glanced over her shoulder to see a shuttle bus had backed into the main driveway, perhaps to block access to the protesters. A screaming woman lay on the ground, next to a sign reading *CULL THE HERD* in blocky letters. Blood gushed from her arm, and her leg was twisted at an odd angle.

The bus's door opened and the white-haired driver stepped down, regarding the scene with surprisingly little distress. The Sister crossed her arms, with apparently no intention of rendering aid to the downed protester.

Ulani wriggled to be let down from Ella's embrace. She wanted to hold on tight, to protect her from any unpleasantness, but she allowed the girl to get down, resolving to lead her away. However, with a determined speed she hadn't expected, Ulani raced toward the injured woman.

"Ulani!" Ella shouted, running after her, not putting it past these protesters to harm an innocent child.

Ulani crouched beside the sobbing woman, not touching her, and closed her eyes. Ella stooped down, wrapping an arm around the girl and keeping the surrounding people in her sights.

Gasps rang out from those towering over them. Ella looked down in time to see the wound on the woman's arm close. Then her twisted leg shifted, and with a soft pop, the bone snapped back into place.

An uncomfortable hush fell across the crowd. For one pregnant moment, everything was still.

Ulani opened her eyes.

"Witchcraft," whispered a tall, bearded man leaning on his picket sign.

The injured protester, a slim woman of about thirty with a mop of curly ginger hair, scrambled to a seated position, running her hand over her leg. Her expression went from astonished to dumbfounded. She gaped at Ulani, jaw open.

Scattered whispers coalesced into a crush of outrage. Ella grabbed Ulani around the waist and hauled her away, back toward the tents. A clamor of disgust and condemnation rose behind them. Half a dozen soldiers ran up to try to calm the situation.

Once they were hidden by a row of tents, Ella put Ulani down and ran a hand across her face, reassuring herself that the girl wasn't hurt.

"You're an Earthsinger," Ella said, pitching her voice to make clear that she wasn't upset or afraid.

Ulani nodded.

Tana ran over and skidded to a stop before them, clutching her younger sister in her arms. “She is . . . not thinking always,” she said in halting Elsiran. “Feels everyone.” The older girl shook her head.

Ella’s stuttered breathing had not yet slowed down. “Ulani, sweetheart, it’s kind of you to want to heal people when they’re hurt, but everyone doesn’t want it. Some people would rather be injured than accept your help.”

Ulani frowned. “No help?” Her bewildered voice trembled.

“Not everyone. They’re afraid.”

“Afraid . . . me?” Her eyes widened so much it was almost comical. If Ella wasn’t tempted to cry she may have laughed.

“I’m so sorry. It doesn’t make any sense.”

Tana crossed her arms, looking angrily in the direction of the parking lot. The storm on her face matched the one in Ella’s heart.

This was just the beginning of what Ella feared could become another war. There may not be a battlefield or tanks or weapons, but there were two sides in conflict and only one could win.

CHAPTER SEVENTEEN

Angry to be abandoned by those who had sent her on this journey, the seeker stayed with the family of Woman-With-Eyes-Like-Fire long after her foot had healed. There was joy and laughter and bickering and cursing. There was life which she had not known before.

As the days passed, the shadows grew long, but she would not be moved.

—THE AYALYA

As the taxicab plodded through heavy traffic, Lizvette could not take her gaze from Tai's scarred hand lying atop Uncle Rodriq's briefcase. He sat across from her, looking out the window and drumming his fingers absently on the smooth leather. His expression was contemplative now, a far cry from the intensity he'd shown when questioning Rodriq.

Lizvette had never been a fan of violence, and she hadn't been around it often in her life. If she'd been asked a few days earlier if she would ever condone such a manner of gaining information, she would have absolutely refused. But seeing Tai leap to her defense and compel Rodriq to shed his superior demeanor had made her pulse quicken.

Tai's hair looked purple in the passing streetlamps, and the tattoos etched into his skin were more intriguing than frightening. Perhaps it was the thoughtful, almost brooding expression he wore that cast him in such a different light.

As if he could feel her perusal, his gaze confronted hers. This time, she didn't look away. Though his eyes were sharp and had likely seen things she couldn't even imagine, they held a kindness.

He'd done it for her.

She shook the thought away as quickly as it had come. He'd been tasked with this mission by the Goddess. Though She wasn't his deity, he'd appeared just as in awe of Her as the rest of them were. Tai likely only wanted to wrap things up here quickly so he could return to whatever business he'd been about before. Lizvette's method hadn't yielded results; Tai's had.

But something lingered in the back of her mind, making her wonder. She wasn't a vain woman and had no reason to believe Tai thought anything of her other than the spoiled, rich princess he derided. But he'd been so zealous when dealing with Uncle Rodriq. When he'd snapped at the man, telling him to not talk to her again, his words had resonated deep within her bones. Did she like the violence? No, she certainly did not, but she *did* like the feeling of being defended, protected. No one had ever stood up for her like that.

Their cab pulled up in front of the hotel. Lizvette broke her eye contact with Tai to find her change purse and pay the fare. She'd been entrusted with the funds from the royal treasury for this mission. On legs leaden from the weight of the day's events, she clambered up the stairs, into the hotel, and up to their suite.

Once inside, Darvyn and Tai caught up Clove and Vanesse on the latest with Verdeel, but Lizvette could not shake the tiredness that had infused her body.

Tai placed the briefcase on the coffee table, and they all stared at it in silence. "Would you like to do the honors?" he asked.

Lizvette nodded, feeling grim. She clenched her hands together and shifted forward to reach it. The lock was engaged, but Tai produced a pocketknife and jiggled the mechanism expertly until it popped open with a snick.

Papers had been thrust inside haphazardly, and she began the job of sifting and organizing them. Financial statements, correspondence, bits of flotsam and jetsam that would take days to go through and understand. Near the bottom, a much larger sheet of paper was rolled up. She unrolled and flattened it on top of the other piles she'd made.

Clove, who had been listening to the radiophonic in the corner, popped up, her interest piqued. "Is that a Caxton M18?" she asked.

On the page were top, side, and angled views of the schematics for an airship, with enlarged callouts for various smaller pieces and mechanics. The words *Caxton M18* were printed in small type in the lower right-hand corner.

"You know this model?" Lizvette asked.

"It's the same as the king's," Clove said. She sat next to Lizvette and studied the renderings intently. Her finger traced the lines and curves of the drawing. After a few minutes, her brow furrowed.

"What is it?" Vanesse asked, inclining her head to take in the design.

Clove leaned forward, nearly pressing her face into the paper. Her eyes blinked rapidly, filling with tears. “You got this from the ambassador?” she whispered.

“Yes,” Lizvette said, a flutter of fear forming at the woman’s reaction.

“Verdeel is a sponsor of one of the ships in the race—a Clinton IV.” Clove’s attention never left the paper.

“So why does he have the plans for a Caxton M18 in his case?” Vanesse asked.

All eyes went to Clove.

“There are three M18s competing—me, Archibald Jaspergrace, and Cardenna Cattleman. Cardenna is widely thought to be the front-runner.” Clove traced a grouping of lines to where pen marks had been scribbled on part of the drawing. “Here is the location of the elevator. On this type of craft, the lifting gas is only used for takeoff. The elevator flaps control altitude at racing speeds. These drawings are for a modification, an extra component attached to the flaps.”

Lizvette’s head spun. “Is that illegal?”

Clove shook her head. “Mods are expected, and many pilots take pride in doctoring up their vessels for an advantage over the competition. But I’ve seen this modification before, and it’s not standard. I thought it was a dampener—they’re often used by newer pilots to cap their maximum altitudes.”

“But you don’t think that anymore?” Vanesse prodded when Clove went quiet.

“No,” she whispered. “I should have looked into it more, but I didn’t even open it up. I never thought . . . These specs . . .” She shook her head and started again, pointing at a small, blocky symbol on the paper. “That is the mark for an amalgamation.”

Lizvette looked up confused, but apparently Tai and Darvyn

were a few steps ahead of her. Both men stiffened. "What?" she asked, looking back and forth between them. "Someone planned to add an amalgam to this ship? What does that mean?"

Clove swallowed. "An amalgam wouldn't be needed to merely cap the ship's altitude, but it could be controlled remotely and effectively take over all height control."

Lizvette looked at the somber faces of the men and women around her.

"Where did you see this modification before?" Darvyn asked.

Tears slipped down Clove's cheeks. "On Prince Alariq's ship."

Lizvette's heart nearly stopped beating.

Clove told them about how she had inspected the ship quickly on the day the Mantle fell, after having been called to pilot the vessel by Jack. He'd been desperate to get to the border and save Jasminda from being forced into Lagrimar.

No one looked at Lizvette accusatorially, not even Vanesse, Jasminda's aunt, but the guilt still burned inside. It was Lizvette's fault that Jasminda had been taken along with the refugees and nearly sent to the brutal hands of the True Father at all, even though she was a lawful Elsiran citizen.

Both Vanesse and Clove bore remorseful expressions. Clove ran a hand through her short bob, mussing it. "I noticed it but didn't think anything of it at the time seeing as Prince Alariq had been a novice pilot. I should have investigated more. If the power of the amalgam hadn't run out, I would have put Prince Jack in danger that day."

She sat back heavily, head in her hands. Vanesse leaned in, holding her close and whispering words of comfort.

Lizvette was numb. The accident that had taken the life of the former Prince Regent—her fiancé—was no accident at all. That day the clear blue sky had turned dark and stormy unexpectedly, and when he'd died, Lizvette had cursed the contraption, cursed the thunder and lightning, and even faulted Alariq and his stubborn insistence on flying. Alariq had never been an irresponsible man. On the contrary, he was renowned for his careful deliberation and consideration of all angles before taking any action. But he'd loved the airship and the feeling of freedom he said it gave him. But that love had come at a heavy price.

"So he was murdered?" Saying the words aloud made her throat close up. Her hand flew to cover her mouth as a sob threatened to wrench itself from her body. She kept it in, barely, as her breathing sped.

"But these plans are not for the prince's ship?" Darvyn asked.

"No," Clove said. "The model is the same but the date is from just last week. The ship Verdeel sponsored hovers between second and third in the ranking, depending on who you ask. If the front-runner had an accident, though . . ."

Vanesse rubbed circles on Clove's back. "Accidents aren't uncommon in the Classic," the Sister said. "It's one of the hardest courses in the world."

"A working elevator is necessary, but no one would think twice of a contender crashing, especially near Rolinor's Peak or in the obstacle course." Clove shivered.

"How can we prove it?" Lizvette asked through shaking lips. The internal barrier maintaining her composure fractured at the thought.

"Verdeel can be made to talk," Tai said darkly. He cracked his knuckles, and the sound shot a thrill of relief through her. She was becoming bloodthirsty, but she couldn't be bothered to care.

"Do you think Uncle Rodriq had something to do with Alariq's crash? Did my fath—" The thought of her father having a hand in the death of the Prince Regent was unfathomable. He'd claimed everything he was doing was for the love of Elsira, the future of Elsira. All he'd ever wanted was for her to be the princess, and she'd been so close. But to kill Alariq before they were married was illogical. She refused to believe that Father could have known, but nothing made sense anymore. "Why?" Lizvette whispered.

Vanesse shifted and pulled her into an embrace. It was awkward for Lizvette, not used to such warmth, but she accepted it, understanding the woman's desire to help.

After a few moments, Lizvette pulled away and stood, wringing her hands. Unsure of what to say, she raced into the bedroom and closed the door. Alariq had been a good prince and a good man. He was kind and would have made her a good husband, even though he'd never held her heart. The knowledge that he may have been murdered—and that people she had trusted could've been involved—cut deeply. She could no longer exert the strict control she'd always had over her emotions, and the dam finally burst.

She lay on the bed sobbing her pain and heartache into her pillow, hoping no one would hear.

CHAPTER EIGHTEEN

When the kindred clan was ready to travel on, Woman-With-Eyes-Like-Fire begged Ayal not to join them. "You have forgotten your mission, you must continue, or I fear there will be much suffering."

The friends looked upon one another with sorrow and love. When Ayal opened her mouth to say good-bye a flame emerged from her lips, flickering wildly in the air between them.

—THE AYALYA

Kyara stepped into her cell, the clang of the rattling bars ringing in her ears. She waited to speak until the jangling stopped and the reverberation inside her skull had calmed.

"Nothing new," she whispered. Though that wasn't precisely true. She was always past the point of exhaustion after having her Song drained, but today she felt much worse. Her limbs were lead.

Even the dim prison lights assaulted her eyes. She needed to wash the blood off, but she didn't have the strength to even cross the short distance to her bed.

Everything was so quiet she heard only the *drip drip* of the blood from her palm hitting the concrete floor. The rattle of a struggling breath pierced the silence. With great effort, she turned her head to witness Varten shuddering on his bed. Dansig and Roshon watched him, hollow-eyed.

True to her word, Asenath had sent medical staff for Varten. They'd come in long white cloaks and whisked him away on a stretcher. Several hours later they had brought him back. He had been pale and sweating still, and even less responsive than before. Since then, he'd grown steadily worse. He hadn't eaten at all and had coughed up much of the water his father and brother had forced down his throat. None of them knew what this illness was, though the symptoms were similar to the onset of the plague, only extremely slow moving.

Kyara closed her eyes. There was little chance she would find a way out of captivity in time to save him. A thorny sensation pricked her eyeballs, and she squeezed her lids tight.

The outer chamber door opened, but Kyara did not bother to open her eyes until she heard a familiar voice. "I'm sorry the doctors will not help him." Kyara looked up to find Asenath standing before the cell, bearing another tray of food.

"Will not or cannot?" Kyara asked weakly.

"It is all a part of their experiments. Without the studies they've been conducting, the Analysts would have killed him and his family long ago." She shook her head sadly and slid the tray into Kyara's cell.

"What kind of experiments?"

"I do not know precisely, only that twins are very rare here.

The Physicks have been very . . . curious." Asenath stood expectantly, looking at the dinner tray.

"I can't eat now," Kyara mumbled. Her jaw felt so heavy, and her mouth was dry. "Perhaps in the morning."

"Come. Try anyway."

Kyara sighed. Sensing there was more to Asenath's request than care for her nutrition, Kyara fell to her knees. A bowl of stew, meaty and aromatic, greeted her along with a thick slice of bread. Her stomach grumbled, but she could not imagine taking a single bite. Then a glimmering bit of metal next to the plate caught her eye. Kyara stared at it, confused, before picking up the delicate, gold-colored hairpin. An empty setting for a jewel sat at the end, and inside, tiny gears were visible.

She stood, a question furrowing her brow. Kyara's hair was done in dozens of thin braids to keep it out of her way. Plaiting it also passed the long hours in the cell, but she had no need for a hairpin to keep it together.

"It's a translation amalgam," Asenath whispered. "Keep it in your hair. They won't check each of your braids." In Kyara's palm, the hairpin seemed to vibrate as the gears moved slowly inside the bare setting.

"Why is she speaking Yalyish all of a sudden?" Roshon asked as he approached the bars between them, suspicious.

"She is?" Kyara took a step back, closing her fingers around the pin. "Why give me this? Is it a trick?"

Asenath darted a glance at the door. "There are some of us who don't agree with what's been happening."

Kyara's only clue that the language she was hearing was not one she natively understood was the subtle vibration in the pin.

Asenath's gaze shot to Roshon. "If you can truly reach the spirits, then one of the renounced prophecies is coming true." This time when she spoke, it was definitely in Lagrimari. The pin was motionless. Asenath's indigo eyes were fearful as her gaze shot back to the chamber's outer door. "The Physicks believe Saint Dahlia guides their hands. She was the patron of healers and aided the sick. But she foresaw the perversion of her followers. We were not meant to live forever. Some of her prophecies were disavowed by those who sought to benefit from eternal life." Asenath's voice grew more urgent. "But there are those among us who did not turn away from that which was not convenient."

"Are you a Physick also?" Kyara asked, bolted in place by the woman's intensity. She'd thought the woman merely a servant, dressed in gray as all the other workers were.

Asenath nodded.

"What is the prophecy?" Roshon asked.

"'The one who walks in the Dark will embrace the Light.'"

Kyara stumbled backward. The words were so similar to her dream. "Embrace the Light? W-what does that mean?"

"Our scholars believe the Dark is the World After, and the Light is the Living World. You've walked among the spirits, have you not?"

Rendered mute, Kyara merely nodded, her body beginning to shake.

A visible shiver also went through Asenath. She donned the hood of her gray cloak. "I will do what I can to help you," she whispered just before the door opened.

A tattooed guard stood there peering into the prison chamber. Asenath motioned for Kyara to take the tray and then shuffled away under the watchful gaze of the guard.

When the door slammed shut, Kyara eyed the bit of jewelry in her palm. The ability to understand what was being said around her was priceless. A grim smile stretched her face. If the old woman could be trusted, then it meant none of the others would even know she understood them.

"What is it?" Roshon asked.

She explained to Roshon and Dansig what the tiny pin did as she placed it at the base of her head, hiding it among her braids. This could all be a trick—perhaps Asenath was merely a test, a way to give her false hope—but she was willing to risk it. The prophecy and the message from the dream were too similar for it to be mere coincidence.

Dansig's expression was thoughtful. He reflexively rubbed Varten's head as the boy tossed fitfully in his sleep, and Roshon stared at the door the woman had left through. Then his gaze fell on the food.

"I can't eat this," Kyara said, sliding the tray to the wall of bars separating the cells.

Roshon looked back and forth from the food to her, ensuring her permission. She waved her hand and hobbled to her bed. By the time she'd sat down, he'd eaten it all.

More than once she'd given the teens part of her rations to supplement their own. Their appetites far exceeded what they'd been living on these past two years. But even with the extra nutrition, Varten had still fallen ill, and his heavy breathing labored on. She missed his easy laughter and attempts to lighten their situation. While Dansig was generally quiet and Roshon irritable, Varten brought balance with his good-natured energy.

Perhaps with the hairpin, she would actually be able to help him.

Kyara didn't remember even closing her eyes, but she soon found herself in the dark place, standing just in front of the Sad Woman.

The whispers rose in volume to surround them, and the words in the ancient tongue were now clear. "Poison Flame," they repeated over and over again.

It was an accusation.

Kyara felt the gaze of the shrouded woman bore into her, and a chill shot up her spine. "Are you a spirit? Are you my mother?" she whispered.

The Sad Woman glided closer, as though her feet didn't touch the ground. She stopped an arm's length away. This close, Kyara could make out more of the woman's features through the inky mask that coated her.

"Your mother has gone into the Eternal Flame," the Sad Woman said, her dual voices competing.

"The Eternal Flame? What is that? Is she being punished?" Horror at the possibility of being responsible for her mother's damnation speared Kyara.

"No, not punished. Consumed. Reborn. The Flame is life, death, the before, and the after. All souls are meant to become one with it when they reach the World After, but some of us resist."

The woman's face was even clearer now, as if it was breaking free of the shadows binding it. There was something familiar about her.

"But why resist? Who are you?"

"I resist to keep the watch; others have their reasons. I am called Mooriah."

Kyara had heard that name before but struggled to remember where.

"My strength wanes," Mooriah said, her arms fluttering around her. "Remember our Light is the only salvation. It is all that can stop what is coming." Her face was clear enough for Kyara to recognize the grimace that crossed it. Then Mooriah shrank in on herself as if in pain.

"What light?" Kyara pleaded. "I don't understand." Mooriah looked up, her brows climbing in surprise.

"You don't know?" she whispered, panic penetrating the melancholy that surrounded her.

Kyara's eyes widened. "How would I know?"

"You *must* know," Mooriah breathed.

The memory of where Kyara knew the name from was just at the edge of her grasp when Mooriah dropped her head and the whispers quieted. "They're coming," Mooriah moaned as she vanished.

"Wait!" But it was too late. Kyara turned, steeling herself to face the arrival of those she'd sinned against.

CHAPTER NINETEEN

The seeker chose a path that led toward the forest and set off on foot in search of her purpose. The road was dark and lonely, but her breath of fire lit the way.

—THE AYALYA

"Another round," Tai called to the waitress who was passing by as he slammed his tankard on the table. The pub was a block from their hotel and seemed to be doing a brisk weekend business of locals and tourists in for the races.

Darvyn shook his head emphatically, motioning that he didn't want any more. He looked sideways at Tai, who ignored the disapproving glance. "How many have you had?" Darvyn's voice pierced the din.

"Who knows," Tai said. "Not enough." He rubbed his head, which had begun to ache a few pints ago, but that was no reason to stop—not when Lizvette's sobbing was still burned into his memory.

Clove tossed back the last of her drink and wiped her lips. That little woman sure could hold her liquor. Vanesse, no longer in her garb from the Sisterhood, still abstained from drinking, though she made fine company, if a bit on the quiet side. They'd left Lizvette to grieve in private, all of them discomfited by the sounds of her anguish.

Tai took in the revelry around them, pausing at the table just across the way where a Summ-Yalyish woman smirked at him. Even in the dim interior, her dark-blue eyes were bright against the rich shade of her skin. He raised his eyebrows in a silent question, and her smug expression turned lascivious as her gaze traveled down his body. Tai looked away, uneasy with an appraisal from the opposite sex perhaps for the first time.

It was disturbing, but he did not want to dwell on it. When the waitress brought around two more drinks and set them in front of Tai and Clove, he grabbed his immediately. "To the race," he said, lifting his mug high. Clove matched his toast. "May you be speedy and have the wind always at your back." Her qualifying heats for the Yaly Classic started the next day, and he truly wished her well. They clinked their glasses together, then downed the cold beers.

The liquid sloshed in his stomach uncomfortably, and he listed over to the side. "Perhaps that *was* enough," he drawled as two Cloves sat before him, laughing at something Vanesse had whispered into their ears.

"Here." Clove tossed something small and dark to him. He reached out to catch it but missed. Darvyn easily plucked it from the air and held it out to him.

"What's this?" Tai muttered. It looked like a short length of black rope.

"Wrap it around your wrist. It will take away some of the pain. The bartender gave it to me."

Tai blinked and tried unsuccessfully to wrap the thing around his wrist.

"What is it?" Darvyn asked.

"An amalgam," Clove explained. "It will last for a few hours and prevent hangovers, too. Apparently they're good for business."

"You're not wearing one," Tai accused.

Clove grinned. "I don't need one." She gulped her remaining beer.

Vanesse reached over and affixed the strap to Tai's wrist. It had a simple loop that he really should have been able to manage on his own.

"Thanks," he grumbled.

Both women laughed. Darvyn merely shook his head, keeping a keen eye on the other patrons.

The crowd appeared mostly made up of Administrators, the bureaucratic class of Yaly, who made things run. Investors, the upper class, didn't populate this part of Melbain City. The outer territories were assigned to the poor souls who toiled in the fields—Bondmen, who most likely would never move past their station.

Everyone in the pub seemed comfortable, well fed, well clothed, and likely ignorant of the world that lay beyond his or her caste. Tai reached for his glass again, surprised to find it empty. His head began to swim, as did the room.

"How long is this thing supposed to take?" He tapped the band around his wrist.

Clove frowned. "Should be instantaneous. You're not feeling any different?"

"Yeah, I feel worse."

The roiling in his stomach became a nasty bile that rose up his throat to coat his tongue. He stood abruptly and ran for the back door, breaking into the alley in a rush just before the vomit spewed from him.

When he was done, he coughed, feeling spent. The buzz from the beer was waning, and his head felt as if it were full of cotton. If only Mik could see him now. His first mate would have a good laugh at Tai's expense.

Was this really all because that princess was crying over her murdered fiancé? Tai had been both shocked and unsurprised to learn that Lizvette had been betrothed to the former Prince Regent of Elsira. She seemed the perfect choice for royalty; his teasing nickname of "duchess" had hit closer to the mark than he'd even known. But realizing that her prospects had been so high . . . It stung and reinforced what he'd known the moment he had set eyes on her in the hallways of the palace of Rosira: she was far outside his reach.

Better for him to accept the unspoken invitation of the woman inside than to be burned by the sun. He had no desire to be reminded that some things were not for him. He already knew it well enough.

And if Lizvette's sorrow cleaved him and sawed at his heart, left him wanting to take on an army just to ease her sadness . . . well, then he just had to ignore it. He was neither a soldier nor a therapist, and he'd only known her for a day. He repeated that statement to himself until it sunk in and turned to go back inside.

A noise at the mouth of the alley caught his attention as two men walked into the pool of illumination cast by the streetlamp. Both looked like average Administrators, dressed in starched button-down shirts and ties as if they'd just come from their offices. The shorter one was Daro-Yalyish, given his wan complexion and golden hair. The other was Pressian-Yalyish, with sun-toasted skin and shoulder-length black hair tied in a queue. Something glittered in his hand in the lamplight. The two appeared to be arguing, though Tai could only make out the angry tone of their voices, not their actual words.

He blinked, and in that briefest of moments, the Pressian disappeared from sight. But the man had not walked away. He was simply there one moment and gone the next.

The Daro walked toward Tai, apparently headed for the back entrance of the pub. Tai leaned against the wall again and closed his eyes, listening to the man's footsteps. He strove to seem in his cups—and in truth, he was—but what he'd seen could not be blamed on the drink.

He waited a few minutes before following the man back into the pub, stopping in the restroom first to clean up. Returning to the table, he noticed that his little band had grown tense.

Darvyn was wound tight as a sail's rigging at full wind, and Clove and Vanesse looked poised for escape. Darvyn's eyes darted to the opposite side of the room where a large group had gathered in Tai's absence. He noted the Daro from the alley among their number.

Sitting down, he whispered to Darvyn, "Who are they?"

"Dominionists," he answered through clenched teeth.

A chill went through Tai. "I saw one of them in the back with another man who disappeared into thin air."

Vanesse raised a skeptical eyebrow, but Clove leaned forward. "Was he using an amalgam?" Her eyebrows rose significantly, and a ripple of confusion swept through the table.

Tai thought back to what he'd seen. The Pressian had been holding something. "Could be."

She nodded. "The Physicks keep the best ones for themselves. I've seen one do that trick before. Handy."

In Tai's trips to Yaly, he'd never purchased any of the magical contraptions. Raunians generally scoffed at such things. And if this useless band around his wrist was any indication, they weren't all that reliable. But the general public in Yaly and Fremia loved them. The items available on the market—translators, devices somewhat like portable telephones for talking over long distances, coins that changed into different currencies, and the like—were all relatively weak and ran out of power in a few days, needing to be either replaced or recharged at Physick-run shops.

But the mage who had boarded Tai's ship two years ago, and apparently had made off with Dansig and his sons, had possessed some very powerful mech—amalgams that weren't available in stores. If one of these things could make someone vanish from sight, that might explain what had happened to his passengers.

"But if the man in the alley is a Dominionist," Tai said, peering at the group across the room, "why would he be associating with a Physick? Dominionists hate magic. They shun amalgam."

The other patrons in the pub grew quiet as a voice from the Dominionist group rose. "Raise a glass in honor of the true path that *The Book of Dominion* offers us." The speaker was hidden among the others, but his voice was high and clear. "Our way does not rely on the supernatural. It is righteous, for right-thinking men. For hard workers who labor for every scrap and coin. No *mage* or *saint* or *goddess* has carried your burden. They have not bled or sweat or cried for you. But they deserve worship? Exaltation? Each man walks his path alone. We are the ones who should be praised, not some long-dead mystics or devious witches."

The group cheered and toasted the speech. Tai looked to the questioning faces of those at his table. The others didn't speak Yalyish, and he translated briefly.

"Dominionist diatribe," Clove said, shaking her head. She took a sip from her cup, which was filled with water now. That was a good idea, Tai decided. He flagged down the waitress and ordered water for himself, as well.

The Summ woman who had been ogling him before stood suddenly, a fierce expression on her face. She opened her mouth and began to sing.

"I'm seeking the land where dear Melba has gone
Her courage was mighty, her faith carries on
She left us with hope that we would stay strong
Walking the trail both narrow and long."

Even the Dominionists were quiet as the woman's achingly sweet voice rang out.

"Melbain's charter song," Tai whispered. "It's the anthem of the commonwealth, honoring Saint Melba."

Others around the pub chimed in, adding their voices to the chorus, opposing the Dominionists' secularity.

"The path that was blessed by dear Melba's wise hand
Is the one that we trod, the one that we trod.
And when we arrive we shall see her sweet face
And we will be awed, we will be awed."

The singing continued, with the many voices creating a resonating harmony. It was inspiring, a moment of shared faith among strangers, fighting back against the faithless.

The Dominionists believed only in themselves and their judgment, labor, and effort. But there was magic in the world, even if they didn't care for it. Tai had seen it and felt it many times, and like most phenomena, it was neither good nor bad. It simply was. Fighting against it was useless.

His dark mood eased as the song continued. Though he didn't share the beliefs of those who praised Saint Melba, he understood faith and knew it to be a kind of magic in itself. And while his had been broken over the years—mainly by his unscrupulous father and implacable mother—it always rebounded. He found it again in the bond he shared with his sister. The trust Ani put in him that he hoped to never betray. Mik's friendship and loyalty was also stalwart.

And love. The more he thought of the word, the more he was reminded of Lizvette's gut-wrenching sobs. He could not bring back her lost fiancé, but he could help find her father and bring him to justice. He could help her shake off the guilt and shame she wore like a cloak. And when the mission was done, he would walk away from her knowing he had done all he could. And that would be enough.

He told himself that over and over, hoping that eventually, he would believe it.

CHAPTER TWENTY

Deep inside the wood, the path Ayal trod forked. She stood at the junction, pondering the way forward. A bobcat emerged to observe her dilemma.

"What should I do?" the seeker asked.

"If you knew the destination at the end of each path was the same, would the decision matter?" the bobcat replied.

—THE AYALYA

Lizvette's tears had long dried. She lay on her bed staring at the ceiling. The suite was quiet. Hours had passed since Vanesse came in saying they were all going out for a drink, pity lacing her voice.

She turned her face into her pillow and slammed her fist down. She didn't want to be pitied, nor did she want her feelings raw and exposed like this, impossible to control. What was wrong with her?

She froze as a question whispered across her mind: what would Jasminda do? The new queen was the strongest woman Lizvette could think of. Jasminda did not seem to be the type to wallow. She took action and had been through much grief, but it had not destroyed her. It was little wonder Jack had preferred her.

Lizvette sat up, determined to pull herself together, when she heard the main door to the suite open. She patted her hair, which must look a fright, and rose to straighten her dress. The sitting room was quiet, so perhaps Darvyn had returned. The others all made so much noise.

She opened her door and froze, the gasp dying in her throat. Her father stood in the entryway to the suite. He'd grown his goatee into a full beard, and new, thicker spectacles graced his face. He removed his hat and stood tall, peering at her through narrowed eyes.

She'd thought it would be days or even weeks before she located him, not that he would appear on her doorstep her very first night in Yaly. She forced herself into action, schooling her features to mask her shock.

"Father!" she said, her hands fluttering uncontrollably. "How in Sovereign's name did you find me?" She scanned the empty room, wishing the others had not left. A ripple of fear cooled her skin. She wasn't sure she knew this man at all.

Her father did not move from his place at the door. He did not smile in greeting, only held up a finger to shush her. From his pocket, he produced a tiny metal contraption that resembled the innards of a watch, all gears and dials. He made an adjustment to the device, turning a clicking cog, then moved forward and placed the amalgam on the sofa table.

"Keeps us safe from prying ears," he said, pinching his earlobe.

As he came closer, she noticed how disheveled he'd grown. As a former professor, he'd always had a tousled, windblown mien—his hair was prone to flying away, and his beard always needed brushing—yet it had grown worse over the past weeks.

He hovered close by but did not reach for her. She had not expected him to. Neither of her parents had ever been affectionate. After all, "proper Elsirans did not run around hugging their children needlessly like the boorish lower classes," or so they'd told her.

She clasped her hands together to prevent their shaking and perched at the edge of the couch. Father stood in front of her, scrutinizing the room with a disapproving gaze. Through his eyes, the comfortable armchairs would be shabby, the wallpaper cheap and loud, the rugs frayed at the edges.

She swallowed, waiting for him to speak.

"So they went through with the exile, did they?" he asked finally.

Lizvette nodded, her mouth dry.

He walked to the bureau and inspected the vase of gillyflowers there. "And Verdeel has been arrested. What do you know of that?"

She swallowed, attempting to bring moisture to her desiccated throat. "That was his own fault. He spoke of things he shouldn't have within earshot of Foreign Service agents. Apparently, he hadn't yet paid off the new men to hold their tongues."

Father sniffed and approached the dining table in the corner, across which the airship plans were spread out. Lizvette held her breath.

"And your current accommodations?" he asked, peering over the rim of his spectacles at the schematics.

She let out what she hoped was a droll chuckle. She worked quickly to come up with a suitable story and wished she'd had the presence of mind earlier to spin a believable yarn.

"A simple kindness extended by a woman of the Sisterhood who's taken pity on me. I was exiled with no funds, you see. Nothing but what I could pack in my traveling case. The Sister has deigned to offer shelter to a number of strange individuals in addition to myself. I was hoping Uncle Rodriq would be able to point me toward a more appropriate situation."

She paused as he leaned toward the table. Was he even listening to her?

"However did you find me, Father?"

He shook his head. "A woman running around in men's clothing? A Raunian? A *grol*? Quite a misfit band you've attached yourself to, my dear." The sneer twisted his face into an expression Lizvette was far too familiar with.

"Necessity makes strange bedfellows, indeed," she murmured, tension still constricting her breathing.

Finally, he straightened and looked at her. "I make it my business to keep track of vessels arriving from Elsira. I should have thought my daughter would have been treated with a good deal more respect."

She barely kept herself from rolling her eyes, and instead stood, gripping her hands together so tightly they were beginning to grow numb. "Are you here to take me with you?" If she was leaving with him, somehow she'd need to get a message to Darvyn or Tai, or at least create a trail they could follow.

Father bent over the table again and brushed the airship plans with a single finger. She drew closer, sensing his fascination. Her father's flaw was one that many men shared—pride.

"Uncle Rodriq had these on him," she said. "I stole them before the police could find them. It seems as if he was responsible for Alariq's death."

"Rodriq had nothing to do with that." Father frowned, making a tsking sound. "And you're a fool if you believe that blubbering idiot could take down a Prince Regent." He shook his head and finally faced Lizvette. "Alariq's death was a shame, but he brought it on himself."

Lizvette gulped, willing her voice not to shake. "W-what do you mean?"

"Oh, I know you two were close, and it was a pity it had to happen. If Alariq had any sense, you would be princess right now and things would be as they should be. I would be the grandfather of the next Prince Regent, the crown back in the hands of our family where it belongs."

She squinted, trying to follow her father's words. "The crown was never in our family. Only the Alliaseen bloodline has ever ruled."

"Ha! Five generations ago, Prince Jerrard had an affair with the wife of one of his Council members—my great-great-grandmother." His eyes blazed. Lizvette fought the urge to step back from him. "My great-grandfather was the firstborn of the Prince Regent, though no one but his mother ever knew. He himself only found out after the prince's death. The Niralls are the true holders of the crown, and it is my duty to make it right."

A lump formed in her throat. "So that is why you wanted me to be princess?" She looked down as understanding dawned. "But if all this is true, how does Alariq's death further your agenda?"

He waved her away as if she were foolish. "Oh, it wasn't *my* idea. He made enemies of the wrong people, is all. It soon became beyond my ability to stop. I did have high hopes for Jack though . . ." He shook his head as if exasperated. "But never mind all that. If you expect me to help you extract yourself from the quagmire you've managed to enter, you will have to earn your keep and find a way to be useful. Though I'll admit I have little confidence that you can do so."

She blinked, remaining silent, not trusting her voice.

"There is yet some good that can come of the fact that you have allowed yourself to be gathered into this den of indigents." He stuffed his hands into his pockets and rocked back and forth. "This Clove Liddelot character . . . she is ranked highly in the airship races, is she not?"

Lizvette nodded.

"Well, she must not win, or there will be serious consequences of the fundraising variety."

"You're . . . gambling on the outcome?"

He sighed impatiently. "You will continue to ingratiate yourself to her. I will gather my resources and have a message sent to you in the coming days with information as to how you can prove yourself a valuable asset to my current enterprise."

Father drew something out of his pocket as Lizvette struggled not to react. "You want me to somehow sabotage Clove?"

He snapped open the object in his hand—a jewelry box. For the briefest of moments, she wondered if he was giving her a gift. Of course, the necklace he produced was nothing she would ever have considered wearing. A garish emerald-and-garnet cluster hung on a simple gold chain. Before she could do more than gape at the ugly pendant, Father had fastened it around her neck.

"A special amalgamation—one that prevents you from mentioning our little chat to anyone." He stood back, a satisfied gleam in his eye. "You won't be able to take it off until its power runs out in about a week or so."

"You don't trust me, Father?"

He opened his mouth to answer when the contraption on the

sofa table let out a soft chime. He turned and plucked it up, frowning at its whirring gears.

"Your party is returning." Placing the device in his pocket, he moved toward the door.

Lizvette jumped up. She couldn't let him leave yet. "Wait, Father—"

"My messenger will find you and give you further instruction. Prove yourself to me. And do take care not to get caught this time, dear girl." He gave the room one last disapproving grimace. Then after the briefest of bows, he disappeared out the door.

Lizvette was left clutching the necklace, grasping at its clasp, unsurprised when she could not remove it. She let out a cry of frustration and fled to her room just before the door to the suite opened again.

Tai stared at the door to the women's bedroom, which had just slammed closed. The others were still downstairs in the lobby of the hotel, watching an impromptu show by a group of roving circus performers, but Tai's head had been done in. He wanted nothing more than to hit his bed and not awaken until morning, perhaps even afternoon.

Lizvette's departure from the sitting room right before he'd arrived had him curious, though. He was ready to ignore it and give her some privacy until he heard her sniffle. His hackles went up. Was she still crying? He stood outside her door and heard the sound again.

Her cool and collected demeanor hinted at a woman who never allowed anyone to see what was hidden inside her. He knew she wouldn't welcome his intrusion. Still, he pushed open the door and found her lying facedown on her bed, hands pillowing her head.

He entered on soft feet, then decided he didn't want to startle her. Earlier, he'd noticed a creaky spot on the floor. He purposely stepped on it now.

Lizvette jerked up at the sound, scrubbing at her eyes. Her gaze turned defiant when she saw him, but it barely hid the sadness within. "What are you doing in here?" she asked, throwing her shoulders back in an approximation of her usual haughty demeanor. She patted her hair self-consciously. "Do you make a habit of barging into women's bedchambers hoping for a gracious welcome?"

Tai crossed his arms, thankful for her sharp words. Perhaps a bit of sparring would take her mind off her troubles. He rocked back on his heels and produced a smirk. "I'm not sure I'd call anything about you gracious, duchess."

Lizvette sniffed and looked down. Her fingers skimmed over a peculiar necklace he hadn't noticed before. The thing was hideous and didn't seem to match her taste. She gave it a tug and looked up at him, all animosity leached from her expression. She opened her mouth, but no words came out. She swallowed and tried again, and then gasped, pulling at the chain around her neck and rubbing the skin where it touched.

"What's wrong?" he asked, rushing to kneel before her.

After a few deep breaths, her hands dropped to her lap. "Nothing. Nothing I can say."

He frowned, scanning her up and down for signs of further distress. This close he noticed the freckles dotting her nose for the first time. They must normally be concealed with makeup. He blinked, not daring to move and upset the tenuous truce that hung between them.

To his surprise, she broke the silence. "Why did your mother sentence you to prison?" The question was quiet, barely more than a whisper.

His gaze dropped to her fingers as they began to fidget in her lap. Long and delicate, they were unvarnished with short, rounded nails. He took a deep breath. He may as well share the whole story. Perhaps it would distract her.

"My father was a smuggler, well known and well respected. I trained with him since I was young, as did my sister." Tai caught her disapproving expression but continued. "In Raun, honor is important. Your word is your bond, and breaking a contract is a serious offense."

Her nose crinkled in confusion. "But you just said you all were smugglers?"

"There's no dishonor in smuggling. The laws of other countries are seen as inferior to those of Raun. Circumventing their regulations and taxes is merely good sense." He smiled, and her lips curved slightly in return.

But the brief moment of cheer dropped away. "Father began secretly gambling," he continued, "and it turned into a problem." Tai clenched his jaw. He of all people should have noticed the change in Father's demeanor, but he'd been blind. "We had a huge shipment of oil linen from the Lincee Isles right before a typhoon devastated the Isles, and ours was to be the last shipment for many months. We had negotiated a good price for it, but a Fremian merchant contacted us, promising fifty percent more. The deal had already been struck with the first buyer, and the contract sworn out."

He paused to clear his throat as the weight of his father's disgrace bore down on him. Lizvette nodded, gently urging him to continue.

"Father's debts were such that he felt he could not turn down the better offer. He told me that the original buyer, a Raunian naval admiral, backed out and so we sold to the Fremian. When the admiral chased us down and challenged my father to a duel, I was shocked."

His chest had grown uncomfortably tight. He rose to his feet and paced to the dresser, unable to look at her. "I stood up for him because I believed him. My father would not have lied, especially not to me, or so I told myself. But the admiral produced witnesses to prove he had never released the original contract. To make matters worse, instead of dueling it out as honor demanded, Father fled."

The shame churned in Tai's belly as he forced out the rest of the story. "He ran, saying it was to protect me and Ani, but the truth was that he was a coward."

A small hand reached out to cover his clenched fists, and Tai hissed out a breath. He hadn't heard Lizvette rise or cross the room.

"What happened?" she asked. Her palm was soft as velvet, her scent entirely too feminine. He pulled his hand away and stepped back to restore his clarity.

"The admiral chased us and killed my father, as was his right. And his debts fell to me, both from the gambling and the squelched deal."

"Oh Tai. I'm so sorry."

He retreated even further from the empathy in her voice, shaking his head to rid himself of it. "At any rate, a year later, my mother agreed to a contract for my sister, promising her as an apprentice to another ship. But the captain was a scoundrel, and I helped my sister flee from him. It was yet another broken contract, so my mother sent me to prison for it. Just another untrustworthy Summerhawk." He spread his arms and shrugged.

Lizvette's keen eyes narrowed. "I don't see it that way. I'm sure your sister doesn't, either. What happened to her?"

Tai smiled. "As it turns out, once she lost her hand in an . . . accident, the captain she was meant to work for decided she was of no use to him. Little did he know she'd be piloting her own ship now, somewhere in the Northern Seas." His chest puffed out with pride at Ani's accomplishments. "I would have gone to meet her, had I not been . . . tasked with this mission."

For a moment, he was afraid she would ask him more, like why he'd sailed to Elsira and how exactly he'd come to the attention of the Goddess Awoken. But Lizvette merely clutched the bulbous pendant and nodded absently.

"It is a difficult thing, to have a reprobate for a father," she said.

"On that we can agree, duchess."

Her smile didn't reach her eyes, but at least she wasn't crying any longer.

Tai was exhausted. Relaying his father's sordid tale had taken much from him. He never spoke of it. All who knew him already knew, and it was far too personal a tale to share with new acquaintances. And yet that was just what he'd done. Shared his pain in an attempt to lessen hers, at least for a short time. That was not something he was used to.

He stood up straight and favored her with a formal bow. "I'll leave you to your rest."

Her eyes followed him as he left the room, and he felt her gaze until he closed the door. He stood on the other side, rubbing his hand where her silken skin had grazed his. Telling himself that one touch could not possibly have felt so good.

CHAPTER TWENTY-ONE

Ayal chose her direction by following a butterfly, trusting its beauty to guide her. She soon met Boy-Who-Passes-Twice, who ran with the speed and grace of a young lion. He earned his name the second time he came by, racing the wind in circles around her. Beware, *she thought,* to try and catch him is to grab the air.

—THE AYALYA

Ella waved good-bye to her last client of the day, pocketing the generous tip she'd been given. She gazed out the front window to the street beyond, bathed in a sunset glow.

The bell over the door tinkled when the paperboy ducked inside to deliver the evening news. Beauticians and wash girls descended on the pile, snagging copies for themselves.

Doreen triumphantly wrenched a newspaper from the grip of a teenage wash girl and sauntered back to her chair. She sat as if she hadn't a care in the world, flipping purposefully through the pages as Ella swept up her station, eager to head home.

"Listen to this," Doreen said. "'We must never allow our country to be overtaken. United as one, the voices of every loyal Elsiran must rise, saying: *Grols* keep moving. Keep moving until you've found a land of your own to do with as you please and leave ours to us.'"

She lowered the paper and shook her head. "Same rubbish, different day. I've got to hand it to whoever's writing these, they know how to keep us reading."

All over the shop, activity had paused while people read over shoulders, eager to see the divisive contents of the latest letter. Ella bent to whisk the loose hair into the dustpan and toss it in the bin. She wished she could do the same with every newspaper in Elsira. The daily letters to the editor weren't signed by the Hand of the Reaper, but the language matched the tone and content of the original note taking responsibility for the bombing.

The hateful words castigating the Lagrimari and calling for a separate land for them had entranced the populace. Whether you were sickened or reassured by the sentiments, they were hard to ignore.

Doreen read on but Ella had heard enough. She felt frayed and worn from having so many emotions at once. Her delight at meeting with the girls the day before bled into the fear that Gizelle would stymie the adoption. That combined with the tension of the ubiquitous protests and the fracturing of public sentiment regarding the Lagrimari—all she wanted to do was fall into her bed and sleep for a thousand years.

With a heavy sigh, she shouldered her bag and left the shop without a word of good-bye to anyone. They were all too enthralled by the newsprint clutched in their hands to notice anyway.

The air smelled of rain. An uncharacteristic hush hung over the streets. Ella welcomed the clouds, dark like her mood. As she neared the Earl Place Park, she was disheartened to find a nest of demonstrators infesting it. The men and women stood shoulder to shoulder, signs raised and voices crying out.

Ella prepared to cross to the other side of the street to avoid them when she got a glimpse of one of the hand-painted signs: GROLS KEEP MOVING.

She paused, staying still even when the traffic semaphore was changed to indicate she could cross and bodies moved around her like a stream parting for a boulder.

The phrase "keep moving" was new. Sure the protesters had shouted variations of the idea that the Lagrimari shouldn't stay where they currently were, but those exact words—the ones Doreen had just read aloud—she was certain she hadn't seen or heard before today.

She moved down the sidewalk, closer to the group, taking a good look at the people and their signs. Those gathered were mostly working-class Elsirans. These weren't indigents or transients rounded up to add bodies and present a good showing. Sincerity and passion shone in their eyes.

A particularly tall man with a bushy beard near the middle of the crowd drew her attention. She recognized him from the day before at the refugee camp. This man had spent his day off demonstrating, and was now here, after normal working hours, standing in the chilly evening, shouting again. These people were not only committed, they were extremely organized.

A youth passed out pamphlets to onlookers. Ella forced herself to accept one and scanned the contents. It was an overview of the key concerns against unification, a rehash of the editorial letters from the papers. She folded it and stuffed it into her bag.

Elsirans were passionate about many issues and protests weren't uncommon, but this level of coordination was unusual. Something felt off here, but she couldn't put her finger on precisely what. And she had no desire to stay and listen to the nonsense any longer to try and work it out.

The young man passing out pamphlets had nearly come to the end of his stack. He motioned to another fellow—dressed almost identically in brown coveralls and a newsboy cap. The second youth, seeing the dwindling supply, straightened from his position lounging against a light pole, nodded once, and turned sharply to head away from the park.

Ella made the split-second decision to follow him. Wherever they got their propaganda materials was bound to offer at least a tidbit of information on whoever was organizing these demonstrators. That could be important in Benn's investigation—an angle they hadn't considered before.

She kept a good half a block between herself and the young man, confident that the crowded streets would also help to mask her pursuit. His destination was only a few minutes away, a well-lit structure two blocks from the docks. Words carved into the concrete above the entry read *The Elsiran Fellowship of Dockworkers*—the union that Benn's father and brother were members of.

The man disappeared inside the front doors, which stood open and welcoming. The building was old, perhaps historic. Not covered in stucco like so much of the city, but built of stone to withstand storms blowing in off the Delaveen Ocean.

A hum of chatter bubbled out from within. Since the doors were open, there could be no harm in taking a peek inside. An inner voice that sounded suspiciously like her husband warned her that it wasn't her best idea, but she shushed it effectively. She'd just take a quick look.

As she ascended the front steps, she ensured her wheat-colored hair was safely hidden beneath her cloche hat, so she wouldn't be immediately recognizable as foreign.

She tried to stick to the shadows cast by the massive wooden doors as she peered inside. A shallow lobby led to an auditorium, all of its doors open as well, as if inviting the city to join the hustle and bustle inside.

Tables had been set up in rows bearing an assembly line of sorts. There were dozens of men and women painting wooden signs and hammering in stakes for handles. Several tables held mimeograph machines with operators rolling papers through, printing up more of the pamphlets. Folding and stacking stations took up much of the rest of the space.

A chalkboard in the corner listed a slew of phrases that Ella had heard the demonstrators hurl. Seated just in front of it were a dozen people of all ages, making notes in little journals, hanging on the words of a woman standing before the board, apparently instructing them.

Ella swallowed her shock and dismay. Not only was this operation highly organized, they weren't even trying to hide it. The act of opposing the Lagrimari—and by extension all foreigners—had been turned into a factory.

She spotted the young man she'd been following coming out of a side door. His head was bent as he spoke to someone in the shadows. Wait, no, the man she'd followed was gathering additional pamphlets into a box near the center of the room. But there was yet another dressed just like him, with the same build and general height standing across the room, watching over the teacher and her blackboard.

With shock, she noticed several more similarly dressed men, appearing to be anywhere from seventeen to twenty-five, scattered across the auditorium. The coveralls and cap they all wore must be more than just coincidence—it appeared to be some type of uniform.

She started to back away, an uneasiness filling her belly. Benn would be home soon, she'd tell him what she'd stumbled upon and get his take on it. When she turned to go, she found her path blocked by a brown-clad chest. She looked up into an unsmiling young face, partially covered by the bill of a cap. He was tall and rangy, without a hint of stubble on his cheeks.

"Excuse me." She attempted to step around him but he placed a heavy hand on her shoulder.

"Mistress Ravel, if you'd come with me please."

Ice numbed her limbs. She tried to swallow through a suddenly dry mouth.

"H-how do you know my name?"

"My employer would like a word with you." His voice was bland, and the grip on her shoulder was firm but not painful.

If she could get her shael out of her bag, she might have a chance to strike him and run for it. But he was doubtless faster than her and there were so many of these men around—in strategic places, as if they were standing guard.

"Who is your employer?"

The young man refused to answer. Ella allowed herself to be turned around and led into the lobby of the union building. She tried to pull out of his grip, but he held firm, his hand moving to her upper arm as if he were escorting her and not forcing her.

A fist seized her lungs, stuttering her breathing. She knew a lot of people in Portside, but she'd made only one true enemy that she knew of. And Syllenne Nidos had never been known to employ a cadre of strapping young lads as guards.

Ella was marched around the perimeter of the room. The only

notice the two of them attracted was from the other guards, whose heads turned in their direction. It was unsettling that their eyes were shaded by the brims of their caps, but it served to make them impossible to tell apart.

Their destination was the side door she'd noticed before. It opened to a short hallway that ended in a door marked *Office.*

"Come in," a pleasant-sounding tenor replied to her guard's knock. Recognition caused her breathing to spike painfully. She struggled to pull herself together as she was pushed into the room. The door clicked shut behind her.

Seated behind a neatly organized desk was Zann Biddel. She should have guessed.

Biddel was the leader of the Dominionist sect in Elsira. She'd only met the man once, but it was clear he remembered her.

"Please have a seat." He motioned to the hard-backed chair in front of the desk. She sank down and perched on the edge.

He offered a somewhat wistful smile. "You look so much like your sister. Not sure how I missed it before."

She jerked at the reminder. Her sister, Kess, had thought herself in love with this man. Had risked everything—including the wrath of Syllenne Nidos—when she'd gotten pregnant by him. When the Sisterhood stole the baby, Ella's investigation into the disappearance had led her to Zann and his small (at the time) group of religious dissidents. But since the fall of the Mantle, the Dominionists had multiplied.

When Zann Biddel lectured, he was able to captivate audiences. His charismatic manner stoked the Elsiran fear of magic into a blaze that burned with distrust of all religion. For them the Great Awakening was something to be feared, and the Goddess's vast power nothing but dubious witchcraft.

Answers began falling into place in her mind. "Are you behind all of the protests? The newspaper editorials?" she asked. Her jaw fell open. Was he a member of the Hand of the Reaper?

He steepled his fingers. "The editorials are anonymous. But quite inspiring. And those moved by the contents within needed a place to come together. I utilized my resources to provide that to them."

"A far cry from the back room of a billiard hall," she murmured, recalling where they'd first met. "What about the bombing?"

"Bombing?" He sat back in his seat and shook his head. "Our protests are peaceful. Citizens exercising their rights to be heard. The bombing was a senseless tragedy that took many lives, both Elsiran and otherwise." His grave expression did nothing to convince Ella.

"And the mimeographs? The supplies? Are those the result of your resources as well?" The copy machines were not cheap to rent or run. Thousands were being spent to keep this operation going. Zann was a fisherman by trade, hardly a wealthy aristocrat. Dominionist rhetoric was all about the working man—no matter how many people his group pulled to their side, their funds could not possibly be so flush.

"We must all provide for that which we believe in," he replied earnestly.

She crossed her arms and settled back. "So to what do I owe the honor of this visit? Is this a social call?"

His gaze never left her, but she refused to become unnerved by it.

"Should I inquire as to your health?" she continued. "That of your family? *Are* you married, Master Biddel?"

A subtle tremor traversed his face; her jab had its intended effect. She hid her satisfaction, knowing very well that his wife had left him, and unlike him, Ella knew where she was. Something he could never find out.

When she'd finally located her nephew and stolen him back from the clutches of the Sisterhood, she couldn't keep him. For one, Kess had created a blood spell on her deathbed and embedded all her memories into her son. Ella was the only one who could access the memories when she touched his skin, but because of that, she couldn't care for the child. The second reason was that the baby had distinctive white hair, a color no Elsiran or Yalyish bore. It was evidence of his father's mixed blood: Zann was half Udlander, but passed himself off as full Elsiran and spouted bigotry and nationalist rhetoric that his own heritage belied.

Revealing the baby would put a target on the child's back, and from what she knew of Zann, he would not hesitate to pull the trigger. Zann's wife had taken the infant out of the country to hide him and raise him safely away from both his father's wrath and the Sisterhood's machinations.

Zann's veil of pleasantness thinned, showing more of the truth beneath. "Mistress Ravel—or is it Mistress Farmafield? It's so difficult to keep up with the peculiarities of foreign naming conventions."

She gave a bold smile. "You, sir, may call me whatever you like."

"Well then, I noticed you hovering at the entry and thought you may want a closer look at our operation. We have nothing to hide." He spread his arms apart. "Your curiosity is well known throughout the city."

That set Ella's hair on end. "I had no idea I was so renowned."

He thumped his hand on the table and another layer of the mask fell away. "You are the type of woman who loves a crusade. We have that in common, you and I."

"I wasn't aware that we had anything in common besides caring for my sister."

His nose flared and something dangerous shifted in his gaze. "It's come to my attention that you have something of a bone to pick with the High Priestess."

Ella just stared back.

"I thought I would share with you that constables are searching the Eastern and Northern temples as we speak. They received an anonymous tip that there might be something worth finding in the storerooms."

She could not let on what she knew of the ongoing investigation. Ella had given Benn the account book to take to the authorities, but she wasn't as certain as Rienne that it was the blow necessary to take down the High Priestess. An anonymous tip though? Could that have been Rienne's work?

"That wasn't in the papers," she said slowly.

"It will be. When they find what they're looking for." His eyes glittered in subtle triumph. Or perhaps the tip had been the work of someone else entirely. She flinched at his smugness.

"You are certainly well informed, Master Biddel," Ella said. "Do you have reason to wish the High Priestess ill?"

"Nothing against her as a person. I'm sure she's delightful," he said dryly. "Her role, however, is the problem. The Sisterhood and the delusions they promote are dangerous to the populace."

"And yours aren't?" She arched a brow.

"I'm not your enemy. We actually have more in common than you know. Your campaign against Syllenne Nidos is nearly over. That is something to rejoice in, is it not?"

She lifted her chin. "Perhaps I'll just have to find something else to occupy my time."

His lip curled into a sneer. "Might I suggest crochet?"

Ella stood, more than ready to be done with this little tête-à-tête. "I'll take that under advisement." Biddel's message had been delivered loud and clear. He had far more reach than he should and was keeping an eye on Ella. She'd have to bear that in mind going forward. She moved toward the door, hopeful no one would stop her exit.

"Did you ever locate your nephew, Mistress Ravel?"

She turned back to him, face carefully composed. "No, I did not. There is absolutely no trace of him."

They stared at each other for a moment. Ella admired his ability to keep everything close to his chest. But she suspected there was a good reason for that—the man was colder than a snake and just as hard to grasp.

"I thank you for your concern," she said. "Have a pleasant evening."

"You as well, mistress. Stay safe." The false regard in his words rippled across her skin.

She exited the office, past the guard who made no move to stop her. Back in the auditorium, the scent of chemicals from the copying machines and paint from the signs clogged her head.

Outside again in the fresh air, she hurried back toward the crowded intersection. There was safety in a group of strangers. She looked over her shoulder, expecting to see a newsboy cap bobbing behind her, but as far as she could tell, no one followed.

Then again, why would they need to? Zann Biddel had his fingers in many pies. He had sources and connections that she couldn't truly imagine. He may well be a member of the Reapers. And he, too, was trying to take down Syllenne Nidos.

Ella didn't relax a muscle until she was home again.

CHAPTER TWENTY-TWO

The dwellers of the forest traveled every year to where Matamere the Builder constructed his castles. When Ayal arrived, their tree-top village was abandoned, save Boy-Who-Passes-Twice, who stayed to stand guard.

"They do not take me with them," he said, voice overripe and bitter. "But I will show them my worth before long."

—THE AYALYA

Lizvette picked up her teacup only to find that the tea had gone cold. Her toast lay uneaten on her plate, and she pushed it away to rest her elbows on the table. Certainly she was too preoccupied to eat, what with her father's threat hanging over her head.

She'd claimed exhaustion and hadn't left the hotel suite at all the day before, hoping to somehow forestall the arrival of the messenger. Though she'd been incredibly bored attempting to focus either on the newspaper or the radiophonic, she had every intention of doing the same today. Likely believing her to be overcome with grief, the others hadn't complained. Darvyn and Tai had been out early both days, having found some lead or another on the Dominionists that they were following up on.

She'd overheard them speaking in hushed tones but hadn't had the energy to really listen. At least someone was doing what they'd come here to do.

She looked up to find Vanesse stalking toward her purposefully. Lizvette straightened to face the other woman, who came to a stop before her. The Sister stood there peacefully, her hands clasped in front of her, and smiled. "You're coming with us to Clove's second qualifying heat today. They're great fun and an exciting preview to the race."

An excuse formed on Lizvette's lips, but then Clove barreled into the room and swooped down on the breakfast table, stuffing a piece of toast in her mouth without butter or jam.

"Hrmph hrmph," she said with her mouth full.

Vanesse elbowed her, shaking her head. "She said we won't take no for an answer. We can't let you sit here moping for another day. It's a terrible tragedy, what happened to Prince Alariq, but we must rally. Grab your cloak. It's a bit chilly outside."

Lizvette's protests fell on deaf ears, and short of grabbing hold of the bedpost and refusing to release it, she had no other choice than to accompany them.

And so she found herself in a taxi, returning to the air station where they had arrived, while Clove described the route of the final race.

The airships in the Yaly Classic would pass through Melbain City and down to the Fremian Canal, then through the outer territories of the commonwealth before ending again in the city.

Melbain boasted a mountain range with jagged peaks and varying climates throughout its territories. Add to that an obstacle course provided by the Physicks, which included such impediments as rain, hail, sleet, and fog, and the course was harrowing, indeed. Eight laps would take about eight hours.

Lizvette shivered to think of all the ways a pilot could be compromised during this race. What did Father have in mind to sabotage Clove? And how did he plan to use Lizvette?

When they arrived, the main tarmac of the air station was closed to commercial traffic, leaving the airbuses to run on a limited schedule from the secondary field. Sleek racing crafts and small, souped-up personal ships now filled the paved area, with pilots in striped jumpsuits milling around.

“Clove came in first in the initial heat. Her chances are very good,” Vanesse said, beaming with pride. The two of them stood off to the side, near the Elsiran ship but out of the fracas of the preparing racers.

“Don’t you get scared for her?” Lizvette asked. “The course sounds terrifying.”

A worried look crossed Vanesse’s face before she shook it off. “I’ll admit, it is different than I’d thought. This is the first time I’ve seen her race in person.”

“Oh?”

Vanesse shrugged. “I’ve always been too afraid to come. Word could have gotten back to my family, and Mother . . .” She shook her head and touched the burn scar on her cheek absently. “At any rate, she’s so excited for it, how can I not be, too?”

Lizvette could see how Clove’s excitement was infectious. The woman positively vibrated with glee as she rushed to her ship to meet a stern-faced inspector bearing a clipboard.

“Today is the final qualifier and will determine racing order,”

Vanesse explained, her eyes on Clove as she spoke with the inspector.

There was no way Lizvette could do anything to hurt Clove. She picked idly at the amalgam necklace hanging like an anchor around her neck. If only she could speak of her father's visit and plans to sabotage the race. Lizvette had tried writing a note, but any action she took to tell others of what had transpired ended in a burning sensation in her throat that physically prevented her from continuing. She'd tried to fight through the pain, but it wasn't just discomfort, it was paralyzing, allowing her only the ability to clutch at her neck and suffer. After several attempts, she'd determined she could not get around the magic that way.

The sun broke through the cloud cover blanketing the city, and Lizvette moved into the shade of the building. The warmth of the sun was welcome, but habit had kicked in without her conscious thought. Staying out of direct sunlight to avoid further freckling had been ingrained in her. She touched her nose and realized she'd forgotten to powder her face today. The freckles she already had would be in full view.

With an inner scoff, she squared her shoulders, hoping her father would be around to see them. Freckles as an act of defiance—how pathetic was she?

She hadn't noticed the boy who sidled up to her until he was firmly in her personal space. She took a step to the side. He edged closer until she pinned him with a glare.

In his early teens or so, he was blond and dark-eyed, wearing knickerbockers buttoned below the knee.

"May I help you?" she asked in her most imperious voice.

The lad kept his gaze forward, peering at the racers as they prepared for the heat. He stuck his hand in his pocket and produced a small, brown paper sack, which he held out to Lizvette.

"I'm not—"

"It's from Nirall," the boy interrupted, his voice cracking with youth. "Place it under the pilot's pillow the night before the race."

He shook the bag impatiently and darted a glance at her from the corner of his eye.

Lizvette looked around nervously before taking the package and hiding it under her cloak. "What does it do?"

The boy shrugged.

"Will it hurt her?"

"Listen, lady. I don't get paid to ask questions."

She swallowed the lump in her throat. "What if it doesn't work?"

"It's guaranteed to work. Absalom's mech always works." With that, he was off, scampering away before Lizvette could ask anything more.

Across the tarmac, Clove laughed heartily. Lizvette's grip tightened around the bag as her dread increased. There must be another amalgamation inside, the purpose of which she was loath to discover. If she used it, she'd gain her father's trust and be that much closer to bringing him to justice. If she didn't, he would never trust her and her chance to capture him could vanish. While both options were terrifying, she knew she had to make a choice.

Darvyn sat on a park bench in a sea of perfectly manicured, vibrant green grass. His fingers gripped a newspaper written in a language he couldn't read. The park was a peaceful respite from the assault of noise and disorder that was Melbain City, yet he still felt frayed at his edges. The press of millions of people packed tightly together battered his Song, leaving him exhausted each day.

Singing took far more concentration here than it did in Lagrimar. Even now, when he had simply shifted the color of his eyes from dark brown to mossy green to better pass for a Summ-Yalyish man, he felt the pull of the spell more than he should.

The disguise he'd crafted for Tai included masking his tattoos, changing his hair color, and broadening his features slightly to better masquerade him as Pressian-Yalyish. The Raunian stood across the paved square at the center of the park, beneath a giant statue of Saint Melba. The stone woman bore a warm smile while she carried an axe in one hand, a sapling in the other. A strange creature sat at her feet comprised of a variety of different animals. Two front paws, the back legs of a bird, the tail of a fish—Darvyn had no idea what the beast was meant to represent.

He scanned the area, both visually and with his Song, searching for the target of their stakeout. The day after they'd visited the pub, he and Tai had returned to question the staff about the identity of the Dominionists who had been there. Since the quest for Nirall had come up empty so far, tracking the group was their next best bet. As it turned out, Tai was nearly as good at coaxing information out of the female waitstaff as he was at intimidating Verdeel. Several waitresses identified one man, Hewett Ladell, as the one who'd begun the Dominionist tirade that night.

Apparently, Ladell was a local instigator, well known in the neighborhood for clashing with Loyalists who worshipped the Yalyish saints. After months of incidents, including several that had turned violent, the priests of Saint Melba began encouraging their followers to fight hatred with love and respond to the Dominionist baiting and criticisms with prayers or songs, like what Darvyn had witnessed in the pub.

Tai had found out Ladell's home address, and they'd begun following him, hoping he would lead them to others in the Dominionist organization. Ideally, someone extreme enough, or with enough authority, to have had a hand in the Elsiran temple bombing. But each of the past two days, they'd lost Ladell in this park. After leaving his workplace in the belly of a giant tower, he would take the streetcar across town to the park. They'd see him enter but never leave, hence the stakeout.

Tai leaned against the base of the statue casually, chomping on roasted peanuts he'd purchased from a street vendor. In his crisp white shirt and vest, he looked like any other Administrator relaxing after work. But he perked up noticeably when a thin man in a black derby hat passed by close to him.

It looked like they exchanged a few words, and then the thin man disappeared behind the statue. Tai straightened, tossed his peanuts in the nearest trash can, then surreptitiously sent two hand signals to Darvyn. The first motioned to his right, where Hewett Ladell was striding down the paved path toward the statue. The second indicated that Darvyn should follow him.

Tai rounded the statue and disappeared. When he didn't reappear, Darvyn stood to follow Ladell. Their target rounded the wide base of the monument just before Darvyn.

Ladell looked up when he approached. Darvyn nodded briskly, the way he'd seen Yalyish men greet one another, and held his breath, hoping this was the right move. Tai had said to follow, so he must know something.

"Autonomy or death, brother," Ladell said, his eyes taking on a conspiratorial glint.

"Autonomy or death," Darvyn repeated. The translator amalgam, which was pressed against the base of his throat, spoke the words in his voice. He couldn't begin to fathom how the magic worked, but it was effective enough that no one suspected he wasn't a native Yalyish speaker.

Ladell smiled tightly, and Darvyn reciprocated. The man then placed his palm on an engraved metal plate bolted to the cement base of the statue. A hidden door, built into the concrete, slid open, revealing a set of stairs leading downward.

The entrance was lit from somewhere below, and the steps were well worn. Ladell descended: this must be where Tai had disappeared to. After a moment, Darvyn followed. They headed through a narrow tunnel toward the sound of men's voices. Darvyn hadn't yet seen any female Dominionists, though it seemed odd for there not to be any.

The tunnel ended at an open door that led to a low-ceilinged basement. As they hadn't walked very far underground, this must be one of the buildings bordering the park. Brick walls discolored with old water stains lined a room large enough to easily house the twenty men inside, many of whom were seated on folding wooden chairs. At the far end of the room, a staircase led up to what Darvyn guessed was the kitchen of a restaurant, if the mouth-watering aromas drifting down were any indication.

Tai stood off to the side next to two men who were locked in a heated debate. One was the man in the derby, who apparently had been convinced that Tai was another Dominionist headed to this gathering. At the pub they'd learned that in a Loyalist city such as Melbain, Dominionists often recruited in secret, only coming aboveground when they were firmly entrenched in their beliefs.

Ladell walked to the front of the room, clapping his hands to get everyone's attention. Casually, Darvyn made his way over to Tai and sat down next to him as the others also took their seats.

"I see some new faces," Ladell said, nodding in approval. "That's good. Glad to know that more of our brothers are seeing through the false promises of the hypnotized. With every new mind unlocked from the tyranny of the saints and the sorcerers, we take another step closer to pure liberty."

"Autonomy or death," the audience said in unison.

Ladell smiled. "Autonomy or death, brothers."

A ripple of unease worked its way through Darvyn. The mood and intentions of the men here were dark. Jealousy, pain, and hatred simmered beneath the surface.

"We are making inroads outside of our borders, as well," Ladell continued. "Let us raise hands of strength to our brethren in Elsira, beset by an awakening deity who was best left asleep."

The men raised both fists above their heads. Tai and Darvyn quickly followed suit along with a few other obvious newcomers in the audience.

"We cannot allow our homeland to be taken from us as theirs has been, drained from them by mages and witches and goddesses. The Physick scourge is growing far beyond the bounds of the commonwealth of Dahlinea. We will all have to dig deep within ourselves in order to fight it off."

A throat cleared loudly from the back of the room. All heads turned to see a tall, dark-haired man standing with his arms crossed. He hadn't been present a few moments earlier, and Darvyn had seen no one arrive from either the tunnel entrance or the kitchen stairs.

Tai nudged Darvyn's arm. "That's the man I saw disappear at the pub," he whispered, sotto voce.

Darvyn took in the man's steely stare and turned back to see Ladell blanch visibly.

"Let us review the words in *The Book of Dominion,*" he said, holding up a leather-bound book. "Chapter fourteen, verse fifty-five. I will be back in a moment."

Ladell looked nervously toward the man in the back and headed for the stairs leading to the kitchen. The audience members stood and began breaking into small groups, dragging their chairs together.

Darvyn tugged on Tai's sleeve and, in the midst of the confusion, backed them both into a corner where he cloaked them in darkness with his Song. Tai froze, the darkness spell blinding him as well as enlarging the shadows, hiding them both from view.

"Follow me," Darvyn whispered. "I'll lead us close enough to hear what they're saying."

Tai nodded. Darvyn grasped his shoulder, pointing him in the right direction. The other men's voices were a soft hum as they began their study groups. Darvyn and Tai hugged the back wall, moving silently toward the staircase where Ladell and the suspected Physick had disappeared.

"And you're sure it will do what you claim?" Ladell's voice was eager.

"I'm sure," the larger man said gruffly. "Only a handful of these have been made. I obtained this at great risk to myself, and I expect top shing for it."

"Of course, of course, but how can I know it works?"

"When has my merchandise ever been faulty? Test it if you want . . . *after* you pay."

"How much, then?" Ladell asked.

"Fifty thousand shings."

Ladell gasped. "That's highway robbery, Absalom. It can't be worth that much."

"I assure you it is," Absalom growled. There was a long pause, and Darvyn strained to hear, not sure if the men had moved or simply lowered their voices.

"Actually," Absalom said, "since you've been such a good customer, I can give you a demonstration right now."

Heavy footfalls thundered down the steps. Absalom emerged from the entry to the staircase and scanned the room.

Darvyn froze only a half dozen paces away. The spell should have made discovery impossible, but when the large man turned, Darvyn's heart sank to see he'd donned a pair of spectacles. When Darvyn had been captured in Lagrimar by the True Father's men, a pair of amalgam spectacles like these had been used to see through his concealment spell. He took a step away from Tai as Absalom locked eyes with Darvyn. The Physick smiled a bone-chilling smile, raised his hand, then tossed something.

"Run!" Darvyn cried, heading toward the tunnel, but the small brown pouch the Physick had thrown hit him in the shoulder. It burned where it touched him and magically unfurled into a net, the webbing spreading out over his body, holding him in place. The brown material began to glow with a brilliant light. Drawing on Earthsong, he crumbled the cement floor around the Physick's feet, trying to lock him in place, but the shimmering netting was draining his Song, rapidly bleeding it from him.

He thrashed against the confines of the net, and every spell he tried fizzled before it could take hold. The thread connecting him to Tai's disguise still held, but barely.

Darvyn turned to Tai, also caught in the amalgam net. The Raunian had produced a knife and was hacking away at the shining mesh. He freed himself quickly, then turned to Darvyn but was hit with a flying chair.

Tai straightened and growled. He used his forearm to block another chair that had been tossed his way. He didn't appear hurt, merely angry.

The Dominionists, including Ladell, scampered out of the basement, leaving only Absalom and the two of them.

Darvyn was so weak—both his Song and physical energy were fading fast—he could barely even lift his head to watch as Tai faced off against Absalom. The Physick pulled a cudgel the length of his forearm, which had been hidden under his jacket, from behind his back and wielded it menacingly. Tai crouched, knife in hand, and beckoned the other man forward.

Absalom chuckled and pointed the cudgel in Tai's direction. A thunderous, head-splitting wall of sound sprang from the weapon. Darvyn covered his ears as his brain vibrated against his skull. The blast of noise was enough to push him backward into the wall, but it didn't seem to affect Tai at all. He didn't so much as wince.

Absalom frowned and pointed the cudgel again, resulting in the same earthshaking clatter. Tai's clothes actually lifted in the breeze that had been produced, but he gave no indication he could hear the horrible sound. Absalom's brow furrowed in confusion as Darvyn's head rattled.

The last of Darvyn's Song dissipated, removing the spell he'd cast on Tai's appearance. The Raunian's hair became blue once more, and his tattoos emerged to stand out boldly on his face.

Absalom tensed his jaw. "Raunian!" he spit out like a curse. He pointed the cudgel at Darvyn directly this time, who cringed as the blast hit him in the chest. His eardrums shattered along with several of his ribs.

When Darvyn opened his eyes, the Physick was gone. Tai was crouching before him, cutting the netting off. He was moving his lips, but the words were lost to the ringing in Darvyn's head. He touched an ear, then the other, to find blood dripping from them both.

Tai helped him stand, and Darvyn stumbled through the tunnel and up the stairs into the open air. Each step was agony, jarring his body. When he reached out to stabilize himself, he found his wrist was either sprained or broken. The pain intensified with each breath, making the journey back to the hotel a blur.

Somehow he had stayed conscious until then, but when his back hit something soft, he closed his eyes and all went dark.

CHAPTER TWENTY-THREE

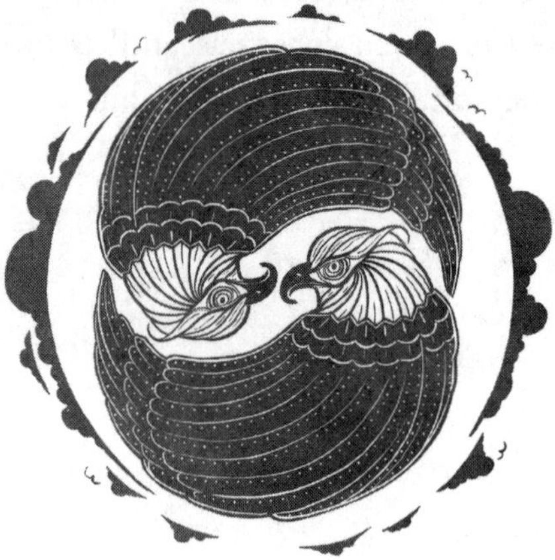

Ayal recognized the seeds of dissatisfaction, well sewn and ready to grow quickly. Its fruit would only nourish the worst in mind and heart. One day while Boy-Who-Passes-Twice was running, Ayal lay a stone in his path. When he fell, she bound his legs, forcing him to remain still and listen.

—THE AYALYA

Kyara paced her cell, giddy with nerves and eager to get things started. She placed and replaced the hairpin several times, and her scalp still stung where she'd accidentally stabbed herself. Unlike all the other days, today she was actually looking forward to being taken from her cell.

Finally, the guards arrived to shackle her wrists and lead her from the prison. She counted the steps as usual, glad to know that they were taking her via the same route, not deviating from the course. Consistency would help any escape plan she was able to form. The long, brightly lit hallways were empty. The freshly polished floors squeaked underfoot. Everything here was radiant and shiny, made of chrome or burnished wood or glass.

A hum of voices wafted from inside the familiar door to the classroom. Kyara wasn't sure if the guards were late or if students had arrived early, but there were not usually so many witnesses for the indignity of her being chained to the stone table. The seats were filled with young men and women in their color-coded cloaks with hues ranging from green to blue to violet. They all stared at her as the guards hauled her in.

The brightness of the auditorium stunned her once again. Electricity must be generated in such vast quantities here that they could waste it illuminating this room far past what was necessary. She squinted as they placed her on the table, then locked her head and limbs in place. Soon the same white-haired Physick as always arrived and sliced open Kyara's palms.

The hairpin did not translate the words he spoke as he cut her—she wondered if it did not know the language of the blood spell. Though she'd learned the ancient tongue from Ydaris over the years, the words he used were unfamiliar.

Her blood flowed from the new wounds as the few remaining seats she could see filled. Then the instructor's droning voice began. "I know everyone is eager to commence today's ceremony. The graduation of a new class of Physick Spellsayers is indeed worthy of celebration. Those of you moving on have worked long and hard to achieve this milestone, and as your instructor, I am proud of each of you.

"As you proceed to your posts of service in the factories, and the valuable work of dedicating every amalgamation that comes off the assembly line with the words of power, never forget that we owe our prosperity to Saint Dahlia the Sanguine. In her name do we work."

"By her grace do we prosper," the audience replied in unison.

Kyara recognized the tone of this call and response. It had been uttered many times during her draining sessions. That the Physicks were some sort of religious order surprised her. Their methods were anything but holy.

"This is the first graduating class to receive quintessence powered by our new donor." Several eyes in the crowd shot to Kyara. She glared back at them. "Not since the Bright One first arrived has there been such a leap forward in our humble art." Now the same gazes were trained somewhere behind Kyara, presumably at the source of the brilliant light that was illuminating the room.

"Now that our supply of Nethersong is as pure and powerful as can be obtained," the instructor continued, "the quintessence is more balanced than ever. Medallions created today will contain enough power to last the rest of your lives."

A murmur of awe rose from the audience, but Kyara's stomach turned sour. If the Physicks were happy about this, it must have been bad.

The voice continued. "In three days' time, we will convene a symposium to share the wonders of our recent achievements due to the new source."

"You're welcome," Kyara mumbled.

"All graduates of the Academie are invited and *encouraged* to attend and bear witness to Saint Dahlia's blessings. And now, with no further ado, my colleague Master Effram will perform the rites. They are as they have been for two hundred years. Since the inception of the Great Machine, we have fed our life's essence into it and, in turn, been rewarded by the glorious gift of quintessence."

Kyara bit her lip, listening carefully, but still not understanding. What was the Machine? And what was quintessence?

"Will the graduates rise and form a line," a new voice spoke. She assumed it to be Master Effram. Then she heard someone draw near to her, and the back of a red-robed figure appeared in her peripheral vision.

All the students in the violet robes rose, while those dressed in blue and green stayed seated. Effram moved farther into her range of vision, standing directly before her in profile. He was pale with blond hair. His age was difficult to determine, perhaps early thirties, but he could have easily been younger or older. In his grip, he held a bone knife already streaked with crimson. It must have been the same one used on her moments ago.

The instructor's voice rang out again from beyond her vision. "You will step forward, one at a time, to make your contribution and collect your medallion. When the rites are complete, place your medallion on the platform so that it may receive the quintessence."

The elderly Physick walked into the edge of Kyara's vision and grabbed hold of a waist-high lever jutting from the ground. With great apparent effort, he engaged the lever, shifting it to the side forty-five degrees. The whirring of gears and motors began and beneath her, it felt like a great mechanical beast was awakening. The stone table vibrated subtly with the hum from the machinery under the floor. This had never happened before.

The students in line gaped with expectation. A small silver plate sitting atop a snarl of copper pipes and tubing rose from somewhere below until it was the same height as the table. Puffs of steam escaped from what must be a hole in the floorboards. The classroom was *built* on top of some kind of machine.

The first student stepped up to Effram. The young man was

about Roshon and Varten's age, with similar coloring except for his yellow hair. Standing tall, he extended his palm. Without any preamble, Effram sliced into it. Kyara's eyes widened, but the student maintained his eager demeanor. He held his hand carefully so that the blood dripped onto the silver plate. There must have been a drain in the center, for the blood disappeared. The piping below the plate shook slightly as another puff of steam rose from below.

"Dahlia's breath is life. Dahlia's breath is death. Dahlia's breath is matter. Dahlia's breath is spirit." Effram reached into a white basket that had appeared at his side and pulled out a circle of gold metal. He placed it into the student's bloody palm and folded the young man's fingers around it.

Then Effram uttered the same string of foreign words that were said every time Kyara's blood was spilled in this room—a blood-magic spell. The tubing coming out of the floor whined and churned and spat out a small, milky-pink stone onto the silver platter. The student pressed his palm down on top of it, and when he lifted his hand, the stone was embedded in the gold coin.

Realization dawned as the student stepped away and was replaced by another. Kyara had seen such a medallion many times—worn around Ydaris's neck.

The "rites" were repeated dozens more times. Students would step to the front, be sliced, and allow their blood to drip onto the silver, then receive a medallion and embed a tiny pink stone in it, delivered from below by the belching machine.

The fatigue from her Song being drained tugged at her. For the first time, she wondered where exactly it was going. Her blood always dripped down below her, but whenever they took her from the room, the floor was clean. There must have been another drain beneath her. Was her blood being fed to the machine in order to drain her Song?

Raal had told her that amalgam magic was the combination of Earthsong, Nethersong, blood magic, and material objects—that would describe what she was witnessing. Well, everything but the Earthsong. She was their source of Nethersong. Was there, even now, an Earthsinger somewhere nearby whose Song was being drained just as hers was?

Dansig had never been taken to this room, had never had his Song drained, though he'd told her once that his was relatively weak. That meant that there was at least one more prisoner here or the Physicks had found some other supply of Earthsong. And what had they done for Nethersong before capturing her? The questions just kept coming.

She had a wealth of new information, though, thanks to Asenath's hairpin. As the ceremony continued, Kyara forced herself to stay aware, determined to gather as much intel as she could before the weariness was too much to bear.

One of the last in the line of students was a short girl with midnight skin and eyes so dark blue they nearly matched the violet in her robe, eyes that reminded Kyara of Asenath. Perhaps this girl was some kin of hers, a granddaughter or great-granddaughter. Did Physicks even have children? Somehow she couldn't picture the ruthless mages marrying and bearing young. But they had to come from somewhere, of course.

Unlike the other students who appeared to view Kyara as part of the furniture, the girl with Asenath's eyes looked directly at her as her palm was sliced and her medallion secured. Did the old woman's entire family share her dissent against the ruling Physicks? Perhaps Kyara truly did have allies here.

After the ceremony ended, the auditorium emptied quickly. The smell of roasting meat and alcohol, along with the sound of merry voices, floated in from somewhere nearby. A celebration for the graduates.

Apparently forgotten, Kyara lay on the table, the machine doing its work to pull her Song from her and serve as a power source for amalgamation magic. She hung on to consciousness for as long as she could, sifting through everything she'd learned. Something here must be the key to escape.

The dream had changed. Kyara stood in the same dark place, illuminated by a source she could not see. But this time, three archways made of smoke and light stood before her. They were each as wide as her arm span and were pulsing with latent power.

A gasp came from behind her; she spun around to find Mooriah, barely visible but shaking her head before abruptly fading back into the darkness.

"Mooriah?"

A blurry image took shape on the other side of the archway on the right. The figure was familiar and male; Kyara's eyes widened, heart racing, as she stared at the man before her.

"Darvyn?" she cried out, reaching for the arch. Could it really be him?

A hand shot out to stop her. Mooriah had reappeared at her side.

The woman's form passed through Kyara's arm, leaving an icy sensation crawling across her skin. "You can only look." Mooriah's voice was desperate.

Kyara nodded sadly. She had so many questions for Mooriah, but Darvyn's presence was foremost in her mind.

On trembling legs, Kyara stepped as close to the archway as she could without going through. "Darvyn?" She stared at his form, which appeared shaky and tremulous, as if not quite certain whether to come into focus or not.

His eyes widened and jaw slackened. He looked around wildly, seeming unable to see her. His mouth moved, but she couldn't hear him.

"Are you real?" she whispered, holding out her hand, longing to touch him. "Have you finally come to judge me?"

His eyes still searching, he turned toward her voice and reached for her. They stood, separated by time or space or worlds—she couldn't be certain—but a flood of yearning threatened to drown her.

She struggled to read his lips, but his form was too indistinct. "I'm so sorry. For everything. The Physicks took me. They've been . . . draining me. Stealing my Song slowly."

He looked like he was shouting now, a vein bulging at his temple.

Her mouth quivered. "I can't hear you. I'm not sure where I am. The World Between? The World After? Maybe it's a place connected to the Physicks' headquarters where they're keeping me prisoner." A ripple went through his form. He came into focus momentarily, his eyes hard and jaw clenched. He was angry, as angry as all the others who came for her to blame her.

She pressed her fingers to her lips. "I'm so sorry."

His image began to fade. "Darvyn!" she screamed, tears forming in her eyes. "I"—he disappeared completely—"love you," she said to the darkness.

She held her hand out again toward the place where he'd been and looked around. Mooriah was gone, too. She'd been dim, hard to see again, and Kyara wondered if the power the woman used to make herself seen and heard was weakening.

Kyara simply stood there, grief beating at her, questions cluttering her mind. Darvyn had looked so fierce. His spirit would never forgive her for taking his life.

Turning away from the arches, she wondered if the others were on their way—the others she'd killed.

She waited alone in the dark for a long time, but they never came.

CHAPTER TWENTY-FOUR

When the forest dwellers returned from their pilgrimage, knees bruised from supplication, they found Boy-Who-Passes-Twice seated calmly. "I will run in circles no more," he said, "instead, I will find a destination. I thank my friend, Ayal, for showing me the way."

The seeker raised her arms in appreciation and watched them transform into the forelegs and paws of a lion.

—THE AYALYA

Lizvette peered inside the brown paper bag before shutting it and tossing it away. It landed on her pillow with a thud. She clenched and unclenched her hands, then crossed the bedroom to wrench open the closed door. The others had gathered in the common area after dinner.

Darvyn was still unconscious in the other room, and Tai stood in the doorway staring down at him. The events at the Dominionist meeting were terrifying. It merely proved how dangerous the sect was, and how desperately they needed to be stopped. And if they had amalgams that could drain the power from an Earthsinger and shatter his bones with sound, what horrors were in store for Clove from the device Lizvette had been given? Lizvette had no idea what would happen if she used the thing, and her father would slip through their hands if she didn't. She needed to find a way to tell the others, but hadn't figured out how to bypass the amalgam necklace around her throat. Scissors wouldn't cut the chain. It didn't fit over her head. She'd even tried to break the clasp with the heel of her shoe. But it was impervious.

She paced the floor, wringing her hands. She was losing time. Clove would be going to bed soon.

"Darvyn is getting better," Vanesse said, looking up from the newspaper's crossword puzzle. "I checked on him an hour ago and his bruises are already fading. It's slow going, but his power is returning and he is healing."

Lizvette nodded but couldn't stop her pacing.

Tai glanced over at her, worry and weariness etched into his face as starkly as his tattoos. He'd been in such a state after dragging Darvyn back into the suite. Lizvette couldn't allow another of their group to come to harm. There had to be some other way to bring her father to justice. But if she didn't use the device, was there some other plan for Clove? Knowing her father and his lack of faith in her, she bet there was a backup plan. She had to warn the woman.

"I have something to say," she announced.

Three pairs of eyes focused on her.

She cleared her throat. "Only . . . you see . . ." She formed the words in her mind. *Father visited me. He knew of the plot to kill Alariq. He's going to sabotage Clove.* But even as she thought the words, the necklace heated up.

She cried out in pain, clutching her throat. Vanesse rushed to her. Lizvette pulled at the chain, unable to speak anymore with the fire in her throat. It now seemed to be obstructing her airway, making it hard to breathe, and she was losing feeling in her limbs.

"What is it? What's the matter?" Vanesse asked.

Lizvette's arms dropped away from the necklace. A dark haze covered her vision. She could feel Vanesse's fingers trying the clasp but knew the woman would have no luck. Her legs collapsed underneath her, and she fell to the floor. This was all useless. There was no way she could warn them, no way to get around the magic searing her body.

Then Tai was there. She felt rather than saw him. Strong fingers moved around the back of her neck. His touch was gentle, though his skin was rough. The path his hands took felt immediately cooler, giving relief from the burning until it stopped completely. Her throat opened, and she sucked in cool, refreshing air. She grasped at her neck and sat up.

Tai kneeled next to her, the necklace dangling from his fingers. She reached up and tossed the thing away, tears burning her eyes.

"How . . . did you . . . ?" she breathed out, then shook her head. "Father . . . came . . . other night . . . I couldn't speak of it . . . because of that."

Tai looked at the discarded necklace with alarm as Vanesse brought Lizvette a glass of water, which she took with gratitude. She sipped it, cooling the remaining heat in her throat. Then she told them of her father's visit and his plans for Clove.

Vanesse insisted they call Jord Zivel. Given her father's escalating actions, they all deemed it necessary to fill in the Foreign Service on exactly what their mission in Melbain really was. Zivel arrived quickly with his second-in-command, Sergeant Kendos.

"Where is the device you were given, Miss Nirall?" Zivel asked.

Lizvette went to the bedroom and returned with the paper sack, holding it gingerly. "Be careful. I do not know what it does, only that apparently it was meant to work overnight and was to be placed under Clove's pillow."

Zivel nodded. "We have a contact we can bring this to. A former Physick who might be able to give us some clue as to its use. We'll take the necklace to him for inspection, as well."

Lizvette nodded, grateful for their businesslike manners and efficiency.

"Are you sure we shouldn't seek medical attention for your friend?" Kendos asked, peering through the doorway at a sleeping Darvyn.

"I think it best not to. He's already healing," Tai said. "It's only a matter of time now."

Darvyn did appear to be in peaceful slumber. Quite different from how he'd looked only hours before.

"Very well, then. We'll put a protective detail on you tomorrow, Miss Liddelot," Zivel said. "And I'll set a guard on your ship to make sure it isn't tampered with overnight."

Clove thanked them, appearing unfazed, while Vanesse was quite pale.

When the men left, silence descended on the suite.

"I'm so sorry," Lizvette said, forcing herself to meet everyone's eyes—Clove's last.

The woman looked up, no change evident in her cheery demeanor. "It's not your fault. None of us get to choose our parents." She shot a measured look at Vanesse, whose scars stood out more than usual against her bloodless cheeks. Clove took her hand and leaned to whisper something in Vanesse's ear.

Lizvette wanted to look away but couldn't, drawn in by the tenderness and care between the two women. Any action against Clove would harm Vanesse, too, and the Sister had clearly been through a great deal already.

"I think ice cream is in order," Clove announced. Vanesse didn't look appeased but allowed herself to be drawn up by the hand and nudged toward the door.

"Would you like any?" Clove asked.

Lizvette shook her head, and Tai denied the offer, as well. Vanesse said something softly that Clove chuckled at.

"Don't worry. We'll find an amalgam that will check for poison." Her dark humor was alarming, but Vanesse seemed somewhat mollified.

In minutes, the two were gone, leaving Lizvette and Tai alone.

She blinked at him, unsure what to say. Shame ate away at her, and she couldn't meet his eyes. They stood in awkward silence until she couldn't stand it any longer and retreated to her room with a mumbled apology.

Tai found his feet moving across the sitting room of their own accord. He stood outside Lizvette's door and listened, but this time there was nothing but silence. He began to return to his room, then stopped and turned around. Lizvette was too quiet, or maybe he was merely rationalizing the pull he felt to go to her. His heart splintered recalling the anguish in her face, the desperation as she struggled against the damnable necklace.

He had no idea how he'd been able to remove it—the clasp had released easily when he'd tried it. Whatever the reason, he was glad. Perhaps he would just peek in to reassure himself that she was all right.

Indecision warred within him, but he pushed through it and knocked.

A pregnant pause left him holding his breath until her quiet voice pierced the silence. "Come in."

Lizvette's eyes were red, but dry. Her composure, however, was slowly crumbling.

Tai wanted to seize her sorrow and slay it like a raging selakki, the ferocious sea creatures harvested in Raun. He wanted to find her useless father and dangle him over the edge of his ship, then toss him in the deepest waters of the ocean. When she'd relayed how her father had spoken to her, what he'd done—saddling her with that amalgamation necklace—Tai had wanted to wring the man's neck. His heartlessness reminded Tai of his mother. The very qualities that had succeeded in making her king of Raun did not make her very maternal. Still, even he couldn't imagine his mother being so hateful and cruel—and she had imprisoned him.

He took the liberty of sitting on the bed beside Lizvette as she stared at him, wide-eyed. Without a word, he scooped her into his arms and held her. He'd expected a protest, perhaps even a slap, but her body crumpled against him immediately. He embraced her, rubbing soothing circles on her back. Her fine gown was wrinkled, her hair sticking out of its neat bun, but he found he liked her best this way. Her body shook with silent sobs, though her cheek, pressed against his chest, remained dry. It was as if she could draw forth no more tears; only these tremors racking her body displayed her anguish.

Soon her muted cries stopped. Her shoulders stilled, and her breathing deepened. He thought she might fall have fallen asleep until she whispered into his chest, "Why do you comfort me? I've been so cold to you."

He stroked her shoulder. It was too thin. The stress of the past weeks had probably caused her to lose weight.

"I can take a bit of coldness, duchess. I can take whatever you're dishing out." He thought she may have snorted, but it was too unladylike a sound to have come from her prim self. But the way she froze afterward made him believe he'd heard correctly.

She sniffed and pulled back. He immediately missed the warmth of her against him but looked her in the eye. "I can't believe Father knew about the plot to kill Alariq and did nothing," she said.

"You mourn your fiancé?" He did not want to hear the answer, but being jealous of a dead man was senseless.

She shook her head. "I am angry about his murder, but my sorrow is only for me. For being a fool."

"You're no fool. And you deserve a far better father than you were given."

She let out a dry laugh. "Perhaps I was given exactly what I deserve. I listened to Father's whispers and cajoling for such a long time. I would have done just about anything to make him proud of me. To lessen the sting of having been born a girl. No wonder he thought I would sabotage Clove." She shook her head. "But it never would have been enough. Nothing would be enough."

Her stare had gone vacant, and her fists clenched so tightly he thought she might hurt herself. He picked up her hand and gently loosened her fingers until they lay flat against his, palm to palm. Her gaze focused on their joined hands. He ran his thumb gently up and down the side of hers, mesmerized by the sensation. No silk could compare to her skin. The small point of contact of their palms was all that tethered him to the world at this moment.

Lizvette made a sound that drew his gaze to her lips, then to her eyes, which were heavy-lidded. She leaned forward a fraction, and he felt himself do the same. When his lips touched hers, it was through no conscious thought of his own. He'd merely allowed his body to do what it did naturally. And it wanted to kiss her.

He would have thought it impossible, but her lips were softer than her hands. They brushed against his, leaving him feeling only the two parts of his body that were in contact with hers.

Their mouths were still closed, but blades of fire licked at him. This was the most chaste kiss he'd experienced since childhood, but somehow also the most erotic. Perhaps it was her scent, dewy like morning rain with a hint of ripe fruit and sunshine. He'd never smelled a woman so sweet, so enticing. He'd noticed it the first time he'd seen her, when she'd passed him surrounded by a phalanx of guards. The aroma had remained in her wake. He'd stared after her, wondering what in this world or the next could smell that good. Now it surrounded him.

He brought his free hand up to stroke her cheek and found it wet. He kissed the tears away, tasting sweetness and salt, wishing to imprint himself on her so that she could no longer remember what had made her so sad in the first place.

He was still surprised that she'd made no move to stop him. Their palms pressed against each other; she curled her fingers around his, locking their hands. He leaned her back until she was fully on the bed, him at her side, hovering slightly above her but keeping his weight off.

She opened her eyes, looking dazed, cheeks high with color, amber gaze piercing him. He simply stared until his breathing was back under control. It was as though he'd just sailed through a flash thunderstorm.

He pulled away, suddenly wanting to run, to put some distance between them, but the warmth of her still attached itself to him, and he found he couldn't move his legs. After a few moments, he was able to push himself to a sitting position and run a shaking hand through his hair. Her eyes tracked the movement, then returned to his, before moving down to his lips.

He huffed out a breath then drew a shaky smile, infusing it with the same cocky bravado as always. But her knowing gaze said she would not be fooled. Not this time. He had to collect himself. He'd never been affected so powerfully by a kiss before—never thought it possible.

Clove and Vanesse would probably be back shortly, he realized, and he should check on Darvyn again. He stood, trying to discreetly adjust his trousers to better accommodate the most tangible results of the last few minutes. But Lizvette's perceptive gaze strayed downward, not missing a thing.

She cleared her throat and popped up from the bed as if suddenly free from a trance. Looking down at her wrinkled gown, she frowned and patted at the skirts in vain.

Tai took a step backward toward the door. "I, um . . ." He cleared his throat as well.

All her attention was consumed by her skirts, and she kept her head bowed. It was just as well. One look into those fire-lit eyes would have undone him again. He needed to go pull himself together. Perhaps even get a drink, though the kiss had left him with a greater buzz than alcohol ever had.

He stumbled backward through the door and into the sitting room. He wanted to say something witty, or even crass, to break the tension, but instead he said nothing at all and retreated into his room as if something were chasing him.

CHAPTER TWENTY-FIVE

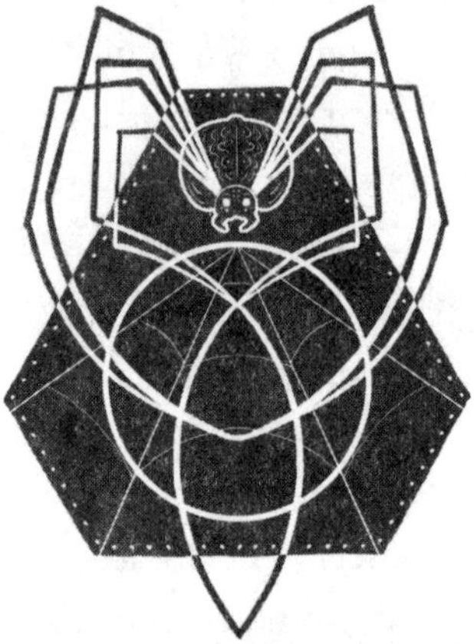

While refreshing herself in a stream, Ayal looked up to the mountain, which rose from the edge of the wood. The peaks kissed the blue of the sky, and she was certain wisdom could be found there. Each step higher was a promise whispered into the stone.

—THE AYALYA

"Is Amber not joining us this evening?" Sapphire asked. The little communication device was absent from the center of the round table.

"Amber has things to attend to," Diamond replied imperiously. "If we want to fund our further ventures, then it's best to allow him to continue uninterrupted. We cannot all drop everything to meet the histrionic whims of a single member. You called this emergency meeting, Sapphire. It's quite out of the ordinary."

"Well this situation is out of the ordinary," Sapphire snapped.

"Constables rummaging around the temples, throwing things into even more chaos. It's unprecedented. The temples have played their part already." The annoyed Reaper's cloth mask featured a peculiar duality: Looked at one way, it portrayed a weeping countenance, eyes and mouth pulled down in apparent misery. But perceived another way, the eyes danced with mirth and the mouth was midlaugh.

"You think me responsible for the trouble at the temples, Sapphire?" Jade sounded more amused than insulted.

"I *know* you are responsible. Never forget, I have eyes and ears in nooks and crannies around town, too."

"Well then you should see and hear the truth. All of this is a means to an end. A little theatre, isn't that what we do?" Jade spread his hands apart. "We have each been given tasks to carry out. I am simply doing my part."

Sapphire leaned forward, bony hands gripping one another tightly. "Your part seems to expand daily. As does your disrespect for this body."

Pearl shifted uncomfortably in his chair. Jade refused to respond.

Diamond cleared his throat to take back control of the conversation. "The plan is working, so we stick to the plan. It is well organized and effective. We have growing numbers moving to our side. Let's stay the course."

He turned to Sapphire. "We have the constables well in hand. This display is just that—misdirection, distraction. Show the audience something wondrous in one hand while the other picks their pocket. You cannot have forgotten the tricks of your youth, have you?"

Sapphire, a childhood pickpocket? Surprising, but the more Jade thought about it, the more it made sense. He filed this information away. Diamond was the only one who knew all of their true identities. Jade knew who Sapphire was and was pretty certain about Amber, but the others were still cloaked in mystery. For now.

"The struggle that this body has fought against for so long is more dire than ever," Diamond said with the conviction of a man overtaken by zealotry. Jade was well familiar with the sensation. "We are needed more than we ever have been, and the eve of victory is nigh."

Sapphire's arms crossed. A scowl no doubt lay beneath the mask.

"We must not falter," Diamond said. "We are so close."

Jade nodded, secure in the knowledge that the statement was true—far more true than anyone else at this table knew.

Darvyn awoke the day of the Yaly Classic to find the suite bathed in quiet with midmorning sunshine streaming in through the window. He rolled over on his side to avoid the glare, relieved to find his body healed. He ran a hand over his ribs, remembering the intense pain of the day before, grateful his Song had returned while he'd slept.

Then the dream came back to him. Snatches of Kyara's voice echoed in his mind. He tried to grab hold of them, but they evaded his grasp. He concentrated on the memory, certain she had told him something vital.

Her face appeared in his mind. Her lips were so often downturned but when she smiled . . . He dropped his head into his hands, allowing himself to be lost in the memory. She was fierce and deadly, braver than anyone he'd ever met. And despite wielding the power of death, her heart was pure.

His chest ached, not from any physical pain but from loss, from finally finding someone he didn't have to hide from only to be torn from her after such a short time.

Her words from the dream suddenly came back clearly. He jumped to his feet. Hearing her voice could not have been simply a projection from his mind. Darvyn had visited the World Between often enough to recognize it—and having lost his Song the day before so quickly and brutally was certainly enough trauma to have thinned the space between worlds, allowing him to communicate with her.

It was odd not to have seen her, though. Her voice had sounded far away. Maybe it was something the Physicks were doing to her. She'd said they were draining her Song.

He raced around the room, throwing his belongings into his bag. He must find the others and tell them he needed to go to Dahlinea. The job in Melbain was not done, but he could not waste another moment now that he had knowledge of Kyara's location.

He opened the door to the sitting room to find Lizvette and Tai, her sitting on the edge of the couch, appearing ready to flee at any moment, him pacing the floor restlessly. Both looked at him sharply. Lizvette's shoulders sagged in relief.

A questioning smile inched across Tai's face. "You all right, mate?"

"Good as new," Darvyn said, tapping his finger on the door frame. A vibrating energy pulsed through him. He wouldn't be able to still himself until he was on his way to Kyara.

"Going somewhere?" Lizvette asked, brows raised, noting the bag slung across his back.

Darvyn nodded solemnly. "I need to head to Dahlinea ahead of schedule."

Tai's gaze was intense. "Has something happened?"

"'Ahead of schedule'?" Lizvette looked back and forth between them with narrowing eyes. "We had no plans to go to Dahlinea at all."

"Well, duchess, you see," Tai began, wincing, "Darvyn and I were given an additional mission." Lizvette frowned. "By the Goddess," he added hastily. "Top secret, but it seems like it's time you knew."

When no one spoke, she spread her arms expectantly. "Well?"

Tai exhaled loudly. "Queen Jasminda's family is alive."

Lizvette's fingers flew to her mouth on a gasp. Darvyn looked away, his face burning with shame. Of course Tai would assume that was the only reason. In truth, Darvyn had been thinking of nothing but Kyara.

"I met them two years ago," Tai continued. "Her father and twin brothers." He closed his eyes. "I watched them die on my ship, killed by a Physick who was hunting them." When his eyes opened again they were red, rimmed with tears. "But somehow they survived."

"How?" Lizvette asked.

Tai shook his head. Darvyn stared at the ground, his guilty eyes unseeing. For the first time in his life, pure selfishness was his only motive. Not Oola's mission. Not bringing the Dominionists who'd helped orchestrate the temple bombing to justice. Not even determining where the next attack would be. Though he'd made vows he intended to keep, they all faded when compared with the thought of Kyara at the mercy of the same vile mages who had killed his mother . . .

No vow could stop him from pursuing Kyara a moment longer.

He squeezed his jaw tight to hold in the rage that was forming, a rage that had no outlet until he found her and made sure she was safe.

"So that is the real reason you were sent?" Lizvette asked Tai. Darvyn struggled to bring himself back into the conversation.

"Yes."

"And you knew this, too?" She looked over at Darvyn, but he had a hard time meeting her eyes.

"I did," he said through clenched teeth. "But there's something else."

Both looked at him with trust in their eyes. He swallowed the knot in his throat as his own eyes filled with tears. Shame was heavy on his shoulders, but it would not deter him. Nothing would.

"I need to tell you about Kyara."

He forced out the story of the assassin he'd met in the desert, a woman who had been tasked with capturing him. He showed them the pendant he wore that had stayed her hand when she was about to strike. Told of how she'd had the matching half of his pendant given to her by his own mother, who'd taken Kyara in long after Darvyn had been sent to live with the Keepers for his own safety.

When he'd been taken prisoner in Lagrimar's glass castle, she had risked herself to save him. Now there was nothing he wouldn't do for her.

"I don't know if I can make you understand," he said, squeezing the back of his neck.

"I understand." Tai's voice was low. "You love her."

Darvyn looked into the other man's eyes. Comprehension lived there, more than he'd given Tai credit for.

A wave of exhaustion tugged at his knees, and he leaned back against the wall.

"You must be hungry," Lizvette said, rising and walking toward the telephone. "We can't go anywhere until you've at least had breakfast."

Darvyn's stomach rumbled just then, punctuating her words. An extra few minutes for food couldn't hurt. Much.

But Tai's brows furrowed. He swiveled around to face her. "We?"

She held up a finger as she called for room service. When she'd replaced the handset, she squared her shoulders and faced Tai. Darvyn sighed. He really didn't need their bickering right now. His Song grazed their emotions, then jumped away sharply. Best for him not to get involved in whatever was going on *there*.

"Yes. It is possible that Queen Jasminda's family is being held in the same place as Darvyn's Kyara," Lizvette said.

His Kyara. He liked the sound of that.

"Possible, yes," Tai said cautiously.

"As that is the best lead we have for the Goddess's mission, it seems prudent to follow up on it immediately." Her hands fluttered in front of her as she moved to the window. "My chance to catch my father is likely gone. The race begins in under an hour, and when Clove shows up right as the river, he'll know he cannot trust me. I don't know how he'll react to that. I don't think I should stay if you all are leaving."

Tai ran his hands through his hair, making it stand up in blue tufts. He muttered to himself in what must be Raunian and began to pace again. "You know I won't let him harm you, don't you?"

The emotions in the room were in flux again, and Darvyn let go of his Song completely. "What's happened to Clove?" he asked.

Lizvette clutched the neck of her gown, appearing flustered. It was Tai who growled out the story of Nirall's scheme for Lizvette to sabotage the race by harming Clove. Vanesse had stuck close by her side all morning, and the Foreign Service had not let the pilot out of their sight.

"I owe Queen Jasminda a debt," Lizvette said quietly. "If I would not be in the way, I would very much like the chance to repay it in some small measure. I'm certain the return of her family would be of great comfort to her."

"Perhaps it would help with your situation," Darvyn said.

Lizvette crossed her arms and lifted her chin. "I'm not looking for praise or gratitude. You don't even have to tell her I did anything. I simply want to help."

Darvyn held up his hands in apology. Tai glared at him, and Darvyn was never more grateful for the knock at the door and the arrival of breakfast.

When the bellman left, Lizvette spoke up. "If we leave during the race, we'll arrive in Dahlinea before it ends." She left unspoken what her father might do to her if she stayed in Melbain and Clove won. Tai looked ready to fight someone.

"Should we leave Vanesse and Clove a note?" she asked.

"No, considering how easily Nirall was able to get in here," Tai replied. "We'll leave a message with Zivel or one of his men."

"So we're agreed? We go to Dahlinea to find Kyara and search for Jasminda's family." Lizvette blinked, waiting for a response.

Tai took a deep breath before nodding slowly. He seemed reluctant to bring Lizvette along, but Darvyn was glad she'd be with them. Though he knew she didn't yet believe it, she'd done well so far and brought a wealth of knowledge and experience they lacked.

He closed his eyes and pictured Kyara. *I'm coming for you. Please hold on.*

CHAPTER TWENTY-SIX

At the summit of the mountain lay an eagle's nest, where a mother bird fed her young. "Best turn back," the eagle said. "Where will you go next, the sky?"

Ayal looked past the clouds, with their portents of doom, trying to see where the sky ended. But she could no more see the top of the heavens than she could the future.

—THE AYALYA

Varten was fully awake and eating for the first time in days. His skin remained ghostly pale and coated in a sheen of sweat that soaked his clothes, but it gave them hope for the first time in a long while. He and Roshon eagerly wolfed down their evening meals. Dansig ate more slowly, watching his sons with a preternatural patience Kyara envied. He turned to her and frowned, likely at the fact that she hadn't been brought any food.

He looked as though he might offer her something from his plate when the outer door opened and Asenath arrived. However, the woman's slow, pained movements were alarming. Kyara approached the bars, regarding Asenath's struggle to shuffle over and place the dinner tray on the ground. It fell with a clatter.

"What's wrong?" Kyara asked. "Are you unwell?"

Asenath remained bent over, one hand on her waist, the other curled around the bar. "Just a bit of weakness." When she looked up, Kyara swallowed a gasp. She hadn't seen the old woman since she delivered the hairpin, but in a few short days, Asenath had aged rapidly. Sagging skin framed her eyes, and her cheeks were drawn and thin. How was this possible?

Kyara's eyes widened. "What's happened?"

"Everything has a cost. Even doing what's right." Asenath's gnarled fingers released the bar. "Here," she said, dropping something into Kyara's hand.

The round, flat gold coin engraved with strange but familiar characters was hot in her palm. Embedded in the metal, a pink crystalline stone winked at her. Kyara stared dazedly at Asenath. "How . . . how did you get this?" She immediately thought of the girl at the graduation ceremony that she'd assumed was Asenath's granddaughter. The girl could have provided the medallion, but given the elaborate ceremony, they must be unimaginably valuable. "What do I do with it?" Kyara asked, pressing it deeper into her palm.

Asenath opened her mouth to answer but promptly collapsed in a heap on the ground. Kyara cried out and reached for her, grasping the woman's frail hand and stroking her tissue-thin skin. Roshon and Dansig began shouting for help. A guard poked his head in and swore when he saw the crumpled body. He rushed over, picked up Asenath, and carried her out of the chamber, hopefully to get her medical attention.

Kyara stared at the door for a long time, but the chances were slim that a guard would bring a prisoner an update on the condition of a servant. Asenath had mentioned others who believed as she did. Was she working with anyone who knew of her ill health? Would they be able to send another to apprise the prisoners?

Both cells remained quiet with unspoken worry. Kyara turned her attention back to the medallion in her palm. Unlike the hairpin amalgamation, this bit of magic didn't vibrate or give her any kind of feeling at all. She wasn't sure how to even use it. Her only other experience with amalgamation magic had been back in Lagrimar, when Ydaris had given her a locket full of stored Nethersong. It had allowed Kyara to overcome the blood spell that bound her actions. But if this medallion contained death energy, she could not sense it.

"May I see it?" Dansig asked on a breath.

Kyara handed it to him through the bars. "It's one of the medallions they created the last time I was drained. Or at least one just like it."

He bounced it in his palm a few times, as if testing its weight.

"I think they must all have them, at least all the initiated Physicks. Ydaris certainly does." She shivered to remember the extent of Ydaris's brutal power, always thought to be Earthsong since no one in Lagrimar knew much of other magics.

Dansig frowned. "If the Cantor had one, then they must be truly powerful."

"I got the impression that some are more powerful than others. They said the ones created using my Song will last the owners their entire lives."

"I wonder if there's a way to discover its usage without the guidance of a Physick." He squeezed his fist around it and closed his eyes. The only sound in the chamber was Varten's labored breathing. Both twins watched their father as long minutes passed. Finally, he opened his eyes and shook his head.

"Maybe the bracelets block the amalgam magic, as well," Kyara offered.

Dansig turned his wrists, encased in the caldera bracelets that obstructed his Song. "Perhaps," he muttered.

Roshon stood up and approached his father. "Physicks have no inborn magic, right?"

"Right," Kyara said, nodding slowly.

"Like me?" He held out his hand. "Kyara said the Cantor mimicked having a Song for decades using something like this. Perhaps it will work for me since I don't have a Song, either."

A moment passed in which something seemed to be communicated between father and son. Begrudgingly, Dansig gave the medallion to Roshon. "Be careful with it. We don't know how it works, son."

Roshon studied the circle of metal. "It must behave like a Song—at least a little bit. How do you sing, Papa?"

Dansig ran his hands through the coils of his hair. He sat down on his bed and leaned forward, elbows on his knees, jaw clenched. Kyara sat, too, her dinner forgotten on the floor. Was it possible only a non-Singer could work the medallion?

"To use Earthsong, you open your inner Song to the source—the endless sea of mingling energy of every living thing. You are essentially dipping your toe into the waves of the ocean and trying to draw in as much water as you can and then hold it in your body and reshape it."

Roshon eyed the medallion. "And Nethersong?" he asked, turning to Kyara.

She sighed. "Nethersong is like holding on to the leash of a wild boar. Its tusks swipe at you and it nearly pulls your shoulder from its socket. Holding on is hardly even possible, but if you don't, everyone around you will die." She could not hold in the bitterness that seeped from her voice. Dansig winced, but Roshon nodded as if he understood.

"And amalgam is both," he added. "So if I have no Song, how would I attempt to weave some mixture of the two energies?"

Kyara shook her head. "The ocean on a leash? I don't see how it's possible."

Dansig rubbed his chin. "The Physicks trap the energies in objects, so instead of connecting with Earthsong or Nethersong and bringing it inside you, I suspect the medallion does that for you. Perhaps use it to focus the combined energy and manage it."

"What's the first thing you taught Jasminda?" Roshon asked. "When you linked with her when she was young?"

Dansig's focus loosened. A pang went through Kyara to watch the softness in his face as he thought about his eldest child. "A bit of wind," he said. "It's easy enough to control, being so insubstantial, and it's something you can feel. A breeze across the face is the first thing my mother taught me, and it's what I showed her."

Roshon stood in the center of the cell, his eyes squeezed shut in concentration. Sweat beaded on his forehead, and his veins stood out in bold relief on his neck. He looked pained but held the rigid posture as the minutes ticked by.

Nothing happened.

Varten stared up at his twin, worry creasing his face. His eyes were heavy, the exhaustion of his mysterious illness weighing him down. He was struggling to stay awake.

She was about to ask Roshon if he wanted to take a break and try another tack when a whistling disturbed the air by her ear. Her head shot around, thinking she'd imagined the sound, but Dansig's astounded gaze met hers. He'd heard it, too.

A puff of air lifted the edge of her tunic. The breeze rose to echo off the stone walls of the chamber. Then the gentle wind grew stronger and swelled rapidly into a violent gust that blew over the cup on her tray and made the whole thing slide nearly out of the cell. Their clothing blew around their bodies. Kyara's braids trailed out behind her as the blast nearly knocked her on her side.

Varten gripped his mattress, struggling to hold on. Dansig stood, reaching for Roshon, whose eyes were wide with terror.

"I can't stop! I don't know how to control it!" he cried.

"Don't try to control the energy," his father yelled. "Control yourself!"

The gale grew even more frenzied. Kyara clung to the rail of the bed, which was bolted into the ground. The sturdy metal creaked and swayed, in danger of ripping out of the stone floor. Her tunic flapped and tore.

"Roshon!" she screamed. "Tighten the leash!"

She squinted against the wind and could only see in flashes. Roshon was barely holding his ground against the storm. She wasn't sure he would be able to reel in the outburst of energy.

Dansig launched himself forward, hurtling his body into Roshon's. The medallion fell from the boy's hand, and the wind died to nothing.

They all lay there gasping for breath, their few belongings strewn around the cells.

A guard came thundering in. "What's all the ruckus in here?" he asked in a gruff voice. The translator buzzed in her hair.

Dansig approached the bars and grinned sheepishly. He motioned to his sons and mimed a fight between the two.

The guard narrowed his eyes, but there could be no reasonable explanation for the condition of the cells. If he suspected any magical involvement, they would be in trouble, but he took another look around, told them to keep it down, and stalked away.

As they put their cells back together, Kyara began to laugh. She shook her head slightly and faced three incredulous faces.

She shrugged. "It really was a valiant effort, Roshon. Next time, we'll have to bundle everything up a bit."

"Next time?" he bit out, his voice rising an octave.

"Oh yes," she said. "The first try is always a little rough. But you'll get the hang of it."

His mouth hung open. It snapped shut at the sound behind him. Varten sat on his bed, arms across his belly, his face turning red as his body shook. Panic stiffened Kyara in place, until she realized what she was seeing. The teen wasn't in the midst of some sort of seizure, he was laughing.

The sound, so little heard of late, warmed and soothed her. It must have had a similar effect on the others, for the tension in the cells dissolved. If Roshon could master the medallion without killing them all, there was still hope.

Tai jerked awake as the slow rocking of the train became a frenzied jitter. To his left, Lizvette peered out the window. Across from him, Darvyn sat ramrod straight, staring at nothing. Due to the Yaly Classic, the air station had been closed, with no airbuses arriving or leaving until late that evening. So they'd headed for the train station in search of passage to Dahlinea. The overnight journey took far longer via rail than through the air, but at least they'd been able to get out of the city quickly and away from whatever spies Lizvette's father may have been working with. Zivel and his men were guarding Vanesse and Clove, but Tai was still apprehensive about Nirall's sabotage plans.

He stole a glance at Lizvette again. Though she sat next to him, it was as if she were a world away. She'd met his earlier attempts at conversation with clipped answers until he left her to her ruminations. Now, as the train shook and swayed, her arm brushed against his. The car lurched and she was knocked off-balance, sliding in her seat. Tai gripped her wrist to stabilize her. She sucked in a breath and stiffened. When he went to release her, she covered his hand with her other palm, locking him in place. He dragged his gaze up to meet her eyes, heart beating out of his chest. His rapid pulse made him feel warm and his hand, sandwiched between hers, was on fire.

"Thank you," she whispered.

He nodded, unable to find his voice with the heat storm raging through his body.

The train's intercom crackled to life, announcing their arrival in Dahlia City. She pulled her hands from his but didn't look away. He couldn't read her expression and wished he knew what was going through her head. Neither of them had mentioned the kiss, but it was not something he could forget. Though he needed to. A Raunian besotted with an Elsiran elite? Such a thing was foolish and impossible. He would have to find a way to squelch this longing before it pulled him under.

Darvyn stood, thankfully pulling Tai's focus away from Lizvette. The Lagrimari man squinted through the tiny window embedded in the door to their compartment, arms folded across his chest. He hadn't relaxed yet, and Tai couldn't blame him for his sense of urgency. What wouldn't a man do to save the woman he loved? Not that Tai had ever been in love.

Lizvette shifted, but he refused to look at her.

The compartment door slid open on a mechanical hinge and the few passengers streamed into the main aisle. Tai and the others followed, exiting the train into the station. They climbed a flight of stairs to the main level and entered a long, sparsely populated lobby, dotted with seating areas and vendor booths, though they were more vacant than full.

"We'll have to change our money to Dahlinean shings," Lizvette said, pulling out her change purse. "I expect the exchange rate will be terrible."

Darvyn looked over from his perusal of the quiet interior. "Why is this place so abandoned? The station in Melbain was overflowing with people."

"Too far north," Tai said, pointing to a map on the wall. Dahlia City was the northernmost city in Yaly, bordered on one side by a treacherous mountain range. The snowcapped peaks were visible through the large picture window next to the map. On the street, people bustled about, bundled up in coats and scarves that hadn't been necessary in Melbain.

"Plus, the Physicks are held in quite low esteem by many of the commonwealths," Lizvette added. "Dahlinea is not a place most Yalyish would visit unless necessary."

"Did something cause a rift?" Darvyn asked.

Lizvette motioned them forward toward the currency exchange on the other end of the station. "Several years ago, Dahlinea sought to contribute soldiers to the confederate defense. Only these weren't men with any combat training, they were mechanical warriors, tin beasts powered by amalgam. The other commonwealths were not pleased. They were convinced to test out the contraptions, assured that they would result in huge financial savings, but the machines went astray, injuring quite a few people in the process, and the entire program was shut down," she explained as they walked. "Many Investors across the country lost a lot of money in the endeavor, and Dahlinea took the brunt of the blame. Ever since then, the Physicks have been stripped of some of their power in the Senate. Many of the other commonwealth leaders don't trust the more powerful amalgams, though the people at large love their toys more than ever."

"'The branches of the tree spread further apart. . . ,'" Tai murmured as they approached the counter.

Lizvette gave him a surprised glance. "You're familiar with *The Ayalya*?"

"I do know how to read, duchess," he said lightly. She pursed her lips and went to respond, then apparently thought better of it.

A door behind the counter of the exchange booth opened, revealing a squat, middle-aged man. Lizvette faced him, offering a radiant smile. "We're just in from Melbain." She slid a handful of coins across the counter.

The dour clerk looked down at the money and nodded, then turned to a contraption before him that had rows of dials and buttons. His thick fingers blurred across the machine.

Lizvette tapped her fingers on her lips, drawing Tai's attention to her mouth until he blinked and tore himself away. "Excuse me, sir. Are there tours available for the amalgamation factories?"

The clerk's eyes never left his machine. "You'll have to check with the foreman of one of the factories or the lead Spellsayer. Though I can't say as I've heard of them giving tours." He shrugged and pulled a lever on the side of his counting machine. A trilling bell sounded, and change began sliding down an incline on the other side of the counter. The Dahlinean shings dropped into several neat piles of shiny coins. Lizvette scooped them into her purse and thanked the clerk for his aid.

"A factory tour?" Tai asked as they headed toward the train

station exit. Lizvette held up a finger and led them behind an empty vendor booth so they were out of sight from the main part of the lobby.

"I was thinking of how we could gain entry to the Physick headquarters. That's where Kyara said she was being held, right?"

Darvyn nodded.

"Well, I doubt they would just allow us to waltz into their facility through the front door, but if we can find someone with access and assume their identity . . ." She raised her eyebrows.

Tai beamed, impressed with her ingenuity. He turned to Darvyn. "Can you copy someone like that? Make one of us into an exact replica?"

He nodded. "I've done it before. With King Jack, as a matter of fact."

Tai did a double take, and Darvyn shrugged. "It's a great plan," Tai told Lizvette. "But why a factory?"

"Well, all we really know about the Physicks is that they've systematized the production of amalgamations. They're all produced in massive factories in this city. A factory worker—someone involved in adding the magic to the machines—would likely have the access we need, but their movements wouldn't necessarily attract notice. It seems like a good place to start getting answers."

Darvyn perked up a bit, nodding at her logic, but worry beat against Tai. "What if the . . . net thing that Absalom character used to steal your Song, what if those are common here? He also had something that allowed him to see right through your cloaking spell."

Lizvette's shoulders slumped. "And the sound weapon. I should have thought about that. Why do you think they had no effect on you, Tai?"

"Wish I knew. Thick Raunian skull, maybe." He grinned and

rapped on his forehead with his knuckles. Lizvette laughed, and he ignored the fizzle in his chest.

"I got the impression that the netting he used to drain my Song was fairly rare," Darvyn said. "I think that's why he was charging the Dominionists so much for it. And the spectacles that make it possible to see through spells . . . ? I've encountered them before." He rubbed the back of his neck and looked off into the distance for a moment. "They won't be expecting us, that's a point in our favor. This may just be a chance we have to take. Lizvette's plan is sound. We will have to be on our guard."

Tai didn't have a good feeling about this, but they had no other ideas, and Darvyn was clearly impatient. Tai hadn't liked Lizvette coming to Dahlinea now that the Physicks had proved themselves so ruthlessly dangerous. However, it wasn't as if Melbain was safe for her, thanks to her miscreant father.

But there was another issue. "Even before we get to the factory, we can't just roam the city as we are. At least I can't—a Raunian is rare and memorable in these parts. And if the Physicks *can* see through a disguise spell, this mission will be over before it begins."

Lizvette looked back and forth between them, again tapping her finger to her lips. How he wished she wouldn't do that. "Perhaps we can use a more traditional disguise for now," she said. "And then see if we can find out how common those devices are."

Her expression turned slightly mischievous, and Tai swallowed. Myr save him, there was nothing more appealing than a woman with a rogue streak.

CHAPTER TWENTY-SEVEN

The chief of the mountain village met the seeker on her way back down the trail. "We have heard tales of your travels. Will you join us in making merry? For we have just left the presence of Gilmer the Hunter, and there is much to celebrate."

She longed to refuse, but her weary feet made the decision for her.

—THE AYALYA

The unholy clattering they were making in the early-morning hours finally brought the guards in, and Kyara exhaled the heavy breath she'd been holding. Dansig spoke urgently in Lagrimari, gesturing wildly toward his son, who lay on the bed writhing in pain. Sweat poured from his skin as his eyes rolled back in his head.

The guard took one look at the boy, pulled out a metal hearing cone from his belt loop, and placed it in his ear. It must be a communications amalgam, for he spoke into it like a telephone, alerting the medical staff that one of the prisoners was incoming. Someone replied, too far away and muffled for Kyara to understand. Not long after, two white-robed servants arrived with a stretcher and carried the twin away. The whole thing had taken under five minutes.

Sitting propped against the wall, his brother looked on without moving. As soon as the outer door clanked shut, he slid back down onto the bed and exhaled loudly.

"Do you think it will work?" Varten asked, his coloring paling to a ghostly hue. The tiny bit of healing that Roshon had managed had faded rapidly. It must be a difficult thing to master with the medallion, for he had only been able to help Varten for a scant few minutes at a time.

"It's got to work. Have some faith, son."

The plan was for Roshon to get to the medical wing and find a way to escape. Earlier in their incarceration, the whole family had been frequent visitors to the infirmary, subject to all manner of testing, and so they were familiar with the layout of the place. Roshon was sure that with the medallion, he could find a way out and then contact the police or the Elsiran ambassador for help.

Dansig placed an arm around Varten, holding him close. He touched his son's forehead and frowned.

The spell Roshon had created for himself mimicked a very dire version of his brother's illness—though Varten's situation was nearly as grim. Seeing Roshon in such a state reminded Kyara of how little time they had, of how this gambit needed to pay off so they could help Varten.

Roshon had practiced nonstop over the past twenty-four hours in order to manage the medallion well enough to enact the ruse.

They had no choice but to place their trust in him as the only one who could wield the amalgam magic.

Peering at the door to the prison chamber, Kyara silently wished him luck. Asenath had not returned, and now Roshon appeared to be their only hope.

She wished she had been able to help Roshon more, but mastering a power like that took time. She could not bear to dwell on her own brutal training at Ydaris's hand. Those days were among her darkest. Dansig, on the other hand, was a patient tutor. He never raised his voice, and his calm demeanor balanced Roshon's impatience and frustration.

Kyara wished she'd had a teacher like him, though it would not have mattered. There were no other Nethersingers for Kyara to learn from. The Physicks had certainly tried to find one, and while Ydaris had hidden Kyara in plain sight for a decade, she suspected the Cantor, too, had sought news of any other Nethersingers for her own gain. After all, it was because she'd delivered Kyara that Ydaris was now accepted by the Physicks again after living in exile for so long.

Kyara sat up as recognition slammed into her. *That's* where she knew the name Mooriah! The memory had niggled at her for days, struggling to come to the surface. During her time with the Cavefolk, an old shaman called Murmur had mentioned another Nethersinger, one who had lived hundreds of years ago, whose name had been Mooriah.

Back in that time, Nethersingers were killed at birth, but Mooriah's father had saved her and brought her to live with the Cavefolk in secret. Kyara strained to remember what else Murmur had told her, but it hadn't been much. Was it possible that the Sad Woman from her dreams was the ancient Nethersinger?

Mooriah had expected Kyara to understand her message: *Em-*

brace the Light. She racked her brain, trying to remember what Murmur had told her deep in those underground caverns where the Cavefolk dwelt. She recalled a vision he'd seen in his youth of the war among the three worlds. He'd insisted that her deadly Song would be needed to fight for the Living World. According to Asenath, the Light *was* the Living World, but was that what Mooriah meant? Somehow Kyara thought not.

Murmur had wanted to teach her how to control her Song, but his teaching style had involved nearly killing Darvyn. Thankfully Kyara had saved him, pulling the deadly energy of Nethersong from his body, a feat she'd never achieved before.

She had to admit that she was stronger at managing her Song now than she was before Murmur's trick, but she still didn't trust him. Being manipulated and controlled was something she'd had enough of. The wound on her chest was a constant ache as it was, and now she suspected there were even more forces at work wanting to use her power. It made her wish the Physicks would just drain her dry and end it. If only the True Father had stolen her Song the way he did so many others'.

"How did you escape tribute and manage to hold on to your Song?" she asked Dansig to fill the uneasy silence.

He looked up thoughtfully. "My mother kept us mobile. She was a peddler. We lived on the highway in a caravan, stayed ahead of the Collectors."

Kyara nodded. She'd lived much of her life on the road, too. Between assignments, she'd preferred staying away from the castle as much as possible.

"My sister was caught by the nabbers when I was fourteen," Dansig continued. "I went straight to the Keepers then. Joined the same week."

Kyara leaned forward. "Did you find her?"

Dansig's eyes were hollow. He shook his head. "The Keepers embedded me in the army—spying, relaying info back to them."

"You fought in the Sixth Breach, right?"

He held her gaze with a considering look. "I came over to Elsira during the Sixth Breach," he said slowly, "but I did not fight."

Dansig looked down at his sleeping son and sighed. "I wanted to leave the Keepers. Not because I disagreed with their mission, but their methods could sometimes be . . ."

"Cutthroat?" A member of the Keepers had betrayed Darvyn, and she'd witnessed his own people collar him when he stood up for her. Freedom fighters they may be, but they were still imperfect men and women.

"People working for a good cause are still people," Dansig said, echoing her thoughts. "At the end of the day, a group is only as good as its leaders, and I had some . . . problems with the elders." He shifted and wiped the sweat from Varten's sopping brow. "It didn't help that I had the Dream of the Queen several times. Some were jealous of that."

Kyara leaned forward. "You saw Her?" She still wasn't sure she even believed in the Queen Who Sleeps, though Darvyn had assured her the deity was real.

"Just before the Sixth Breach, I asked Her for help leaving. She guided me to a tear in the Mantle, a weak point in the magic. I slipped through and lived in the mountains for a time. After the fighting ended, I found the prisoner of war camps where the Lagrimari soldiers trapped in Elsira were housed. That's where I met Emi."

The twins' Elsiran mother had been a member of some sort of religious order that worshipped the Queen Who Sleeps.

"Why do you think She did it? Helped you leave?" Kyara asked.

Dansig's expression slackened. The emotion drained from his face. "She never does anything without a reason." The words were cold. "I believe She wanted me in Her debt. I wonder if my child's life is payment enough." The last was a bitter whisper likely not meant for Kyara to hear. The mission that had landed his family in prison had been undertaken at the Queen's behest.

"They like to meddle in our lives, don't they?" Kyara mused. Dansig looked up questioningly. She waved her arm in the air. "The powerful. The strong. The gods. They push us this way and that way, and for what? Sometimes I just want to push back."

Dansig scratched his jaw. "I do think they have their reasons. Sometimes we are sacrifices for the greater good. What is it you're struggling with, Kyara?"

She dropped her head into her hands, running her fingers through the rows of braids. Darvyn's face flickered in her mind briefly before fading away. "I just want to choose. I want a choice in what happens to me."

Dansig was grim, his voice heavy and low. "All I can say is this: when you get the choice, choose wisely. More wisely than I did."

His hand went back to Varten, who murmured restlessly in his sleep. Kyara closed her eyes. She would remember his words and hoped she lived to see the day she could heed his advice.

For Lizvette, Dahlia City, while large and teeming with people, had a very different air from Melbain City. She and the others left the train station and emerged in the modern metropolis of the central business district. Like in Melbain, towers rose into the sky around them, though these were considerably shorter and less grand. But after only a handful of blocks, the architecture changed drastically. Worn-down buildings with brick facades lined the streets; the neighborhood was dingy and unkempt. Even the automobiles charging down the street were all older, without the gleam of regular polishing.

"Those markings," Darvyn said, scanning the people going about their business on the streets. "What do they mean?" He turned to peer at a woman who had just passed them, her head covered in a colorful scarf. A blocky tattoo was emblazoned on the back of her neck. Several of the people they'd seen in the commonwealth bore the marks. Men often had them on shaved heads, while women bore them on their necks.

Lizvette faced forward, her stomach churning. "Those tattoos are how the Dahlineans mark Bondmen—the lowest caste in Yaly. Investors use an ink that fades away after seven years, the period of their indenturing."

"Indenturing?" Darvyn asked.

"It's like slavery," Tai spat. "The commonwealths keep the lower classes, the poor toilers, tightly controlled. The workers are required to use commonwealth banks and stores, and are paid in a currency that is worthless elsewhere. Yet somehow they always remain in debt. They nearly always have to extend their indenturing."

Darvyn looked troubled, and Lizvette couldn't blame him. It was an abominable practice.

"Let's go in here," she said, coming upon a store with coats and winter gear displayed in the window. Her autumn shawl was doing nothing to protect against the colder northern temperatures.

Once arrayed in a warm—if utilitarian—woolen coat, Lizvette led them on foot to the nearby arts district. Her plan was to find a costume shop to purchase the type of heavy makeup that would cover Tai's tattoos. A wig for him and one for her own distinctly Elsiran hair color would help, as well. But as they crossed deeper into the neighborhood of colorfully painted shops, they found it nearly deserted. Stores that should be open at this time of the morning were barred with the windows shuttered. Trash lay piled up in cans that had not been emptied in weeks, from all appearances. The arts district seemed dead. They turned a corner onto Theatre Row. The marquee of a single hall was lit, but it advertised a photoplay. *Experience the Talkie Revolution!* proclaimed the poster in bold script.

Lizvette looked down the desolate street. The wind whistled through the air, blowing bits of trash from the overflowing cans. She shook her head. "Perhaps we'll have to take our chances disguising ourselves with Earthsong. It doesn't look like we'll find what we need here." She wrung her hands, both in frustration and to bring warmth to her frozen fingertips. She should have purchased gloves.

Darvyn's grim expression didn't change. He was coiled tight with tension, and her heart went out to him. But Tai tilted his head to the side. "Do you hear that?"

Lizvette closed her eyes but only made out the sound of the wind.

"There are people in that theatre over there," Darvyn said, pointing across the street.

The lights on the marquee were dark, but the lettering advertised, A SIDE-RIPPINGLY HILARIOUS ROMP. NIGHTLY.

"We could get what we need from the theatre's makeup supply. If they'll sell to us," Lizvette said, leading the way across the street.

The front doors were barred, but she could hear music now, coming from around the side of the building. She turned down the narrow alley next to the theatre only to be stopped short by Tai's hand on her shoulder.

"Not so fast there, duchess."

She shivered from his touch before steeling herself and turning around.

He looked down the dark alley with suspicion. Whatever unsavory things might be hiding nearby could certainly not stand up to the fiercely protective look in his eye. He stepped around her so that he was in the lead.

They marched down the alley. Other than being perilous to the cleanliness of her hemline, it held no visible threats. Behind the theatre's side door, loud music played. She knocked and waited a minute, but no one came. She was raising her hand to knock again when the door swung open on creaking hinges.

The young woman on the other side was about her age with straight, black hair that fell past her shoulders. Violet eyes took up half of her heart-shaped face. Lizvette saw the exact moment she caught sight of Tai. Her eyes, at first filled with vague curiosity, widened, tracking him up and down, no doubt taking in the dusting of hair on his chest, exposed by the way he insisted on unbuttoning the top few buttons of his shirt, regardless of the temperature.

Lizvette cleared her throat, bringing the woman's attention back to her. "Hello. We're so sorry to bother you, but we're—"

"Come in," she said, speaking only to Tai.

Lizvette shot an annoyed glance over her shoulder. Darvyn appeared to be holding back a smile. She was glad someone found this so amusing. Meanwhile, Tai's eyes twinkled. He unfurled a roguish grin upon the woman, who ushered them into a chaotic room beyond the door.

Two dozen people lounged about a cluttered space littered with wardrobes, tables, boxes, discarded furniture, and contraptions she couldn't identify. The front half of an automobile lay next to a miniature cardboard replica of the city's skyline. The music was courtesy of a phonograph blaring from the corner.

In the center, an enormous bearded man was engaged in a very bawdy jig with a voluptuous blonde. Others gyrated suggestively with partners or alone. Everyone here was in a costume of some kind—colorful breeches, fur-covered jackets, formal gowns. One man even wore a boar's head over a tuxedo.

Lizvette clasped her hands in front of her, taking it all in.

"I'm Brigit," the woman who'd ushered them in said. "Are you here for the party?" Once again, she had eyes only for Tai.

Lizvette fumed. "No, we're—"

"I'd never pass up a good party," Tai interrupted, his smile broad.

Darvyn looked considerably less amused now. His jaw was locked, eyes scanning the partygoers, arms rigid at his side. His single-minded focus on rescuing his Kyara had kept him tied in knots since the day before.

Lizvette stared at Tai, trying to communicate to him that they needed to hurry, but his attention had been captured by Brigit.

"What are we celebrating?" Tai asked.

"The end of our fair theatre," she replied with a dramatic curtsey, designed to allow Tai the optimal angle to see down her dress, no doubt. "Our last show is tonight, and then we go the way of the rest."

"What happened to them all?" Darvyn asked. His voice sounded strange and tinny. Perhaps the communications amalgamation around his neck was running out. Lizvette made a mental note to pick up a new one after they left. If they could get what they needed and get out.

Brigit shrugged. "Ticket sales have been down for months. Everyone wants to see the talkies instead. But a few days ago, word came down from on high that all government allotment for the arts has been pulled. Without those stipends, we can't pay the bills here."

Lizvette watched the revelers more closely. Though they laughed and danced and acted cheerful, careful inspection revealed gloomy undertones.

"What will you do?" she asked. She had to repeat the question as Brigit was staring at Tai and didn't hear her the first time.

"Take jobs in the factories, I suppose. They're on a hiring kick. No one turned away. Production is way up." She took a step closer to Tai, tilting her head. "You aren't from around here, are you?"

Tai laughed as if her question was the funniest thing he'd ever heard. Lizvette rolled her eyes, gritting her teeth when Brigit looped her arm through his and dragged him over to a table laden with food. Red clouded Lizvette's vision.

"Let's get what we need and go," Darvyn said tightly.

Lizvette couldn't have agreed more. She tore her gaze away from Tai's broad back and looked around. Thick, black curtains indicated where the stage was. They stood in the backstage area, and far on the other side was a hallway.

"Dressing rooms are most likely through there," she said. From being in a few productions at school, she knew the basic layout of a theatre.

Darvyn motioned that she should lead the way. They skirted the edges of the rowdy affair. No one seemed to pay them any mind.

"Why do you think the Dahlinean government is pulling funding from the theatres?" she asked, thinking out loud.

"And increasing production at the factories? Maybe they're diverting the money there," Darvyn said. "More amalgams on the market . . . it must be significant somehow." He shook his head.

Soon they were in the long hallway, peering through the doorways. The first led to a storage closet, but the second appeared to be a dressing room.

Lizvette quickly found a blond wig for herself and stuffed it in a paper sack that had been lying on the ground. A pair of tinted spectacles would do to mask the shade of Darvyn's eyes. It was Tai who stood out the most and would need the most work. Lizvette sighed as she opened jar after jar of heavy, tinted face paint. "If he were here I could better match his tone, but this will have to do," she said, choosing one she thought would work. She grabbed a black wig to cover his blue hair, then left a few coins on the table so she didn't feel like they were stealing. With their supplies now procured, they headed back to the party.

Tai and Brigit were on the dance floor, where the latter was rubbing her considerable cleavage on him like a cat in heat. Lizvette crossed her arms over her own more modest chest and sighed.

When Tai looked over, she pointed to her wrist, though she wasn't wearing a wristwatch. He had the nerve to grin at her and swing Brigit around one more time before whispering something in her ear that made the woman blush redder than an apple. Then he disengaged from her and approached them.

"Having fun?" Lizvette snapped.

"Did you get what you needed?" he asked, oblivious to her mood.

"I think so, though if you end up looking chalky it's only because I couldn't match your coloring with you out here . . . gallivanting."

"Gallivanting?" He chuckled in the most irritating way and plucked the paper sack of supplies out of her hand. "After you," he said with a bow. Lizvette marched toward the door. She thought that Brigit would stop their exit, but they made it back outside without incident.

"I'm surprised you weren't roped into a full bacchanal before we could leave."

Darvyn lengthened his stride, now in the lead. "I sang a small spell to avert everyone's attention."

Lizvette stopped in her tracks, mouth agape. "You couldn't have done that when we first went in?"

With a furrowed brow, he motioned to Tai. "He didn't give me a chance."

Tai spread his arms out, not looking remorseful at all. "What?"

She reached into the sack he held, pulled out the black wig, and tossed it in his face. Then she stomped down the alley back to the street.

CHAPTER TWENTY-EIGHT

The mountain villagers praised the good fortune brought by the Hunter long into the night. Man-With-Voice-Like-Nightbirds sang a warbling melody with many verses. Though darkness hung like a cloak, Ayal felt a sliver of longing—joy such as this was infectious. She wished it didn't have to end.

—THE AYALYA

Darvyn winced as the stench of exhaust from the factories became impossible to ignore. Metallic and rotten, it soured the meager contents of his stomach. He sang a bubble of fresh air around their heads whenever the stink became too much.

The factory district was bordered on one side by a placid lake and on the other by a wide highway that cut through the city. They'd taken a cab to the edge of the district, then walked the streets on foot, unsure which factory to enter.

The buildings were concrete behemoths, each taking up an entire city block. There were no names over the doors, no indications of what types of amalgams were produced inside. Just pockmarked streets and sidewalks separating enormous structures, each at least seven stories tall.

"Maybe we should just pick one at random and knock on the front door?" Tai asked, though his voice held no confidence in the suggestion. He'd applied the face paint in the taxi and looked a bit plain with his tattoos covered.

Anger still rolled off Lizvette in waves, and she had not yet spoken up with any proposals of her own. Tai's performance with the woman in the theatre was unfortunate, but Darvyn clearly sensed the fear and longing within Tai when he was around Lizvette. Those two were going to give him a headache with their volatile emotions.

Darvyn rubbed his forehead as an image of Kyara tethered in chains played in his mind. They were close to her. Though he could never sense her with his Song, some other knowledge he couldn't define made him certain.

A lightning bolt splintered the sky far ahead of them. The city's smog obscured the weather conditions, and Darvyn felt no storm in the vicinity. Although the day was cloudless above the haze, another strike of lightning fell to the earth, and a dark cloud spontaneously formed amidst the smog about a kilometer away.

During his time in Yaly, he'd learned that the Physicks were able to command the weather with their amalgam magic, but the tiny storm they were witnessing appeared random and uncontrolled. It reminded him of his own early experiments with his power as a small child first learning the limits of his Song.

When another flare of lightning flew sideways, Darvyn picked up his pace. Something wasn't right. "We need to see what's causing that." The others followed without question. Soon they were running through the barren streets, tall, graceless factory buildings towering over them.

Another strike hit quite close to their party, sizzling the pavement in front of them. They raced along until the road ended at the edge of the lake. The asphalt of the ground crumbled into a gravel shore of the murky waters. Several dozen paces away, clouds roiled and spun, dumping rain over an area no wider than Darvyn's arm span. Huddled in a wet mass on the rocky coast was a shivering figure dressed in black.

"Hello?" Darvyn called out. He spoke in Lagrimari from force of habit, then winced. No one in Yaly knew that language, and he hadn't yet replaced the dead communications amalgam around his throat with the new one they'd purchased.

He was digging in his pocket for the thing when a voice answered in the same tongue. "Who's that?"

Still too far away to see the figure clearly, Darvyn's heart leaped. An Earthsinger! He prodded with his Song and found it was a teenage boy, cold and frightened but uninjured.

Where had he come from and what was he doing here?

Tai and Lizvette thundered up behind Darvyn to stop a few paces from the boy. A cloak covered him completely, the hood obscuring his face. His dread was palpable, but mixed with a cautious relief, probably at meeting another Lagrimari.

"My name is Darvyn ol-Tahlyro. I'm also known as the Shadowfox." He thought announcing himself would calm the young man, but it did nothing. There was no recognition flowing through him. How long had the Physicks had him in their clutches? Certain that he spoke to an Earthsinger, Darvyn stumbled backward in shock when the teen pulled down his hood to reveal red hair and freckled cheeks.

Both Lizvette and Tai gasped to see the Elsiran. So many emotions were flying around now that Darvyn couldn't parse them all out. "What's your name?" he asked.

"Roshon ol-Sarifor!" Tai exclaimed, relief loosening the man's shoulders. The boy's head snapped over to Tai, and his jaw dropped.

"Tai?" he said, incredulous, at the same moment Darvyn asked, "You're Jasminda's brother?"

Roshon jumped to his feet and ran for Tai, embracing the man. His fear was immediately replaced by amazement and a flood of hope. "What are you doing here? How did you know? And what happened to your face?" Tears escaped his eyes, and he ruthlessly scrubbed them away.

Tai chuckled and thumped Roshon on the shoulder a few times. His reply was cut off by a deep, ear-piercing horn blowing from across the lake. Darvyn turned toward the origin of the sound and noticed the island in the middle of the lake for the first time. On it stood a small stone castle with no shortage of turrets and spires. The structure was older than anything he'd seen in Dahlinea.

Men in black coats gathered on the island's shore outside the exterior walls of the castle. Roshon took a hasty step back.

"They're looking for you," Darvyn said, already certain.

Roshon nodded, eyes round and full of fear. "My family is still inside."

"And we will get them out," Tai promised.

Darvyn stared at the stone structure again. "Are there any other prisoners? A woman—"

The horn sounded a second time, drowning out his question; the lake water began to churn and froth, as if it were being heated from within. White, bubbling foam seeped onto the gravel beach, making the rocks sizzle. Darvyn and the others scrambled away, dashing back from the boiling waters and out of sight behind the nearest building.

The lake grew more and more violent; across the water, the black-clad men were now splitting into groups. Large metal-plated boats pulled around from the back of the island. They must be starting a search.

"We need to get out of here," Tai said.

"But my brother . . . and Papa . . ." Roshon whispered.

Tai clutched the boy's shoulder. "I promise we'll come back for them, but we're vastly outnumbered right now and staying here isn't safe."

Roshon nodded. "We have to hurry. Varten is so sick, and I don't think Kyara can last much longer, either."

Inside Darvyn's mind, all went silent. The earsplitting horn and the stewing lake ceased to exist. "Kyara," he mouthed, at once grateful for the confirmation that she was there and unwilling to leave now that he was so close. How had the boy escaped? And what did it say about Kyara's condition that she had not?

Something jostled him. Tai grabbed his upper arm and hauled him down the street. Darvyn shook away the paralysis that had gripped him at the mention of Kyara's name and increased his pace. As much as it hurt to move farther from her, they needed to regroup before they could save her and the others.

They raced down a street lined with the bleak faces of factories. Tai grabbed Lizvette's hand, helping her along when she fell behind. Up ahead, a pair of massive steel doors creaked open. The empty street was quickly flooded with black-coated men, all larger than the average Yalyishman.

"Security," Roshon whispered.

Each man wielded a cudgel about the length of Darvyn's

forearm. He flinched. They looked just like the weapon Absalom had used on him, the one that had shattered his bones with the force of concentrated sound. He could only hope none of the men was carrying anything like the netting that had drained his Song so quickly.

It didn't take long for the small army to spot the only other people on the street. The leader wore a gold band around his upper arm. He spoke a few words into a curved cone before replacing the device at his hip.

"You there!" the man shouted. "Stay where you are." He raised the cudgel and it discharged a blast of sound, though far weaker than what Absalom had unleashed. Expecting such an assault, Darvyn had pulled the air tight in front of his group, creating an invisible wall, much like the barrier he'd used against the deadly palmsalt gas. It stopped the force of the noise before it could harm them.

Alone, he could protect them from the sound weapon, but with another strong Singer, perhaps he could neutralize all the men at once, slowing their heart rates until they all fell asleep.

"Link with me," Darvyn said, holding out his hand to Roshon. Though the boy appeared Elsiran, he must be a Singer if he was responsible for the weather changes by the lake. From the corner of his eye, he saw the teen shake his head.

"I'm not an Earthsinger. But I can try to use this." He opened his fist, revealing a gold coin. "It's an amalgam, but I'm not sure what to do."

Darvyn didn't know what the small coin *could* do, but if Roshon had somehow used it to escape, it might be helpful. "Do whatever you can think of to keep them away."

Tai stepped protectively in front of Lizvette, whose eyes darted around as the security force closed in. The men brandished their weapons, beating against Darvyn's barrier. They approached in formation, discipline evident in every deliberate step.

Darvyn flooded his Song with Earthsong, pulling from the source of power, and felt for the ground beneath the black-tarred road. He pulled on the earth and forced it up, cracking the pavement and shooting hunks of it into the air.

A scraping noise began and a gust of wind raced by and blew the pieces of asphalt toward the guards, hitting several of them in the chests and faces. Darvyn shot a glance at Roshon, whose expression was taut with concentration. The wind must be his, then.

The guards stumbled back, doing their best to avoid the onslaught. Darvyn heated the asphalt beneath their feet until it was gooey and sticky. Their opponents' boots were now caught in the muck, locking them in place as their arms windmilled wildly.

"Behind you!" Lizvette shouted.

Darvyn turned and realized the scraping sound was from boats coming ashore. Three of them, each with ten men, had arrived from the island at amazing speed. These men bore rifles. They hopped from the boats and quickly took up firing positions.

The water had quieted at some point, so Darvyn stirred it up again. He did not have much experience spelling bodies of water, though. Liquid always seemed to have a mind of its own—it was slippery and difficult to control.

He managed to create a gigantic wave that crested above the men and pounded down on them, washing a good number back into the lake. Those who were left scrambled up, cocking their rifles and firing, only to find the weapons waterlogged.

When Darvyn turned back, Tai was carrying Lizvette down an alley like a sack thrown over his shoulder as she struggled and kicked at him. Darvyn grabbed Roshon's arm and took off after them. The security force would no doubt regroup quickly.

After a few blocks with Lizvette slapping at Tai, he finally put her down. They raced back toward the merchant district bordering the factory area. Darvyn scanned the surroundings with his Song, directing them off the main streets and into the darkened alleys between factories when he sensed others nearby. They exited onto a busy street and blended into the crowd, and he released a sigh of relief. They walked for several blocks hidden in plain sight.

"We'll need to find somewhere to talk privately," Lizvette said.

Tai looked around then pointed down a side street. "What about there?"

Painted on the wall of a red brick building were the words *Rooms Rented Hourly.*

"I don't think that would be an appropriate place." Dull horror coated Lizvette's voice.

"No better spot for privacy." Tai shrugged. "Those hotels forget your face the moment after they've taken your money."

"I suppose you'd know all about how such establishments operate," she snapped.

Darvyn held up a hand before the two of them could get started. "It will be fine."

He led the way to the building, and the bickering, thankfully, ceased. He didn't care where they made their plans. The sooner they debriefed, the sooner they could go back for Kyara.

CHAPTER TWENTY-NINE

When dawn broke, the revelers began sharpening swords and spears. Man-With-Voice-Like-Nightbirds sang to her of how they planned to make war with the people of the foothills before sundown. Though the sun rose steadily higher, the darkness in the seeker's heart deepened.

—THE AYALYA

The inside of the "hotel" was far worse than Lizvette had feared. A peculiar odor had sealed itself into the walls under the frightfully stained wallpaper. The carpeting was so faded and torn that spots of plywood showed underneath. The room Tai had acquired from the one-eyed man at the front desk featured a lumpy bed, a couch made up of more springs than cushions, and two hard, wooden chairs. Not trusting the laundry facilities of such a place, she chose a chair, which had been constructed in such a way as to numb her bottom after only a few minutes of use.

Roshon sat across from her on the couch, poor boy. He resembled his aunt Vanesse so much, but the intensity of his eyes reminded her of Jasminda.

Once they were settled—Darvyn standing sentry at the window and Tai lounging comfortably next to Roshon—Lizvette broke the silence. "How is your family?"

Roshon looked down at the scarred, wobbly coffee table as a shudder went through him. "My brother, Varten, is very ill. He's dying."

Lizvette swallowed painfully. Tai's dark eyes filled with emotion, but he blinked it away when she turned toward him.

"And Kyara?" she asked, gaze darting to Darvyn, whose face was grim.

The corners of Roshon's lips curved up. "Strong. Brave. But they're draining her Song. Over and over. Each time seems worse than the last."

Darvyn closed his eyes and dropped his head. Lizvette wanted to comfort him somehow but knew it would do no good.

Roshon cleared his throat. "When we were first taken, the Physicks wanted to know about the stone we found—the death stone. Papa wouldn't tell them anything and so they thought . . ." His eyes hardened and his fists curled. "They thought they could use my brother and me against him."

She didn't want to hear any more but forced herself to sit through Roshon's tale of the painful experiments he and his brother had endured.

"I don't think women bear twins here," Roshon continued. "One of their physicians spoke Elsiran, and he seemed fascinated by the fact that Varten and I are identical. They would do things to us and then compare our reactions."

His eyes rimmed with tears. It was a moment before he could continue. "I think they gave us both the disease and tested different cures to see what would happen."

"Is it plague?" Darvyn asked.

Roshon shrugged. "It's similar, but it's slow. It's been weeks now since he's had a normal appetite. He coughs up blood and sleeps all the time. When he's not sleeping, he's in pain."

Lizvette winced. The people who had done this to him were monsters.

"Before Kyara arrived, the physicians would come every day and take him. He told us they would just keep him on a cot in an infirmary with a lot of other sick people with some kind of equipment strapped to their chests."

"But they stopped taking Varten once Kyara was brought in?" she asked.

He nodded. "They take *her* every few days instead. And he's just grown worse and worse." Roshon placed the curious gold coin on the table. "Then a servant gave this to Kyara. The old woman claimed that there is a faction within the Physicks that doesn't agree with their methods. She's been helping Kyara. These medallions give the Physicks their power. I guess they mimic a Song, sort of, but a Singer can't use it.

"Once I got the hang of it, I pretended to be Varten basically near death, and they brought me to a private room in the medical unit. I feigned unconsciousness, and they left me on a cot. I think they were calling in the ones who had first experimented on us. There was a guard there, but I knocked him into the wall with a blast of wind, stole his cloak, and jumped out the window."

Lizvette's heart leaped into her throat. "How did you know you wouldn't break your neck?"

Roshon shrugged again. "I fell into the water. It's not normal water, though—it's thick and rank. Heavier than it should be. It leaves your skin tingling and burning." He shivered as the memory crossed him. "I didn't think I'd make it across, but I tried using the medallion. I didn't know what I was doing but somehow found myself on the shore."

"In the middle of a tiny thunderstorm," she said. The corner of his lip rose a fraction.

"And what was your plan after that?" Darvyn asked.

"Get help. Find a place where I could get word to Elsira. Call the ambassador. We weren't sure if the Yalyish police would help, but Papa said the Queen would provide."

Tai frowned. "Your sister?"

"What?" The young man's brow furrowed.

Lizvette shook her head. "He means the Queen Who Sleeps. He doesn't know."

"Know what?" Roshon asked, looking back and forth between the two of them.

"The Queen Who Sleeps is awake," Lizvette said. "Your sister awakened Her. And then she married the Prince Regent, and now they're king and queen."

Roshon's eyebrows slowly rose until they nearly hit his hairline.

"And your aunt—your mother's sister, Vanesse—she came on this mission with us, too, though she doesn't know you're here," Tai said.

Roshon paled so much that Lizvette thought he might pass out.

"Much has happened, and we'll tell you all of it, but we need to know more about the Physicks' castle in order to save the others. Everything you can remember," Darvyn said.

It was a moment before Roshon could speak. "They call it the Academie. It's some sort of school for them."

Roshon explained what he knew, along with things that Kyara had observed. Rescuing them would be quite a thorny proposition. Part of Lizvette wished that they'd been able to accept Zivel's offer of assistance. But the Goddess's order of secrecy about this mission extended to the Foreign Service agents, as well, and all they were able to tell Zivel was that Lizvette and the others had gone to Dahlinea on official business.

She stood as the conversation turned to the various options for entering the Academie. Tai's voice rumbled whenever he spoke, causing an odd sensation in her chest. She wished she could escape the small room. Even now, she felt his eyes on her. Probably because she was the only woman around. Had there been a pretty brunette present, he'd likely be looking at her.

She sighed, feeling petty for her jealousy. There were much more important things to think about now than the meaning of a kiss neither one of them had even acknowledged. She could only imagine that he regretted it. But did she? She should—it had definitely been a mistake. A simple moment of weakness and nothing more.

Lizvette looked around the room. She noticed a crumpled copy of this morning's newspaper on the chipped night table beside her. She dared not think who had used this room before them. Emblazoned on the front page was a story about the Yaly Classic. With all that had happened, she had nearly forgotten.

CATTLEMAN CARRIES THE DAY

Cardenna Cattleman rose to the expectations of many to take first place in the Yaly Classic Air Race.

After falling behind in lap three in a particularly vicious obstacle course that took out sixteen other competitors, Cattleman regained her pace in lap six. But in the eighth and final lap, Elsiran racer Clovette Liddelot swooped in to take the lead.

The battling Caxton M18 airships duked it out, with Cattleman winning in a photo finish.

The paper dropped from her fingertips and fell to the floor. Someone called her name, but it sounded far away. Clove had nearly won. Lizvette couldn't help but wonder if there had been some other reason for the woman's loss.

Tai was there suddenly, peering at her, worry creasing his face.

"I'm all right," she said, straightening her spine. "Look." She pointed to the paper.

He crouched to grab it and scanned the article. "This is good, right? If she'd won, that would have spelled a lot of trouble for your father and he would likely have retaliated in some way."

"I know, it's just . . . did she really lose? And just barely like that? Do you think something happened at the last minute?"

Tai frowned, looking back down at the paper. "The article doesn't mention anything about her being harmed in any way. Do you want to call and check in on her?"

A grateful smile spread across Lizvette's face before she could stop it. She was still mad at Tai, but it was of little importance.

It turned out that the telephone, like the bathroom, was in the hall, encased in a booth for privacy. Tai trailed behind her as she left the room to make the call. Though his presence irked her, she was grateful for it when a seedy character with a soot-covered face passed by silently. At the telephone, she wiped down the handset with her handkerchief before pressing it to her ear.

The operator connected her with the hotel in Melbain where she was directed to their suite. The other line was open, but silence crackled through the receiver.

"Hello?" she said, thinking that she heard someone breathing.

"Lizvette, is that you?"

Her breath hitched. The familiar male voice made her skin crawl.

Her jaw moved but no sound came out for a moment. "F-Father?"

"Where are you? You've made things very inconvenient for me, young lady."

She swallowed, widening her eyes at Tai, whose glower was intense. She pulled back the handset a bit, so he could hear. "I-I was able to find other accommodations. What are you doing in Clove and Vanesse's hotel room?"

"Never mind that. You couldn't even manage to accomplish a simple task. Fortunately, the Liddelot woman didn't win the race—no thanks to you. My associates were not impressed by that little display of incompetence, however. Not in the least." His voice was harsh as ever, but Lizvette felt a spark of hope. He was angry but didn't seem to suspect her of being anything more or less than ineffectual. After all, he would have no way of knowing she'd removed the amalgam necklace and shared his plan with anyone.

"I'm sorry, Father. I wasn't able to place that . . . contraption as you'd wanted. I-I lost it and had no way to get back in contact with you. Perhaps the task was too much for me." She held her breath.

On her side, the only sound was the cracking of Tai's knuckles as he flexed his fists, looking for all the world like he wanted her father's neck squeezed between them.

Father grunted. "I suspected as much. Fortunately, the outcome of the race was still profitable. I've managed to devise one more chance for you. But after this, you truly will be on your own, child. I cannot carry you along if you continue to be maladroit. And why did you not tell me the Sisterhood woman was Jasminda's aunt?"

"I . . ." Her head whirled. What did that have to do with anything?

"It doesn't matter. That information came my way and is very valuable indeed. Now she and that pilot are accompanied by the Foreign Service at all times, and I don't have the resources to hire additional manpower, so I'll need you to draw the Sister out."

"Draw her out? For what?"

He let out an exasperated sigh. "So we can ransom her, of course. How much do you think Jack and Jasminda would pay for the safe return of one of the queen's remaining kin?"

For a moment, she was weightless with shock. "You want to kidnap Vanesse?"

"Keep up, my dear."

Lizvette looked over to find Tai's expression lit with an inner fire. She closed her eyes to focus on her father's words as he relayed his plan. This was the chance she'd thought she'd lost, but it would mean using Vanesse as bait. However, if Father could lead them to the temple bombers, and knew of any future attacks, the queen's aunt would certainly want to do her part to bring the perpetrators to justice and stop another tragedy.

Lizvette mumbled responses when necessary, still reeling. Finally, Father named the time and place where she was expected to bring Vanesse later that evening.

"Tonight?" Lizvette gasped.

"We must do it quickly," he replied. "There's no time to waste."

"But it's so soon. You need the money that badly?"

"I have people depending on me."

A pang hit her heart. There was a time when she'd depended on him, too, but not for a long while.

Dazed, Lizvette agreed to the details of the plan. Her father hung up without saying good-bye. Beside her, Tai was rigid.

"I'll take the next flight back to Melbain and coordinate with Zivel," she said, her eyes staring forward but unseeing. "It will all be fine. We should go and tell the others."

Tai remained silent as they trudged back to the hotel room and informed Darvyn and Roshon of the new development.

"I don't know that I'd be of much help here anyway," Lizvette said. Next to her, Tai snorted; she raised an eyebrow at him. What was *his* problem?

"You are very valuable, Lizvette," Darvyn replied. "But I agree. It makes the most sense for you to go and wrap things up with your father. Do you think it will be safe for you to go alone?"

She gave a humorless chuckle. "I don't believe Father will harm me now, if that's what you're worried about. It seems he needs me."

Tai and Darvyn shared a glance. They worked well together, able to communicate in some silent man language she would likely never crack. After a moment, Tai spoke up. "That necklace certainly caused you harm. I'm not sure we know the full extent of what your father is capable of, Vette." His words annoyed her, but the nickname made her heart stutter. Only Jack had ever called her that.

She should tell him not to be so familiar. But the memory of how familiar they had been the other night overcame her, causing her cheeks to warm. She quickly banished the thoughts and focused on the task at hand.

"The rescue mission here is of the utmost importance," she said, "but I cannot simply allow Father to slip through our hands. Especially when he may know the plans of future attacks."

Tai's expression was grave. "We will get Nirall, hold him accountable, and find out what else he knows."

"Well, we can't all be in two places at once," she said. "I will go and meet him. The rest of you can stay here and rescue the queen's family and Kyara." She sat back a bit too firmly in the hard chair and held in a wince. Neither man could argue with her logic—it was sound.

"You can't go back to Melbain alone," Tai said, lowering himself onto the couch.

"Zivel will be there. And his men."

Tai shook his head. "Not good enough. I'm going with you."

"But . . ." She frowned. Tai had only come on this mission to rescue the new queen's family. Her father was of little concern to him. Apparently, he thought her too incompetent to bring Father in, as earlier he'd acted as though she were unfit to run from danger on her own two legs. Never mind that he'd claimed to approve of her plan with the factory. She had no desire to have him along out of some misplaced sense of duty, or worse, pity.

Darvyn shifted forward. "Roshon and I can free the prisoners, especially since we know we have an ally inside the Academie—perhaps more than one. You two go back for Nirall. You're right, Lizvette: your mission is no less important than ours."

She was grateful for Darvyn's cool head when her own emotions were running so erratically.

"Then it's settled," Tai said, leaning back and crossing his arms. He didn't look very pleased about things, but neither was Lizvette.

She copied his movements, crossing her arms. The last thing she needed was an angry, intemperate Raunian by her side wishing he were somewhere else.

"Fine, then," she said, petulantly. "We'll both go."

CHAPTER THIRTY

The battlefield was bathed in the glow of the setting sun. Ayal rushed to stand between the two forces, willing them to stop.

Man-With-Voice-Like-Nightbirds sang a battle cry. Ayal raised her lion's paws and breathed fire into the air. The song cut off, both sides gaping in shock.

—THE AYALYA

Jasminda stormed from the assembly hall, fire nipping at her heels. She worked to cool her raging emotions. Royal Guardsmen lined the corridor, faces impassive but noticing every detail. All she wanted was a few moments to herself.

A door marked *Library* caught her attention.

"Is this room occupied?" she asked the Guardsman standing next to it.

"No, Your Majesty."

She nodded and ducked inside. It wasn't a proper library, just a small office lined with bookshelves, most of them only half-full, but the familiar surroundings grounded her.

Only a minute later, the door opened, revealing her husband. He was formally dressed, military medals lined across his chest. As much as she loved seeing him in his uniform, her feelings were just a little too hot. She turned to face a shelf.

"I don't want to talk to you right now."

His footsteps approached slowly. "I know you're angry."

She spun around so fast, hair hit her cheek. "Angry?" She pointed back in the direction of the auditorium where the Elsiran Council's public town hall meeting had just adjourned. "Anger doesn't even begin to describe the utter disgust and complete fury I feel for those people."

The Council members—the same vile men who had voted unanimously to expel the Lagrimari refugees from the country just before the Mantle fell—were falling firmly on the side of dividing the country. And the Elsiran citizens in attendance were split on the issue.

Jasminda's heart hurt for the Lagrimari in the audience. She had personally translated much of the meeting so that they could understand. Repeating the hateful words voiced by the Elsirans made her stomach churn violently. Eventually, she'd had to stop, giving the duty over to Jack.

Her husband hung his head. "I did not expect so many to fall on the side of division."

"And yet you gave them this opportunity to gain support for their cause."

"You think we shouldn't have held the meeting?" he asked, incredulous. "This issue won't go away by ignoring it."

"No, but aren't we supposed to lead? Giving everyone who

believes their horrid thoughts have some validity a chance to speak isn't helpful. It legitimizes their views."

"Jasminda, part of leading is listening to offensive opinions. The people have a right to their beliefs."

"Even if those beliefs are outrageous?"

"Especially then. If we lead by stifling their ability to speak their minds, how are we different than the True Father?"

Jasminda dropped her head and crossed her arms, squeezing them. She didn't want to admit his point. Exasperation and dejection rolled through her. "Perhaps they're right. Who wants to live side by side with people who spew such filth?"

Gingerly, Jack reached out a hand to touch her shoulder. She didn't brush him away; she needed his comfort.

"In my heart," he said, "I don't believe most of the citizenry agrees with the division. We already know the people are being manipulated by the Reapers. The newspaper editorials have stirred up dissent. And given what Benn and Ella discovered, I think that if we cut the strings of the puppet master, some of this will die down."

Jasminda shook her head. "I'm not so certain."

A knock rattled the door. Jack crossed the space to open it, revealing two familiar Lagrimari faces: Rozyl and Turwig.

"How did you know we were in here?" Jack asked, eyes wide.

Rozyl thumbed over at Jasminda. "That one's emotions are a tornado. A Singer could feel them from the other side of the city."

Fighting for composure, Jasminda greeted the newcomers.

"*Uli,*" Turwig said, reaching for her hand and squeezing it kindly. He and Rozyl were among the first Lagrimari Jasminda had ever met, aside from her father. For a moment, she wondered what it would be like if Papa were here. Turwig had known him, though he'd been tight-lipped about it. The two didn't resemble one another, but Turwig's energy was warm and paternal. It helped her to rein in her feelings.

"What did *you* think of the meeting?" she asked.

The two Keepers shared a look. Rozyl raised a shoulder. "Went about as well as could be expected. I was hoping for a little more action, truth be told." She cracked her knuckles.

"Physical violence will never solve this. Centuries of war hasn't, and the peace may just need a little push in the right direction," Turwig advised.

"You have an idea?" Jack said, settling next to Jasminda.

"Yes. Something that would do double duty, provide the Lagrimari with much-needed justice and perhaps even soften the Elsirans toward us." The elder's eyes sparkled.

"What is it?" Jasminda asked.

"As we understand it, by Elsiran law, a sitting monarch may delegate a special tribunal for crimes committed during wartime."

"Yes," Jack said, nodding.

"Since the Council has not yet authorized trials for the members of the True Father's regime, the leadership of the Keepers of the Promise would like to request such a tribunal. We have already collected a massive amount of evidence against those already in custody and are ready to enact swift justice."

"How swift?" Jack asked, brow furrowing.

"Immediate."

The word sent a chill down Jasminda's spine. "Trials here can take weeks."

"We don't need weeks," Rozyl said. "We've endured years of treachery, and have gathered no less than one hundred victim affidavits for each of the accused, as well as those who have yet to be apprehended. The crimes are well documented and detailed."

"And what of a defense?" Jack asked.

Rozyl shrugged, but Turwig spoke up. "That is the Elsiran way, we understand. In the few cases where we've found witnesses willing to speak up for the accused, we've obtained affidavits for them, too. But there have not been many."

Jasminda thought through the implications of what they were proposing. "I know that you all want the Lagrimari to be responsible for judging the criminals, but the Keepers cannot be both the prosecution and the adjudicators—that doesn't sound like justice to me. However, if we appoint a tribunal made up of Elsirans *and* Lagrimari to review the evidence, I think that would be acceptable."

Jack nodded.

"We think that hearing what the Lagrimari have gone through under the True Father's rule would help the Elsirans view us in a different light," Turwig added. "Empathy can work wonders to soften the heart."

"It is a hopeful sentiment," Jasminda said, unconvinced.

"I agree such a tribunal would greatly help the Lagrimari face the past and move forward," Jack said. "And don't count our people out so quickly. There are plenty who support unification. Their voices just aren't screaming the loudest."

As much as she loved Jack, there were simply things he'd never understand. He'd never felt the sting of being called a *grol* witch, had never been shunned, ostracized, hated. His optimism was both endearing and naive.

"We'll need to find Lagrimari candidates to make up the judges," Jack said. "But the tribunal will be our top priority."

"Thank you, Your Majesties. This will help heal a great wound," Turwig said.

Jasminda felt Rozyl's scrutiny. Her shield was up, keeping out intrusions from other Singers, but something in the other woman's perceptive gaze let Jasminda know she couldn't hide completely. She gave a weak smile, which was met with a snort.

"This will help, Jasminda," Rozyl leaned in to whisper before taking her leave. "It must."

Lizvette's hopes of returning to Melbain and telling Vanesse all about the plan were dashed as soon as she and Tai arrived at the hotel suite. As they entered, a bellboy was leaving, bearing the afternoon tea service. Lizvette startled when she recognized him as the same teen who had delivered the amalgamation to her at the air station. His blank expression betrayed nothing, but she held her breath until he'd passed. She entered, looking around the room uneasily.

Could the boy have planted some kind of listening device in the suite? One of Zivel's men was posted out in the hallway, but she was suddenly too apprehensive to speak of the new developments aloud.

Tai noticed her distress and raised his brows in question. She shook her head slightly and pointed to her ear, hoping he would understand her meaning. His gaze darted around the suite, and she thought he did, for he remained quiet.

"That was a quick jaunt. Where's Darvyn?" Clove asked from the couch. She did a double take when she saw Tai. "And what happened to your face?" He was still wearing the makeup that hid his tattoos and his black wig. With a grimace, he pulled the thing from his head and flung it across the room.

Clove snorted and returned to flipping through a stack of cards, which Lizvette quickly discerned were congratulatory messages. Vanesse sat beside her, pen and paper in hand, likely making a list of the well-wishers so that thanks could be sent. That was what Lizvette would have done, at any rate.

"Darvyn found something to capture his attention," Tai said in a light voice. He plucked the pad from Vanesse's hand and scrawled a message on a new page:

Has Zivel checked for listening devices?

Both women froze. Vanesse looked warily at Clove, who shook her head.

Tai returned the paper and pen to Vanesse and shrugged. "I thought it best not to delve too much further into Darvyn's affairs. I'm sure we'll see him back here soon." He settled in the armchair, appearing relaxed, but Lizvette did not miss the guarded clench of his jaw.

She perched on the edge of the chair opposite him. "Were you all planning on going to tonight's gala? It's sure to be . . . elucidating."

The entire spectacle of the Yaly Classic Air Race was a week-long affair. The qualifying heats and actual race were only half of it. Following were days of celebrations and parties honoring all the participants. But that night's event was where Father had insisted she meet him, with Vanesse in tow.

Clove slowly looked from Tai to Lizvette, appearing to catch on that there was something more happening. She grabbed the pad from Vanesse and began scribbling furiously.

What's going on?

Lizvette took a deep breath before writing her response.

Father plans to kidnap Vanesse and ransom her. He needs my help. It is how we will catch him.

Clove must have been an incredibly fast reader for she tore the sheet off and crushed the paper in her fist almost as soon as it hit her hand. The diminutive woman's disposition changed rapidly as a storm cloud raged in her eyes. Vanesse plucked the paper from her hand and smoothed it out. She visibly paled as she read it.

Lizvette's gaze went to Tai, who watched the exchange intently.

Clove held out her hand expectantly, and Lizvette gave her back the pad.

YOU WANT HER TO PLAY ALONG???

When Lizvette nodded, the second page went the way of the first, disappearing into Clove's taut-knuckled fist.

Vanesse's expression was pinched, her eyes pained. "I don't know that I have anything to wear to a gala."

Clove stood and stalked over to the radiophonic. She clicked it on and chose a station playing bright, syncopated music—the kind favored in Yalyish dance halls.

"I have several gowns that would be appropriate," Lizvette said, raising her voice to be heard over the music.

Clove leaned over the radiophonic, facing away, tension evident in the hunch of her shoulders. Lizvette felt even worse than she had before. She vehemently wished her father hadn't brought anyone else into his scheme.

A brittle smile barely graced Vanesse's face. "Very well, then. It appears as though we're going."

Lizvette thought she saw Clove shudder. She expected Vanesse to question her more via written message, but the woman just stared at the congratulatory cards piled on the coffee table, her brow furrowed. Nervous energy clung to her like thin satin. Every so often, her gaze would dart around the room as if expecting someone to pop out from behind the dining table, and when the horns in the song swept into a crescendo, Vanesse jumped.

"Perhaps you'd like to look at my gowns," Lizvette offered a bit lamely. She could try to assuage the woman's fears by assuring her that Zivel's men would be enlisted to ensure her safety, but she suspected that would fall on deaf ears.

When Vanesse looked up, her eyes were a bit vacant. "Yes. I suspect it will take me quite a while to get ready for something as elegant as a gala." A life in the Sisterhood certainly left little opportunity to acquire clothing. Then Vanesse raised a hand absently to her scarred cheek, revising Lizvette's assumption of the Sister's worry.

She wanted to offer to do Vanesse's makeup, though little could be done to hide the burn marks. "Look through my closet, and choose anything you like."

Vanesse smiled gratefully and rose to head for the bedroom. Perhaps overpacking for this trip hadn't been a waste after all.

Tai stood. "Well, now that that's settled, I'll go make the arrangements." They had agreed on the airship back to Melbain that he would inform Zivel of the plan and assist with security.

Lizvette's ire at Tai had melted away on their journey, too. She didn't have the energy for it, and she was grateful he was there. Though tension hovered in the air, clashing with the buoyant melody of the music, his presence was oddly calming. She could only hope that Father fell easily into the trap, and she wondered if it was possible for her to be so lucky.

CHAPTER THIRTY-ONE

By the time darkness had fallen, the would-be enemies had laid down their weapons to listen to the seeker's words of peace. Surprise and wonder wove harmony into years of distrust. When Man-With-Voice-Like-Nightbirds began to sing a new song, Ayal's two legs remade themselves. Flesh and skin grew feathers and ten toes tipped themselves with talons.

—THE AYALYA

The taxi stopped in front of the Melbain City Children's Museum. Sergeant Kendos held the door open as Lizvette, Vanesse, and Clove climbed out into the warm evening. Vanesse had chosen to wear one of Lizvette's favorite gowns. It was peach silk with a hand-beaded bodice of crystals and sequins. The Sister seemed a bit uncomfortable with the plunging neckline, perhaps because it revealed more burn scars on her neck and chest. Lizvette had given her a cream shawl that she wore like armor, though it was a pity to cover the beautiful beadwork.

Clove looked smart in a fitted tuxedo that was quite flattering. Her short hair was styled in thick finger waves molded to her skull, something Lizvette's locks would never do. For herself, Lizvette chose a full-length gown that was sheer black over a pale-pink shell. She felt like she was walking into battle, regardless of the finery.

Captain Zivel and his men were around somewhere, hopefully being inconspicuous. Lizvette hadn't seen Tai since he left earlier that day and found herself wishing for him. His presence would give her a shot of much-needed confidence. Standing on the sidewalk amid the other arriving guests, she looked up at the building that had been one of her favorite places to visit during her childhood trips to Yaly. Tonight it gave her chills.

The museum's facade was whimsical, painted in bright orange, pink, and purple and constructed in an avant-garde architectural style. Big and blocky, the structure matched neither the steel-and-glass monstrosities of the skyscrapers nor the classic columns and pure white stone adorning the city's oldest buildings. Rather, it resembled giant wooden children's blocks stacked on top of one another with a few tossed slightly to the side. Very strange, but she had always loved it.

Inside were story booths, drawing stations, and places where you could construct and engineer buildings and bits of mech from an assortment of parts scattered across enormous tables. Contests and games were held, pitting the children against one another, or forcing them to work in teams to accomplish a goal.

Had Father selected this particular gala at this particular location because he remembered her fondness for this place? There were other parties going on tonight he could have chosen. That thought created the tiniest kernel of doubt within her. But she'd never known him to be nostalgic.

Vanesse appeared composed on the outside, if a bit rigid. In the taxi, which Kendos had thankfully swept for amalgamations, the Foreign Service agent had repeatedly reassured both Clove and Vanesse that no harm would come to any of them that night. Lizvette trusted the men. They had served in the army under Jack, and *he* trusted them, but she didn't put it past her father to engage in something horrible that no one had predicted.

Kendos led them to a line of attendees entering the museum. Inside, they passed the same interactive exhibits Lizvette had once loved. As she grew older, she understood that the staff monitored the games and puzzles closely. This "museum" was just an elaborate method for screening children with special talents or certain skills in order to help place them in careers that would benefit the commonwealth. Those excelling in activities that displayed a predilection for engineering or mechanics were filtered to specialized training programs. The rest of the children were funneled toward Administration careers or the factories, depending on their classes. Nothing was ever as it seemed.

At the center of the building was a great atrium where the upper levels of the museum were visible. As a child, she'd been afraid of heights, but she recalled bravely peeking over the edge on one of the upper levels to see the beauty of the museum spread out below.

Now the ledge of every level was decorated with strands of lights. Below, a five-piece band sat on a raised stage with space for dancing in front. Round tables dotted the space, cloaked in starched white tablecloths and place settings rivaling those of the Elsiran palace.

Laughter and gaiety surrounded them, but Lizvette and her friends were grim.

"Clove!" several voices shouted from nearby. Suddenly there was a flurry of people encircling them, offering hearty congratulations. They were jostled and bumped by at least two dozen partygoers in various states of sobriety. Lizvette stiffened her limbs against the onslaught and grabbed Vanesse's hand. A flashbulb popped, and she thought Vanesse might just jump out of her skin.

Something brushed against her bare arm, and Lizvette felt a tug on her hand. She pulled it back, glaring at the crowd, but couldn't tell which of the surrounding people had grabbed her. Pressed into her palm was a piece of paper—someone had just passed her a note.

A bit panicked, she caught the eye of Kendos and was glad when he jumped into action, cutting a swath through the revelers and leading her and Vanesse to a relatively quiet part of the atrium.

"What about Clove?" Vanesse asked, craning her neck for a look at the other woman.

"We've got someone assigned to her," Kendos said. "She'll be safe." Vanesse pursed her lips, not appearing entirely mollified.

While the others watched the celebrants, Lizvette took a step back and surreptitiously opened the slip of paper.

Change of plans. Meet in thirty minutes in the Ancient Beasts exhibit.

She checked the clock on the wall. Father had moved up the meeting time by a full thirty minutes. Certain she was being watched closely, she scrutinized everyone in her range of sight.

Were there listening devices near them now? Could she communicate the change to Kendos so he could tell Zivel and the others?

She schooled her features carefully so as not to betray any of the fear coursing through her body. If Father suspected something, he would slip the net for sure, and any hope of bringing him to justice would be gone. Lizvette breathed deeply, hoping to stop the shivers that racked her, as she noticed several men nearby watching her with unusual interest.

What in Sovereign's name was she going to do?

Tai stayed hidden in the shadows of the third floor of the museum, peering at the atrium below. He'd kept Lizvette in his sights since she'd entered, looking stunning in her formfitting gown. She played her part well, but he was able to recognize the subtle signs of her nervousness. Fidgeting with her dress. Touching her hair. Wringing her hands.

Vanesse was little better. She was skittish as a mouse with a cat on the loose. Her head darted around wildly, trying to take in the entire room at once. They sat at a table in a far corner, away from the worst of the chaos.

Kendos had not yet left their side. At first he'd stood, making it clear that he was guarding them. Though Nirall was expecting the guards, the sergeant needn't be so obvious. After a few words from Lizvette, Kendos sat down on Vanesse's other side. The man was vigilant, and Tai couldn't fault him for that. He and the other agents sprinkled throughout the room took their jobs and the safety of their charges seriously. Still, Tai had a bad feeling.

He located Clove, who was as she had been for the past thirty minutes—in the center of a group of fans that hung on her every word. To all appearances, she was having the time of her life, holding court for a collection of admirers. But her head turned often to the corner where Vanesse sat. Clove wore her mask of merriment well and hid the toll it surely was taking.

As Tai watched, Clove stopped midsentence before concealing her shock quickly and continuing. In the corner, Lizvette and Vanesse were on the move, heading toward the restroom. That was the plan, but they were early—very early—and the knot of uneasiness he'd been carrying loosened into a skein of dread.

Could Lizvette have misunderstood the timing? He wished the Elsirans used some sort of communications amalgam so they could talk to one another over distances, but Zivel had shot down the idea, looking affronted by the mere suggestion. Tai shook his head. Elsirans and their hatred of technology . . . He was no lover of the magical contraptions, but efficiency was efficiency, and right now they were off script with no way of knowing what was really happening.

The women bypassed the restroom as expected, but instead of veering left toward the outer door where Nirall had told Lizvette to meet, they went right, swiftly moving out of Tai's field of vision. Thankfully, he and Zivel's men had done reconnaissance on the building ahead of time. Three exhibit halls were on this side of the building, as well as a number of offices and storage rooms.

In the atrium, several men—dressed in tuxedos but with the stiff bearings of soldiers—peeled themselves away from the party. Surely the agents had noticed that something was amiss, but Tai left his post anyway and raced down the stairs, sticking to the shadows as he headed for the corner where Zivel had indicated he'd be lying in wait for Nirall. He found the captain at the side door leading to the loading docks, whispering furiously to another man in his command.

"What's happening?" Tai asked. "Something's wrong."

Zivel's eyes narrowed. "They slipped into the side hall and we lost them. I'm not sure Miss Nirall has been entirely truthful with us."

A tic flickered in Tai's jaw. "We don't know what's happened or what her Father has set up. If she went off book, there must be a reason." He couldn't imagine that she would betray Vanesse and fall victim to her father's manipulations again. It just wasn't possible.

Zivel didn't seem convinced. "We're searching all the rooms on that side, but it will take some time."

"I'll help," Tai said through clenched teeth. "If we assume Nirall changed the plan at some point, then he must have found another way out since your men are guarding all the exits."

"There are no other ways," Zivel said. "We reconned this building."

"I know, but we must have missed something." Tai turned, eager to begin the search.

Locked doors were no barrier to him. One of Zivel's men looked flummoxed as Tai easily picked the lock to an office. The room had no window and was dark as pitch. He listened for any sound before closing the door and moving to the next one.

They checked one windowless room after another until a door snicked open to reveal a space lit by the moon shining in through a skylight above. The soft moonglow lent a dreamlike quality to the large, bulky objects cloaked in shadow spaced across the floor. Could the skylight be how Nirall planned to escape? It wasn't likely that a man of his age would be able to shimmy up any kind of rope and exit that way—the exhibit hall was three stories tall—much less with a victim in tow. He must have some other plan.

Muffled voices reached him from nearby. Tai recognized Lizvette. Her tone was low and urgent. He scanned the room and noted a door in the corner that was open a crack. A pale-blue glow, just a shade darker than the moonlight, streamed out.

He motioned to the man behind him, who disappeared back

into the hall to get reinforcements. Tai moved cautiously toward the door.

"Who else are you working with?" Lizvette asked.

"The messenger boy has been useful, but I could ill afford anyone else. But now, the entire Elsiran treasury will be at our disposal."

Tai's skin crawled at Nirall's smug tone. He strained to hear more and made out a soft shuffling sound.

"She's fine, she's fine. No need to hover. It's just a simple anesthetic. She'll wake in an hour no worse for wear."

"What did you use on her? Another gift from the Physicks?" Though Lizvette's tone was conversational, Tai didn't miss the tightness she was trying to hide.

"No, this is very nonmagical. A simple spray, easily obtained."

"And how do you and I get her out of here past hundreds of people?"

Tai looked behind him to see if Zivel's men had arrived. But when Lizvette gasped, he slid forward, ready to throw open the door. He withdrew the knife he kept sheathed at his back, holding it at the ready.

"What is that?" Lizvette asked.

"I don't know its name, but Hewett Ladell assured me it would serve my purposes nicely."

"For what?"

"Patience, child."

Lizvette stayed quiet for a moment while a series of clicks sounded. Tai frowned. What was Nirall doing? He wished he could see inside the room.

"Is Hewett Ladell a Physick?" Lizvette prodded.

"No. But he deals with a rogue Physick mercenary called Absalom who can get his hands on just about anything for a price.

I've never met the man myself, but I've seen his products and they've always been reliable."

Tai tightened his grip on his blade. Absalom was the same Physick they'd faced at the Dominionist meeting who had injured Darvyn. Tai would love a chance to get back at him.

"Ladell did warn me that amalgamations apparently don't work on Raunians. Absalom mentioned it the last time they met for some reason." Nirall's voice was light, but Tai hung on every word. He was immune from amalgam magic?

"Whatever happened to that barbarian you were with when you arrived, anyway?" Nirall asked.

"I-I'm not quite sure. I expect he went off to loot something or other." Tai grinned at her words. He was glad he'd maintained the disguise covering his hair and tattoos. If Nirall had people watching them, they wouldn't have marked him as a foreigner. "I wonder why the magic wouldn't work on Raunians, though."

Nirall sighed. "The Physick told Ladell some foolishness about magical fish canceling out the enchantment."

Magical fish? Could he mean the selakki? His people used virtually every part of the enormous sea creatures in some way. The deck of the *Hekili* was covered in selakki skin, as it absorbed the sun's energy to power the engine, and its bones were used for the frames of ships in general. Aside from the legends, they weren't known to have any magic.

But an immunity to amalgam magic would explain why he'd been able to remove Lizvette's necklace and hadn't been affected when Darvyn had been injured by the Physick weapon. He wondered idly if the Goddess Awoken had known. Was that why She'd really included him on this mission? She *had* said it would be helpful to have a Raunian along. He filed the question away for later.

Lizvette seemed to be stalling for time, which he was glad for as backup had still not arrived. Tai had no problem taking on an old man alone, but the Elsirans wanted to arrest Nirall, not kill him. If the man did anything to harm Lizvette, Tai couldn't promise to leave him in any state to face a trial. Where was Zivel?

Lizvette spoke up again. "What does it do? And how did you afford it? I thought—"

"Shut up! I can barely think with you nattering on." Nirall exhaled testily.

Tai's patience reached its end. He crept forward to peek through the crack in the door. It was a small closet, no more than eight paces across, lined with crates and shelves. A globe of blue light illuminated the space. Perhaps an amalgam of some sort. Lizvette stood on one side, her back against a metal shelf with Vanesse unconscious at her feet. Nirall stood closer to the door.

When Tai caught sight of the device Nirall clutched, his breath left him. Innocuous looking, it could be mistaken for a pocket watch. In fact, the last time Tai had seen such a thing, that's exactly what he'd thought it was—a broken one at least. Its open, gold-plated face was a mass of winding gears. It clicked softly, and Tai's panic mushroomed.

If this did what he thought it did, when the clicking stopped, it would trigger an explosion and bring the room down around them. The Physick who'd boarded his ship searching for Dansig ol-Sarifor and the death stone had carried such an amalgam. It must be a magical transporter. Roshon had said that when the Physicks had taken them, he'd felt the heat of the explosion, but it never touched them as they were already away, somehow being taken across thousands of kilometers to Yaly.

Tai's gaze shot to Lizvette, who saw him. Her only reaction was a shimmer of relief in her eyes. Nirall stood between them, reaching for his daughter. Tai jerked the door open and jumped forward, tackling the man before he could touch her. They toppled into the side of a metal shelf, dislodging several small wooden crates, which crashed onto Tai's back.

He ignored the pain. The clicking of the watch had grown louder. "Run!" he screamed at Lizvette, but he didn't dare look up to see if she'd complied.

Nirall's hand, bearing the device, was lodged between the two men's bodies. The clicking stopped, and Tai squeezed his eyes shut and hunched down. Hopefully he could absorb much of the blast and save Lizvette and Vanesse.

Acrid smoke filled his nostrils. He waited, but no explosion came.

Unless it had already happened and he was dead.

Someone was calling his name, and a firm grip held his shoulders. The hands pulled him aside, revealing Nirall beneath him, whimpering like a child.

Tai looked up into the face of Jord Zivel, which was immediately replaced by that of Lizvette. Her eyes were wet and astonished. He looked down to the front of his shirt and found it merely singed. Patting his chest and abdomen to be sure he was whole, he smiled nervously.

"Must have been a dud?" he whispered. Or his immunity to the magic made it one.

Lizvette crouched before him, pulling his hands into her own, but whatever she was going to say was lost by the shouting from Nirall.

"Unhand me! Who do you think you are?" he spat as Kendos and another man slapped handcuffs on his wrists. Disheveled appearance notwithstanding, Nirall knew how to turn on his aristocratic manner like a tap.

Zivel stepped forward with an official air. "I'm Captain Jord Zivel, Elsiran Foreign Service. Meeqal Nirall, you are under arrest for conspiracy to murder Prince Alariq Alliaseen, for crimes against the Elsiran people, and high treason."

Nirall sputtered. His venomous gaze shot to Lizvette. "You would betray me?" His face contorted into a sneer. "My own flesh and blood!"

"You betrayed me first, Father."

"Idiot girl, have you no thought of your homeland? No sense of honor? You're as useless and stupid as I always thought."

Lizvette winced, dropping her head. Tai refused to hear any more. He stood and rounded on Nirall. "You will never speak to her that way again, or so help me . . ." The older man shrank back into Kendos, who held his arm.

Lizvette reached for Tai. He dragged her to his side, crushing her against his body. His breathing was shallow as a haze of rage clouded his vision. "Your daughter is one of the most intelligent, cunning, and capable women I've ever encountered. It's a miracle that she even shares any of your blood. I don't know what manner of idiocy you're afflicted with, but if you cannot see what an amazing creature she is, then I don't know how you've managed this far in the world."

Nirall's jaw hung open, but Lizvette's arm squeezed tighter around Tai's waist.

Zivel and Kendos jostled Nirall forward, pulling him from the storage closet into the main exhibit hall. Another man carried Vanesse's limp form.

"Wait," Lizvette said as the agents dragged Nirall toward the door. She pulled away from Tai and stepped up to her father warily. Then she wrapped her arms around his neck in a hug he could not return.

Tai moved closer to hear the words she whispered in her father's ear.

"When you're in your cell, think of me, the daughter who was good for nothing except marrying a prince and bearing an heir. Nothing more than another piece on the board to manipulate. Then remember why you are in prison in the first place. For the rest of your short life, I will love you as my father and hate you as the man who tried to destroy me and our country."

The look on Nirall's face was nothing short of murderous. The agents hustled him away, followed by the man bearing the unconscious Vanesse. Tai and Lizvette stood alone in the darkened exhibit.

"Lizvette?" He reached for her, but she shrank away.

"Please don't." She blinked rapidly, as if holding back tears.

Pain speared him at the rejection, and he stared at her as she slowly brought herself back under control. Her head lifted, her shoulders straightened, and her breathing deepened. Was she retreating? He desperately didn't want that to happen, but what could he do?

The mission was over. Very soon they would part. Perhaps she was girding herself for that now. All he knew was that he wasn't ready to let her go.

He could only guess at the path of her thoughts as she visibly refitted her emotional armor. But when she spoke, her voice was shaky. "Did you mean what you said to him, or were you merely trying to push Father's buttons?"

He blinked and shook his head. "What do you mean?"

She cleared her throat, averting her gaze. "When you said those things about me. That I was intelligent . . . and capable."

This time when he reached for her, he would not let her retreat. "Yes, I meant every word." His hands untangled her tightly gripped fingers. He slipped his palm under hers, enveloping her smaller hand in his. "How could you doubt that?"

Maddeningly, she wouldn't meet his gaze. "I thought you disliked me."

"Disliked you? I don't believe that I have ever liked anyone more."

Finally, she lifted her head. Her expression was still guarded. "You like me? Truly?"

"Yes, duchess." The nickname he'd once meant as a barb was now a term of endearment.

Her eyes narrowed. "More than Brigit?"

Tai schooled his features so they wouldn't show the joy he felt at her jealousy. He brought his fingertips to her chin to hold her gaze in place. "Since the day I first saw you in the palace, surrounded by guards, I can't tell you what any other woman even looks like." He released her chin to stroke her cheek. "I got . . . overwhelmed. And I tried to pretend I was the man I used to be, but he doesn't exist. The only version of Tai Summerhawk presently drawing breath is the one whose heart belongs to you."

CHAPTER THIRTY-TWO

The people danced the dance for her, their feet pounding the ground. At first, she shied away, afraid the cheer was too close to praise. But soon, she rose on her new legs, slowly feeling their rhythm. She spun and danced and laughed and sang. And learned to love it all.

—THE AYALYA

Lizvette was speechless at Tai's admission. She still hadn't uttered a word by the time Kendos came looking for them.

"Are you ready to go, Miss Nirall?" the man asked. "Miss Liddelot is asking for you. She wants to know if you have any information on the sleeping agent used on Sister Vanesse."

Nodding mutely but unable to tear her eyes away from Tai, Lizvette followed Kendos from the exhibit hall.

A flurry of activity followed. The police arrived to coordinate with Zivel about Nirall's imprisonment until they could transport him back to Elsira. A doctor was called to see to Vanesse. Lizvette and Tai gave their initial statements to both the Foreign Service agents and the Melbain police.

Lizvette thought she'd spoken clearly, tried to be as detailed as possible, but her mind was still in that moonlit hall where Tai had confessed his true feelings. Her confusion and worry had been replaced by exhilaration, but she had no idea what to do with the new emotion.

Vanesse woke as Nirall had promised, with no lingering side effects, and they all left the clueless revelers at the gala behind and headed back to the hotel.

Their little suite now seemed ominous to Lizvette as soon as she walked in the door. Father had infiltrated it one too many times, and Sovereign only knew if there were other surprises hidden inside. The others must have thought so, too, because Clove called to the front desk to see if they could change rooms. Now that the race was over, the accommodations were more plentiful and she was able to book three rooms on another floor.

The other women left quickly, having far less to pack. They said their good nights and planned to meet up the next day for the trip to Elsira.

Half an hour later, when Lizvette emerged from her bedroom, traveling case in hand, the door to Tai's room was closed. She moved toward it, fear tightening her stomach, when the bellman arrived to take her bag to her new room. The older man smiled at her kindly and plucked her heavy case from her hand.

She looked at Tai's door longingly, then turned to follow the bellman. Her steps were heavy as she walked away. She had nearly been the princess of Elsira, and he was a smuggler and an ex-convict. True, they had imprisonment in common, though hers had been inside a majestic palace and his on some sort of floating penitentiary where he'd worked from sunrise to sunset. At least his conviction had been for something righteous. She wished she could say the same about her own.

And there was the rub. While an outsider may see the two of them and imagine a well-bred Elsiran to be outside the grasp of a brash Raunian, to Lizvette she was the one who was unworthy of him. Tai had proved his honor in protecting his sister, and he'd sacrificed much to come on this mission to save Jasminda's family. And when Lizvette had been in need, he hadn't thought twice about protecting her tonight.

Those things he had said about her had been flattering, and while he appeared to truly believe them, she could not.

"Miss?" the bellman said from the doorway.

She looked up, realizing she'd stopped walking and had been lost in thought for some time. Her cheeks heated. She scanned the room again to make sure she hadn't forgotten anything, and her gaze fell to Tai's door once more.

"Please drop my things off in my room for me. I'll be along in a few minutes."

"Certainly, miss," the man said, then left, closing the door behind him.

Lizvette's feet were leaden. She forced herself to walk the few paces to Tai's room but couldn't bring herself to knock. What would she say? As she stood there trying to come up with something, the door flew open.

Tai stood before her, looking as surprised as she felt. "I thought you'd left," he said. The wig and makeup were gone. The dark swirls and lines on his chin, cheek, and forehead drew her in. They were beautiful. She'd missed them when he'd covered up.

"I was leaving, but . . ." She clasped her hands and squeezed. "I couldn't."

For a moment, they stared at each other, her eyes drinking him in, maybe for the last time. Then his lips crashed down on hers. His hands encircled her waist, pulling her tight. She slipped her arms around his neck, pressing their bodies together, standing on her tiptoes to get even closer. A sigh escaped her as he prodded her mouth open farther, and then his tongue invaded, plundering, looting, owning her mouth.

Her legs left the ground. Tai lifted her until her back was pressed against the wall. She tried to wrap her legs around him, but her skirt was too long and fitted. It did not seem as if she was a burden, though, and she settled into his strong embrace, heat building within her. The need to touch more of him, to feel his skin on her fingertips, grew wildly. She drew her head back and sucked in a breath, then wiggled until he released her back to the floor.

Tension coiling within her, she eyed the bed behind him. Then, feeling decidedly wicked, she clutched the hem of his shirt and pulled it up, revealing smooth sun-kissed skin, along with more tattoos. The intersecting lines and curves started under his belly button on each side of his torso and disappeared underneath his trousers.

She traced the ink, wondering what it meant and how far it went. When she leaned down to kiss the path her finger had taken, Tai stopped her with a hand on her arm.

"Duchess, I—"

Lizvette straightened and pushed on his chest. "I think you should get on the bed."

Tai blinked. After a moment's pause, he walked backward until his legs hit the mattress. He still looked a little unsure, but at some point in the last few moments, Lizvette had made a decision. Or maybe she'd made it days ago, she couldn't be certain.

He sat, and she pulled his shirt off over his head. Her hands explored the planes of his chest and the crop of dark hair there. Tai closed his eyes as she explored his upper body. But then he stilled her motions with a hand on hers.

"Have you . . . done this before?" He winced at his own question.

She bit her lip and nodded, looking away. Raunians weren't known for being prudish. She hoped he wouldn't think poorly of her. "Once the wedding was near, it just didn't—"

"You don't have to explain," he said, taking her chin and forcing her to meet his gaze. "I only asked because I don't want to cause you pain."

Alariq had been kind, considerate, and gentle. And while Lizvette wasn't surprised that Tai was so thoughtful, it only made her want him more. Her gaze dropped to his lips, and her fingers curled, grasping the hair on his chest.

In the morning, they would head back to Elsira. She would drink the sylfimweed tea that prevented pregnancy and cherish the memory of this night. She didn't know what the future would hold, but the chance to feel like this, with someone who looked at her the way Tai did, was not to be wasted. She smiled at him before lowering her head to taste his skin.

Tai sucked in a breath as Lizvette's tongue followed the swirls of his *naikko,* the traditional tattoo that covered him from waist to midthigh. She seemed fascinated by it, and he wondered what she'd think in a few years when it would cover his legs and buttocks.

As her lips heated his skin, the tips of her nails skimmed over his nipple. He hissed. Her gaze narrowed, and she did it again, learning quickly to read his body's response. He grasped her wrist, stilling her hand, and pulled her arms around him, leaning her back on the bed and hovering over her.

Her eyes searched his. He met the stare, needing her to be sure this was what she wanted. He opened his mouth to ask, and she swiftly freed her hand to cover his lips.

"Don't second-guess me, Raunian. This is what I want. With you." Her eyes held a challenge, one he was determined to meet. She would not need to tell him again.

He pulled at the tiny buttons of the dress she'd changed into after the gala, not wanting to destroy the beautiful garment. But then he reasoned that she had other gowns in her overstuffed traveling case, and he would simply buy her a new one if she wanted. He tore the delicate silk down the middle, ducking a flying button.

Lizvette drew in a breath, then chuckled, squirming out of the skirt and bodice. Only a thin satin slip lay between them now. Tai slid his hand up her thigh, pushing up the smooth fabric to reveal her skin. Even there it was covered in freckles. He moved down her body to follow the path of the hem of her slip with his lips, starting at her knee and kissing his way up her thigh.

Her underwear was simple white cotton, which made him smile. Under all her airs and graces was something solid and real. He kissed a path up her hip to her stomach, breathing in her addictive scent. He looked up to find her staring at him with wide eyes, lips slightly parted, an expression of shock mixed with arousal coloring her cheeks. He grinned before lowering his mouth again and making her moan. The sound shot straight through him and he pushed the slip the rest of the way up and over her head.

She was bare now except for the panties. A blush crept up her skin, starting at her chest and going both up to her face and down farther and farther.

"No need for embarrassment, love. You are the most beautiful creature I've ever laid eyes on." She pursed her lips as if she didn't believe him, but it was true. He would show her if she wouldn't believe his words.

Patiently he demonstrated his reverence for her with his touch and his kiss. She urged him to move faster, but he batted her greedy hands away, enjoying taking his time.

"Tai," she growled, gripping his hair to the point of pain.

He chuckled, and in moments, his pants were shucked off and her panties were gone. He hovered over her, her eyes locking onto his. The connection sizzled straight to his heart. She leaned up and captured his mouth at the same moment he sank inside her.

There was no other place he wanted to be. The rhythm he set was slow. She arched her back as if trying to take in more of him, urging him to go faster, but he wanted to savor this for as long as he could. His control was fraying, but he did not want to be a wanton beast. She deserved so much more.

The sounds of pleasure she made gave him goose bumps. She scratched her nails down his back. He could tell the mark was deep and felt a trickle of blood seep from it as her eyes flashed intensely. Just like that, the barrier holding him back crumbled away.

Sweat dripped from his brow as he increased his pace. Lizvette was not a delicate flower that would break in two. She begged for more, tightening around him, making him feel as if he'd lost his mind.

They crashed into their orgasms like a ship battered against the rocks. Both gasped for air in the aftermath. Her hair had come completely out of its knot and lay messily across the pillow. He'd never seen her more disheveled and another pang of lust shot through him.

This is the real Lizvette, he thought as he stroked her face and they tried to catch their breath. He moved to lie at her side, while she threw her hand over her eyes. Her chest rose and fell, the motion hypnotizing him.

Elsirans may have no magic, but Lizvette had cast some sort of spell on him.

He held a hand to his chest where his heart beat wildly. With each pulse, he wished for the night to never end.

CHAPTER THIRTY-THREE

The morning found her on the journey, still humming tunes of joy. But clouds rolled in, thick and heavy, and the skies emptied themselves of rain. She sheltered under a fallen tree and burrowed into the soft earth. She dug until she was no longer alone, having discovered a serpent's nest. "Ressst awhile," the serpent said. And she was so tired, she did.

—THE AYALYA

Darvyn raised the hood of his crimson cloak to protect against the biting chill. A crisp wind blew across the lake, rippling the water around them. Beside him, Roshon scratched above his ear, near where the blond wig hit his scalp. Darvyn nudged the teen, who lowered his arm, looking away sulkily. They sat squeezed on a ferryboat crossing the small lake to the Physicks' island with a dozen others, all clad in robes of varying shades of red.

After Tai and Lizvette's departure the evening before, Darvyn and Roshon found a nearby tavern at which to dine. There they overheard talk that Physicks from all parts of the city and commonwealth were converging at the Academie in the morning.

"I recall this happening before, about a year ago," Roshon had said as they discussed how to use the news to their advantage. "They held the event to show off a new discovery to the other Physicks."

"What was the discovery they presented on before?" Darvyn asked, but Roshon didn't know.

The decision to sneak into the Academie along with the other visitors was easy. They'd purchased a new translator amalgamation for Roshon and managed to find the cloaks the mages wore at a secondhand store.

The ferry docked at the tiny island, and the passengers streamed forward. A guard clad in black blocked the gated entrance to the castle. He held up a thin, metal hoop—two handspans across—in front of each person he questioned.

"What is that?" Darvyn asked.

"It's the lie-detector amalgam I told you of," Roshon whispered. "They used it on us when we first got here."

Darvyn mulled over a way to trick the device, but all too soon they were near the front of the line. The guard questioned a tall man ahead of them whose well-used cloak had faded to mauve.

"Name?"

"Moises, Spellsayer Corps."

The guard waved the wand in front of the man, then peered at it closely. He checked his list and crossed off a name. Darvyn and Roshon were only two people away from being queried. Lying was out of the question, but the truth would be disastrous.

Unless, it wouldn't . . .

Something Oola had said to him the day of the temple bombing came to mind. *You cannot force a man to do what he would not. You may, however, impel him to prioritize certain actions.*

What if Darvyn told the truth and the guard believed him?

He took a deep breath and closed his eyes. He pictured Kyara's face—she was his priority. The only way to gain entry and save her and the others meant violating his firmly held beliefs. All men had the right to free will, but now his principles were at odds with his priorities. Doing the right thing had always been second nature to him, but before, the right thing had always been clear. The lines were now blurred, and he was forced to admit that he cared less about right and wrong than he did about seeing Kyara again alive.

He reached for Earthsong, stretching his Song to dip into the endless source of power. When he faced the guard, he shivered from the amount of energy he held at his command.

"Name?"

"Darvyn ol-Tahlyro and Roshon ol-Sarifor."

The guard frowned at the foreign names, but the lie detector apparently approved the truthful messages. He looked down at his list, mouth still downturned.

"I don't see you listed among the invited guests."

"Look again." Darvyn spoke quietly so no one else in line would hear him. Using his Song, he focused on the guard's energy and intentions. The man was a servant, not a Physick, and weariness hung over him. Those in service to the mages were conscripted for seven-year terms, often forced to leave their families in order to provide for them. Hopelessness saturated the guard's emotions, along with grief, pain, and loss. Darvyn prodded at the man's heavy burdens. Someone like him could be easily manipulated.

With a pang of remorse, Darvyn flooded the guard with a feeling of recognition at the two men before him. Added to it was the pride so lacking in his sentiments about his position. The fear embedded in the man by his superiors was easily bested by the notion that they would appreciate him for a job well done. That ensuring these two honored guests gained entry would bring the man the acclaim and gratitude he so desperately sought. Bring him closer to getting back to his family.

"Let us in," Darvyn said. He increased the onslaught of emotion, refocusing the guard's priorities until the man was exhilarated by the idea of letting them through, convinced it could only mean good things for his future. He stood up straighter. His eyes flashed with a boosted sense of self-worth. With a wave of his hand, he allowed Darvyn and Roshon to pass without further questioning.

Darvyn walked on, prolonging the guard's forced emotions until he and Roshon were well inside. Then he released the swell of power.

"What did you do?" Roshon whispered as they followed the mass of people.

Darvyn shook his head. "Something I shouldn't have. But it was necessary."

Roshon peered at him intently, then nodded, seeming to understand. The forward movement of the crowd paused, giving Darvyn the chance to look around. They stood amid a sea of red robes of every shade, with some clad in green or blue mixed in. A few wore white, while the black and gray of guards and other servants peppered the edges. All were being ushered into a vast auditorium.

The gleaming wood that covered every surface made Darvyn's head spin. He'd first seen forests in Elsira, but it must have taken the wood from a dozen forests to finish this building.

Roshon led the way to the middle of the seating area. They sat as the auditorium quickly filled. Darvyn's stomach turned sour when he caught sight of the gray, stone table at the front of the room. It was just to the right of center and positioned in front of a black curtain hanging from the ceiling, covering the back half of the main area. From this distance, he couldn't make out the carvings engraved on the table's border, but he guessed they were similar to the ones on the identical table in the Cantor's library in Lagrimar. A chill rippled through him. He knew exactly the sorts of things that took place on those tables and became anxious about what was in store for them.

It was several minutes before everyone was seated. A figure he recognized stood in the front of the auditorium, waiting for the audience's attention. Ydaris, former Royal Cantor of Lagrimar and second-in-command to the True Father, stood regally next to an older, white-haired man in a ruby cloak. It seemed laughable that the Lagrimari had thought Ydaris one of them, her green eyes were so bright and foreign looking. Now that he'd seen they were traits of the Summ, it was ridiculous for the Lagrimari not to have known. Then again, few had ever seen the Cantor and lived to tell of it, and no Lagrimari knew what anyone outside their land, save the Elsirans, even looked like.

Darvyn wondered if the True Father had known what she was. He must have. Had he simply not cared? He shook off those thoughts and looked around. His curiosity was piqued by the large gathering, but he still needed to be on the lookout for a way to find Kyara and the others.

Roshon whispered in Darvyn's ear in Lagrimari. "This must be the room Kyara told me about. The one where they bring her to be drained."

His gaze was drawn like a magnet to the stone table, and a new rip rent his heart. The white-haired Physick approached a podium to the left of the stone table. At the same time, the curtain hiding the back of the stage area drew to the side, flooding the room with light. Gasps sounded throughout the auditorium as the full room was revealed.

At first, Darvyn didn't know what he was looking at. The blinding shine stole his vision. He made out thin vertical columns of bluish-tinged light, evenly spaced. It was like a cage made of light built to house the sun, for a brilliant orange glow sat behind the bars.

"What is that?" Darvyn whispered. Roshon shook his head.

"Praise be to Saint Dahlia. In her name do we work," the old Physick intoned.

"By her grace do we prosper," the crowd responded as one.

"It is my honor as Grand Instructor to welcome you here on this most glorious day." He swept his arm toward the cage of light where the golden blaze trapped inside seemed to grow brighter. "Witness the Bright One, the Lifebringer, who has served Saint Dahlia for so long."

Then the Instructor brushed his arm to the other side where the outer door to the auditorium flew open. "And the Deathbringer who is responsible for our latest success." A hush fell across the crowd as four guards dragged in a shackled and bound Kyara.

Darvyn leaned forward in his seat to watch her be roughly chained to the stone table. Her face was as defiant as ever. His greedy gaze was locked to her form, tracing over the lines of her body again and again. She'd lost weight, her cheekbones were more prominent, and deep circles hung under her eyes. He cringed when the Instructor sliced her palms with a pale knife. The memory of a similar knife cutting into his own flesh was still fresh.

He had lain on a table such as this, bruised and bleeding, and it had not taken long for his will to flicker and nearly give out.

But Kyara was strong. Her eyes flashed even as her blood dripped to the ground, where small draining holes had been cut into the floorboards. The Instructor ambled back to the podium to address the crowd again.

"Saint Dahlia has truly been benevolent. She has finally sent us all we need to complete our most sacred goal. The barrier between the three worlds has kept us captive here. We cross to the other side only on a one-way trip, unable to bring back the secrets from the World After to elucidate our quest in this world. Well, that ends today."

Another red-robed figure, hood drawn up, walked up to the podium to stand beside the speaker. "We welcome Raal to the gathering."

Murmurs of welcome went up from the crowd. Darvyn's pulse quickened as the bald man removed his hood. His fists tightened involuntarily at the sight of his mother's murderer.

"Seeker Raal spent many years in far-flung places, searching for a stronger source of Nethersong. Over the years, he improved the extraction process substantially, discovering the right balance of serums to bring about a slow enough death to provide Nether to run the Great Machine and thus produce the quintessence blessed to us by Saint Dahlia. But the old way required hundreds of vessels. Men and women were continually infected and healed over and over again, coming near death and then being restored. It was slow and resource intensive. Inefficient."

Many around him shook their heads, mumbling their agreement. Darvyn fought to keep his body steady as rage built within him.

"A new way was needed. By Saint Dahlia's grace, we were able to make contact with a denizen of the World After over two years ago. He pointed us in the direction of a greater source of

Nethersong—the death stone. But as you know, we had no success. Seeker Effram searched the seas for it, but it remained hidden."

Roshon tensed beside him when another figure joined them up front, thin and blond. "He's the one who captured us," he whispered to Darvyn, a look of pure murder on his face.

"But then Seeker Raal and Seeker Ydaris located the Deathbringer," the Instructor continued. He waved toward Kyara, lying motionless on the table. "A true Nethersinger is so rare and valuable. And the Machine is revitalized, powered by her essence, pulling the energy of death from her at more impressive rates than all our previous sources.

"Production of amalgamations is up sixty percent due to the increased quantity of quintessence being created. And the Great Machine is now powerful enough that we can open a portal to the World After and gain the knowledge we seek. We will bring back those who have crossed over to that world and, at last, learn the secrets of eternal life."

Roshon shot Darvyn a glance full of skepticism and fear. Were they serious? Could their magic do such a thing?

"You all traveled here to bear witness to our greatest accomplishment! Let us wait no longer."

The Instructor moved to the center of the room where an enormous lever jutted up from the floor. He pushed until it shifted forty-five degrees in the opposite direction, accompanied by the sound of gears and cranks churning. A great grinding whir began from beneath the floor, and the wooden boards shook from the vibration.

Kyara cried out softly; however, no one but Darvyn seemed to notice. This machine was responsible for draining her Song and using it along with the mysterious source of Earthsong to create their amalgamations. He'd never heard of quintessence before today, but whatever it was seemed vital to the Physicks.

He reached for Earthsong and felt a strange presence to the energy. Here in this room, its texture and vigor were different. Dully, he could sense a siphoning of the power and something more that he couldn't quite define.

His gaze shot to the glowing brightness caged behind Kyara. It was difficult to make anything out, but he felt a draw toward the light.

What was it? Did it just move?

He blinked several times to try to clear his vision when the jangling of bells rang out overhead. The air below the ceiling rippled with a series of pulses and then began to shine. A brilliant golden mirror, like a pool of water reflecting the sky at dawn, opened. Though he could not see clearly into it, he got the sense of a flurry of motion on the other side.

The attention of the entire crowd was locked overhead. Roshon sucked in a breath when a tendril of black smoke slipped through the mirror and into the room. The undulating column of vapor churned, creeping through the air with jerky movements. It hovered for a few moments, then like a snake, darted toward Seeker Effram and disappeared inside him.

As one, the audience gasped. Effram jerked forward. His eyes clouded over and darkened until the whites were as black as if he'd been stricken with the plague. Then his whole face transformed, remolded itself into an entirely different image. Effram's features rearranged themselves before their eyes. His skin and hair darkened and his eyes cleared. Now a slightly younger man stood before them. He was Pressian in appearance, with a toasty complexion and a shaved head. A mark of indenturing was tattooed onto the man's scalp.

The crowd was rapt, motionless with wonder, until the possessed hands of Effram's new body reached out from the folds of his cloak to grasp hold of the man next to him—Raal. The former Effram began choking the other Physick, growling low like an animal.

The Instructor broke out of his shock and moved to stop the attack, but before he'd taken two steps, his feet shot out from under him. He flew backward and smashed into the wall with a *crack*. Several people in the front row jumped up, some heading for the exit and some to lend aid. They were all tossed back into their seats, though, all without Effram—or whoever he was now—ever lifting a finger.

Screams rang out as the crowd realized that this joyous, momentous event had turned deadly. Not-Effram released Raal, who collapsed to the ground in a lifeless heap. Darvyn felt for the man's energy, finding it gone. He was dead.

Chaos erupted as people stood and began trying to escape. Darvyn was on his feet, too, dragging Roshon behind him. "We have to get Kyara," he said, leaping down the stairs.

More columns of black smoke pierced the shimmering hole in the air. One veered into a female Physick in the front. Her eyes blackened, and she transformed into a pale woman, another mark of indenturing emblazoned on the back of her neck. The possessed woman lurched forward, grabbing the closest Physick and pulling him up by his hair with incredible strength.

Others in the crowd were being possessed by the smoke and transforming before attacking their neighbors—punching, biting, kicking, choking. All the possessed became altered into tattooed servants, back from the World After and, by all appearances, intent on revenge.

Low incantations rose all around the auditorium, and power crackled through the air as some Physicks began using their magic against the attackers. Flashes of light and balls of fire flew through the air, poorly targeted and hastily created.

"Close the portal!" someone shouted.

Still more spirits entered the Living World from the World After, seeking hosts. Behind the stone table, the bright glow inside the cage dimmed slightly—enough for Darvyn to see that the light appeared to be in the shape of a man.

Darvyn raced toward Kyara as the illuminated form drew nearer to the boundary of the cage.

Behind you, a hushed voice whispered via Earthsong inside Darvyn's head. He turned and ducked, pulling Roshon down, too, as a column of smoke barely missed their heads. The spirit veered and entered a Physick nearby.

Darvyn gulped and stumbled forward, finally reaching Kyara. She pulled and struggled against her bonds, bloodying her wrists.

"Kyara," he said. She froze, staring at him. "Hold still, I'll remove them."

But her face was a mask of horror. Did she not recognize him?

He had no key with which to release her, so he drew his Song to him and crumbled the metal of the locks on the leather bands until they fell off. She jumped from the table, running around to place the stone between them. She leaped to the lever in the ground, then yanked it hard. The whirring below them stopped, and the golden hole in the air above shrank until it disappeared.

All the errant spirits had found bodies and were now battling against the remaining Physicks in the room as guards entered to fight the possessed. They battered the spirit hosts with the black cudgels, releasing blasts of sound that cracked bones on impact.

"Kyara, we have to get out of here," Darvyn urged.

She whipped her head around, shock now tinged with fear. "Darvyn?" she asked, eyes wild.

“We need to find the others,” he said. He motioned to Roshon. When she looked at the young Elsiran, her brow descended in confusion.

“Get away from him, Roshon. He’s one of them,” she said.

Darvyn’s jaw dropped.

“One of who?” the teen asked.

“The dead . . . come back for revenge.” Her voice shook. She took another step back.

“No, Kyara,” Roshon pleaded. “I met him yesterday. He’s not a spirit. He’s here to help.”

Tears pooled in her eyes. She shook her head again, still backing away until she stepped into the path of a possessed Physick who had raced over with preternatural speed. The man grabbed her from behind and closed his hands around her neck.

Kyara’s eyes bugged. She clawed at the hands squeezing her, pushing and kicking as Darvyn and Roshon rushed to her aid.

Desperately, Darvyn grasped for his Song and vaulted forward, only to be thrown back by a bruising, invisible force. He was tossed across the floor and crashed into the cage of light. Its solid bars bit into his shoulder as his Song stuttered and began flowing out of him at an alarming rate. This cage must have possessed the same magic as the netting.

This time, though, he was able to pull away. Once he was no longer in contact with the bars, his Song stabilized, now much weaker. He struggled to his feet as the room spun. Roshon was down, as well, and Kyara still frantically fought her attacker. Her movements were furious. She had forced the possessed man backward until he was up against the cage of light. Then all of a sudden, Kyara was free and the man who’d been choking her lay slumped on the ground.

At the edge of the cage, the figure of light stood, dimmer than before. Darvyn could make out the shape of a man again but no features. Somehow, this being had stopped the possessed Physick.

Kyara gripped her neck, staring up through the bars of the cage. "Embrace the Light," she whispered, eyes wide. Chaos still held the room in its grip as the fighting continued behind them.

"What?" Darvyn asked, approaching cautiously. She shot him a glance that said she still didn't trust him and wasn't sure he was really alive. He held up his hands to appease her.

"Your dream?" Roshon guessed, rising unsteadily to his feet.

Darvyn took control of his Song and checked the teen for injuries, healing a few fractured ribs.

"How do we release you?" Kyara asked the man of light.

The cage is powered by electricity.

Darvyn heard the voice clearly in his head. He jogged around the side of the cage to find the electricity source. A thick cable emerged from a hole in the floor and ended in a receptacle on the far wall.

"Watch my back," he called to Roshon. Darvyn tugged at the cable, pulling it from the wall. The cage disappeared immediately, leaving only the bright, golden light in the shape of a man.

Kyara, Roshon, and Darvyn stared, the sound of fighting crashing around them in the background. In the blink of an eye, the man of light darted forward with blinding speed and took down each of the remaining possessed Physicks attacking the crowd. Each man or woman fell where they stood, unconscious, their bodies transforming back into their original selves. Whatever the man of light had done had banished the spirits.

He stood before them again where the cage had been, as if he'd never moved at all. His form was still too bright to see clearly, but he tilted his head to the side, regarding Darvyn.

"Who are you?" Darvyn asked.

"I am called Fenix. I thank you." He spoke aloud in Lagrimari.

"How long have you been trapped here?" Kyara whispered.

Fenix turned to face her and dimmed until his light was nearly extinguished. In his place was a man, maybe in his late thirties, like no one Darvyn had ever seen before. His skin was the color of burnished gold and his eyes were fire. He wore light like clothing. "I have been a prisoner here for generations."

"They stole your Song?" she asked.

He nodded sadly. "And trapped me in that form to do so." A sparkling golden ripple disturbed the air behind him. The portal was almost identical to the portal to the World After, only smaller and not breeched by angry spirits. He turned toward it. "I must go now."

"No!" Kyara cried. "In my dream, Mooriah said the Light is the only salvation. What did that mean? Did she mean you?"

Fenix's impossibly bright eyes swirled orange and red and gold. "You have spoken to Mooriah?" His voice held a tinge of longing. He looked back at the shimmering rift in the air with an expression that appeared torn.

Fenix shook his head slightly and backed away from them. "I must go back now to renew my strength. But I will return. I owe you a debt." He bowed formally and stepped toward the portal. "Tell Mooriah—" He shook his head, appearing unsure. "Tell her I vow to return."

"Wait! Where do you come from? What are you?" Kyara asked. Darvyn's mouth hadn't closed since Fenix had been freed. He was impressed at her ability to articulate her questions when confronted with something so unbelievable.

But Fenix was gone in the blink of an eye, and the portal disappeared as soon as he stepped through it.

They were alone in the auditorium—the only ones conscious,

at any rate. The possessed Physicks had done a lot of damage to the survivors of the onslaught. Darvyn considered healing them but thought better of it. There were others far more deserving of his power.

Kyara looked at him cautiously. He raised his hands in a defensive position. "If I were dead, I'd be attacking someone like all those others, right?"

Her brow furrowed. "You could be biding your time. I saw you die. I killed you."

"What? No." He took a step forward, longing for nothing more than to bring her into his arms, but her rigid body kept him at a distance. "Why do you think that?"

"Everyone died that day in Sayya. I killed them all!" she shrieked.

"No, you didn't. Myself, Farron, Zango, all of us on the street, we woke up that day to find everything smashed to pieces, but no one died. There were cuts and bruises, some broken bones, but nothing more serious."

She stared at him in shock for a moment, then crumpled in a heap, tears streaming down her face, desperate sobs wrenching themselves from her chest. Darvyn sank down beside her, holding her up and pulling her against his chest. Slowly her arms found their way around him.

"I'm flesh and blood. I'm real," he whispered into her hair. "I've been looking for you."

She looked up, hope shining in her eyes.

"Someone's coming," Roshon said from near the doorway, his voice low. Kyara took several stuttered breaths and then withdrew from Darvyn, still staring in awe as if she couldn't believe he was real. She stood on wobbly legs and turned toward the door. Darvyn placed himself in front of her protectively, but she settled a hand on his arm as if to remind him who she was and then moved next to him.

Racing footsteps drew closer, and they stood side by side to face the new threat.

CHAPTER THIRTY-FOUR

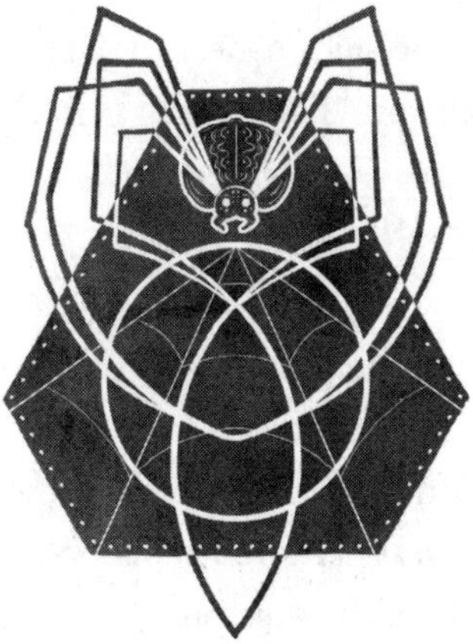

Ayal found the serpent staring back at her when she first opened her eyes. "Where does this tunnel lead?" she asked, noting the branching routes underground.

"Any course you take becomes your own. Make of it what you will."

—THE AYALYA

Kyara's heart beat rapidly, throbbing against her ribs in a stuttering rhythm. Her shoulder touched Darvyn's, and the contact made her buzz. Darvyn! Alive and next to her. She still couldn't bring herself to believe it. They were far from out of danger, but she couldn't stop glancing at him every few seconds, to assure herself that he really was there.

A figure appeared in the doorway. She, Darvyn, and Roshon tensed as one. But the girl standing before them held her hands out. Her violet eyes were wide with shock as she took in the carnage around them. This was the same girl who was related to Asenath, the one who'd provided the medallion from the graduation ceremony.

"Come quickly," she said, ushering them forward while peeking back into the hallway. "Everything is in chaos now, but they'll be sending more guards shortly."

Kyara moved to follow, but Darvyn grasped her arm. "You know her?"

"In a way," she answered. His brow furrowed, but he nodded, trusting her, and began to move.

"What's your name?" Kyara asked as the girl directed them down the empty hallway. Her red robe looked old and worn, unusual since it should be new as she was a recent graduate. She paused at an intersection, fingering the medallion around her neck, then darted to a door around the corner and led them in.

"We should be safe in here for a short while," she announced, then held her finger to her lips. Footsteps thundered past outside as what sounded like a squad of guards ran by.

Kyara turned to find they were in an empty classroom, much smaller than the auditorium. The stale smell indicated it hadn't been used in quite some time. A few broken, wooden desks lined the wall, but otherwise the space was empty.

The girl stood near the door, still listening. "Did Asenath send you?" Kyara asked.

With a smile, the girl fingered her medallion again. Then she uttered a phrase in a low, guttural tone. The language Kyara recognized—it was the tongue of blood magic—but the words the Physicks used for their spells were foreign to her.

Before her eyes, the girl, who appeared no older than Roshon, transformed. Her skin thinned and sagged, her form hunched over. Within seconds, the resemblance between her and Asenath had become clear. They were the same person.

Beside her, Darvyn stiffened, and Roshon cursed.

Kyara scrutinized the woman. "Which form is the true one?"

"Sadly, this one is." Asenath shook her head and settled into a creaky chair beneath a shaded window. "You will find that nearly all Physicks of any experience have true appearances vastly different from those we present to the world. Such is the price of amalgam magic."

Darvyn's voice shook. "I don't understand."

Asenath took a deep breath and rubbed a gnarled hand over her face. "Many years ago, after Saint Dahlia passed from this land, her followers—the physicians and healers she had taught and cared for—sought a way to continue without her guidance. They traveled across the world, studying other forms of magic. In the east, they learned blood spells. In the far north, necromancy. They came back and combined this knowledge with the magic of the saints and turned it into something the world had never seen before."

Her eyes took on a faraway look, and she leaned forward in her chair. "The Great Machine was built two hundred years ago when they had finally found a way to reliably combine Earthsong, Nethersong, and blood magic to create these." She pointed to her medallion. "The Machine produces a substance known as quintessence, or Dahlia's breath. This is the source of our magic. Each amalgamation made in the factories contains a small quantity of quintessence. The more an amalgam has, the longer it lasts. But these . . ." Her fingers stroked along the worn edges of her old medallion. "The quintessence in our medallions is connected to our own life *and* death energies."

"The blood," Kyara said, recalling the ceremony where the new Physicks were initiated.

Asenath nodded. "During the rites of passage, we gift our blood to the Machine. So the quintessence we use draws from our own natural stores of life and death. It pulls them both from us, shortening our lives and then extending them very unnaturally, and our bodies can't keep up. We live longer than most, but age much more quickly. After only a decade or two of using amalgam, this is the result." She motioned to her face.

"How old are you, Asenath?" Kyara asked softly.

"Forty-two," she said with a smile.

Kyara's eyes widened slightly. She had thought the woman perhaps thirty or forty years older than that.

"That is why they seek answers from the World After. The current board of directors believes the key to eternal life—and youth—can be found by communing with the spirits. They have interpreted Dahlia's prophecies to mean that there are spirits waiting to share their secrets with us, and then amalgam magic can undergo yet another revolution. One without such drastic side effects."

"Looks like the side effects of talking with the spirits were more than they expected," Darvyn said.

"Yes. I'd wager they never thought that all the people they'd killed would be waiting for revenge," Kyara said bitterly. A chill moved through her, but she pushed her dreams far from her mind. At least none of the spirits waiting on the other side of the portal had been there for her.

"Those spirits were all killed by the Physicks?" Roshon asked.

Asenath looked down. When her head rose again, her eyes were filled with tears. "Their deaths fed the Machine. Obtaining life magic was always much easier. At first they used Earthsingers, captured from within Lagrimar. Then they found the Bright One and trapped it. Nethersong was always far more difficult to obtain. True Nethersingers are exceedingly rare—we've never known more than two to be alive at the same time. The Physicks spent a long time experimenting and perfecting the right blend of diseases and cures to create a continuous supply from the population, but it was always difficult."

Roshon shuddered visibly.

"When a Physick is close to death, he can often commune with the spirits. It was one such spirit who first alerted us to the existence of the death stone—a powerful supply of magic created by trapping the Song of a Nethersinger. It was everything we had ever wished for." Asenath shook her head. "When that could not be retrieved and you were brought here"—her gaze met Kyara's—"there was much rejoicing."

Kyara shivered, pushing away all thoughts of her time on the stone table. "When did you break with them?"

"Not soon enough, I'm ashamed to say. Becoming a Physick is a great honor, especially for the daughter of servants. I went along with all they were doing for many years. Too many," she said with a wince.

Kyara felt a pang of anger and then sympathy. She certainly had no right to judge another when she was guilty of so much.

"Now that they've seen what comes through the portal to the World After, do you think they will keep trying?" Darvyn asked. He stood close to her. His presence was a comfort considering all she was learning.

Asenath took a deep breath. "I believe they will. A few angry, vengeful spirits cannot be allowed to stop progress. Especially when the Physicks have convinced themselves they are serving Saint Dahlia's will."

"And what of those, like you, who believe the prophecies were perverted? That what they're doing is a mistake? Is there any chance you all can talk some sense into the others?" Kyara asked.

"Perhaps after today there will be more wanting to join our numbers. But some will only ever be self-interested. No one wants to grow old so quickly, and it becomes more difficult to hold the glamours—the appearance of youth—as you age, especially with weaker medallions. The strongest are always reserved for those in charge."

"But I saw the initiates getting the new medallions," Kyara said. "The instructor said they would last the rest of their lives."

Asenath pursed her lips. "Pretty lies. They were switched out for weaker ones after the ceremony. I managed to hold on to the one I gave you, but barely."

Darvyn crossed his arms and began to pace. "If they continue to use the Machine, they will need a new source of Earthsong—and Nethersong, once we get Kyara out. If the Physicks managed to enter Lagrimar in the past, there is nothing to stop them from capturing more of my people." His fingers curled into fists. "I can't allow that to happen."

"What do you want to do?" Roshon asked.

Kyara met Darvyn's gaze and instinctively knew. "You want to destroy it."

He nodded. "The Machine, the building, the whole bloody island. It all needs to go."

Asenath looked up at him, but her surprise was quickly replaced with resignation. She nodded. "Saint Dahlia would not have wanted these travesties to continue."

"Is there another Machine somewhere?" he asked.

"No, this is the only one. It is the full source of the power of the Physicks. Its loss would be devastating."

"Devastating enough that it might prevent the war among the three worlds?" Kyara asked.

The old woman stroked her chin. "Perhaps."

"Then we have to get Dansig and Varten free and find a way to wipe it out," Kyara said.

Asenath struggled to her feet, and Roshon rushed over to aid her. She gripped her medallion again and with a few whispered words, changed back to her youthful form. Kyara flinched internally, wondering what that had cost her. How much life, how much of the function of her body? Her younger form moved more easily, but now that Kyara knew what to look for, she could see its slow speed and the pain Asenath tried to hide.

"I will show you the servants' passages to the prison floor. You should be able to get down there unnoticed and free the others. Getting out will be the hard part."

"We'll find a way," Kyara assured her. "What are you going to do?"

"I will gather whoever I can and destroy the Machine," she said. "You will have to move quickly. The entire Academie will still be in upheaval after the attack. Use that to your advantage."

She leaned toward the door and closed her eyes, listening. Kyara strained her ears and heard nothing, but Asenath stayed motionless for several moments before opening the door and leading them briskly down the hall to a staircase. In the middle of the steps, she paused and opened a hidden door.

"Before this was a school, the castle rulers never wanted servants to be seen in the main hallways," Asenath told them as she led them through a cramped and narrow passageway with low ceilings. "Some of the corridors have been blocked off and most aren't used any longer. They're easy to get lost in, so be careful."

Darvyn shuffled in front of Kyara and grabbed her hand. The corridor narrowed so that they had to walk sideways to fit through the tight space. Soon enough, they came to a fork in the path.

"That way leads to the prison floor," Asenath said, pointing. "It will let you out just before the guard station."

Kyara peered down the other path. "And you're headed down there?"

The now-young woman nodded grimly. "The Machine is that way."

They stood silently for a moment. Kyara was deeply afraid that she would not see Asenath again.

"Do not worry," Asenath said. "Dahlia will guide my steps."

Kyara nodded, her gratitude too much for words.

"Thank you," Darvyn said simply.

"You are most welcome. May we meet again before the end of things." With that, she shuffled away into the darkness.

CHAPTER THIRTY-FIVE

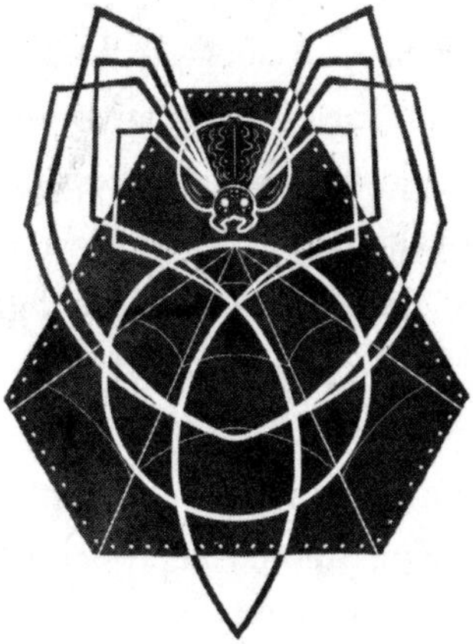

The seeker chose a passageway and crawled underground for quite some time. Her lion's paws shifted the dirt, but her bird's legs scrabbled for purchase. Frustrated, she looked up and decided to forge her own way out.

—THE AYALYA

Kyara followed the ball of light that Darvyn had conjured to illuminate the depths of the Academie. The temperature lowered steadily and the floor slanted downward, descending as a chill invaded the air. She wished she, too, could access her Song, but when she reached for it, she was met with the agonizing pain of the blood spell carved into her chest. Though she felt like it was almost in her grasp, she stopped trying, panting until the pain faded away.

Ydaris must have believed that Kyara could overcome the spell since she had made a point to reinforce it every few days. Perhaps with enough effort she could do so, but it would be exhausting and they had little time to waste. Still, traveling blind and powerless made her uneasy.

They stopped in front of a doorway. With her Song, she could have detected the presence of any guards on the other side. She never thought she would miss her abilities before.

"There are four of them," Darvyn announced as if reading her mind. His eyes were shadowed in the low light, making his face fearsome. Behind her, Roshon shifted and muttered under his breath.

"Hold on," Darvyn said. He inhaled deeply and let it out slowly. "All right. They're down." He pushed open the stubborn door. It complained on loud hinges. It likely hadn't been used in decades. Kyara tensed, hoping the noise wouldn't bring more guards. Then again, the chaos upstairs had probably pulled all reinforcements.

They walked out still hunched over from the tight space and stood upright in the gloom of the entry chamber to the prison cells. Through the doorway, the bodies of four men lay slumped over—two on the ground, two at the main desk.

Roshon rushed forward and scrambled for the key chain attached to one of the fallen men. After only a few tries, he located the proper key and wrenched open the door to the cell block. They ran inside and stopped short to see Dansig sitting on the bed and cradling Varten's head in his lap.

Kyara sucked in a breath. "Is he . . . ? Are we . . . ?"

Roshon stepped up and began trying the keys, searching for the correct one. He let out a curse after the third try and slapped the bars with his hand.

"Let me," Darvyn said, gently pushing the boy aside. He

brushed the lock with his fingers and the door snicked open, the scent of burning metal singeing the air.

Roshon charged inside and dropped to his knees before his brother. Varten's chest rose slowly, though he looked so near death that Kyara's heart ached. She stayed outside the cell, knowing there was nothing she could do to help.

Darvyn knelt next to Dansig. "You are a Singer?" he asked.

Dansig pointed to the red bracelets adorning his wrists that prevented him from accessing his Song. Darvyn nodded. "We need the key for the bracelets. Is it on the ring?"

Roshon flipped through the many keys in his hand. "They all look too big. The keyhole is so tiny."

"My son doesn't have much time left," Dansig said to Darvyn. "Can you heal him?"

Darvyn placed a hand on Varten's forehead and closed his eyes. Within moments, the teen's color returned. His freckles faded once his cheeks lost their pallor, and the dewy sheen on his skin disappeared. His labored breathing eased as his eyes blinked open.

Darvyn dropped his hand and propped himself up, nearly keeling over. Kyara rushed forward to assist him. "Are you all right?"

He nodded but allowed her to help him up.

"Darvyn?"

"I'm fine, I'm just . . ." He rubbed the back of his neck and seemed to pull himself together. "Let's get out of here." Kyara eyed him suspiciously. If one healing had him so weak, his Song must have been taxed more than he was letting on.

Dansig and Roshon propped up a still-unsteady Varten and helped him out of the cell. Kyara thought she heard a noise. She held up a hand to halt their progress, straining to listen. "Footsteps on the stairs. Can we make it back to the servants' passage?"

Darvyn squinted, tilting his head to the side, listening, and shook his head.

"I'll hold them off," she said. "You help the others."

She ran forward and picked up a cudgel from one of the downed guards, then raced to meet whoever was coming down the staircase. She wasn't certain how the weapons operated, but a tiny dial on the side displayed five levels. She set it to level three and hoped for the best.

Two guards thundered down the steps and paused in shock when they saw her. She raised her cudgel high, then swung it toward them. The club emitted a rumbling boom that struck the guards in their chests, forcing them back to crash against the stairs.

Kyara regarded the weapon with wide eyes. Her ears rang from the force of the sound. More steps came from above. She turned to see the twins and their father disappearing into the hidden door. Darvyn leaned against the wall, obviously exhausted, waiting for her.

"Get in," she said in as loud a whisper as she dared. His hard eyes glittered defiantly.

Two more pairs of boots descended the steps. She raised the cudgel again, swooping it forward, somewhat more prepared for the blast of sound it emitted this time. It felled the newest reinforcements. Only then did she race back and push Darvyn into the passageway, closing the door behind her.

They caught up to the others quickly. Varten was regaining his strength, yet moving through the narrow tunnel was slow going.

"What's the best way out?" Dansig asked.

"After what happened today, the medical wing is likely to be full—that's how I got out before," Roshon replied.

"There's an intersection up ahead," said Darvyn. "Turn left. It leads to a wing of the building where I sense few people."

They shuffled through, following Darvyn's directions until they reached a dead end. A very small door, only waist high, met them.

"Where does this lead?" Kyara asked.

"I'm not sure," he admitted. "There's someone in the hallway ahead—just one person. We'll have to take our chances."

Kyara gripped the cudgel tighter, toying with the idea of raising it to level four, then thinking better of it. She didn't know what kind of damage it would cause, and the guards were merely servants. There was no reason to hurt them more than necessary.

The others stepped aside so Kyara could exit first. Darvyn insisted on being right behind her. She ignored her annoyance at his stubbornness and opened the door.

These hinges were quiet, and the door opened easily. She crouched to get through the low doorway then sprang into the brightly lit hallway and stood, wielding the cudgel in front of her like a sword, ready to face whoever was in the hall. A bark of laughter escaped her lips when she saw her adversary.

Ydaris's eyes went wide. She froze, staring at Kyara and Darvyn beside her. The others crept out of the passageway to stand behind them, and the woman took a shaky step back.

Kyara raised her cudgel and swept it forward before a single word could escape Ydaris's lips. She could not allow her to utter a blood spell.

The woman shot backward and smashed into the wall. A moan rose from her. She was still conscious.

Kyara advanced. All it would take was a word from Ydaris and Kyara would be compelled to hurt her friends, or worse, use her power against them. She'd only just now gotten Darvyn back; she would not harm him again.

She raced toward her tormentor, intent on ending the woman's life once and for all and finally freeing herself from the spell. But footsteps followed her.

She turned to Darvyn angrily. "Get away from me. Don't you know what she could make me do with one word?"

Darvyn looked back and forth from the fallen Cantor to Kyara.

"I have to kill her," she said. "It will end the blood spell."

"Wait," Ydaris's soft voice said. Kyara stepped away from Darvyn, dropping the cudgel, afraid she'd be made to use it against him.

"Pick it up," Kyara breathed. Darvyn bent and grasped it. "Remember your promise to me." She held his eyes and saw the recognition there. In Lagrimar, she had made him swear to disable her—to do whatever was necessary—if she ever became a threat to him.

She turned to face Ydaris and her jaw dropped in horror and surprise. The woman's medallion must have come off when she'd crashed against the wall for instead of the regally imposing beauty Kyara was used to seeing, an ancient hag lay in her place. Her green eyes were dull, her skin worn and lined with advanced age, and her eyes sunken into her head. She looked like a corpse.

Ydaris reached for the medallion, which lay several paces away. Darvyn stalked over, picked it up, and held it over her.

"I will crush this if you do anything to command Kyara."

Blood spells like the one that bound Kyara were ancient magic requiring no amalgam or Earthsong. Ydaris's frightened eyes blinked rapidly. She looked to Kyara and nodded silently.

"Please don't kill me." The woman's voice was little more than a rasp.

"Why not?" Anger filled Kyara's voice. She couldn't believe

Ydaris had the nerve to beg for her life after all the lives she'd taken.

"I will release the spell. I vow it. Just . . . just return my medallion and let me live. I have information the Elsirans will want to hear."

Kyara snorted and crossed her arms. Bargaining now was cowardly. But Darvyn seemed interested. He crouched so he was closer to the woman's level and spoke low. "Release the spell now, and then we'll talk."

Ydaris swallowed. Much to Kyara's surprise, the woman began speaking in the language of blood magic. A long spell, with some familiar words—*binding, command, girl.*

The skin of Kyara's chest began to cool, and she pulled her ragged tunic away to find the wound healing before her eyes. It felt as though she'd been carrying an anvil around her neck for the past ten years and now it was finally gone. She rubbed her breastbone and sank to her knees. Tears she couldn't control overflowed to stream down her cheeks.

"It's gone." Darvyn's gaze found her, and Kyara spoke directly to him. "It's gone."

He smiled sadly, then turned to Ydaris.

"What do we do with her?" Kyara asked, hoping the answer was *kill her.* But she suspected Darvyn had something else in mind, especially if Ydaris truly did have useful information.

"The Lagrimari people have a deep need for justice," he said. "Ydaris has wronged us—you more than most. However, her death belongs to all of us. Just as the True Father's does."

He stood and came over to Kyara, helping her stand. They had barely touched since he'd come to rescue her, and she gripped him hard.

"There will be trials. It is what our people need to move on. Seeing the Cantor brought to justice will help many."

Kyara looked at the pathetic old woman before them, who was cowering in disgrace. It did not seem right to let her live, but Kyara understood the truth of Darvyn's words.

"No matter what she says, we can't allow her to keep the medallion," Kyara said.

Darvyn regarded Ydaris again and nodded.

"Put her to sleep," Kyara suggested. "We will have to carry her, but it will be safer."

"Wait!" Dansig cried out.

They turned around to face him. He held up Varten with one arm but raised the other. "Does she have the key?"

Kyara faced Ydaris again, and the woman's hand lowered to the skirt of her dress.

"Slowly," Kyara warned, worried about some hidden amalgam in her pocket. But Ydaris merely pulled out a key chain. Her knotted fingers slipped through the keys until she held up a tiny one.

"Roshon, come get it. Make sure it works," Kyara called out.

The twin ran up and grabbed the key. Kyara began to search Ydaris's pockets, ensuring she had no surprises hidden within. An intake of breath sounded behind her. Kyara turned in time to see the two red bracelets clatter to the floor.

Dansig's face was shot through with relief. "*Now* put her to sleep," he said to Darvyn.

In a moment, Ydaris slumped to the ground. Kyara marched over to pick her up and cut her eyes to Darvyn as he rushed over. "Save your strength," she said. "*All* of it. I can carry this bag of bones." She pulled the woman over her shoulder. "Let's get out of here."

Their footsteps thundered down the staircase at the end of the hall. The weight of Ydaris on Kyara's shoulder felt like nothing in comparison to that of the blood spell. They reached a landing where glass doors led to a terrace overlooking the lake.

Darvyn kicked the doors open, and they all charged outside. "We'll have to swim for it," he said. "That's really how you escaped, Roshon?"

The teen nodded. Kyara smiled to know that Roshon had done so well.

Below them, the island's shoreline was in upheaval. Physicks were piling into boats left and right; some were swimming away. They must not have realized that the threat of the spirits had been extinguished.

A giant boom sounded and the building began to shake. Kyara's head snapped up as the castle's stone walls vibrated and ripples extended across the lake. "That would be Asenath," she said, pride in her voice.

"Do you think she destroyed the machine?" Roshon asked.

Thick smoke began to pour from somewhere below, and Kyara scrutinized the shore again. "That's a safe bet."

A rectangular, metal-encased boat sailed into view from behind the palace. "Look!" Kyara said. "I don't think Varten can make the swim, and this old crone certainly can't." She hefted Ydaris, repositioning her on her shoulder. "We can get away in one of those."

The boats were large enough to carry all of them twice over. She stepped to the edge of the terrace, which was only one story off ground level. Below, dark sand met the lake's edge. "We'll have to jump."

"If we use a pocket of air, we can soften our fall," Dansig said. Darvyn turned to him with surprise. "Link with me, and we'll do it together."

Darvyn assented, and the two men held hands. Kyara led the others to the terrace edge.

“On three.” Darvyn swung a leg over the railing.

“One.” Kyara gripped Ydaris’s limp form more tightly, eyeing the ground below them warily.

“Two.” Roshon and Varten linked arms and looked down.

“Three.” She leaped. In her mind, Kyara screamed, though her voice was silent. A soft cushion of air cradled her, and it slowed her descent and supported her until she reached the ground with a soft thud, not a head-splitting crash.

She breathed deeply, looking in shock at the others who wore similar expressions.

Varten smiled big. “Why haven’t we ever done that before, Papa?”

Appearing a bit queasy, Roshon elbowed his brother in the side. The other twin was much improved, though he wore the evidence of his recent illness in the deep circles under his eyes and his thin frame.

Nearby, guards, servants, and Physicks alike were racing to the marina behind the castle where the boats were docked, chased by the smoke pouring from the Academie. Cracks were forming in the stone walls, and groans from inside warned that the structure was about to collapse.

Kyara and the others hid behind a low wall dividing the castle grounds from the shore. “They’ll see us if we get any closer,” she said.

Darvyn’s keen gaze took in the chaos around them. “Roshon and I are dressed as Physicks already. We just need three more robes for you, Varten, and Dansig.”

“Roshon, give me yours,” Dansig said. “I’ll get the rest. You all find a boat for us.” He took his son’s robe and rushed off into the fray before anyone could stop him.

Kyara set Ydaris on the ground, trying to be careful with

her. Her anger had morphed to cold pity as she gazed at the old woman's face. All the magic she'd used over the years had done this to her. Her medallion must be very powerful, indeed, to allow her to do so much.

Kyara refocused on the vessels before them, which were quickly dwindling in number as people escaped, some with only a few on board.

"That one," Darvyn said, pointing to a boat set off from the rest. "Everyone seems to be avoiding it."

"That's probably because it looks damaged. It may not run," Kyara said. The crafts were motorized, but whether it was with amalgam or just regular mechanics, she wasn't sure.

"We don't need it to run. We just need it not to sink. Dansig and I can spell the waves to do the rest."

Kyara shrugged as Dansig returned, clutching three robes to his chest. They donned them quickly, then raced to the lonely ship.

With another frightening boom, one of the spires of the castle fell forward and crashed down, taking huge chunks of the floors below with it and smashing into a cloud of smoke.

"Not a moment too soon," Roshon said as they piled into the boat.

The craft was some kind of speeder with a bank of controls to manage the engine. Except it lacked one important component—the actual *engine*. But they had something better . . .

Darvyn and Dansig linked hands again as another spire from the castle moaned and detached itself from its foundation. The boat thrust into the water, moving swiftly. Kyara turned back to watch another section of the castle crumble away into the water and thought of Asenath. Had the woman gotten out? Kyara hoped so with all her heart, wishing they would meet again one day.

She swallowed, hard, and looked at the men around her. The

Earthsingers in control of the vessel pointed it toward a wooded section of the far shore, away from where the other escaping Physicks were headed.

Kyara held on to the side of the boat, the wind rushing against her face. For the first time, she allowed herself to contemplate freedom. There was no wound restricting her actions, no chains binding her, and Darvyn—her Darvyn—was alive.

She was afraid to allow herself to enjoy this moment, afraid of her first taste of joy in a very long time.

CHAPTER THIRTY-SIX

Ayal tunneled upward through rock and soil, passing the deep roots of an old tree. She emerged in brightness and confusion, surrounded by a sea of white sand. Heat pummeled from the relentless sun, and she wandered, lost, until Girl-With-Hands-Like-Ice found her.

—THE AYALYA

Ella held her breath as she pushed the door to her flat open. Next to her, Tana and Ulani stood in the doorway, peering cautiously into the room.

"Come in, come in," she said, shooing the girls forward. Nerves bit her belly as she took in their reactions.

"It isn't much, just one bedroom, but we'll only be here for a few days. My friend Anneli is renting us one of her townhomes, which has much more space, but she's had to get it cleaned out first. It's been empty for a few years. However, we should be able to go in there by Sixthday."

Aware that she was rambling, she clamped her lips shut to cut off the stream of words. How much did the girls even understand? Gratitude for Anneli and her rental property threatened to burst from her seams. The older woman was eccentric to a fault, but kindhearted, and she was giving them a great deal on the lease of a town house they otherwise couldn't have afforded.

"For the next few nights, you two can take the bed; Benn and I will sleep out here."

Benn had borrowed two cots, which sat folded in the corner, but Ella wanted the girls to sleep in a real bed after so many weeks in the refugee camp lying on mats on the floor. She and Benn would survive for a few nights of relatively rough living.

The adoption approval had been a very welcome surprise, but they'd barely had any time to really prepare for the arrival of the girls. Her fear that Syllenne Nidos would stop the adoption had proved unfounded. She wasn't sure who she had to thank, Gizelle or the High Priestess herself. Though the raids on the temples meant that the woman had bigger problems to deal with. Ella certainly rated low in comparison to suspicion of being involved in an act of terrorism.

After walking the perimeter of the small sitting room on wobbly legs, Ulani settled into a perch on the edge of the couch. Tana stood next to her, taking in their surroundings.

"Sit, sit—please," Ella said, motioning the girl down. Tana sank awkwardly onto the cushion, but both girls looked uncomfortable.

"Would you prefer to sit on the ground?" Ella took the third cushion, placed it on the floor, then sat on it cross-legged. Ulani smiled and did the same, followed somewhat begrudgingly by her older sister.

"Benn will be here soon." At that, Tana looked up with interest. "We both want you to feel comfortable. It's a lot to get used to. We want you to be happy here."

Ulani nodded vigorously. "Happy. Very happy."

Ella's smile hurt her cheeks. Her nerves began to settle a fraction when a resounding knock on the door startled everyone.

She rose to answer the door and had to force herself not to close it again immediately. "Vera," she exclaimed, though dread slid down her spine. "What a surprise. Benn didn't tell me you were visiting."

Vera Ravel stood before her, cheeks red from the exertion of the climb to the third floor. "I get a call from my son saying he's adopted two—"

"Girls!" Ella called out brightly. If this woman called either of her daughters a *grol,* things would get ugly fast. "This is Benn's mama." She presented Vera with a sweep of her arm. The girls stood up and executed neat curtsies.

Ella's brows rose. "Where did you learn that?"

"Elsiran . . . manners," Tana said, glaring at Vera.

"How lovely," she said, making a note to distinguish formal greetings from informal ones at some point in the future. For her part, Vera's jaw still hadn't shut. She'd probably never been curtsied to in her life. Reluctantly Ella stepped aside to allow her mother-in-law into the flat.

"Girls, this is Grandma Vera. Vera, this is Ulani and Tana." She tried to inject some cheer into her voice, but Ulani was already regarding the woman judiciously. The child's ability to sense emotion would be a blessing and a curse.

Still, Ulani came over and wrapped little arms around her new grandmother. Vera stiffened and patted the girl's head lightly, appearing perplexed.

Tana approached like a skittish cat, keeping to the side of the room. She didn't touch Vera but reached out to pull Ulani back to her side. How interesting that Ulani was the Earthsinger, aware of Vera's feelings, but Tana exhibited far more caution.

Ella took some satisfaction in Vera's dazed expression. Until the woman pulled herself together enough to regard the room with blatant disapproval.

"I don't know what in Sovereign's name inspired you to adopt two . . . refugee children when there are plenty of motherless Elsirans about. But you can't possibly think you're going to raise them *here*?"

Ella took a deep breath. "No, of course not. We're renting a house on Port Hill Road."

Vera's eyes widened, impressed. While no section of Portside could be considered posh, Anneli had bought her property in the nicest part of the neighborhood. Vera sniffed and sat in one of the two armchairs. Ella pursed her lips and motioned the girls back onto their cushions.

Vera's visible alarm at the approximation of traditional Lagrimari seating made Ella restless. "Can I offer you some tea?"

The woman wearily accepted with an incline of the head. But if Ella thought she would get a reprieve in the small kitchenette, she was wrong.

"Do you think it's wise to bring these sort of children into your home?" her mother-in-law called out. "The witchcraft they're capable of. Why, they could murder you in your sleep."

Ella counted to ten before turning around, a fractured smile plastered to her face. "These are my children, mine and Benn's. And they are learning Elsiran, so I would kindly thank you not to accuse them of murder on their first day here."

Vera waved her hand, dismissively. "Oh, I'm sure you lead that boy around by the nose enough to get him to agree to anything. He hasn't been right since he met you." She *tsk*ed and sat back farther in her chair.

The girls looked on with wide eyes, and Ella prayed they weren't understanding much. She, however, was used to Benn's family, having dealt with them for the past six years.

Initially, she'd hoped to foster a close relationship with them considering she hadn't seen her own parents since she was a young teen, but that was not to be. She could only hope that with her own daughters, she would be able to create the sort of family she'd always dreamed of.

Brushing away the sting of the old disappointment, she opened the icebox, pulled out the two colas she'd splurged on at the market, and set them before the girls. They looked at the glass bottles curiously, and Ella realized they didn't know what they were.

She opened the top of one and handed it to Tana. The girl took a measured sip and then rewarded Ella with the biggest smile she'd ever given. Tana handed the bottle to Ulani who sipped the beverage and then began giggling infectiously.

She said a word that Ella didn't understand. "Bubbles," Tana said, translating. Ella laughed along with the girls.

"Good, isn't it?" she said.

Ulani offered Ella the bottle; she took a small sip before returning it. "Very good," Ulani replied, grinning.

Ella turned to find Vera gazing at the girls, an unreadable expression on her face. She was prepared to kick the woman out on her arse, mother-in-law or not, if her hostility toward the children continued, but Vera looked more flummoxed than anything else, so Ella held her tongue.

The door burst open revealing Benn, who skidded to a comic halt as he took in the scene.

Tana abandoned her soda to jump up and give him a hug, with Ulani right behind her. Benn produced two candies from his pocket and then leveled a gaze at his mother, eyes guarded.

"Mama, I see you've met the family." Each girl clung to him with one hand while trying to unwrap their treats with the other.

"Yes, I have," Vera replied. "I wish you'd spoken with me and your father before making such a big decision."

Benn shrugged. "The decision was Ella's and mine. I didn't see the need for more opinions."

"You keep bringing foreigners into our family," she said, shaking her head.

Benn stood straight, dashing and severe, for all that the girls still hung from his legs. "I keep bringing *family* into our family." His seriousness broke as he looked down. "All right, girls. I need my legs back." He gently plucked them off and approached Ella for a hug.

"I'm sorry, I didn't know she would show up immediately," he whispered into her hair as they embraced. The teakettle's whistle cut off her response.

As she prepared the tea, Benn settled at the kitchen table, tossing down the evening newspaper he'd brought in with him. Vera rose from her chair to settle herself at the table, then gasped, reading the headline.

"'High Priestess Arrested'?"

She dragged the paper closer and straightened the folded page. Ella stood next to her, teacup in hand, reading over her shoulder. A sickening feeling spread over her as Vera read.

"It says that they found palmsalt residue in a storeroom at the Eastern temple. There is overwhelming evidence pointing to Syllenne as the orchestrator of the bombing."

Papers rustled as Vera turned the page. Frozen, Ella found the cups removed from her hands and herself drawn down onto Benn's lap. She stared unseeing as Vera read aloud.

"'Officials suspect that with the Great Awakening, High Priestess Syllenne found her power in the organization diminished. Though she still ran the day-to-day operations of the Sisterhood, the spiritual needs of the people are now being ministered to by the Goddess Herself. This reduction in her influence and esteem caused a break in her mental status, says one source close to the investigation.'"

The paper fell from Vera's shaking hands. "The stress of the Awakening must have caused her to lose her mind. Imagine that . . ." She stared out the window into the distance.

Ella gave a sidelong glance to Benn. Vera was lost in her thoughts and the girls were chattering quietly to themselves as they shared their colas.

She motioned for Benn to follow her into the bedroom, where she left the door open a crack. "As much as I'd like to see Syllenne Nidos behind bars, something isn't quite right about this."

"I know," Benn said. "I finally cracked the code in Hak Floodhammer's account ledger today." He pulled a piece of paper from the inside of his jacket pocket. "It was a complicated cipher, but here are the entries from five weeks ago."

"'Zero point five kilos palmsalt sold to a C. T. Herd.'" Ella frowned. "C. T. Herd? As in 'cull the herd'?"

Benn's lips firmed to an angry line. "The constables investigating the bombing had already taken Syllenne into custody. I brought this to them, but they weren't interested. I sent it along to

Director Dillot at the Intelligence Service. I hope they can inject some sense into this."

"What did they find at the temple? What sort of evidence could there have been against Syllenne?" Ella asked.

"Palmsalt leaves a residue when stored for a long period of time. They tested the storerooms and found small traces. That coupled with the ledger convinced them."

Ella dismissed that with a wave of her hand. "That sounds circumstantial at best."

"Well, they also have a witness," Benn said. "A young Lagrimari acolyte to the Sisterhood said she witnessed the High Priestess overseeing the transfer of several large bags that were stored in the location they found the palmsalt residue. Her testimony was damning."

"That's not in the papers."

"No, they're trying to preserve the girl's identity from any backlash. And Syllenne isn't speaking to anyone—not the investigators, not her attorneys, not even her Sisters."

Ella's foot vibrated. "Something's wrong here, Benn. I know that Syllenne is monstrous, and I wouldn't put anything past her—but if they have the wrong person here . . ."

Benn placed a hand on her shoulder. "I know. This could all be a distraction to turn our attention from what the Reapers are planning next."

Ella peered through the bedroom door to find everyone still in the same positions as before. But she shouldn't leave Vera alone with the girls for any length of time. She shook her head at Benn and went back out to the sitting room.

Vera was still dazed. As a devout follower of the Goddess, she had spent her life viewing the role of High Priestess with an almost godlike fervor. Benn sat beside his mother and put his arm around her. Silent tears leaked down the woman's face.

"It just doesn't make any sense. I wish we could see inside the High Priestess's mind to know what she was thinking. How could she have done something so awful? My next-door neighbor had gone to temple just the day before it exploded. *I* could have been there that day. Any one of us could have been harmed in the bombing." Vera's expression was so desolate, Ella almost felt sorry for her.

"We may never know," Benn said, rubbing his mother's arm. "She's refusing to answer any questions, so it's possible we won't ever know her side of the story."

As Vera shook her head and blew her nose on one of Ella's good napkins, the spark of an idea formed in Ella's mind. If the High Priestess was being railroaded or framed and wouldn't speak to her advocates or friends, perhaps she would speak to an enemy.

CHAPTER THIRTY-SEVEN

The desert people welcomed her, having even there heard of her exploits. "We are shortly to visit Ysari the Artist and will tell your tale and receive Her grace." Their painted pottery, jewelry, and decorated fabrics proclaimed the Artist's influence. Ayal thrust her head in the sand, wanting to burrow away again.

—THE AYALYA

Ella pressed her nose to the window of the borrowed town car as Benn navigated Rosira's steep streets, taking detour after detour. Whole sections of the city had been blocked off by two competing protest marches: one led by those supporting a separate Lagrimari state, and the other by those in favor of unification. Each was headed to the palace for a face-off in front of the seat of government.

"Do you think we'll be able to get there?" Ella asked as they turned down a narrow side street.

"Eventually," Benn replied, grimacing as the car ascended a sheer incline.

The vehicle—property of the Royal Guard—handled the near perpendicular slopes with ease. Ella's nerves fired rapidly as they drove closer to the palace.

That morning, they'd completed the move to the town house. It had been a fairly simple affair since they'd had so little to take with them. The home was already furnished, and far too fine for their old, secondhand furniture anyway, so that had all been given away. Moving their clothes and personal items had barely taken any time at all.

And then the girls were off to school, a language immersion course for Lagrimari children housed temporarily in a leased storefront. Eventually, the Sisterhood hoped to integrate the adoptees into the Elsiran school system. Ella shuddered to think of what that would be like for the girls given the current climate.

If she could fix the country with a snap of her fingers, she would. For an assurance that Tana and Ulani would be safe and accepted in their new land, she would do anything, face down any monster—even one in a blue robe and topknot.

The route Benn took led them to a back entrance to the palace. They pulled into a vehicle depot and parked amidst rows of shining automobiles used by the army and Royal Guard, which both had stations here.

The High Priestess was being kept in the palace's dungeon, a place reserved for high-value criminals too important or dangerous to be housed in a normal jail. Syllenne Nidos had still refused to speak to anyone, so it was likely that today's excursion was an exercise in futility, but Ella was determined to at least try.

She'd never seen the palace before, never seen so much of Rosira before, and though she hadn't gotten a glimpse of the front facade and majestic gates, even the side entrance was awe-inspiring, embellished with carved figures of animals greeting the Lord and Lady who had first settled Elsira.

Benn led her through hallways filled with finery, each distinctly decorated with mirrors, or tapestries, or paintings, or carvings. His pace was such that she did not get time to linger at the beauty and wealth on display, but she hoped one day to persuade him to give her a proper tour.

Soon enough, they were moving down a series of stairways, and down farther to what was obviously an early section of the building. Kerosene lamps projected pools of illumination on stone walls and a chilled dampness filled the air. An intricately filigreed brass gate loomed before them, manned by a small group of Guardsmen.

Benn conferred with a guard who soon opened the clanking door and ushered them into the cells. The dungeon itself was hardly the gothic horror novel nightmare she'd expected. It was no worse than the city constabulary she'd briefly been remanded to after being arrested while searching for her nephew. Though it was well kept and clean, the stone walls and iron bars still made her shiver.

The Guardsman led them through a series of corridors. Ella was surprised the dungeon was so large. Many sections were full—mostly men with a few women—though some halls were completely empty. They stopped in one such empty section that only housed a single prisoner. Seated on a cot that looked not dissimilar to the one Ella had been sleeping on the last few nights was Syllenne Nidos.

The woman looked up and regarded the visitors imperiously, her sharp, angular features more pronounced in the harsh lighting. Her hair was loose about her shoulders, the graying bulk thick and long, still red around the temples. Narrowed eyes regarded Ella before looking away.

The Guardsman left her and Benn alone with the prisoner. Benn, wearing his black uniform, took a position near the end of the hall, out of Syllenne's line of sight. Ella stood straight, burning the vision of this woman into her memory.

"I've longed to see you here," she said. "You deserve to be in prison. You've harmed many people and are guilty of more crimes than even I know. But are you guilty of what you've been put here for?"

Syllenne's gaze snapped forward; she peered at Ella with a hint of intrigue.

"I know you're not speaking to anyone. Not the attorneys brought in to defend you nor any of your Sisters. Not even Gizelle. I wonder . . . would you have spoken to Kess?"

Syllenne's expression changed slightly, betraying a hint of suppressed emotion.

"Would you have confided in my sister, the one who knew all of your secrets?"

The High Priestess snorted.

"All right, maybe not all, but enough of them."

Ella placed a hand on a bar, resting her weight on it. "For all that she regretted following you so blindly, near the end, my sister still cared for you. Loved you like a mother." She was skating a little too close to secrets she would never share with the woman, no matter what. The manner by which she'd gained access to Kess's history and remorse was something Syllenne could never know.

The High Priestess's jaw tensed, and her eyes went soft for a moment. "Where is her baby?" Her voice was rough after days of disuse.

Ella swallowed, startled that she'd actually spoken. "Somewhere neither you nor Zann will ever find him."

"A shame. We could have used Zann's bastard child right about now."

The little sympathy that had seeped into Ella for the woman burned away. She'd hidden her infant nephew precisely so he wouldn't be used as a pawn. It was the one last thing Kess had asked of her.

Ella kept her voice light; she wasn't here to antagonize. "We'll have to use something else, then. So is Zann Biddel responsible for you being in here?"

"Many have had a hand in my current circumstances. Including you." Syllenne's voice was ice. "Didn't you turn in the supposed account registry 'found' by that shrinking little shrike, Rienne?"

"It wasn't yours?"

Syllenne snorted. "I have been the High Priestess for close to twenty years. I've never left anything even mildly incriminating written down."

Her indignation made Ella smile. "It didn't seem like your style."

"Certainly not." Syllenne's gaze turned hazy. "Never trust a man, Mistress Farmafield. No matter what they say."

Ella glanced at her husband who, while out of sight, was still within listening distance. "Were you hurt by a man?"

A brittle trill of laughter drilled the air. "Why are you here? A hairdresser. A nobody. What is it that you think you can do?"

Ella straightened her shoulders. "I'm here to protect my family. I'm here because I stumbled onto something big that I didn't understand, that affects us all. I want a country I can live in safely with those I love. I—"

"Don't you think I want that, too?" Syllenne spat, leaning forward. "Everything I've ever done is for Elsira."

Ella's temper rose. "Every despot says the same lines. 'It was all for love of country.' You helped kill Prince Alariq! Was that for Elsira?"

"You think you know so much," she hissed, rising from the cot. "Prince Alariq was close to signing a deal with foreign mages—Physicks from Yaly—to create a direct transportation channel from their state across the southeastern mountains. Some kind of magicked airtrain." Her eyes rolled with disgust. "That kind of thing could destroy Elsira."

"A train? Carrying goods and people between lands? How would that ruin us?"

"We survive because of our unique and insular nature. It's what makes us great. Alariq had no respect for our ideals and values. It wasn't my decision for him to die, but those in Yaly who oppose the Physicks and wanted the prince dead were powerful enough that no loyal Elsiran would have reasonably stopped them. Even better to assist and be owed a favor." Syllenne's lips snapped shut. Her nose flared with anger and, perhaps, the recognition that she'd said too much.

"Are you a member of the Hand of the Reaper?" Ella asked.

"Do you think I'd tell you if I were?" Syllenne waved off the idea with a flick of her wrist. A peculiar sapphire ring on her index finger flashed in the cell's low light. "I wouldn't make it to my own execution if I admitted something like that. There are rules. Checks and balances."

Ella stared, understanding settling over her. Syllenne hadn't admitted it, but her lack of denial was clear. "You *did* bomb your own temple." She shook her head in disbelief.

"Me, personally? If you thought that, you wouldn't be here." Syllenne clenched her jaw. "However, in military strategy, one must often accept a strategic loss. If it supports the greater good."

Ella turned away. "You knew about it. You gave your approval for the murder of the Prince Regent *and* all those worshippers. *Your* worshippers. I don't know why I would expect anything less."

"Ask yourself, if your theory is correct and I am a Reaper, then how am I here? Why have I been offered up like a sacrificial lamb for this . . . misery?" She motioned around the prison cell.

Arms crossed, Ella regarded the woman silently.

"I walked into a trap." Syllenne's expression was wry. "I knew Zann Biddel couldn't be trusted, but I thought I had enough leverage to properly manage him. I underestimated him. Don't you do the same."

The High Priestess turned and made her way back to the cot, sitting heavily. "I see a lot of myself in you, Ella. An intractable will. A sharp mind. Just like your sister. You two are very much alike. Very much like me."

Gripping her arms tight, Ella shook her head. "I'm nothing like you," she whispered. Syllenne shrugged and waved the statement away.

Ella's heart beat painfully in her chest. "So if not you, who carried out the bombing?"

Syllenne kept her head turned, staring at the stones in the wall.

"If they have abandoned you as you say, why protect them?"

"I protect no one but myself." Syllenne's voice was low.

"So why talk to me at all?"

She peered across the cell down her angular nose. "Call it nostalgia. How do you know so much; I assume Kess left some sort of diary? Thought I taught her better than that."

Ella rubbed her arms, suddenly cold. She couldn't go there. "I want to stop the next attack. You can help me. Make up for some of what you've done."

Shrewdness entered the woman's gaze. Her posture straightened. "Where is the baby? He's the last card to play against Biddel."

"No." The word vibrated against Ella's lips.

Syllenne spread her arms. "Then I cannot help you. The herd must be culled. For Elsira."

A growl of frustration left Ella's lips. "Do you even believe that nonsense?"

"I believe that men have ruled tyrannically since the beginning of time. I fought and clawed my way into power to stand up for us, for the women of this land. For our children and grandchildren. At every step I was opposed, mocked, disregarded, and belittled. I finally landed in a place of influence, with a hand on the wheel to direct where we were going, and then the Great Awakening happened and it all went to shite.

"The Goddess set us on this path with no direction. Absorb a horde of foreigners who don't speak our language or know our ways—that's a recipe for utter destruction. And then She disappears, unreachable, unwilling, and unconcerned. You should be grateful for the Reapers. You should thank your ineffectual saints for people like me, willing to do what must be done, regardless of the consequences."

Ella listened to the diatribe, her will turning steely. "The same consequences that landed you in here? Where are your Reapers now? Why aren't they helping you?"

Syllenne refused to respond. Frustration warmed Ella's blood. "Do you know the plans for the next attack or not? I don't care who's behind it. I just want to stop it."

The High Priestess made a show of pressing her lips together.

"You'll only help me if I let you use my nephew in some vengeance scheme against Biddel?"

"The child is proof that Biddel is a liar. A foreigner, like those he rails against. Do you think the people would follow him so blindly if they knew his secrets?"

"I won't use the baby that way," Ella said firmly. "Zann would kill him to keep the truth about his own heritage hidden, as you well know."

Syllenne crossed her arms and leaned back against the wall. "Strategic loss. Greater good."

Tears gathered in Ella's eyes. She was done here. This woman was hopeless. She had no conscience and no heart.

"I hope you rot in here, Syllenne. For every bad deed you've ever done, and those still to come. I hope you never see daylight again."

She spun around and raced toward Benn, eager to be out of this underground prison that she hoped would be Syllenne Nidos's crypt.

CHAPTER THIRTY-EIGHT

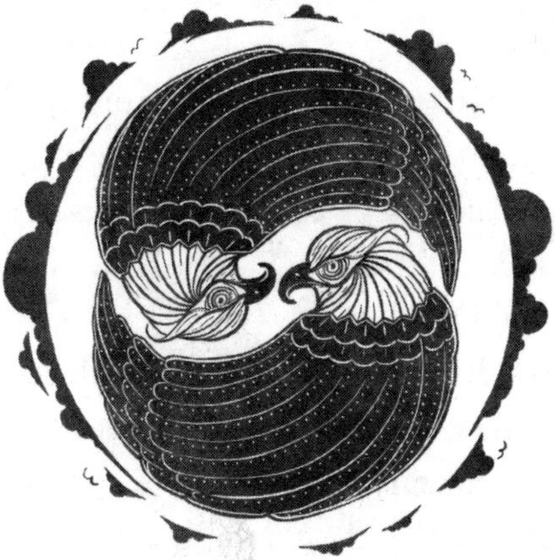

The heat of the sun made her skin feel like clay, baked and cracking. Girl-With-Hands-Like-Ice pressed her palms to Ayal's cheeks, cooling them. This comfort was a kindness, and the seeker found herself profoundly grateful. "Are not gratitude and praise two sides of the same coin?" the girl asked.

—THE AYALYA

Lizvette clasped and unclasped her hands repeatedly. She straightened her skirts for the fiftieth time, then adjusted the sleeves of her dress. Next to her, Tai sat motionless, staring straight ahead. When her fingers threaded through themselves again, he gently settled one large hand over hers. The tension bubbling inside her melted away at his touch. She inhaled deeply and closed her eyes, willing herself to be calm.

She and Tai sat just outside of Jack's office in the waiting area.

Around them, the sounds of normal palace life rang out. The hard-soled boots of servants and guards clapped across the marble floors in the outer hallway. Phones rang in nearby offices, and Jack's secretary answered a call a few paces away.

Clove had flown them to Elsira, and then she and Vanesse had gone back to Melbain City to await word of Darvyn and the others. Lizvette and Tai had been sent to see the chief of the Intelligence Service and had given their accounts of everything that had transpired in Yaly.

Well, not everything . . .

Lizvette stroked the underside of Tai's palm with her thumb. Even the tiny contact sent a thrill through her, further relieving her anxiety. His scent surrounded her, and while she hadn't seen him since they'd arrived at the palace that morning and been hustled off to separate debriefings, he had never been far from her mind.

Jack's secretary, Netta, looked up, phone to her ear. "The king and queen will see you now," she said, and gestured to the office door.

Lizvette stood, straightening her shoulders and tilting her chin up until she felt the strain in her neck. That was how Mother had taught her to stand.

Use the discomfort, channel all your feelings into it until they are just sensations. Like water rolling over you but not a part of you. Things are only real if you make them so.

With that reminder, she strode into the king's office, nearly prepared to come face-to-face with him.

Jack and Jasminda sat side by side behind his grand desk, presenting a united front. Lizvette executed a deep curtsey and then rose, keeping her eyes steady.

For the first time in a long time, setting her gaze on Jack didn't hurt. She looked upon the planes of his face—only glancing so as not to stare—but the old ache in her heart didn't flare to life. A tiny prickle of jealousy flickered when she took in Jasminda's beauty—the queen's hair was arrayed magnificently, full and bold; she was quite imposing—but the gnawing suffering her presence had once delivered was no longer present.

Tai took a step closer. Her heart twitched at his nearness. They weren't touching, but she wished they were. Wished it were appropriate to take his hand right now.

A movement on the side of the room caught her attention. Her cousin, Zavros Calladeen, stood next to the chief of the Intelligence Service, Luqos Dillot, whose walrus mustache was almost comical. But the way Dillot looked at Tai could only be described as malevolent. Lizvette shuddered before reluctantly turning her attention back to the king and queen.

Jasminda broke the silence. "Miss Nirall. Master Summerhawk. Jack and I are both extremely grateful for your service to our nation." She set her dark eyes on Lizvette, who tensed under the scrutiny.

"To bring in your own father under such circumstances is worthy of much praise. We thank you."

Lizvette bowed. When she rose, she noticed Jack's jaw was tensed as he looked off into the distance. He appeared harried, and she hoped he was coping well with the strain of the position. But she dropped her gaze when she felt Jasminda's stare burrow into her.

"It is my honor," Lizvette said. "I hope this serves to prove where my true loyalties lie, Your Majesties."

"We continue to take your case under advisement," Jasminda said. "Your reports both stated that Darvyn stayed behind to attend to a personal matter?"

Lizvette swallowed, unwilling to lie to the queen.

"Yes, Your Majesty," Tai said. "He found that the Physicks were holding someone very close to him and stayed to rescue her."

Jack frowned at this but stayed silent.

Dillot stepped forward. "I have personally questioned Nirall, and he claims to have no specifics about any further terrorist plots. He also has not been able to shine a light on the identities of the temple bombers. According to him, all his Dominionist contacts were Yalyish, not Elsiran. We need to be certain he did not mention anything more to you, Miss Nirall."

Lizvette's nostrils flared, but she quickly brought herself under control. "Chief Dillot," she began, "I assure you that I relayed every word my father said to me. I tried diligently to find information regarding future acts of violence and destruction, but either he does not truly know, or he would not entrust me with the details."

Dillot frowned, looking ready to respond, but the queen cut him off. "Thank you, Lizvette. You may return to your apartment. Your house arrest is lifted, but we ask that you do not leave the palace for the time being."

"As a safety precaution," Jack added, the first words he'd spoken.

Lizvette curtsied again, then shot a look at Tai. He winked at her, and she felt herself blush. She turned quickly and exited the office with Zavros stepping up to escort her. But she longed to speak further with Tai. He lingered outside the office doors, but Zavros was urging her away down the hall.

He turned to her, his eyes bright. "Well done, Lizvette. I don't know how you managed it."

"It's easy to do things when everyone underestimates you." She was a bit snappish but didn't feel like withstanding Zavros's superciliousness at this moment. They were walking away from Tai. She would have to find him later, perhaps send a servant to suss out where he was staying.

"How is the king handling the news about Alariq's murder?" she asked, veering the conversation in a different direction for her own sanity.

"Surprisingly well. Though, of course, it was a great shock to everyone on the Council. It just goes to show that you never really know people." He shrugged it off as if it were only a small matter. Then again, he had never been very emotional, though he had certainly liked Alariq a great deal better than he liked Jack.

"Do you think this is the end of it, then? I'll be free?" she asked as they walked through the hallways back to her family's apartment.

"I suspect so. I have done my best to advocate on your behalf, cousin. For your sacrifice, I think a full pardon is the least you deserve. I always thought the charge of treason quite severe. I mean, any of us would have acted similarly in your position, with foreigners infiltrating the palace and whatnot."

Lizvette held back a grimace. There was no love lost between the queen and Zavros—he was one of the Council members who was least friendly to the Lagrimari. Lizvette also didn't bother to remind him that Jasminda was an Elsiran-born citizen, not a foreigner.

"And besides," he continued, "I'd think forcing you to take the journey with that pirate was punishment enough. I'm surprised Jack would agree to such a thing. Who knows what he could have done to you? Those Raunians are brutes."

"Master Summerhawk was a perfect gentleman, I assure you. He was extremely helpful in capturing Father."

Zavros grunted and waved off her defense of Tai. "I'm just glad he managed to bring you back in one piece. The whole event was very unusual, indeed, sending an unmarried young woman of your status off with such questionable company. If I'd been consulted, I would certainly not have allowed it."

Lizvette gripped her skirts tightly and worked to reroute her growing rage.

"The situation will make securing your future a bit more difficult, given your association with those foreigners, however brief," he said. "But there are still respectable families who will overlook that, as well as Nirall's difficulties, in order to align themselves with someone so close to royalty."

Lizvette stopped short, nearly crashing into a passing Guardsman. "What are you talking about?"

Zavros frowned and stroked his goatee. "Do be careful, dear. I'm talking about securing you a marriage after you are pardoned. The news has spread quickly. Aunt Mari has already received calls from several families with eligible bachelors, though many are far too lowborn to be acceptable and only interested in the gossip. The key is to find someone in just the right circumstance—with enough money to provide for you and your mother, and well bred enough not to be an insult."

Lizvette swallowed the lump in her throat. Zavros went on, rattling off the names of families that would be acceptable who had sons of the right age and education. Apparently, Mother had made a rather miraculous recovery from her dubious illness once she'd been apprised of Father's capture. She was certainly well enough to entertain correspondence with Rosiran aristocracy.

"This is the perfect opportunity to redeem the family name, and with a strong association, your children may not feel the effects of this scandal. At least not too deeply."

Lizvette frowned as they reached the hallway leading to her apartment. "And what if I don't want to marry any of them?"

Zavros looked at her incredulously. "Then what will you do with yourself? Join the Sisterhood? Seriously, Lizvette, I thought you were shrewder than that." He chuckled and held the door open for her. "This unsavory business will follow you for the rest of your life if you don't erase it with a good marriage. And when Nirall is convicted, your family wealth will be forfeited to the crown treasury. That's the way it is with traitors. Then what will you do? How will you survive? How will Aunt Mari survive?" He shook his head, muttering under his breath. "Do give her my love," he said before turning and striding off down the hallway, his black coat billowing behind him.

Lizvette stood in the entryway for several minutes, thinking about Zavros's words. Would the daughter of a traitor even be allowed to live in the palace? Hardly. And when their money was confiscated to the state as part of Father's penalty, what *would* she do?

She leaned against the door and closed her eyes. Tai winked at her from the darkness behind her lids, and she opened them again.

A tattooed, blue-haired, Raunian smuggler would never be thought of as an acceptable choice. Falling in love with the pirate was probably the worst thing she could do.

A pity it was already too late.

Jasminda stared sightlessly out the window. Normally, she loved the view of the gardens below. The carefully tended greenery stretched out to the base of the mountain, which towered over the

Rosiran palace. It was her favorite place in the city, but the worries weighing on her mind blinded her to the beauty outside.

On the other side of the palace, protestors blanketed the main lawn, some supporting unification and some opposed. Though she could not hear their cries and shouts from here, they were like a swarm of insects gathering, ready to blight the land and rend it in two.

Jack approached, his presence warming her back. He placed his hands on her shoulders, kneading gently against the tension stored there.

"Catching Nirall is a huge step," he murmured close to her ear. "I think he'll tell us more eventually and lead us to the rest of the Reapers."

Begrudgingly, she had to admit that she owed Lizvette quite a lot for doing what no one else had been able to accomplish. And though Jasminda couldn't have imagined it a few days ago, Lizvette's earnestness and dedication did inspire some level of confidence, and, perhaps one day, forgiveness.

"I'm worried by the time Nirall decides to talk, it will be too late." She leaned back, enjoying the strong press of his fingers on knotted muscles.

"Maybe if we take execution off the table, he will be induced to give up his conspirators." His voice was shot through with pain. Justice for his brother's death was still a long way off.

"And Syllenne Nidos isn't talking. I doubt she'll confide in Benn's wife again." Jasminda pressed her forehead against the glass to cool her fevered skin. "Even with two suspected Reapers in custody, why don't I feel any safer?"

Jack sighed slowly. "We're watching Zann Biddel and his organization closely. If he so much as jaywalks, he'll be brought in for questioning."

"Why can't we take him in now? We *know* he's involved. Can't we stuff him in a hole somewhere so he won't stir up so much trouble?" Frustration bubbled within her. She was only half joking.

"You'd make a fine little dictator, my love. Biddel is squeaky clean. His operation is tight and by the book. We can't yet tie him to the anonymous newspaper editorials—and even if we could, there's nothing illegal about those or his protests. Plus, if it looks like Biddel's being targeted, he could turn into a martyr. Pull even more people onto his side."

She pursed her lips, unhappy with the reasonableness of his logic. "The right to spew hate is all well and good, but there are always consequences."

"Yes, and we'll have to deal with them as they arise."

She shook her head. "And then there's the tribunals . . . I'm worried agreeing to them was a mistake. It's all happening so quickly."

"They certainly haven't wasted any time. Then again, they're used to things happening on a much faster scale in Lagrimar. Accusations and sentences were carried out on the same day there."

"Yes, and don't they see why that's a problem?"

"This morning's poll shows ninety-six percent of the Lagrimari approve of the way justice is being handled. They're feeling seen and heard. And the number of Elsirans supporting unification is up by five points as well. Turwig was right, seeing the witness testimonies published in the papers is helping Elsirans understand more about what the Lagrimari went through for so long." He ran a hand over his hair, and blew a breath out. "But it is fast."

These speedy trials and judgments—often held without the defendants even present—did not feel like justice to Jasminda. The sentences were death—nothing to be taken lightly, no matter how grave the crimes. She crossed her arms tight, the feeling of unease growing stronger in her gut.

Jack turned her around to face him, keeping his hands on her shoulders. "The Lagrimari public trusts the Keepers and deserves closure on the painful parts of their past. In a few months, we'll begin revising the constitution and can reassess issues like this."

Jasminda nodded, still unconvinced. "Their plan for the True Father's trial sounds like a circus."

Jack frowned.

The "immortal" king of the Lagrimari remained hidden away deep in the palace dungeon. Instead of a mere tribunal, the Keepers wanted him shamed publicly and humiliated—someone had even suggested weekly public floggings. Jasminda would never stand up for the True Father, but the idea of such a spectacle being called *justice* didn't sit well with her.

She leaned into Jack's embrace, grateful for it. He kissed her temple, lingering at her hairline. She breathed in the scent of him.

A crackling from the direction of his desk interrupted the moment.

"Your Majesties," Netta said through the intercom. "Captain Zivel is here with an urgent message."

Jack sighed, then dragged Jasminda back to his desk with him. The captain had stayed for debriefing after delivering Nirall from Yaly.

"Send him in, Netta," he called out.

In a moment, the office door swung open and Jord Zivel stood there, his face solemn.

"Has something happened?" Jasminda asked, breaking out of Jack's embrace.

"Yes, Your Majesty," he said, blinking rapidly. She'd met the soldier only once, before he was deployed to Yaly, when it was clear their intelligence there had been compromised. But his rigid, officious demeanor was cracking. Something had shaken him.

He swallowed. "I-I have heard from Miss Liddelot and Sister Vanesse."

"Do they have Darvyn?" Jack asked. Jasminda held her breath.

"They do." Relief loosened her shoulders, but Zivel's expression did not change. He pulled a sheet of paper from his pocket and unfolded it, then cleared his throat. "Sister Vanesse bade me give you this message. They are in the air right now, else she would have given it to you herself, but she did not want you to be caught unawares."

Jasminda stepped forward, eyes on the paper in his hands. "What is it?"

He handed it to her and stepped back.

> My dear niece. The Goddess has blessed us again, and though Her ways are mysterious, we enjoy the good fortune of benefitting from them. Your father and brothers are alive.

Jasminda's knees weakened; she clutched the corner of the desk. Jack was there helping her into the chair. She swallowed and kept reading, with him looking over her shoulder.

> Unbeknownst to all save Darvyn and Tai, the Goddess placed them on a private mission to retrieve your family. All three are alive and well, and I have had the immense pleasure to be able to confirm it directly.
>
> I met Dansig, Roshon, and Varten, and we will be back to Rosira in a few short hours. May She bless your dreams and waking hours.
>
> Love, Vanesse

An empty space in Jasminda's chest opened up, threatening to suck her in. She blinked back tears and tried to grasp hold of one coherent thought.

Papa? The twins? Alive?

Her mouth couldn't form words; it quivered and her eyesight blurred.

Jack said something to Zivel, but it was just noise in her ears. Then she was being carried to the couch, nestled in Jack's arms.

Only a few hours until they arrived. Finally, the joy broke through the astonishment, and she smiled.

"They're alive," she whispered.

"They're alive," Jack repeated.

He pressed a kiss to her forehead and she closed her eyes.

Alive.

CHAPTER THIRTY-NINE

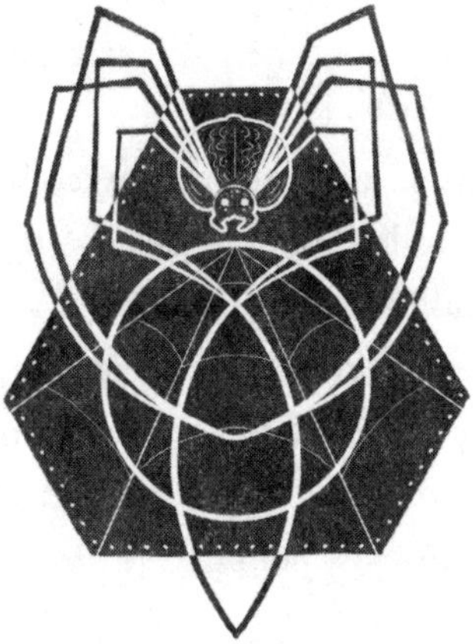

"We are happy for your visit, seeker," the desert people said. "You honor us and we will paint pictures of your deeds to immortalize your accomplishments." Ayal shrank away, ready to flee, when Girl-With-Hands-Like-Ice stopped her.

"No thrones, no dynasties," Ayal whispered, and the girl nodded solemnly, turning back and convincing the people to lay down their paint brushes.

—THE AYALYA

The airship hit a good amount of turbulence on the way back to Rosira. It shook and swayed, slowly deteriorating Darvyn's good mood. Kyara lay in his arms for the entire journey, sleeping soundly, while across the narrow aisle, Ydaris slouched against the window, still unconscious. Next to her, Varten slumbered peacefully.

The ship only seated four, aside from the pilot and copilot, but Dansig and Roshon had squeezed aboard and sat cramped on the floor. Darvyn had sensed Clove's worry over the weight of so many passengers, but Vanesse's joy at meeting her nephews and brother-in-law for the first time overcame any protests the pilot might have made.

Darvyn had pulled Clove aside and asked if it would be a problem. "I won't let there be," she'd replied. "It's too important. A strong tailwind wouldn't hurt, though."

Exhausted as he was, arriving home in one piece was vital, and so he used the last of his Song to call the wind and help push the airship along. Every fiber of every muscle in his body ached, and a throbbing behind his eyes pounded the way it did whenever he was nearly depleted.

Those who were awake remained quiet on the trip. Vanesse kept turning to look over her shoulder. Her reaction to the twins had been intense. Her whispered words to Dansig replayed in Darvyn's mind: *They look so much like Emi.* Dansig had nodded and closed his eyes. The man's Elsiran wife had been gone for a long time.

Varten was doing much better. He needed sleep after his healing, but Darvyn had completely destroyed the disease that had tormented the boy. Jasminda would have her family again, whole and hale.

And yet, as the ship rocked and he forced what power he had left into the wind to keep it moving forward, his anxiety grew. He squeezed Kyara more tightly to reassure himself that she was here with him and safe. He touched his forehead to hers and closed his eyes, just enjoying her nearness. But fear for what lay ahead gripped him. The Poison Flame would not be greeted warmly by the Lagrimari. He hoped providing them with the Cantor would satisfy their desire for justice, but worry nagged at him.

As the tiled roofs and colorful stucco facades of Rosira came into view beyond the mountain ridge, Darvyn perked up. This was home for now. The future would bring what it would, and he would face it the way he always had.

Clove brought them to a smooth landing on top of the palace. Everyone but Ydaris roused and tumbled out of the airship's carriage. A door on the far side of the roof opened and Jasminda ran toward them, her hair streaming out behind her. She wore a dress of fine blue silk edged in lace with heavy boots on her feet. Her father captured her in his arms and spun her around. Soon the entire family was locked in a long embrace.

Vanesse looked on with tears in her eyes. In fact, no eye was dry. It was impossible not to be moved by the reunited family. Kyara gripped his hand, and he turned to her. Whatever she was about to say was drowned out by the pounding footsteps that approached them.

Five Royal Guardsmen marched up, the lead man fringed in gold epaulets to indicate his high rank. "The prisoner?" he asked sharply.

Darvyn pointed at the carriage where Ydaris still slept. "She will be out for several more hours," he said. Two of the guards peeled off toward the old woman.

"And the other?" the lead guard snapped.

Kyara squeezed his hand. Darvyn shook his head in confusion. "What other prisoner?"

More footsteps approached. This time four familiar faces greeted him: Turwig, Aggar, Talida, and Rozyl. Aggar's eyes were wild and Talida looked ready to spill blood. Rozyl and Turwig, on the other hand, appeared dispassionate.

"That's her," Aggar said, pointing a finger at Kyara. Two Guardsmen stepped forward, and Darvyn moved in front of Kyara protectively.

"Stand down, *oli,*" Turwig said to Darvyn.

"No one is laying a hand on Kyara," he said through clenched teeth, staring down his mentor.

Aggar's face contorted in anger. "By the order of the Royal Tribunal of Elsira, Kyara ul-Lagrimar, the sergeant in the True Father's army known as the Poison Flame, is under arrest for crimes against the people."

Darvyn cursed and reached for his Song, but his power had been exhausted.

"Jack!" he shouted. The king strode over, and the lead Guardsman looked cowed.

"What's going on here?" Jack asked.

"Your Majesty," Aggar gritted out. "A tribunal judgment has been delivered for this woman."

Darvyn took a step back, forcing Kyara to do the same. Desperation sped his heartbeat. Jack appeared to understand that Kyara meant something to him. The lead Guardsman produced a sheaf of papers from his inner pocket.

Jack stood to his full height. "Let me see those," he said, plucking the pages from the guard's fingers and scanning them. He sighed and looked up at Darvyn, eyes heavy. "The paperwork is in order. I signed them." His voice was apologetic as he held the papers out for Darvyn to see.

Darvyn made out the scrawled signature at the bottom. His chest rose as his breath quickened. Jack's eyes were pools of sadness, and Darvyn had to look away. Kyara's hand loosened in his, but he held on to her.

With her other hand, she touched his arm, forcing him to look at her. "It's all right, Darvyn. We both know this is what must happen."

He shut out the others to focus solely on her. "We don't know that."

She cupped his cheek. "I did what I did."

"What you were *forced* to do." He spun around to face Aggar again. "When is the trial scheduled?"

Aggar's expression was smug. "The trial has already been held. The Poison Flame has been convicted in absentia. The Goddess Awoken has chosen the date of her execution Herself."

A chill raced down his spine. "She *what*?"

Talida spoke up, aiming an icy glare at Kyara. "She is guilty. Dozens of witnesses confirmed a mere handful of her kills, but hundreds more were willing to come forward. She must be executed."

Rage heated Darvyn's blood until he could barely see straight.

"I deserve it," Kyara said, pulling out of his grip. The guards approached and clamped manacles on her wrists. "You know I do."

He shook his head, everything in his body rejecting her sentence. He needed to save her. If his blasted Song weren't spent, he would tear down the entire palace to free her. A knowing look from Kyara settled him a fraction. How could she be so calm?

"I can't just let them take you away," he cried, and the two guards on either side of her looked nervously at each other.

Jack placed a hand on his shoulder, likely in warning.

"If you love me, you must," she said, and all the fight went out of him. The guards directed her across the rough surface of the roof and disappeared down the stairwell. His knees threatened to buckle. As if Jack sensed it, his grip on Darvyn's shoulder tightened. It was a show of solidarity.

Darvyn was barely aware of Roshon, Varten, and Dansig speaking up, asking what was going on and pleading Kyara's case. His entire being was with Kyara, hating that she was once again a captive. Hating that he could not escape being stabbed in the back by those who had been like family to him.

First the Keepers had kept him from his real family for years, denying his mother her attempts to find him before she died. Then an old grudge had resulted in someone he'd thought a friend giving him up to the True Father. Now they took Kyara from him.

And where was Oola? He should have expected something like this from Her. Send him to rescue the woman he loves only to sentence her to death upon return. The so-called Goddess's machinations were endless.

He turned to Jack. Anger tightened his throat, but he should not direct it toward the king. Jack hadn't known what signing that order would mean to Darvyn. "Make certain she's treated well, Jack," he said, voice strangled.

"I promise," his friend replied solemnly.

"I will fix this." He pushed past the other Keepers to go find Oola.

Darvyn tore through hallways, stopping every Sister he came across until he found Tarazeli, Oola's robe mistress, whatever that was.

"I need to see Her. Immediately." The girl flinched, and he realized he'd been shouting. He needed to calm down. This wasn't her fault. He took a breath and tried again. "I apologize, but it's urgent."

Zeli nodded and turned on her heel, rushing in the opposite direction. Darvyn kept pace with her as she wound her way through the snarl of hallways. She ushered him outside and across the breathtaking gardens, which he barely noticed, to a spot at the base of the mountain. There, a dark-haired figure sat on a stone bench, surveying the city spread out below them.

Darvyn felt more than saw Zeli's retreat. He stared at Oola's back for long moments before he trusted himself to proceed.

"Is there a heart beating in your chest, or just a shriveled, empty hole?" His voice shuddered with bitterness.

She did not turn when he rounded on Her. Her eyes stayed on the city and the sea beyond it.

"Did you send me there to get her just so you could kill her?"

Oola's demeanor was infuriatingly tranquil. "The people need healing. They need to see that there are consequences."

"And so you set her execution date? You haven't been involved in any aspect of governing for weeks, and yet you step in for this? I brought back Jasminda's family. I've done everything you asked. They are all alive and well, and that family is whole again. Will you not make mine whole, too?"

She quirked an eyebrow. "What family do you have?"

"Kyara." His voice broke on her name. The emotion welled up inside him, and he fell to his knees before Oola. "Do you want me to worship you? Venerate you like the others? What would it take to save her?"

Dark eyes sliced him when She looked at him for the first time. "Do not kneel before me, Darvyn. Not you, too. You are the only one who sees me as I am."

"A lying, conniving bitch?"

Her teeth unfurled from behind Her lips in an embittered smile. "You remind me of someone. Your eyes are so similar, but Yllis's face was even more severe. He assaulted me with silence, not with curses and threats. And that silence nearly broke me. But he saw *me* when others saw only what they wanted to see. Someone who could save them, not someone who led them into harm's way in the first place."

Her smile was nearly mad. Had She truly gone insane? Was he dealing with a crazed, omnipotent creature? Her words made little sense. Whoever this Yllis was, he must have been wise to shut Her out.

He stared at Her with venom in his heart. "Do not do this, Oola. I know that you can stop it. She doesn't deserve to die."

Oola stood and brushed off the seat of Her gown, then clasped Her hands. "In three days, Kyara will be executed. She will be hung by the neck until she is dead. The first sacrifice from the True Father's regime. That was the ruling of the tribunal. And that is what must occur."

With a gust of wind, She rose into the air. Darvyn shouted and screamed and cursed Her up one side and down again, but Oola was soon only a dark spot in the sky.

He sat on the bench She had vacated and did something he had not done in a very long time. He cried.

CHAPTER FORTY

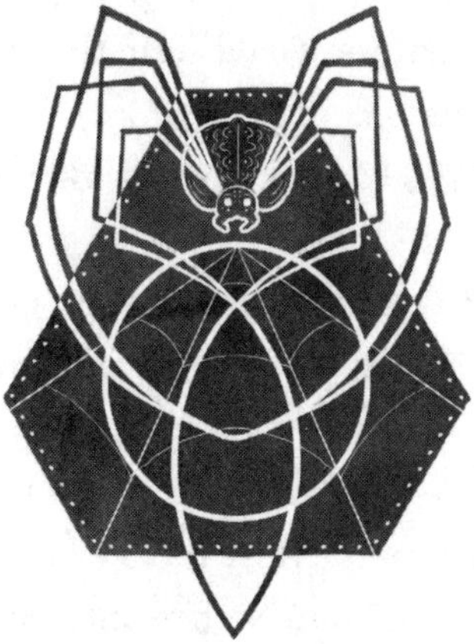

Before she fled the desert, Ayal collapsed onto the sand, her skin burning and hardening. When she rose again, her body had transformed, soft flesh hardening into the form of a lizard. She coughed a flame into the air and continued on her way.

—THE AYALYA

As far as dungeons went, Kyara had been in worse. Kerosene lanterns from the hallway illuminated the stone walls and floor, and an elevated pallet for sleeping featured a surprisingly clean mattress. It wasn't modern and sleek like the Physicks' prison, but it was head and shoulders above the dungeon in the glass castle of Sayya. She would count her blessings while she still could.

Waking from an uneasy night's sleep, she stared at the stone ceiling, restlessness filling the hollows in her bones. For a few moments on the airship, she'd thought her days of confinement were over. At least now she had an end date. Two more days and it would all be over.

Her back ached from lying down, so she stood to pace the cell. The scrape of her boots over the rough floor captured her attention for a little while. She could hear the murmurings of other prisoners—they mumbled or sometimes shouted in Lagrimari—but unlike in Yaly, she could not see or interact with anyone else from her cell.

If she wanted, she could kill everyone here. Everyone in the entire castle, most likely. When the guard came with dinner, she could knock him unconscious or deliver a vomiting attack, steal his keys, and free herself. The tribunal who had convicted her had no idea of her true power. Most thought the Poison Flame used actual poison on her victims. Nethersong was virtually unknown. Darvyn wouldn't reveal her secret, either. If the others knew what she was capable of, her two remaining days would likely evaporate. They'd do away with a formal execution and kill her right now—if she let them.

For a moment, she considered actually killing the other prisoners. They were probably all pay-rollers and, like her, guilty of atrocities done in the True Father's name. Many of those working for the immortal king had reveled in the depraved tasks he'd demanded of them. Kyara weighed the benefit to humanity of taking them out now against her desire to live the rest of her short life without blood on her hands. With a sigh, she settled back onto the pallet and rested her head against the wall. She was not judge, jury, and executioner.

The coolness of the stone was a relief for her pounding head. But she winced when the rusting hinges of the iron gate to this section of the dungeon creaked and the gate swung open. She wondered idly who she'd see passing by her door, then scrambled up on wobbly legs when an imposing figure stopped just on the other side of the bars.

The Queen Who Sleeps—no, the Goddess Awoken—stood regally before her. Kyara had never seen Her before, hadn't even heard anyone describe Her, but recognized Her on sight. It was impossible not to sense the power crackling around the woman, even for a Nethersinger such as herself.

Not knowing what else to do in the presence of a deity, Kyara fell to her knees, bowing her head.

"Stand." The Goddess's voice filled the cell, echoing off the stones. Kyara rose, keeping her head down, then peered up at the woman through her lashes. She was tall, a head taller than Kyara. Her skin was richer and so vibrant it almost glowed from within. Tightly coiled locks cascaded to Her shoulders, and Her eyes stabbed Kyara with their intensity.

"Why do you kneel when you are not a believer?"

Kyara had no idea what she believed anymore and struggled to find her voice. "Just because I lack faith does not mean I lack respect."

The Goddess drew closer to the bars until She gripped them with long fingers. "And what is it that you have respect for? Certainly not human life."

The statement stung, and Kyara had no response.

"You have allowed yourself to be captured. Will you let them execute you?"

Kyara swallowed around the lump of dread in her throat. "Yes."

"In my youth, those with your power were killed as babies. You should never have been allowed to live in the first place."

Ice raced down Kyara's spine as her vision tunneled, the words from the Goddess's lips echoing in her head. "You're right," she whispered. She gripped her head in her hands and shivered.

"So you are here to be a martyr. You think that will bring you some peace." Her cold voice chilled Kyara's skin even more.

"Will it?" She forced herself not to look away from the Goddess's fierce stare.

The Goddess narrowed Her eyes. "Do you think *he* will forgive you?"

"Who?"

The Goddess released the bars and held out her hand. In Her palm lay a tiny red stone. A caldera. Blood magic. Ydaris used such things all the time for various purposes, from communicating over long distances to changing the temperature of a room.

Shaking her head, Kyara backed away. Whatever the stone did, she didn't want to know. But it levitated into the air, following her across the cell. The little caldera hovered in front of her face before pressing itself into her forehead.

Images of Darvyn flooded Kyara's mind. Him tied to a table screaming in pain, his skin sliced to ribbons by a wicked blade. The sounds of misery fading as unconsciousness took him under. His limp form being dragged away, then it starting all over again.

She couldn't escape the barrage of images. Pain seized her, and she dropped to the ground, curling into a ball, whimpering against the onslaught. The wound on her chest had been agony when used against her, but somehow, reliving Darvyn's suffering was worse.

"Please stop!" she gritted through clenched teeth. "Have mercy!"

The images ceased. The caldera clattered when it fell. The cold of the stones seeped through her tunic, the fabric doing nothing to warm against the chill of the dungeon floor. Still, she lay there, the discomfort a balm after the anguish of the vision.

"Mercy?" the Goddess asked. "The same mercy you gave your victims? Mercy is reserved for those who do good. I wonder if that is possible for you."

Kyara shivered violently. "I can give them their justice. Wouldn't that be good?"

The Goddess smiled coldly without showing any teeth. Her eyes sparked with inner light. "We shall have to see if that is enough."

The whispering darkness surrounded Kyara, though this time her senses were clearer. She was cold. Her teeth began to chatter as the voices grew louder, then quieted.

Then *they* came.

Ahlini, her only friend. The only one to disregard the customs shunning the *ul-nedrim*—those in the harem who were daughters of the king. Ahlini had played by her side, shared what she learned in the classroom she went to every day, and treated Kyara like a person. Now Ahlini stared up at her, eyes blacked out by Kyara's power, asking why her friend had killed her.

On and on it went. Those the True Father had ordered her to kill. Those she'd accidentally killed in the early days before she'd learned the little control she managed of her deadly power. Her Song beat against her ribs now, longing to be set free.

The circle of her victims grew larger, their pleas louder.

"My children starved without me," one man cried. "My wife killed herself."

"I did nothing but try to survive," another said. "And then the True Father grew tired of me and sent you. Didn't you know what he was?"

She covered her ears, but the words penetrated. She held herself tightly, trying to maintain control, but something shattered within her and her Song leaped forward eagerly. It sprang to the waiting Nethersong that filled the darkness, drinking it up. If this truly was the World After, then this was the origin of her ability. Maybe she did belong here.

Bursting with power, she opened her eyes to find all her victims frozen around her, staring. She stood, turning around in the circle, eyeing them. The current of strength running through her bolstered her.

"I met the man of light," she called out. Mooriah was nowhere to be seen, but Kyara knew she must be nearby. She always was.

"*Embrace the Light.* Did that mean him? Fenix?" She spun around again. None of the men and women had moved a hairsbreadth. "I freed him. He went away—disappeared—but said he would return. Will I find salvation now?"

The people surrounding her disappeared. She turned to discover Mooriah behind her. She was draped in black from head to toe as always, but somehow she was set apart from the gloom now.

"You spoke to Fenix?" she asked, a note of hope in her voice.

Kyara nodded slowly, feeling the Nethersong swell inside her. "Please tell me. Is that what you meant? Does releasing him stop what's to come?"

Mooriah tilted her head. She was clearer now than she ever had been. Her features were regal, with a high forehead and proud nose. She was so familiar, odd as that seemed.

"Freeing him will help, but it has stopped nothing. You must learn to control your power. It is the Light."

Kyara groaned in frustration. "My power is death and destruction—nothing close to light. You sound like Murmur. Besides, who is there to teach me?" she demanded. "There is no one else like me. The Cavefolk claimed they could help, but they are manipulators. I would rather die than be controlled by another puppeteer."

"Die?" Mooriah sounded incredulous.

Kyara folded her arms over her chest. "I'm to be executed in two days."

"Why would you allow yourself to be executed? You are controlled no longer by blood magic."

"Because of them." Kyara waved her arm toward where her victims had been moments before. "Because I deserve to be punished for my crimes."

Mooriah shook her head and glided closer. "None of that is important. You have seen a taste of the war to come, have you not? Can you imagine what will happen when it is not just a handful of angry spirits breaching the veil between worlds? What about when it is untold thousands, all vying for another chance at life?"

Kyara released her Song. The Nether that had been buoying her slipped away, and she deflated. "What can I do against that? What can any of us do?"

The hand that reached for Kyara was covered by the sleeve of Mooriah's dress. But unlike before when the woman's touch had been just an echo of icy sensation, this time the contact was substantial. Still cold and not quite solid, but tangible.

"You must learn."

The touch was likely meant to be comforting, but it was the opposite. Kyara stepped back, out of Mooriah's reach. There was no one to teach her. And without more control, she would always be a danger to others. She could exile herself to some far-flung place or accept the punishment she deserved, even if Mooriah and Darvyn didn't agree.

Mooriah flinched, and her hands flew to her midsection as if she was in pain. "Not yet!" she cried, appearing as though she was trying to fight whatever force it was that made her disappear so suddenly. "You must not—" But her words were lost when she vanished.

If the war she'd spoken of truly was coming, Kyara wished she could help. But her own people wanted her dead and she couldn't disagree with them. She was still a danger. And while she would love to learn to control her power, she'd been trying on her own for a decade with only moderate success.

The destruction she'd wrought in Sayya the day Raal kidnapped her could have been so much worse. She wished she could see Mooriah again and explain it to her, but it made little difference. Kyara's time in the Living World was nearly at its end.

CHAPTER FORTY-ONE

She emerged onto the grasslands, throat parched and heart numb. A rushing river swept by, wider across than she could see. Stopping on the sloping bank to slake her thirst, she saw Child-Who-Gathers-Water swim by. She called out in warning, but the child ignored her, diving down, then flying from the water like a dolphin.

Ayal's worry turned to wonder, tinged with fear.

—THE AYALYA

Darvyn paced the small room, wearing out the woven rug in front of the fireplace, where the dying embers gave off a light smoky scent. He leaned on the mantel and let his forehead hit the wood.

Papers rustled behind him. Jack and Jasminda stood at the massive desk, paging through the law books they'd had brought in from the library.

"There is precedent here, I think." Jasminda's voice was low and insistent. "After the Princeling's Scourge two hundred years ago, the new Prince Regent declared the wartime trials null and void."

"I don't think so," Jack said, shaking his head. "He nullified the tribunals set up by the previous monarch. We're talking about trials we ourselves approved."

Darvyn turned around. He moved to a chair in front of the desk and fell into it with a thud. Jasminda's kind gaze held pity. Jack's brow creased as he read over the enormous book before them.

"Nothing?" Darvyn asked.

Jasminda stood. "The ruling monarch *can* reverse the judgment of a wartime tribunal, but we'd need to prove some sort of wrongdoing took place."

"They've been . . . unusual," Jack said, "in their speed and efficiency. But nothing that is illegal by current law."

Darvyn sank back into the seat farther, cracking his hands. His whole body ached from head to toe.

"The judgments have brought some measure of peace to the Lagrimari," Jack explained. "And has made the call for two states more nuanced. Sympathetic Elsirans learning of what the people suffered under the True Father's rule have been supporting unification. Given the current division, for us to nullify a ruling . . ." He looked at his wife, who looked at Darvyn with anguish.

"No, I understand," Darvyn said, leaning forward to put his head in his hands. "You would look capricious. It could undo what little goodwill exists toward my people. There could be chaos and riots by Lagrimari already wary of rulers and their whims. It would be a disaster."

Jack ran his hand through his hair and nodded.

Jasminda rounded the desk to sit next to Darvyn, taking his

hands in her own. "I believe she didn't want to do any of those things and that the True Father forced her with magic, and I know that she saved your life . . . but even if Ydaris testifies to that effect, it doesn't look good. I've spoken with the Keepers. As the prosecutors, they could petition the tribunal for a retrial if new evidence came to their attention. But even telling them how Kyara helped save my brother's life has done no good. They said no good deed can erase the bad ones."

Her jaw tensed, and she looked away. "I don't know what we can do that won't make things worse."

Darvyn's eyes clouded over.

"We are teetering on the edge of unification and division," Jack added. "A gust of wind in the wrong direction could be disastrous."

He couldn't just accept this. He understood the king and queen had tried their best, but Darvyn wasn't done yet. He jumped up from his seat. "You say it was the elders of the Keepers who gathered the evidence?"

"Yes," Jack said. "Why?"

"I would like to have a word with them myself."

"I should have a place among the elders." The door to the assembly hall's meeting room had barely shut behind Darvyn before the words were out of his mouth.

Six faces looked up at him with expressions ranging from bewilderment to shock to disapproval. At the table sat Turwig, Aggar, Talida, and Rozyl, along with two additional elders he was familiar with, Lyngar and Hanko.

Darvyn did a double take at Rozyl. "Are you an elder now?"

She nodded gravely. "Fresh meat," she said, quirking her lips.

Darvyn cracked a smile, grateful for another cool head among the leadership.

He turned to Turwig, whose rank was the most senior of those gathered. "I believe the Shadowfox should have a seat here. I think the people, were they to be consulted, would want it to be so."

Turwig remained impassive, but Lyngar, seated beside him, frowned. From the corner of his eye, Darvyn saw Aggar puff up, as if he'd been personally insulted.

No one spoke for a few moments.

Finally, Hanko swiped at his face and shrugged. Unruly tufts of hair clung to the sides of his bald head. "The boy has a point. For all he has done, I think Darvyn has earned his place here."

"Arrogant one, isn't he?" Lyngar said. He was the eldest of the elders and looked even older due to the permanent scowl etched into his deeply lined face. "I'm not sure we should make any change just now. Could throw things into confusion."

Darvyn gritted his teeth to hold back any unwise comments. He took a breath and waited for the others to have their say.

"A powerful Song does not make someone ready for leadership." Aggar spoke up, his voice like gravel. "And I think Darvyn has proved very recently that his judgment is suspect."

No surprise there. He hadn't expected any support from that quarter.

Rozyl leaned back, appearing uncomfortable in the Elsiran chair. "I agree that the people would want the Shadowfox to represent them. And I think Darvyn's judgment has been just fine."

"You weren't there in the days before the Mantle fell. You didn't witness his wild temper."

Aggar's gruff tone didn't appear to bother Rozyl at all. "And who made the decision to collar a fellow Keeper?" Her low voice was unemotional, her face placid, but steel edged her words.

Aggar's nostrils flared as his jaw worked silently.

Talida squared her shoulders, looking between the two of them. "The Shadowfox has been an important tool. But I agree with Aggar: The decisions we make here go beyond his expertise. He is not ready for a place at this table." She ignored him as she spoke, as if he was unworthy of addressing directly.

"Should we hold a vote, then?" Turwig asked.

"Fine," Lyngar spat. "Let's get this over with so we can get back to more important matters."

"All in favor of elevating the Shadowfox to the rank of elder?" Turwig asked. He touched his hand to his forehead to indicate his vote. Rozyl and Hanko did, as well.

With a grimace, Lyngar added his vote to the mix. Aggar and Talida didn't move a muscle.

With that, Darvyn was in.

"Have a seat, young man," Hanko said. Darvyn dragged over a chair from against the wall and sat between Rozyl and Turwig. Waves of bitterness flowed from Aggar along with icy disregard from Talida, the Keeper here he knew the least.

Turwig picked up the top page of a stack of papers before him. His voice filled the awkward silence. "The order of business now is the trial of Osyn ol-Krastigar, former Commandant of the Enforcers. What discussion is there?"

Talida cleared her throat. "Witness affidavits have been notarized and delivered to the judges. All that needs to be decided is the manner of his defense. No witnesses have come forward on his behalf, and due to his position and the nature of his crimes, none of the settlers who speak Elsiran are willing to translate a statement for him for the Elsiran judges. I propose we submit a waiver of his right to defense to the tribunal."

"I agree with Talida," Aggar said, spiking a vicious gaze at

Darvyn. "Really, none of these swine should be allowed the privilege of a defense. If no one can be found to speak up for them, why force the people who have been their victims to hear another vile word from their vile mouths? We all know what he's done."

Darvyn blinked back his shock. "That isn't justice. That sounds more like a continuation of the old regime, not a new way forward. Elsiran law requires a sincere defense for all accused of a crime."

"Yes, but a defendant can waive their defense if they have no statement to give and no witnesses," Talida said, jaw tight.

Darvyn shook his head. "Osyn's crimes may be undeniable, but we sink to the True Father's level when we subvert the law in the name of justice and deny him the opportunity to speak on his own behalf. I'll translate for him if no one else will do it."

Stunned faces peered back at him.

"In fact," he said, soldiering on, "I think all those who have been convicted in absentia, and thus denied a defense, should be retried only when they are located. No one should be sentenced to death without having had the chance to have their say."

"You're referring, I take it, to the Poison Flame?" Aggar asked, unmoved.

Darvyn met his hard eyes. "Why should she not get the opportunity to speak up for herself?"

Aggar scoffed.

"What could she possibly have to say?" Rozyl asked. "What defense is there for crimes such as hers?"

"Blood magic." Darvyn's words were met with silence and bewilderment. He continued. "When Kyara was only a child, the Cantor carved a spell into her skin that made it so she could not disobey the commands she was given. She could not even raise a hand against herself to take her own life and escape her bondage. Her life was not her own."

He curled his hand into a fist, staring at nothing as he relayed Kyara's tale. "She was forced to become an assassin. Yes, she killed for the True Father, but it was not by choice. Even the pay-rollers had free will. What they did, they did of their own volition. The soldiers were trained from childhood but still chose to embody the brutality they were taught. It was not so with her."

"You seem to know quite a lot about her," Turwig said, sitting up straight.

Darvyn looked over at the old man, pleading with him. "She saved my life. More than once." His gaze went to everyone around the table. "At the least, she deserves a new trial so that she can tell you all this herself. If we're creating a new way forward, we must embrace justice, not just revenge. You all can petition the tribunal."

The silence stretched on and on. Darvyn waited, his heart beating faster, his body taut with anticipation.

Aggar snorted. "This changes nothing. It does not take away the lives she's stolen. You speak of justice for her, but what about justice for them?"

"A dog that's been trained to kill must still be put down," Lyngar said.

"She's not a dog," Darvyn gritted out.

"I don't think we can go back on this," Hanko said, his voice kind. "The True Father manipulated with many methods, some magical, some not. But the victims still deserve to see the perpetrators held accountable."

"She saved my life," Darvyn plead. "At her own peril, she saved me."

Rozyl spoke quietly from his side. "I'm sorry, but the others are right. If the Poison Flame is allowed to walk the streets free, imagine how the people would react. We need to show a united front and prove that the old regime is gone. Forever."

"Then exile her," Darvyn said. "Send her somewhere far away where no one will ever see her again."

"She's too dangerous," Turwig said in a low voice.

Not him, too. Darvyn wanted to scream at them all. If they knew how dangerous Kyara truly was, how much restraint she practiced every day, they would never get a night's sleep. What they knew about her could fill a thimble.

"None of you will listen?"

"I'm sorry, *oli*," Turwig said, resting a hand on his arm.

Hanko looked down, pursing his lips. Lyngar scowled, and Aggar closed his eyes before shaking his head.

On his other side, Rozyl inhaled deeply. "I'm sorry, Darvyn. We wouldn't be safe with her on the loose."

He jerked out of Turwig's grip. Anger burned through him, throwing a haze across his vision. Briefly, he considered using Earthsong on them and trying to change their emotions, but he knew that wouldn't work. They were firmly entrenched in their bids for vengeance.

He had done everything he could within the system. Now he would just have to go outside of it.

CHAPTER FORTY-TWO

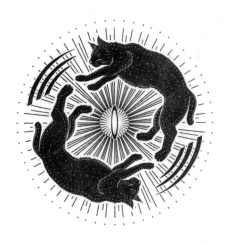

The child's family gathered, coming back from their fields and crops. "Is the young one in danger?" Ayal cried.

"There is no danger," the father replied. "The water is as much our home as the land. Sit and share our meal."

But when she saw their paltry supply of food, she balked as there was not enough to go around.

—THE AYALYA

Ella stepped out of the taxi, anticipation wrapping thick fingers around her middle. She brushed the wrinkles out of her best dress and patted her cloche hat, ensuring it was in place. Benn straightened beside her, and helped Ulani and Tana out of the car. The girls' hair was freshly plaited, with ribbons on the ends. Each wore new dresses, Ulani's in a soft pink and Tana's in seafoam green.

The Eastern temple loomed before them, majestic and serene.

The street and sidewalk were crowded this afternoon. Other families were climbing the steps, Elsiran parents with their Lagrimari children in tow. The Sisterhood had put together a special ceremony to celebrate the first wave of adoptions.

The last to exit the car was Vera, who had insisted on accompanying them. Ella had warily agreed, vowing to watch her interaction with the girls carefully. So far, she had praised their outfits and hair, much to Ella's surprise.

As the taxi sped away, Ella scanned the busy street. The sight of the Lagrimari children was raising eyebrows from passersby. A trio of women walked by swiftly, putting a wide berth between themselves and the girls. Tana and Ulani, staring up in awe at the temple, had yet to notice, but Vera did. She sniffed, squared her shoulders, and took Ulani's hand. "Come on girls, we don't want to be late."

Ella blinked and shared a bemused glance with Benn. He lifted a shoulder and followed his mother up the steps, with Tana close beside him.

Shaking her head, Ella started after them, only to be nearly plowed down by a man rushing down the sidewalk. She stumbled to right herself after the force of the collision.

"Excuse me," she said, shaking off the blow and taking a good look at him before he hurried away. His face was obscured by a newsboy cap and he wore brown coveralls with heavy work boots. The outfit was common enough, but an inner voice told her this was one of Zann Biddel's guards.

She turned to stare at the man's retreating back. He hadn't said a word to her, hadn't acknowledged her at all. Déjà vu rippled over her. Another day, another sidewalk, another young man dressed in the same way who had nearly run her down.

Or maybe the same one, they were all so interchangeable—

probably by design. That man and a companion had been fleeing the warehouse belonging to Hak Floodhammer. The two had likely killed him. What little investigation there'd been into Floodhammer's death had yielded nothing, and had never even made the papers.

Ella whipped her head around, scrutinizing the other people on the street. Brown coveralls and caps were common among the working men, but she didn't see any others with the distinct combination that so resembled a uniform. Zann Biddel's little army. Could they be up to something here? Was this the site of the next attack?

She raced up to the entry, searching for her family. Everyone was being directed downstairs to a meeting room on a lower floor. Forced to slow her pace by the press of bodies in the stairwell, Ella's anxiety rose. There were less than two dozen families adopting children in this group; would it be a likely terrorist target? The young man who'd bumped into her hadn't been coming from the temple, so perhaps she was just being paranoid.

When she finally reached the meeting space, she tried to calm her racing heartbeat. The room had been decorated with balloons and streamers, and a table full of finger food stood to the side. She searched for Benn's tall form through the small crowd, then gasped when a hand gripped hers.

Ulani looked up at her, concern in her eyes. The child could sense her distress with her Song. Ella took a purposeful deep breath and crouched down beside her daughter. "I'm all right, sweetheart. I'm okay."

The girl looked unconvinced, and Ella chastised herself for getting so worked up. After the temple bombing, attacking a handful of parents and children would be anticlimactic. Surely the next target would be bigger and more public than a basement room in the smaller temple.

She stood and allowed Ulani to lead her to where the rest of the family had gathered, talking to a pair of Sisters. After a few minutes, Ella was totally calm again, trying to enjoy the afternoon.

A teenage Lagrimari acolyte to the Sisterhood approached, a huge smile on her face. Ulani jumped up and down and raced to embrace the girl. "Zeli-yul!" she said. "Mama, meet Zeli. She is friend."

Ella's heart stuttered to be called Mama. She reached for Zeli's forehead to greet her. "Pleasant to meet you," she said.

Zeli nodded and held her palms out for an Elsiran greeting. "Pleasant to meet you," she said with a thick accent.

The three girls began chattering excitedly in Lagrimari, and the sight warmed Ella all over. Benn and Vera were locked in conversation with a Brother, the first man Ella had ever seen in the Sisterhood. He wore the same blue robe and his long hair was in the same topknot as all the women wore.

A tap on her shoulder had her turning around. "Sister Rienne," she exclaimed.

Rienne beamed. "Such a wonderful sight, I'm so pleased. How is the transition to parenthood going?"

"It's been quite a change, bringing the girls home, moving house—all in such a short period of time. But I'm deliriously happy. I know it won't be easy, but they're mine. I feel like it was meant to be."

"The Goddess provides," Rienne said, looking over at the girls. "I see you've met Tarazeli, one of our new recruits. She's the Goddess's personal robe mistress. Very promising." She lowered her voice and pulled Ella slightly to the side. "You know, she's part of the reason Syllenne is behind bars."

"Oh, really?"

"Yes, Zeli was the main witness. She saw Syllenne transferring the bags of palmsalt with her own eyes. Her account was quite credible."

Ella regarded the girl anew. She was certain that while Syllenne was involved, she had protected herself from any direct connection with the crime, as she'd done for many years. So what had Zeli actually witnessed?

"So much to be grateful for," Rienne exclaimed, clapping her hands together. "Syllenne's entire operation has been taken down and all her cronies, even Gizelle, have either fled or been arrested." Ella had never seen the woman so upbeat.

"And look, the ceremony is about to begin." With a trill of laughter, Rienne excused herself. The Sisters present began to gather the adoptees together at the front of the room.

Ella approached Zeli before she could move away. "Do you speak Elsiran?"

"Not well," Zeli replied. "Learning still."

"You saw Syllenne Nidos . . . in the storeroom." Ella enunciated each word, watching the teen carefully for recognition.

Zeli nodded. "Yes. I see her." She brought her arms out to represent something big. "Bags. Large bags."

"They found the traces of palmsalt where the bags were stored."

The girl squinted, not understanding. Ella tried another tack. "Do you know Zann Biddel?"

Zeli frowned. "A man?"

"Yes, a man. Elsiran." *More or less,* she thought.

Zeli shook her head. Ella didn't detect any sort of subterfuge, though she couldn't be sure. What she wouldn't give for a Song to be able to distinguish truth from lies.

"Tarazeli was not involved in any conspiracy." The rich voice came from behind her. Ella's hair lifted on end with the force of an overpowering energy crackling in the air. She turned around slowly to find the Goddess Awoken standing behind her.

"Your Excellency." She dove into a deep curtsey, keeping her head down as she rose.

The Goddess was clad in a flowing white gown. When Ella dared to look up again, she found the woman tall, regal, and imposing, Her hair shifting from a mysterious breeze.

Whereas Ella would have expected the arrival of the Goddess to draw a crowd, all behind her was strangely quiet. She chanced a look around to find a veil of darkness between her and the rest of the room. It was like she and the Goddess existed outside of time and space.

"You have questions, Zorelladine Farmafield." The Goddess's statement was flat, Her voice mellifluous and musical, but commanding.

Ella had no desire to question the Goddess Awoken about anything, but it was obvious that's what the woman wanted. Her fingers fidgeted as she worked up the nerve to give voice to her suspicions.

"I believe that Zann Biddel set up Syllenne to take the fall for the bombing. I think she was involved, but he was, too. Do you know of this?" She kept her voice as respectful as possible, but fear of reprisal bloomed in her chest.

The Goddess peered at Ella intensely. "Zann frightens you."

"He's grown powerful. He has many at his command and his views are . . . divisive." Her voice shook a bit at the end as she was subjected to the severe scrutiny.

"Zann's time in the spotlight is temporary. He is like a rodent that comes out of its warm, dry nest just before a storm. He will squeak and squawk while frightened women with brooms race after him, but when the storm hits, all of that will be forgotten."

Ella shivered. Was she the woman with the broom in that metaphor? The Goddess's lips curved in an almost smile as if She'd heard Ella's thoughts. Perhaps She had. Ella couldn't conceive of the power She possessed.

"So you're saying Zann is nothing to worry about?"

"Will worrying help?"

Frustration beat at her. This conversation was surreal on so many levels. "But . . . he's on the brink of splitting the country in two. He can't just be ignored."

"A wise woman once said that a strategic sacrifice is often necessary for the greater good."

Ella's heart nearly stopped. Every muscle froze in shock and a growing sense of fear. Her mouth worked soundlessly, unable to even respond.

"You, yourself, wanted Syllenne behind bars, did you not?"

Ella nodded, still unable to form words.

"What does it matter if Zann put her there or someone else did?"

Rienne's words from so many days ago came back to her. *Don't you think the Goddess can sense the heart of Her own High Priestess? If something could be done, wouldn't She do it?*

Clarity poked through the fog. "Someone else . . . like . . . you?" She thought of Zeli, the Goddess's personal servant, the one who had witnessed Syllenne's misdeeds. The account ledger found in the Eastern temple—that Rienne had been the one to find it. Someone with a specific grievance against the High Priestess. All so improbable, so calculated.

Ella swallowed and took a step back.

"Discomfort is a part of change. Do not fear it, Zorelladine." Oola's stare pinned her in place. A surge of power flowed over Ella's skin. She'd never felt anything like it and couldn't say it was pleasant. Then, it was gone. The cocoon of darkness that they'd been enclosed in lifted. Sounds and scents from the room rose to greet her. And a wave of gasps indicated the presence of the Goddess had been noted.

On wobbly legs, Ella stepped aside, allowing the Goddess to glide past her. Instead of joining the fray, she hung back in the corner, trying to make sense of the way the world had shifted on its axis.

She was not a follower of the Goddess, did not worship in Her temples or read Her scriptures. But Ella was a woman of faith and had respect for the power of all deities. The Goddess Awoken was something entirely different.

Eventually, she made her way to Benn and witnessed the ceremony in silence. Each adoptee received a satin sash and had their names entered in the Book of Records, where the Sisterhood kept genealogical data on the populace. The new interim High Priestess arrived and said a few inspiring words. The Goddess declined to make a speech, but stayed on the sidelines, watching the event.

After it was over, Tana and Ulani raced up to her, grinning widely. Tana's rare smile was something Ella hoped to see much more of. Vera was cooing over their sashes, acting every inch the doting grandmother. But Ella could barely spare the emotion to be shocked at her mother-in-law's turnaround, she was still in so much turmoil.

Benn's gaze indicated he'd noticed her strange mood. She shook her head slightly, indicating she didn't want to talk about it now. Later, when they were alone and she had processed things a bit more.

When the crackling energy hit her skin, tears formed in her eyes. Couldn't She just leave Ella alone?

But instead of targeting Ella, the Goddess bent to regard Ulani. Ella held her breath, scared for her daughter.

"Do you remember me, little one?" the Goddess asked.

Ulani nodded and reached out to touch the woman's forehead.

"It is good that you have found a family. There is nothing more important." She spoke in Elsiran, but Ulani appeared to understand perfectly.

The Goddess then turned to Tana. Her hand reached out toward the child as if to stroke her cheek, but stopped, hovering there in the air. Tana's eyes were wide, not with fear, but awe.

The Goddess stood sharply, all of Her intense regard focused exclusively on Tana. When She spoke, Ella knew it was directed at her, though Her gaze never moved from the girl. "Your daughters will need to be trained. Their Songs are strong and must be focused."

Ella cleared her throat. "Tana doesn't have a Song, Your Excellency."

"All Lagrimari have Songs. Some are just different than others." She turned to face Ella. "Her Song has been bound; for that you should be grateful. When the viper regains her venom, it will be something to behold."

Without another word, She turned and disappeared into the crowd.

Ella gathered her daughters to her, one in each arm, holding them close to overcome the trembling.

"What did that mean?" Benn murmured behind her.

"Wait until everyone hears that my granddaughters received special attention from the Goddess Herself!" Vera sounded beside herself with joy.

Ella just squeezed the girls tight. She had thought long and hard on how to protect her family. To shield them from the scheming and the power hungry, from those who wanted to manipulate or harm them. From the cutting glances and biting words and the people shouting against them in the streets.

But the reality of being a parent was just starting to set in. Sometimes protection was impossible. Some threats were far too big to grasp, much less battle against. All she could do was hold them tight, and love them as much as she could.

And pray it would be enough.

CHAPTER FORTY-THREE

The child emerged from the river bearing an armload of wriggling fish. "We have plenty," the sister said. "Jasper the Farmer has made it so."

Ayal ate with the family, enjoying the veritable feast. But inside her full belly lay a dark foreboding.

—THE AYALYA

Tai found Darvyn standing at the edge of the vast car park, black vehicles stretched out beyond. The Lagrimari man was hunched over, stiff as a board, staring toward the mountain rising behind the palace. Tai crossed the gravel underfoot to stand next to him. In their brief acquaintance, Darvyn had proven himself to be an excellent ally and a good friend.

"If there's anything I can do, mate," he said, "I *do* smuggle things for a living. Occasionally that includes people."

Darvyn's eyebrows rose a fraction.

"Only those who want to be smuggled, I assure you," Tai said, holding up his hands.

A flicker of amusement crossed Darvyn's face but soon died.

"I'm very serious, though. My ship is yours if you need it. I'm headed out in two days' time. I've been summoned home by my king." His mother's furious cable message had been singeing its way through his pocket. It was already a week old, having arrived while he was in Yaly. He would have to do quite a lot of groveling to avoid prison again, unless she was in a generous mood.

"I appreciate that, Tai. I'll keep it in mind."

They stood for a few moments more before Tai decided to leave the man alone with his solitude. Sometimes that was the greatest gift of all—time to think.

He'd been doing a lot of thinking himself. The hedge maze beyond the main garden was good for that. He'd wandered it for hours the day before, his mother's summons in his hand. He had no love for the city of Rosira, for the fancy palace and the residents who, as a whole, turned their noses up at him. If not for the Goddess's mission and then the king and queen's consent, he would not even have been allowed into this place. Mik had firmly refused Tai's invitation to join him, preferring the cheap Portside inn. There was only one thing that made the thought of leaving shred him inside: Lizvette.

Though she had not invited him to her apartment in the palace, Tai had made sure as soon as he arrived that he knew how to get there. A bit of talking up certain members of the kitchen staff—more intrigued than appalled by his rough looks—had ensured he knew Lizvette Nirall's location. He sought her out now, walking through the finely appointed labyrinth until he reached her door.

He was glad her house arrest had been lifted and her rooms

were not under guard. Imagining her locked away, even in an opulent palace apartment, grated him. He knocked and waited several minutes before Lizvette herself appeared on the threshold. She broke into a grin when she looked up at him. He leaned against the door frame, drinking her in. But instead of inviting him inside, she stepped out, closing the door softly behind her.

"What are you doing here?" she asked, still smiling.

"What do you think?"

"How did you know where to find me?"

He winked. "Are you having a party in there or something? Too busy for old Tai?" He made his voice teasing, but her obvious reluctance to invite him in spoke volumes.

"No, I'm not busy. Let's go somewhere, though. I hate being stuck inside all day. Shall we visit the gardens?"

He forced a smile and waited in the hallway while she grabbed her shawl. Once she was suitably covered, they headed out.

Tai wanted to reach for her, to hold her hand, but her crossed arms offered little chance of that. He wondered if it had been a mistake to come see her. She hadn't contacted him since they'd been back at the palace and he hadn't seen her for two days, not since she'd left the king's office after their meeting.

As soon as Tai and Lizvette cleared the palace walls, however, her shield seemed to come down. They paused at the entrance to the main garden, where the path split off in three different directions.

"Come this way," she said, pointing to the left. She took his hand in hers, and a weight dropped off his shoulders.

Her hand was soft and delicate. The memory of it stroking him heated his blood, blasting away any chill. Her cheeks were rosy, as well. He wondered how often she thought of their night together. They had yet to speak of it.

“I have to leave in two days.” He’d thought it best to be direct, not dance around the issue, but she paled rapidly and nearly tripped over the gravel pathway. He steadied her with an arm around her waist and pulled her to his side.

“S-so soon?” Her voice was small. He regretted having to tell her, but it was for the best.

“Mother is angry with me. If I don’t go quickly, she will no doubt send me back to prison.”

Her eyes rounded, and she sucked in a breath. However, she didn’t draw away at the reminder of his past. Instead, her expression turned melancholy, her eyes wide and sorrowful. “Do you have to go?” she whispered.

He couldn’t stop himself from caressing her cheek. “Unfortunately, yes.”

She nodded, leaning into his palm. The knot inside him tied itself tighter, joining him to her in an invisible bond. He wanted to kiss her, but something held him back.

“Come with me.” He spoke the words before he’d even finished thinking them, but once they were said, they felt right. “You don’t have to be stuck here surrounded by memories of everything that’s gone wrong. I believe I can convince my mother that I’m sufficiently sorry, and then we can go anywhere you want. We can sail the Delaveen Ocean to every port. You’ll see things you’ve only read about.”

Lizvette closed her eyes, as if picturing the trip already. Color returned to her cheeks, and she smiled. When she opened her eyes again, though, sadness still overflowed.

“That sounds wonderful, but I can’t. Father will surely be convicted, and my mother . . .” She shook her head. “She’ll be left with nothing.”

Tai stroked her cheek. "Do you think she would . . . harm herself?"

Lizvette chuckled bitterly. "Not a chance. She's already trying to marry me off to a rich merchant's son, or anyone with coin who will still have me, really." Her tone was wry, but Tai stiffened.

"Marry you off?" He searched her face for some clue she was joking.

Lizvette looked away, then took his hand, tugging him down the path. They passed through gardens whose buds had already closed in preparation for winter.

"My mother and my cousin believe I can still secure the future of our family through marriage." She shrugged with stiff shoulders.

Tai's head ached suddenly, pounding inside his skull. "And what do you think of that? Aren't you tired of being their pawn?"

She turned on him, her face full of fire. "This isn't Raun, Tai. There are limits to what women can do here. I could work and provide for her, or I can marry. And I've never had a job." She looked around helplessly. "I don't even know what it is I could do to earn enough for Mother to be comfortable."

"Maybe she needs to be a little uncomfortable," he muttered.

Lizvette squeezed his hand. "I didn't say I *would* marry someone Mother chose. But I don't know what I'm going to do. I just don't know."

The desperation in her voice melted Tai's anger. He drew her to him and breathed in the scent of her hair.

"Perhaps you can come back here. Once you appease your mother," she said. The hope in her voice only saddened him.

He forced his voice to be cheerful when he responded. "Rosira has always been a busy port. I will certainly be back."

She nodded against his chest and wrapped her arms around him.

"Are you cold?" he asked.

"Cold to my bones," she said.

"You know, even though we can't go to your room, we could always go to mine," he said cheekily. He fully expected her to refuse and was surprised when she pulled back with a giant grin on her face.

"Why, Master Summerhawk, that's an innovative idea."

He gave a mock bow. "I have those every now and again, duchess."

He led her back to the palace and to his room and kept her there, between his sheets, for as long as he could.

Footsteps passed Kyara's cell fairly regularly, but there was something about these particular ones that caught her attention. She shifted on the mattress to see who was there and lost her breath.

Eyes red, face inscrutable, Darvyn stood before the barred door. He didn't say anything, merely raised his hand to grip the iron, holding it so tightly the skin around his knuckles lightened.

She scrambled up, hurried over to him, and stroked his fingers. She smelled burning metal, and then he was pushing open the door, hauling her into his arms, burying his face in her hair.

Tears streamed down her cheeks at his closeness. She'd washed up and been given a new set of clothing—an Elsiran dress that hung off her awkwardly—but she wished she could meet Darvyn looking her best for once. Though she had no idea what that would even look like.

"Is there any way I can persuade you to come with me?" he asked. "To walk out this door and just leave? We could go anywhere. Tai would sail us away and we could just be gone, like specters in the night."

His voice stoked the longing in her. "They would stop us," she said, shaking her head.

"They couldn't stop *you*."

"You don't think I should be punished for what I did?"

His eyes bored holes into her. "Would you have done it without the spell?"

She shook her head silently.

"Then no. You were forced. Besides, the trial was a sham. You had no chance to represent yourself. At worst, you should be retried with an adequate defense."

Kyara leaned her head against Darvyn's chest and ran her hands up and down his back. "And if I follow you out of here, how many would get hurt?"

"No one has to. You don't have to use your power if you don't want to. You never have to use it again. I can get us out. Just tell me that's what you want."

She stared up at him. If the choice was between death and Darvyn, then there wasn't one. Her resolve to go through with the execution wavered. "I don't want to kill anymore," she whispered. "I don't want to hurt anyone. No more spirits." She shivered, pushing away the memory of the dream. "And we'd have to go far away from people. I can't risk . . ." She swallowed hard.

"Whatever you want." Darvyn gently took her hands and led her out of the cell. As they passed the other compartments, she peered in to find the occupants all asleep. The guards at the front station were in the same condition.

She looked at Darvyn askance, and he shrugged. "I've been forbidden from the dungeons by the Goddess."

"And where is She now?" Kyara asked.

"Not here." He hurried up the staircase leading away from the damp stone prison. The dark passageway was empty, but footsteps ahead drew them up short. She jerked Darvyn's hand back when the intense concentration on his face made it look like he was gearing up for a spell.

"You can't put everyone in the castle to sleep."

"Why not?" he asked.

She drew him toward a door. When the handle wouldn't turn, she motioned for him to do his unlocking trick. He complied, and they slipped into the dark room just as the footsteps drew nearer.

He sang a ball of fire to illuminate the space. They were in a storage room. Shelves lined the coarse walls, and discarded tables, chairs, crates, and boxes filled the floor. Footsteps thundered by in the hallway outside. Darvyn led Kyara to the back of the room, and they settled on a thick, scarred table.

"They must have discovered what you've done," Kyara whispered.

"It doesn't matter. I won't let them kill you." He said it with such vehemence, such strength, but Kyara was torn. Was her life worth so much more than those of the people she'd killed? Did she even deserve Darvyn's loyalty or his love?

If she lived, what would she do? And what would happen if someone else took an interest in her powers? More Physicks or some other type of mage out in the world? She was one blood spell away from being made a killer again. She knew all too well how short-lived freedom could be.

But she couldn't explain any of that to Darvyn. His pain was raw and exposed. She knew he felt the need to make this right. Isn't that what the Shadowfox did? He'd spent his whole life saving people he didn't even know, and she loved him all the more for his determination to rescue her, even when she didn't deserve it.

She stroked his cheek and brought his head around so she could brush his lips with hers. It wasn't even a kiss, just a graze of their mouths, but it opened up a well of longing. Darvyn let the fire spell go, plunging them into darkness. But she didn't need to see him, only to feel him. He kissed her properly, thoroughly, plundering her mouth with his own and leaving no part unexplored. She was soon on her back on the table, ignoring the discomfort of the hard wood as he fit himself above her and between her legs.

She could still hear activity in the hall. Then the door to the room rattled as someone tried it.

"Darvyn," she murmured.

"They won't get in. No key will open that door."

She wanted to protest more, but then his lips moved to her neck. She stretched back, pushing everything else from her mind. She trusted her safety to him. And her time was nearly up anyway.

Impatient, she dragged up the hem of the dress to her waist and tried to move his hand to where she wanted it. He chuckled against her mouth before pulling back to help remove the irksome clothing. She was left only in her underwear, shivering in the cool air.

The intense darkness, together with the noises just outside the door and her overall sense that this would be the last time for them, made her greedy. Her emotions were at war, her body on fire, and her heart breaking.

The rustling beside her must have been Darvyn shedding his own clothing, for when his body met hers, it was all smooth skin and hard muscle. He kissed her senseless until all thought melted away. She stroked every bit of him she could reach, running her palms down his back and over the firm globes of muscle below, down the backs of his thighs and around to the front until she gripped him in her hand and guided him inside her.

There was never enough time for them, there never would be, but she relished the perfect fit as he invaded her body. She bit her lip and then his shoulder as they came together, rocking the table into the wall with each movement.

Darvyn shifted them so that the table was quieter and he was somehow deeper, no longer just inside her body and her heart, but now penetrating her soul, too. The darkness, the fear, the longing all combined, and when she went over the edge, bright stars lit her vision, piercing the blackness.

She heard and felt his heavy breaths against her and pulled him even closer, wishing she could slice herself down the middle and store him inside her. She never wanted to be without him and mourned the fact that nothing, not even love, was allowed her.

She only realized she was crying when he separated himself from her and cradled her in his arms and wiped her tears. His lips glanced off her cheeks, kissing the wetness away.

Whoever was at the door had long since moved on, apparently deciding that if they couldn't get in, neither could anyone else. They had a little more time, then. She took advantage of it and found Darvyn's lips again. This time she would savor him. Taste him everywhere she wanted to.

She gently prodded at his chest until he was lying on his back, then crawled on top of him, holding his arms in place as she took her time exploring the length of his body with her tongue. When he moved to shift positions, she silenced him in the most pleasurable ways. This time when they made love, it was slow and lingering.

After she asked, he brought the flame back so she could look into his eyes and burn the expression on his face when they came together into her memory.

CHAPTER FORTY-FOUR

When it was time to leave, the family offered her their horse. "To carry you on your way," said the grandmother.

"Your generosity is too much," Ayal said. "I cannot take your only horse."

"Do not fear," the horse replied. "I will return to them once I have seen you off." And so she accepted the gift.

—THE AYALYA

"The hallway is quiet now," Kyara said. She opened her other sight and found no Nethersong nearby, indicating no one lingering about. They had lain together quietly for a long while in the darkness, but if they were going to leave, now was the time to do it.

Kyara was still unsure what she should do. Was it possible to live happily with Darvyn when so much guilt assailed her? His touch and his presence convinced her to try, for him.

They made their way to the door. Darvyn melted the lock completely away, releasing it. He peered into the hall, then motioned for her to follow.

They sprinted down the corridor, which ended in a set of stairs going up. Kyara headed for them, but he pulled her back. Reaching out with her Song again, she sensed two people waiting on the floor above.

"This way," he breathed into her ear.

He guided her to a narrow area behind the stairs that she hadn't noticed before. At first, it appeared to be a crawl space, but it ended up being a low tunnel. They crept a dozen paces on their hands and knees when the ceiling rose suddenly. The passage ended in a small vestibule that, judging by the dust and musty odor, hadn't been used in quite a long time.

A small window, completely clouded over with dust and grime, was embedded into the stone across from them. They crouched beneath it, and Darvyn used the corner of his sleeve to wipe away a small circle of muck near the bottom.

"It just leads to another storage room," he said.

Kyara scanned the small area, then tugged on his sleeve and pointed to the ceiling in which a wooden trapdoor had been fixed. Neither could reach it standing, so Darvyn wrapped his arms around her legs and lifted her up. She pushed against it, but it wouldn't budge. "Do you feel anyone on the other side?" she asked.

"No."

"Let me down," she said. Once on the ground, she tugged Darvyn back from underneath it. She reached out for the Nether in the dead wood and multiplied it, smashing the trapdoor into pieces that rained down on where they'd just been standing. Darvyn's eyes widened in surprise. Then he grinned at her. He hoisted her up, and she climbed through the opening to find herself surrounded by delicious aromas.

In moments, Darvyn was by her side. Shelves overflowing with food surrounded them. Fresh vegetables, most of which she couldn't identify, lay out next to tins painted with colorful fruits. Burlap sacks stuffed with grain and cartons of mysterious dry goods burdened the shelves, some of which sagged under their weight. Light shined from a bulb overhead, and the pantry was further lit by a round window in a door on the far side of the small room. She sensed at least a dozen people on the other side of the door. Low chatter could be heard from the staff along with the sounds of chopping.

Darvyn stood to the side of the door and peered into the kitchen. Kyara moved to him and caught a glimpse of white-clad men and women, all engrossed in their tasks. Darvyn grabbed an apron from a hook and tossed it to Kyara.

She raised her eyebrows. The workers all appeared to be Elsiran.

"The palace has hired several Lagrimari over the past weeks. I'll divert their attention, and no one will look at us too closely if we act like we belong here," he said.

If she weren't a Nethersinger, he could change her appearance completely, but she shrugged and tied on the apron, covering her drab, blue prison garb. Darvyn donned a white chef's coat and covered his hair in a white cap to match. Once their meager disguises were in place, he opened the pantry door and they made a beeline for the exit, walking purposefully.

The outer doors led to a covered porch with a driveway just beyond where the kitchen received supplies. They stepped onto the pavement, and Kyara couldn't believe that she was nearly free. The late-afternoon sunshine warmed her cheeks, and she breathed in the fresh air.

But a storm of energy crackled nearby. She turned to the shadows of the porch and was somehow unsurprised to find the Goddess Awoken standing there, lit by the sun as if She were on fire.

Darvyn gripped her hand, but Kyara's shoulders slumped. The one person stronger than Darvyn faced them down. The Goddess's eyes held no anger. She wore no expression at all. She merely stood, Her hair moving in a breeze Kyara didn't feel.

Darvyn's expression brimmed with betrayal as he looked at the Goddess. When She raised Her hands, Kyara gasped at what She held and pulled Darvyn behind her to protect him.

"It is for his own good," the Goddess said, approaching Darvyn with a collar.

"How could you?" Kyara asked. "Don't collar him! I will go back. Please!"

A great wind whipped up where the day had been so calm and sunny just a moment before. Dark clouds manifested. Lightning struck, and thunder roared.

A storm beat down on the palace out of nowhere, growing more furious by the second. Even under the cover of the overhang, Kyara was suddenly soaked to the skin. She turned to Darvyn to find his eyes shining with power, using more Earthsong than she could ever remember him using before.

The Goddess didn't say anything, nor did She appear to grow angry. Darvyn's outburst didn't halt Her, though. Fireballs popped into existence, immune to the rain, and pelted Her, but they disappeared before they touched Her. The mountain behind the palace rumbled and the earth shook, yet none of it fazed Her.

Darvyn didn't move. His hand on Kyara's was as unyielding as stone. Veins bulged in his neck and forehead, but he didn't try to run. Perhaps he couldn't. Was the Goddess freezing him in place?

She floated closer, Her feet not touching the ground until She was near enough to affix the red collar around Darvyn's neck. His attack abruptly ceased.

With a wave of Her hand, the clouds disappeared. Kyara's clothes dried in an instant and no evidence of the storm remained. Kyara wrapped her arms around Darvyn's rigid form as footsteps sounded behind her. Rough hands pulled her away and placed shackles on her wrists.

"Those aren't necessary," the Goddess said.

The Guardsman next to her widened his eyes, but didn't speak and removed the shackles. Kyara rubbed her wrists. She stared at Darvyn, whose eyes had gone cold and hard.

"I love you," she said.

His gaze slowly moved to her, and his eyes gentled a fraction. "For always."

She nodded as the guards tugged on her arm and led her away. "For always."

She kept her eyes on him as she was led backward, around the corner of the palace. At the last second, the intense look he gave her morphed to one of venom as he shifted his gaze to the Goddess.

CHAPTER FORTY-FIVE

As she rode away, she turned back to witness Child-Who-Gathers-Water take a running leap into the river. An innocent delight overtook the seeker, causing her to wriggle and move on the horse's back.

"Be still," the horse admonished.

"I can't," Ayal said. For she had grown the tail of a fish.

—THE AYALYA

"You can't be serious," Lizvette's mother said from her perch on the settee. She clicked off the radiophonic and stared down her nose at her daughter.

Lizvette responded as she always had, by steeling her spine to ensure no ounce of emotion showed in her eyes. It was harder now than it ever had been. "Yes, Mother. I'm going. It's a horrible display, and I just don't believe that they'll actually go through with it."

Mother pursed her lips and sighed dramatically. "You should not be down there among the rabble watching an execution. It's unseemly."

"The king and queen will be there."

Her mother gave a scoff just short of a snort. Lizvette's eyes widened a fraction. Then Mother fell into a fit of coughing that sounded fake even to Lizvette's ears.

She remained motionless near the door until the racket ceased. "I am going to support a friend in his time of need."

Mother rolled her eyes. "Cavorting with Lagrimari men . . . What is the world coming to? You will undo everything I'm trying to put together here with your ill-considered associations."

Lizvette pulled on her gloves and straightened her dress, then wrapped her shawl around her to keep out the autumn cold. "I will see you when I return, Mother. Stay well."

"Wait a minute, young lady!" But her next words were muffled by the door that kept the apartment insulated from the sounds of the palace. Lizvette closed her eyes and sighed with relief, only to startle when something soft brushed her lips.

She smiled into Tai's kiss and took a handful of his shirt in her grip to draw him closer. Today she didn't care a whit about the eyes that might see them, about what they would say. Today was the day. He was leaving this evening, sailing off at sunset like a true pirate.

He pulled away and grabbed her hand; she grinned up at him like a lovestruck fool. What did anything matter when today was their last day?

"Looks like you're escaping," he said with a smile that didn't quite meet his eyes. He'd been doing everything he could to make this easier for both of them—she knew he felt far more than he was letting on.

"The apartment never felt so small before. Mother's impeccable health is positively suffocating."

Her mother had not reacted at all when faced with Lizvette's role in capturing her father. In fact, she refused to speak his name or respond to any conversation about him. It was as if Marineve Nirall was determined to put her husband out of her head and ignore his perfidy forever.

It was just as well. Lizvette had no desire to speak about her father. He had apparently not given any more information on future plots against the monarchy and faced trial in a few weeks. Elsiran justice moved quite a bit slower than that of the Lagrimari.

Tai firmed his lips, looking like he wanted to say something then thinking better of it. Perhaps he would repeat his invitation to her. It was a fantastic notion, her sailing away to Raun, but she just couldn't conceive of it. Regardless of how Mother treated her, Lizvette would not let her be put out onto the streets because of Father's disgrace.

She grasped Tai's hand like a lifeline as they left the palace.

A large crowd of palace dwellers and servants accompanied them down the winding streets to the park square where the public execution was to take place. Elsirans rarely executed their prisoners, and when they did, such affairs were usually done in private. However, the law did allow for conspicuous exhibitions such as this, a fact that the Lagrimari demanding Kyara's blood had exploited.

A chill went through Lizvette. The whole idea was barbaric, but so many of the curious—and the bloodthirsty—had gathered. An empty wooden platform had been erected with a large pole jutting up. Her eyes glanced off the attached rope, watering at the thought of what it meant.

"Where is Darvyn?" she asked Tai.

"I'm not sure. I think—wait, there he is." He pointed to the other large platform in front of the crowd that held two chairs of minimal ornamentation. This was where the king and queen would observe. Four Royal Guardsmen stood in a rigid line in front of it with more behind it. On the ground to the left of the stage stood Darvyn, a scowl marring his normally placid face. He wore a strange bit of ruby jewelry around his neck, which twinkled in the sun.

In wordless agreement, she and Tai made their way through the crowd to the royal stage. Surprisingly, they were allowed through security without comment and rushed to Darvyn's side. He acknowledged them with a nod, but the misery in his eyes was so intense it made Lizvette's breath catch.

"I don't—I'm so sorry," she began. He looked away, and she clamped her lips shut. Words were not enough for the situation, and she had nothing more to give. Tai moved to Darvyn's other side and stood, shoulder to shoulder, in solidarity with him. Lizvette took his cue and lent Darvyn her quiet support.

An imperious throat-clearing sounded behind her, and she craned her neck to see Zavros standing with several other Council members. She inclined her head at him, ignored his glower, and turned back around.

Darvyn appeared calmer for the next few minutes, but a sudden tensing of his body alerted her that Kyara must be near.

She wasn't sure what she'd expected, but the woman being led to the gallows was not it. Her hair was braided in thin, dark plaits that brushed her shoulders. She was beautiful in a wholly different way than Jasminda. Her face was lean and almost sharp, but at the same time graceful.

Kyara's eyes searched the crowd. When they landed on Darvyn, a visible shudder went through her. The longing and misery in the look she gave him brought tears to Lizvette's eyes. She had spent a lifetime hiding her emotions, numbing herself to pain and injury, but the strength Kyara displayed made her feel like a lowly jester in the presence of a master performer.

Suddenly, she wasn't sure if she could go through with watching this woman be killed. The presence of the gathered crowd seemed mercenary. She longed to squeeze her eyes shut and retreat from it all, but though she'd never met her, she felt she owed it to Kyara to bear witness. It was the very least she could do.

Kyara was stunned by the number of people who had gathered to watch her die. Hundreds stood in what looked like some sort of park where a wooden scaffold had been erected. A noose swung ominously from the crossbeam.

In Lagrimar, observing executions was compulsory; however, from what the teenaged Lagrimari girl in Sisterhood robes who'd prayed for her during her last meal had told her, Elsirans generally did not attend such things. Kyara squinted at the audience, surprised to find a nearly equal number of Lagrimari and Elsiran faces. For her people, old habits must die hard. Or perhaps they just wanted to see the famed Poison Flame punished. Most of the Elsirans looked vaguely perplexed and unsure of why they'd come at all. It was something new, a rare public hanging in their land. Hers was to be the first of many, so they'd best get used to it.

Her hands were unbound—the Goddess must have ordered it. Yet the mighty Earthsinger knew that Kyara could wipe out all these people with a thought. It was amazing She had enough trust in her to allow her this small bit of freedom. Kyara only hoped her Song would not betray her. It had the habit of lashing out, trying to protect her when danger arose. But it was small and quiet within her now, cowed perhaps by Kyara's own acceptance of her fate.

She scanned the crowd. Those assembled were oddly quiet. Only a low murmur rippled through them—nothing like the forced cheers of a Lagrimari Mercy Day execution. But those were folks afraid that their noncompliance or lack of enthusiasm would mean death or worse. These people were mostly just curious.

To her left, another wooden platform stood, bearing two ornate chairs for the king and queen. The entire crowd bowed low in response to some signal Kyara had missed, and the two royals ascended the short staircase to their stage.

The queen looked like any other Lagrimari girl, only playing dress up in a fine gown with a delicate crown on her head. Next to her was her Elsiran husband. If those two could make it work, perhaps there was a world in which she and Darvyn could have, as well. It just was not this world.

Darvyn stood between a beautiful Elsiran woman and a strange man with blue hair and markings all over his face. This must be the pirate, though she couldn't recall his name. She was glad Darvyn had friends near him—especially since his Lagrimari comrades had turned on him—but her eyes stung to see him collared, trapped.

A third person alighted the royal stage—the Goddess Awoken. She stood serenely, Her hands clasped in front of Her. Naked awe spread through the crowd as they caught sight of Her, but Kyara was numb.

Over a loudspeaker, a gruff voice began to list the crimes of which Kyara had been convicted at her trial. A trial that she had not attended because she had been locked in another dungeon half a world away.

A bitter smile cracked Kyara's lips. She'd been born in a cage and had never left. Would death finally free her?

Once the recitation had been repeated again in Elsiran, the Goddess left the king and queen's platform and crossed the distance to the gallows where Kyara stood. She raised Her arm to silence the murmuring crowd, and the quiet that resulted was harsh and immediate.

"Kyara ul-Lagrimar, your sentence will be carried out directly." She spoke in Lagrimari this time, the king translating for the audience.

Kyara's gaze was torn away from the Goddess's potency by a movement on the other stage. Queen Jasminda clawed at her throat, her eyes growing wide with obvious distress. The king reached for her and gripped her hands as she slumped down in her chair. Royal Guardsmen leaped onto the stage, blocking Kyara's view and preventing anyone else from approaching.

"Do you think that you can do some good, Kyara?" The Goddess's low voice was ice on Kyara's spine, making her shiver.

"What's happening?" she asked.

The swarm around Queen Jasminda expanded, the crowd growing more and more panicked.

"Do some good." The Goddess pointed in the queen's direction and stepped back.

Kyara frowned. What was She talking about? Through a break in the bodies, she saw the queen's limp body being held in the king's arms. Kyara sank into her other sight to seek out the Nethersong within the queen. Jasminda was easy to locate; the light from her death energy burned bright and hot. Poison coursed through her veins—a formidable compound that had been lingering in her bloodstream for several hours.

Kyara reached for the toxin and recoiled. The sheer force of the Nether was alarming. She grasped for it again, taking hold and pulling it from the queen's body, drawing it into her own Song.

The world faded as she focused on the queen, rerouting the deadly energy as quickly as she could. But the bright glow of Jasminda's body continued to shine as Nethersong multiplied within her. The king was hustling Jasminda off the stage now and down to a waiting car. Kyara, blind to her surroundings, moved to follow, but strong hands held her back. Frustrated with being stymied in her quest, she let loose a burst of energy and the hands left her.

Realizing what she'd done, she looked around and found the people within twelve paces of her down on the ground. The Nether inside them was fading fast; they must just be unconscious, not dead. The only person still standing was the Goddess, who looked at her inscrutably.

Kyara once again moved toward the stage, noting the vehicles lined up behind it. She locked eyes with the king, who held his wife in his arms. Darvyn was next to him, speaking urgently in his ear.

"Can you help?" King Jaqros asked in a strangled voice, tears streaming down his face.

"I think so." Kyara approached. "Set her down."

"She has no heartbeat," the king said as he sat right there on the ground at the curb with the queen's head cradled in his lap.

Kyara's gaze shot to Darvyn. He pulled at the collar around his neck, and it snapped off and floated back to the Goddess. Darvyn spared the Goddess a savage look, then touched Queen Jasminda's forehead.

He shook his head slightly. "I can't feel anything."

"Sit back," she told Darvyn, feeling instinctively that an Earthsinger should not be in contact with Jasminda while she tried to help.

She closed her eyes and took one of the queen's hands. Sinking into her other vision, she was blinded by the Nethersong. Drawing it from her was having no effect. It had taken over Jasminda completely. The new queen was, by all appearances, dead.

Still, Kyara tried harder, pulling at it all, breathing it in like air. But there was no Void rushing in as there had been when she'd done this before when Darvyn had been poisoned, just more Nether. This poison must have some sort of magical properties to it. Amalgam had to be at work here. It was the only answer.

Though it seemed futile, Kyara refused to give up. She gathered her strength and tugged with all her might on the energy. It filled her, like a crushing wave pulling her under. Her other sight blanked out, and she stood inside a doorway made of smoke and light. All around her was blackness, and cold rattled her bones. She recognized this place from her dream—she had traveled to the World After. Queen Jasminda stood before her.

Kyara took a step forward, and the whispers started in earnest. She was only a few paces from the queen, whose back was to her, but each step she took seemed to put her farther away.

"Your Majesty?" she called out.

The queen turned, her expression frightened. "Where am I?"

"The World After."

The queen's face crumpled. "What happened? All of a sudden I felt . . ." She grasped at her neck.

"You were poisoned. It felt magical to me. I think it was some kind of amalgam poison from the Physicks. Maybe the same kind they used to generate Nethersong before they captured me, only more potent."

The queen's arms fell to her sides, and a look of despondency came over her. "Jack."

"Your Majesty, I think I can bring you back."

Jasminda looked up, surprised. "How, when we're both dead?"

"I'm not. I mean, they didn't . . . execute me . . . yet. But did Darvyn tell you I'm a Nethersinger?"

Jasminda turned around again, lost in her own grief. Kyara could still see the glowing doorway behind them. She felt that if she could get Jasminda back through it, the queen would live again. Kyara reached for her, only to be frozen in place when a young girl entered the circle of light in which they stood.

"Ahlini?"

The girl walked up to Kyara, closer than she'd ever come in one of the dreams.

Kyara kneeled to face her. "I'm so sorry, Ahlini."

The others came again—her victims—forming a circle around her, only this time, unlike in her dream, they were quiet. No one threw out accusations or blame. They all stood staring silently.

Jasminda turned around, obviously able to see them, too. She chuckled harshly. "What is this, the welcoming committee?"

"Ahlini," Kyara said, "let me help her leave. She doesn't belong here. If I can do this one thing, then you all can do whatever you want to me. Take whatever vengeance you feel you need."

She saw Jasminda freeze in her peripheral vision. Ahlini extended her hand and Kyara took it. She'd expected cold, frigid skin, but instead, the young girl was as warm as she'd been in real life.

"You have to save them," Ahlini whispered with urgency.

"Save who?"

"The living. Both of you do. You *must* go back."

Kyara shook her head, trying to make sense of the words. "I don't understand." She looked up to see all her victims looking at her imploringly. "Where is Mooriah?"

"Go now. Save them. Embrace the Light."

A new doorway appeared behind the spirits, this one made of flame. Its flickering light danced along Ahlini's pleading face. One by one, her victims passed through the doorway of fire and disappeared until just Ahlini, Jasminda, and Kyara remained. Then Ahlini pulled away, following the others until she, too, was gone, the fire along with her.

Kyara swallowed and stood. This was so different from her dream. She couldn't begin to parse it, and the softly glowing doorway leading back to the Living World was beginning to fade. Queen Jasminda stared at Kyara, a thousand questions in her eyes. Hopefully, there would be time for answers later. She grabbed the queen's hand and tugged her toward the doorway.

Stepping through the shining arch of light felt like walking through soup. The space around her resisted her passage, sucking her sideways as if trying to lead her elsewhere. She felt the Void at the edges, a powerful yet ambivalent force. It wanted her for some reason, but she shrank away.

Full of Nethersong from the World After, Kyara was strong enough to push her way through the doorway, past the density of the Void. She made sure to have a strong grip on Jasminda and pulled her along.

Kyara's vision blurred. When she blinked her eyes, she was once again looking at the Living World through her other sight, still drawing Nethersong away from Jasminda's motionless body. Only now the staticky visual noise of the Void was rushing in to take its place. Kyara sucked in a breath. The Void was neither death nor life, but at least it was progress.

"Earthsong!" she called out. "Darvyn, she needs Earthsong. Flood her with as much as you can." She couldn't see him with her other sight, but she was certain he would assist.

Kyara redoubled her efforts, pulling the bright Nethersong out of the queen's lifeless body and watching in her mind's eye as the static of the Void was replaced with the darkness of Earthsong.

Soon the queen's body responded. The life energy within her multiplied until just a tiny spark of Nether remained—less than an adult of her age normally held. She must be a powerful Earthsinger.

Kyara sat back on her heels and focused her physical vision back on the Living World. Within a few moments, Queen Jasminda's eyes fluttered open. Her chest rose and fell rapidly, and she gasped for breath only to be crushed against the king as he embraced her.

"Jasminda," he breathed as their tears mingled.

In a small voice, the queen reassured him that she was all right. He sobbed against her and Kyara looked away, exhausted from the effort of dragging Jasminda back from death. She wavered and found herself propped up by Darvyn, his sturdy arms lending the physical strength she lacked.

"Thank you," the king said to Kyara. "I didn't think it was possible."

"Yes, thank you," Jasminda said, reaching for her hand, squeezing with a tight grip, and Kyara smiled wearily.

"You're welcome. It wasn't your time to go." She knew that instinctively.

Behind them, the agitation of the crowd bubbled. Kyara dragged her head up to see the queen rise.

"We need to leave," the king said, motioning to the Guardsmen near the long, black town car.

Jasminda placed a hand on her husband's chest. "No, not yet." She shook her head firmly at his aggrieved expression. "They tried to kill me, and I want them to know I'm not cowed."

She turned toward the stage. After a moment's pause, the king followed, his face a hard mask. They climbed back onto the platform to assure everyone of her well-being. A cheer went up in the audience.

Regardless of what some thought about the half-Lagrimari queen, she was evidently popular. Both Elsirans and Lagrimari shouted and rejoiced. Few eyes were dry.

The Goddess stood at the base of the stairs peering out into the crowd. She turned and nodded Her head in Kyara's direction. Kyara held Her gaze and nodded back.

Do some good. She'd done her very best.

CHAPTER FORTY-SIX

And so the girl with the lion's paws, bird's legs, lizard's body, and fish's tail, whose breath was edged in fire returned to Siruna the Mother. Lemuel the Wise One met her as she approached her home. "How did you find the world, child?" he asked.

"Stranger than I ever could have imagined," she replied.

—THE AYALYA

Darvyn stood, his hand in Kyara's, considering the reaction of the crowd. Competing emotions battered him, full as he was of Earthsong. Shock, fear, relief, and desperation each vied for dominance. He looked around but could not get a bead on who was feeling what. Someone had just tried to kill the new queen. Was the traitor still here watching? Had he or she already fled?

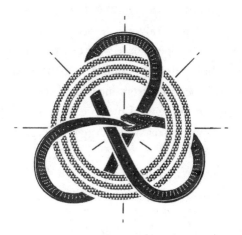

Near the stage, Lizvette and Tai stood side by side, their eyes wide with concern. Darvyn and Tai shared a glance and it was like the Raunian knew just what he was thinking. Tai put his arm around Lizvette and led her toward the street behind the square. Danger could still be lurking here. There was no way of telling friend from foe, and the perpetrator could have easily identified all of them from their trip to Yaly.

To his right, in the open space between the platform and the gallows, Aggar's bulky figure stepped up, a bullhorn in his hand. "I'm quite certain I speak for everyone when I say how glad I am to see our new queen faring well. I propose we postpone this execution until a more appropriate time." Aggar's words penetrated the cheering of the crowd.

"Postpone?" Darvyn bellowed, incredulous. Were they still going through with this madness? "Did you not see her save the queen's life?"

Shocked expressions surrounded him. These people had no clue what had just transpired. To outsiders, the queen had fallen suddenly ill and then arisen a few minutes later.

He turned to Oola who stood behind Jasminda.

You must do something.

Oola's cool gaze slid over him. *You think that I am doing nothing? Kyara needs to learn to use her power or we are all doomed.*

He shook his head slowly. *You did this on purpose? To . . . to* help *her learn her power?* He couldn't comprehend the callousness of the plan. *Did you know that someone was poisoning Jasminda? Did you let it happen? Why didn't you say anything?*

Oola blinked, and Her expression hardened. *There are mistakes that have been made that cannot be repeated. Over five centuries, I have found that people learn not with their ears but with their hearts. Words mean little.*

No. No! Darvyn shook his head over and over. Kyara reached for him, worried. *You cannot move us around like puzzle pieces. You cannot play our lives as you would a flute.*

His knees sagged, and Kyara held him up. He would lean on her for just a little while. Oola's games and riddles were nothing new to him, but this was too much.

Jasminda's clear voice pierced the fog of his mind. "This woman—Kyara—has saved my life," she announced. She looked at Jack expectantly until he translated, though she could easily have done so herself. "Her case will come back under the consideration of myself and the king. For now, her execution is stayed." Her gaze turned to Darvyn, and he knew, just knew, that she would not let Kyara die.

We will find a way to save her, Jasminda sent to him. *I owe it to her and to you. My thanks will never be enough.*

Darvyn took a deep breath and stood up straighter. He would go back to the elders. He had to make them see reason. Perhaps he might even persuade Oola to speak to them. Now that he knew She'd never really wanted Kyara dead, She would have to break Her silence.

Kyara vibrated with tension beside him, and he placed an arm around her shoulders. She would not want to break down in front of an audience, but her emotions were clearly running high.

Turwig, Hanko, and Talida approached Aggar. They whispered animatedly, and a strong anger cut through their numbers. Talida gestured emphatically next to Aggar. Turwig and Hanko were shaking their heads, but Talida pushed Aggar forward.

"Your Majesty," he said. "I understand that you believe this criminal saved your life, but it cannot make up for the many, many lives she has taken."

Jasminda turned in her seat, eyebrows raised.

"Now is not the time, Aggar," Turwig muttered, resting a hand on his shoulder. Aggar jerked away.

"If not now, when?" Talida snapped.

"Kyara's case will come under our advisement," Jasminda repeated. "You have had your say and submitted evidence to the tribunal, but we take executions very seriously here and she was offered no opportunity for defense. Part of the evidence against Kyara was that she was incapable of remorse for her actions. Saving my life today, in front of all these witnesses, seems to prove otherwise. That is reason enough for her case to be given a second look." Jasminda eyed Aggar, challenging him to talk back again.

His eyes flashed, but he clenched his jaw, gave an abrupt bow, then turned and stalked away with Talida at his side.

Darvyn swallowed. Fighting among the elders had been rare when they strategized against the True Father. But now with freedom, the unified front of the Keepers appeared to be cracking.

He shook his head and turned back to Kyara, whose arms flew around him. He lifted her, holding her close and drowning in her scent. The rest could wait, at least for another day.

The crowd chattered curiously, as if unsure what to do now that there would be no execution. Darvyn, however, was eager to retreat from the bloodthirsty masses.

In his arms, Kyara squeezed back tighter. He shut his eyes to the rest of the world and focused on what mattered most to him: her.

And then there were three.

The round table, meant for five, was down two members. Satisfaction filled Jade to bursting. He felt like an overripe peach.

To his left, Pearl fidgeted nervously, picking at his nails. His mask was slightly askew, hastily put on. The smooth-cheeked, featureless face was even more ridiculous at an angle.

"I don't know what happened," Pearl said, miserably. "The queen's drink was dosed last evening. I supervised it myself. I think we need some answers from our Yalyish contact. Didn't he guarantee results? We should get our money back. Obviously the claims that an antidote didn't exist were greatly exaggerated." The pompous fool was blustering. "This is all Amber's fault. He brokered the deal—"

"Yet it was you who failed," Jade spat. "Amber's incompetence is clear. It's why he's sitting in a jail cell now. And why are we persisting with the code names? There's little use for them anymore. Nirall's ineptitude matches only Nidos's. They sit in the dungeon because they were not up to the tasks they were given."

Diamond leaned forward, gloved hands pressed firmly onto the table. "We will not disrespect this body any further, and will keep to our rules and traditions. *Amber* and *Sapphire* are victims of the foreign plague that has swept our nation. A plague that the Hand of the Reaper has vowed to snuff out. We take care of our own and they will taste freedom again soon."

Jade sniffed. "Freedom? The only freedom they'll see is in the World After when they're executed. You seriously believe you can get them out of prison?"

"The Hand of the Reaper is held together by sinew and bone of loyalty. That is part of our strength." Diamond's voice was low and fierce.

"Loyalty to what? An ineffectual windbag?" He motioned to Pearl. "A blue-blooded blowhard?" He pointed to Diamond.

"Now you wait just a minute—"

"I seem to be the only one getting results, and I don't need either of you to do so." Jade pushed back from the table. "Lads!"

The doors opened, illuminating the windowless room with bright lighting from the hallway. Six identically dressed young men entered, faces partially hidden by the bills of their caps. Quickly and efficiently, Diamond and Pearl were lifted from their chairs and had their hands bound while they sputtered in protest.

"Your service to your country has been noted," Jade sneered, "but your methods are no longer necessary. Thank you for inviting me into your secret society. It's been very interesting to see how the rich and elite have gotten things done over the years. But personally, I prefer my way."

He allowed their masks to stay on a while longer. He didn't care about their true identities anymore, having already made sure the playing field was leveled. Whether Diamond was a man of import like Pearl, the Director of the Intelligence Service, or like Jade himself, just a bastard fisherman, was of little consequence.

"Look at it this way, gents. Even if *Amber* and *Sapphire* decide to confess during their few remaining days on this earth, your legacy is secure. There will be nothing for anyone to find. The Hand of the Reaper is no more."

With that, Jade ripped off his stifling mask. Zann Biddel was done hiding. There was no reason to play in the shadows anymore.

The *grol* queen was still alive, but soon it wouldn't matter. There wouldn't be any *grols* left in Elsira to destroy his country. He would make sure of that. And once the witches and their dangerous magic were safely ensconced in a place far away, then he would target the elites. The ones in their ivory towers who had kept down the working men for so long.

Like Pearl and Diamond here—even their code names told of wealth and disregard for the backs on which such treasure was found.

"Elsira for Elsirans" was the motto, but more than that, Zann wanted an Elsira for those who had worked so hard for everything they built.

The time for secrets was over.

CHAPTER FORTY-SEVEN

Tales of her travels overtook the land, and the route she had trod became sacred. The branches of the tree, so long divided, grew intertwined once more, thick and strong the way we all had hoped they would be.

—THE AYALYA

Tai adjusted the cravat strangling his neck. Mainland formal wear rivaled any torture he'd ever heard of. He smirked to find Darvyn pulling at a scrap of silk that was choking him, as well. The frustration on the other man's face mirrored his own.

Kyara stood by Darvyn's side, arrayed in a simple white gown borrowed from Lizvette. It was elegant yet understated. Kyara's limbs were stiff, and she ran the smooth silk of the skirt between her fingers nervously. The three of them were equally uncomfortable in Elsiran finery.

They had all been called to the throne room again this afternoon after the bewildering events of the morning's thwarted execution, with the only instruction being to dress formally. Tai was to set sail as soon as he was done here. He believed he could talk his mother out of sentencing him to prison, though every day away from Lizvette would feel like captivity on its own.

Tai's fidgeting stopped the moment the woman in question glided into the throne room. Lizvette moved with a divine grace, like a creature from another world sent here to live among the mortals. His mouth went dry.

Her eyes caught his and held. The sadness in her gaze made his entire body ache, but he couldn't contemplate it and, instead, turned his attention to the polished floor.

Captain Zivel entered in full military regalia with lots of shiny bits on his chest. Tai nodded and Zivel strolled over, holding his palms out for an Elsiran greeting.

"Do you know what this is about?" Tai asked.

"I've some idea," Zivel replied with what could almost be considered a smile. Tai's brows shot up. "I've been to a couple of these before."

When the man would say nothing else, Tai merely shook his head. "Do you know anything more about who poisoned the queen?"

Whatever joviality the captain had possessed disappeared. "A warrant is out for the arrest of Chief Luqos Dillot."

"The head of the Intelligence Service?"

"The same. One of the new Lagrimari maids—an Earthsinger—pointed us toward a footman who she said was gushing guilt like a hose. The young man admitted that Dillot had been blackmailing some of the staff. Had forced him to add a 'sleeping draft' into the queen's tea last night. Dillot's in the wind, but we'll find him." Zivel's face was grim. "And I intend to petition the Council for a few Earthsingers to be added to the Yaly Foreign Service. They could help us identify threats over there."

Darvyn must have made quite an impression. Tai had no idea what Zivel's politics were, but he seemed the practical sort. If an Earthsinger could help him do his job, then why not?

After a few more polite words, the captain wandered away and Lizvette drifted over. Her perfume was a sweet greeting that arrived slightly before she did. Tai closed his eyes, inhaling deeply, trying to commit it to memory. It was unlikely he would ever scent something so refined and delicate again. Lizvette's fragrance would likely haunt him for the rest of his days.

Certainly he would return to Elsira as soon as whatever obligations his mother had cooked up for him were done, but he could not expect Lizvette to wait. There would doubtless be proposals headed her way. And she was a practical woman—what use would waiting for him to sail into port every few months be to her? What kind of life would that make?

Finally, feeling as though he was in control of the emotion flashing behind his eyes, he met her gaze. Everything he was feeling was reflected in her face.

The murmuring in the throne room ceased as the king, queen, and Goddess entered. Clove, Vanesse, and Jasminda's family had also arrived, and they all stood before the monarchs.

A liveried attendant strode up to the dais with a large cushion in his hands. The king examined the contents of the cushion, then nodded in approval. He addressed those gathered. "For your service to the state, I, Jaqros Edvard Alliaseen, High Commander of the Royal Army and King of Elsira, grant you our most cherished distinction—the Order of the Grainbearer, an ancient honor that few have achieved." From the cushion, he picked up a sash with a golden medal attached.

"Vanesse Olivesse Zinadeel. Clovette Mozelle Liddelot. Lizvette Marineve Nirall. Darvyn ol-Tahlyro. Tai N'dogo Summerhawk. Kyara ul-Lagrimar. You are all hereby inducted into this great legacy. Elsira gives you our thanks."

They each stepped forward to accept their medals. The queen placed Tai's over his head and smiled beatifically. He was a bit dazzled and stumbled as he moved away.

He noticed the Goddess standing behind the thrones, peering down at them with glittering eyes. She nodded once after they'd received their medals, then left the room.

Other attendants and servants milled around. A photograph was taken, for which Tai had to stand stiffly until the exposure was complete. He fingered the ribbon around his neck absently. On one side it bore the great seal of Elsira, a fish swimming around a tree, its branches spread wide. On the other, the profile of a man wearing a crown with the words: *In Feast and in Famine We Sustain.*

A Summerhawk had never received an official honor before. His mother having ruthlessly clawed her way into the role of king of Raun notwithstanding, his family name had been tarnished by his father. The respect a medal of this kind represented meant more than he thought such a thing could.

Roshon and Varten approached him then as their father stood next to their sister, speaking quietly. The twins congratulated him and smiled wide, though Roshon's expression was a bit guarded.

Varten spoke up on his brother's behalf. "So, word is your sister has her own ship now?"

Tai hadn't gotten the chance to see the boys since their rescue, but he'd located a dolphin messenger and sent word to Ani that Roshon and his family were alive and well. A response had not yet come back.

"She blew through her apprenticeship even faster than I thought she would," he responded. "She should be in the north of the ocean now, shuttling goods from Raun to Udland."

Roshon's amber eyes darted back and forth. He was trying admirably to hide his emotions, but the nerves broke through.

Ani's mourning after Roshon's disappearance had consisted of throwing herself into her work, making captain at an unprecedented speed. And while the king claimed that the teenagers' betrothal was invalid—due to Roshon being assumed dead—Ani had never accepted the ruling.

"I would expect that she will be making a detour to Rosira, though," Tai added. "Once she receives my message . . ."

Only then did Roshon's eyes light up, though he attempted to keep his face neutral. "Is that so?" he asked casually. Varten elbowed him in the ribs, causing him to stumble.

"I'd give her about a week," Tai said.

Finally, a grin overtook his face. "One week?" he asked as his brother snickered.

Tai nodded. Roshon's cheeks flushed as he tried to contain his emotions.

"Jasminda's eager to meet the girl who had to whup Roshon in order to secure a betrothal," Varten said.

Now the grin that split Roshon's face was huge. "Jasminda will love Ani. They might even get into a fistfight—I think they'd both enjoy that!"

Tai looked skeptically at the demure and sophisticated queen, trying to compare her to his energetic sister.

"Don't let the dress and crown fool you," Varten said. "Jas used to wallop us good. She gives as good as she gets. She and Ani will get along just fine. And they could both use a sister."

Tai nodded and slapped the boys on the backs before they returned to their family.

He felt a presence behind him and knew it was Lizvette. But he didn't have the nerve to turn around. Instead, he waited as Darvyn walked up, loosening the silk around his neck, appearing as though he was ready to leave.

"You getting out of here, mate?" Tai asked.

"Yeah, Kyara needs some time away from people." He motioned over his shoulder to where she stood near the door. "She's still coming to terms with everything that's happened."

Tai nodded, relief and pity for her mixing within him.

"If I don't see you before you go, then . . ." Darvyn gave Tai a hug, complete with several thumps on the back.

"Until the next time, mate."

"Until the next time," Darvyn repeated and then ambled away.

Once he was gone, Lizvette spoke to Tai. "Are you leaving now?" Her voice was crystal clear and melodic, with a note of worry at the end.

He gathered his courage and turned to face her. "Yes. In a few moments."

Her eyes darkened, and she remained quiet.

"Does this medal mean that you're pardoned?" he asked.

She looked at the adornment on her chest. "The crown has dropped all charges against me." Her lips curved in an abbreviated smile, though it did not reach her eyes. The anguish there made his chest tighten. "Tai—"

"No need for good-byes, duchess," he said around the swelling in his throat. His eyes prickled in a strange way that must have meant the throne room was especially dusty.

He took a step back and gave a deep bow. "My lady," he said

formally and reached for her hand to give it a kiss. The softness of her skin against his lips brought back all sorts of memories that he couldn't bear to dwell on just now. They would no doubt keep him company on the journey ahead and the long days and years without her. He had to leave. Now.

"Until the next time, duchess," he said. He waited for her to repeat the Raunian greeting, but only silence met him.

He chanced a glance to her face and saw more emotion there than he was prepared for. Instead of giving in to the desire to beg her to come with him, he bowed again and released her hand, then beat a swift retreat from the throne room.

Lizvette's heart cracked inside her chest as Tai's broad back retreated. Her feet wanted to chase after him, but they couldn't. She was stuck. Perhaps exile would not have been so bad after all. Could she have been exiled with Tai?

She shook off the feeling and turned only to gasp at finding Jasminda standing directly beside her. As quickly as possible, she gathered her composure and sank into a curtsey. When she stood fully, she was Lizvette Nirall again, self-possessed former almost-princess, at least to the outside world.

"I owe you more than this medal," Jasminda said, motioning to the ribbon around Lizvette's neck. "I owe you a debt of gratitude. My family has been returned to me."

Lizvette shook her head. "That had very little to do with me, Your Majesty. I only wish that I could have ferreted out the threat against you sooner and more completely."

Jasminda tsked. "What's done is done, and your aid was invaluable. I have spoken to the others and know what you were able to accomplish. None of this would have been possible without you."

Lizvette did not know how to respond to that, so she remained silent.

Queen Jasminda's dark eyes glittered as they regarded her. They did not look particularly angry, but not particularly friendly, either. "You and I will never be friends," she said.

Lizvette paled. Yes, that would be too much to ask for. She dared not apologize again for her actions before the Mantle fell.

"But I no longer count you an enemy," the queen continued. "And my husband is still very fond of you, though he is afraid to admit it to me." She snorted. "Loyal friends are difficult to find. And I believe you are loyal, Lizvette." The queen grabbed her skirts and walked toward the window at the edge of the throne room, motioning for Lizvette to follow. "However, that does not mean I have any wish for you to be around the palace day in and day out."

Lizvette gripped her hands in front of her. "So we're to be put out, then?"

The queen raised an eyebrow.

"With Father's trial approaching, the crown will seize his assets. I'll just need time to secure a dwelling for my mother and myself. Would that be possible, Your Majesty?"

Queen Jasminda looked at her askance. "I would not throw you out into the street, regardless of what Nirall is guilty of. We've already established that you had nothing to do with that. Your home is not at risk. Your mother may live there for the rest of her days."

A burst of air escaped Lizvette's lungs. Mother would not fare well away from the place she'd called home most of her adult life. But then the entirety of the queen's words sunk in. "My mother, but not me."

The queen pursed her lips.

Lizvette took a shaky breath. "I can understand if you don't forgive me. It is your right. I cannot apologize more earnestly or truthfully than I have already done. I was wrong . . . about a great many things. If I could have found an amalgam in Yaly that would turn back the hands of time so that I could change things, I would. But do not forget that your presence on that battlefield the day the Mantle fell is the only reason the war is over. It doesn't excuse my actions, but perhaps it is proof of a larger plan at work. And if your heart is still so hardened against me that it can never be softened, I will leave. You won't have to see me again."

She steeled her spine against the queen's fiery gaze. Her skin tingled, and she felt as though she were almost outside of her body. Had she really said such a thing to the queen? Searching her heart, she found no part of herself that wanted to take it back.

The corners of the queen's mouth tilted up a fraction. Was it Lizvette's imagination or was that a modicum of respect shining in the monarch's eyes?

"I was going to say that your abilities on this mission have proven that you are an asset to our country. There are several ambassadorships open at the moment, and our weakening relationships with certain neighbors necessitate installing diplomats we trust. Would you be interested in serving in such a role?"

Lizvette snapped her mouth shut as her heart raced. "Yes, Your Majesty. I would be honored. I am eager to serve in any capacity—"

"Good," Jasminda cut her off.

"Am I to return to Yaly, then?" They had need of a new ambassador there certainly. Everyone in that land seemed to be corrupt.

"It is your choice. We do need someone there, but the situation with Raun has become untenable. The embargo must be lifted if Elsira is to recover financially. Their king is not known for being reasonable, but perhaps if we had a woman negotiating, it would be more effective." The queen raised her chin. She faced the window, but Lizvette had the distinct impression that *she* was the subject of Jasminda's scrutiny. "The Raunian culture is rather strange, from what I've learned, but their women take on very strong roles."

Lizvette worked to loosen her frozen jaw. "Raun?"

"Yes. And if that is your choice, we'll need you to leave immediately. Though I know you've only been back a short time, this cannot wait. We will have a nurse tend to your mother if she is still ill, and your written deposition should serve for your father's trial."

Her breath stuttered in her chest. "Raun?" she repeated.

The queen raised an eyebrow. "I believe that many of the common Elsiran fears about the Raunians are likely unfounded. But Yaly is still an option, if you'd prefer."

"No, Your Majesty. You're right. Raun is the far more pressing situation, and I do feel a woman's touch may be needed when dealing with their king. And time is of the essence. In fact, I know of a vessel that is leaving today."

Jasminda looked a bit startled by the speed of the words shooting from Lizvette's mouth.

"If I may be excused, Your Majesty?"

"Certainly." The queen stepped aside, and Lizvette did her best to walk out of the throne room in a dignified manner. Once outside, however, she tore through the hallway at a dead sprint until she reached her rooms.

When Lizvette arrived, she found Mother sitting in the window with a sour look on her face. Lizvette called her maid and told her to pack as if her life depended on it. She didn't have clothing appropriate for weeks on a ship, but perhaps clothing would not be entirely necessary after all.

CHAPTER FORTY-EIGHT

The hand of Ylajah the Scholar keeps this record, so all may bear witness and recognize. The seeker herself, did not stay long in her home. She is out there even now, wandering among the people of the land she united. Journeying still, so the past remains history and the future secure in our outstretched hands.

—THE AYALYA

Tai reviewed the ship's manifest and waited for the dock inspectors to finish their scrutiny. He'd already completed his check on the engines. There was nothing more for him to do as Mik had prepared everything on the *Hekili* in expectation of having to leave quickly.

"Are you ready to face your mum again?" Mik asked.

"Are you?" Tai shot back, trying for levity. Ignoring the pain that had settled onto his heart would be his main pastime now. It certainly wasn't going anywhere.

Perhaps after he'd fixed things with his mother, he would be able to return and find that Lizvette was still willing to see him, that she had not chosen another. The admittedly weak hope would have to last him for the weeks and months ahead.

He sat on the bridge of the ship, the instrumentation blurring in front of him. Beyond, the vast ocean spread out. Thousands of kilometers away lay Raun, and between here and there, the sea separated him from the woman he loved. He'd never thought to utter those words before, but the reality of his feelings settled across him as he stared at the waves.

Never before had the ocean been anything other than home for him. Now it was an impediment. Yet another challenge to overcome.

Love. He shook his head and wiped a hand over his face. Swallowing the uncharacteristic surge of emotion, he pulled out his navigation charts and the latest weather predictions. Whoever had generated these was an idiot, he thought, as the storm coming surely wouldn't be as strong as all that. Would it?

The inspectors had finally signed off and left the ship. "Are your final checks done?" Tai shouted to Mik.

"Aye. Ready to lift anchor," the man replied.

Tai took a deep breath, preparing himself to depart. With no cargo aboard, the ship was unusually light, so at least that would help them make good time. The sooner he got to Raun, the sooner he could grovel at his mother's feet the way she wanted and return to Elsira. Then he would tell Lizvette he loved her.

He prayed to Myr it would not be too late.

The ship shuddered as it came to life. He pulled himself onto the broad deck to reel in the ramp. The thermoelectric engine was quiet, though a froth began to churn in the waters around it. But the gentle hum of the port activity was interrupted by a disturbance on the boardwalk lining the docks.

Grizzled sailors and dockworkers lined up, and all heads turned toward someone tearing through the crowd. A peach-colored silken gown decorated with wispy lace and beading was being held up in one small fist as its bearer raced across the creaking boards. A pair of fine legs ending in delicate shoes that had no business being in Portside were exposed in the mad dash.

The leers from the passersby broke Tai out of his daze, and he crossed the ship's deck in three steps and ran down the ramp. Lizvette barreled into his arms, nearly knocking him off-balance. He gripped her tightly, his hands fighting against the slide of her silk gown. Lizvette was out of breath, her chest heaving, but she wrapped her arms around him and buried her face in his chest. Soon she was planting kisses up his neck to his jaw until she found his mouth.

He was frozen in shock but thawed quickly under her ministrations and gathered his senses enough to kiss her back.

"Room for one more?" she asked once she came up for air.

Tai grinned and hauled her onto his ship before she could change her mind.

"How long do you think it will be until someone tries to kill you again?" Roshon's voice pierced the haze clouding Jasminda's mind.

She turned to her brother. "One would hope for at least a week between assassination attempts."

He didn't smile.

"Come here," she said. "Both of you." Varten appeared from

behind the doorway to the sitting room in the royal suite. He looked unsure about stepping on the thick, woven rugs—something Jasminda could relate to.

"Listen," she said, "if someone doesn't try to kill you at least once in your life, then maybe you're not making a big enough impact in the world."

Roshon stared at her for a beat before shaking his head. "It isn't funny."

"No, it's not, but sometimes you have to laugh anyway. Especially with a world gone mad."

Varten stepped up to them, already beginning to gain back the weight he'd lost in captivity. He slung an arm around her and she wrapped her other arm around Roshon, dwarfed by the two of them for the first time. They'd grown so much. They stood before a picture window looking out over the front of the palace, to the city and ocean beyond.

"What would Mama say about all this?" Varten mused.

Jasminda tried to come up with something, but couldn't. "I wish I knew."

Varten squeezed her gently. "We can ask Papa."

"Where is he anyway?"

"With Clove and Vanesse," Roshon responded. "Clove's teaching him an Elsiran card game with some of the Guardsmen."

Jasminda shook her head, smothering a smile. In the distance, storm clouds darkened the horizon. Heavy and full of gloom.

On the lawn below, protestors took up another chant. Their words were muffled, but the sharpness in their tone still stung.

They came every day now. Dominionists and sympathizers with their picket signs and tongues full of hate. And Lagrimari, along with a growing number of Elsirans supporting unification. They bore no signs, cried no slogans. They just marched and stood on their side of the field. Existing. Right in front of the faces of their detractors.

There were skirmishes here and there in the city. Some Lagrimari were not content to silently make their presence and their displeasure known. But more and more, for every street corner filled with separatist demonstrators, there was another on the other side, filled with quiet protestors. Living and breathing. Surviving. Hoping for a chance to thrive.

Jasminda held her brothers tight as the sound and its answering silence rose to meet them.

"I heard there was a swimming pool here," Varten announced, mischief in his voice.

"I think there are three," Jasminda answered.

"Bet I can beat you in a race."

Roshon snorted. "Neither of you know how to swim."

"It's not that hard," Varten scoffed.

"You'll drown and Jas will just float herself across the water. What's the point of that?"

"Then we'll make a rule—no Earthsong."

"How would you know if she cheated?"

"I'd know. I'd feel it."

The boys bickered on and Jasminda had never heard a more wonderful sound in all her life. The ocean before them was still calm—for a little while longer. For now, she would enjoy the peace and the chaos.

For as long as she could.

EPILOGUE

If you come upon the seeker in a twilight wood, or near a babbling brook, or under the glow of the morning sun and she asks you "What is freely given, but expects a reward?" remember to make no supplication and bend no knee. For the answer is "a prayer."

—THE AYALYA

The endless ocean stretches out before me, blue and serene. I sit on the bench at the edge of the palace gardens, the one that I have come to think of as my own, watching a small ship sail away to the west. Once upon a time, I used to stand here in this spot and dream of visiting the lands across the sea. But that path is closed to me. My home is here. My remaining days on this earth will be spent on this soil.

I tilt my head up to enjoy the warmth of the sun on my cheeks, to soak in this brief moment without anyone fawning over me or requesting something of me. I tune out the sound of turmoil on the other side of the palace. Now may be the last chance for a moment of solitude before the tempest arrives and the skies open up.

I feel Tarazeli's approach several minutes before she appears at my side. Her agitation is palpable. I had thought her knot of trepidation around me had finally loosened after the past weeks of her service.

"Is it done?" I ask her.

"Yes, Your Excellency, but—"

"You delivered the death stone to Kyara exactly as I instructed?"

Zeli comes into view in my peripheral vision, twisting her hands together. "Yes, Your Excellency. I placed the box holding the stone at her bedside for her to find when she returns to her room. Though anyone could go in and—"

"No one will disturb the box."

Besides, the death stone will drive an Earthsinger mad if they touch it for too long. And if a Silent comes upon it, they will see little more than a red rock.

"Very well, Your Excellency. But there is something you need to see . . . in the dungeons." Her anxiety has grown to such levels that it nettles my skin.

"Show me." I rise and follow her back into the palace. She doesn't make a sound as we walk through the halls, but her disquiet is deafening.

We descend into the dungeon, each step on the old stone stairway echoing in the dank depths. The barred cells blur as I pass them—nearly all are filled with the victims of my brother's madness and evil. My beloved twin has committed more atrocities than I can fathom. I observed the effect of his tyranny for centuries, locked in a prison of my own making in the World Between;

however, I created his prison, too. Ultimately, I am the reason he is locked away here. The gift of power I gave him was the catalyst that caused him to spiral out of control. I will always bear the brunt of the blame.

An echoing whisper behind me causes me to turn my head. I almost thought someone was saying my name, but no one calls me Oola anymore, save Darvyn. Even now, he is with his little viper. It is as it should be, but still I feel as though I am being watched. The hairs on the back of my neck rise with the tension. The hallway contains only the Guardsman assigned to this section who would not dare use my name. Even if he knew it. And yet I hear the whisper again, more of a rasp than a true voice.

Oola. Oola.

Zeli looks at me curiously to see what has made me stop walking. I turn back around, a shiver running down my spine, and continue to enter the deepest part of the dungeon.

What she wanted me to see is immediately evident. The wooden door to the old storage room is cracked in two, with one piece hanging at an odd angle as if it was blasted open from within by an incredible force.

And my brother is gone.

Zeli's eyes are wide and round. My Song infuses her with calm, irritated by the chafing of her emotions against me.

Earthsong could have split the door in this manner. That or an incredibly strong kick. One thing is certain, my frail brother, weakened by depression and despondency, could not have done this.

At least I do not think he could have.

"Who else knows?" I whisper.

"No one, Your Excellency."

I remember the boy he was, sweet and kind. How we used to

visit the water's edge and sit by the fire, dreaming of our futures. None of those dreams came true. Instead, the power I gifted him destroyed us both.

The splintered wood of the door taunts me. I extend my senses to try to locate Eero. The pull of hundreds of thousands of people in the city tugs at me. I swim through an ocean of emotions, searching for one man. I stretch, feeling the surrounding areas, the sea, the mountains, the farms beyond.

But I do not find him.

My heart beats faster. For the first time in centuries, I do not know where my twin is.

Again I hear the murmur of my name. Zeli is glassy-eyed behind me, lips sealed shut, and we are the only two here.

"Tell no one."

She nods absently. I may have softened her emotions a bit too much. I undo the magic, freeing her feelings once again.

The cold of the stone walls seeps into my skin. I leave the bowels of the palace to seek the last rays of sun. The storm is nearly upon us. I can only hope that I will not come to regret the things I have done.

Only later will I learn of the snaking column of whispering black smoke that follows me. Only later will I discover what it portends.

Mooriah was drawn to the tall woman gliding down the darkened hall. But as much as she longed to, she could not approach the woman called the Goddess Awoken. Not yet.

She needed a body first.

Her spirit floated through corridors of stone, seeking a convenient host. Moving outside of the inmates' notice, she undulated through the shadows like an airborne snake. But one woman looked up at her, squinting into the darkness. An ancient crone, she looked older than death itself; however, her green eyes sparkled with sharp alertness.

Mooriah moved swiftly, invading the woman's body and absorbing her memories. Her name was Ydaris, and after a glimpse into her past, Mooriah felt no remorse for choosing her.

The body's long limbs shortened. Wasted muscles swelled and hardened. Sagging skin tightened and bone regenerated until Mooriah flexed her arms and legs, reintroducing herself to a physical form she had not worn in centuries.

The consciousness known as Ydaris was locked away in a corner of Mooriah's mind. Unseen, unheard, and unharmed—at least for now.

The locked cell door, made of ancient iron, was but a small impediment. She scraped her finger on a jagged corner of rock jutting from the wall. The sting was invigorating after so long without senses. After a few muttered words of a blood spell, with her own blood as payment, the lock disengaged.

The guard standing straight-backed at the end of the corridor startled when she approached. Then he slumped down in a heap as she manipulated his Nethersong.

She passed cell after cell of Lagrimari criminals, but paid them no mind. The war between Elsira and Lagrimar was over. She was far more concerned with stopping the war to come.

Unsteady legs carried her out of the dungeon as she slowly became used to the feel of true flesh and skin again. Nethersong invigorated her all the way down to her bones. It was the Light shining in the darkness, illuminating the way.

The Light Kyara needed to find and master. Embracing the Light, and all that went with it, was the only way forward.

First she had to find the other Nethersinger. They had much to discuss now that Mooriah could do so freely. Only afterward could she give in to the longing in her heart and finally meet the woman they called a goddess. A woman Mooriah had never gotten the chance to call "mother."

ACKNOWLEDGMENTS

As always, I owe deep gratitude to those who have helped make this possible:

A huge thanks to the readers who have taken this journey with me. If you've made it this far, you are my people! Some of you have been waiting for this book for a very long time. I did my best to make it worth it.

To all My Imaginary Friends, both old and new, thanks for being there.

My editor, Monique Patterson, and the entire team at St. Martin's, including: Mara Delgado-Sanchez, Meghan Harrington, and Beatrice Jason. It takes a village to put these book-children out into the world. I appreciate everything that you all do.

My agent, Sara Megibow, an incredible cheerleader, guide, and friend.

To my writer friends, Nakeesha, Cerece, Cynthia, and Denny,

who regularly hold me up, inspire, and challenge me, I don't know what I'd do without y'all.

My family, who knew I was a writer before anyone else did, and gave me the tools I needed to grow.

And to Jared, who is always willing to wrangle dogs and slay trolls so I can live my dream.

About the Author

Valerie Bey

L. Penelope has been writing since she could hold a pen and loves getting lost in the worlds in her head. She is an award-winning author of new adult, fantasy, and paranormal romance. She lives in Maryland with her husband and their furry dependents. Her books include the Earthsinger Chronicles (*Song of Blood & Stone, Whispers of Shadow & Flame, Cry of Metal & Bone*).